Operation Devil's Fire

Also by Ronn Munsterman

<u>NON-FICTION</u>

Chess Handbook for Parents and Coaches

Available on Amazon.com

Operation Devil's Fire

Ronn Munsterman

This book is a work of fiction. Names, characters, places, and incidents are the product of the author's imagination or are used fictitiously. Any resemblance to actual events, locales, or persons, living or dead is coincidental.

OPERATION DEVIL'S FIRE – A SGT. DUNN NOVEL

Cover Design by Ronn Munsterman
Atomic Bomb photo: Public Domain-U.S. Department of Energy
Photograph of Ronn Munsterman: Berta Munsterman

www.ronnmunsterman.com

Manufactured in the United States of America
10 9 8 7 6 5

ISBN: 1-453-61363-3
BISAC: Fiction / War & Military

Acknowledgments

No book arrives at a completed state by itself and this one certainly took a good long while to get here. Through it all, thanks to my wife, Berta, my best friend, for her love, encouragement and support. Every day brings joy because of my children and their spouses: Stefanie–Eric, Nathan–Jessica, and my granddaughters: Ali and Julia.

I believe we all owe a debt of gratitude to the men and women of the Greatest Generation for their sacrifices both on the battlefield and at home. May we never forget.

Special thanks to Colonel C.E. "Bud" Anderson (USAF Retired), WWII Triple Ace.

To my *FAITHFUL FIRST READERS*:

Thank you for your encouragement and insightful suggestions that made this book better: Steve Barltrop, Dave J. Cross, Jim Engstrom, David M. Jones, John Skelton, Steven White, and Derek Williams.

To you, the reader: at the end of the book are Author's Notes where I give you some insight into where this story came from, and some of the technical, historical, and geographical research done to make this as realistic a story as I could. However! Promise me you will NOT read the Author's Notes, until, well, *after* you read the book. There is a spoiler . . . don't say I didn't warn you.

In Loving Honor

Amos Munsterman – U.S. Army, Silver Star

In Loving Memory

Olga Munsterman – U.S. Coast Guard
Norman Munsterman – U.S. Army
Hugo Munsterman – U.S. Army, Bronze Star, Purple Heart
Maxwell Elder – U.S. Army
Lester Knisley – U.S. Navy

1944

May						
Su	Mo	Tu	We	Th	Fr	Sa
	1	2	3	4	5	6
7	8	9	10	11	12	13
14	15	16	17	18	19	20
21	22	23	24	25	26	27
28	29	30	31			

June						
Su	Mo	Tu	We	Th	Fr	Sa
				1	2	3
4	5	6	7	8	9	10
11	12	13	14	15	16	17
18	19	20	21	22	23	24
25	26	27	28	29	30	

CAST

Americans

Adams, Lt., Samuel	Colonel Kenton's aide
Clark, Lt., Bob	C-47 copilot
Cross, Cpl. Dave	Dunn's squad member
Donovan, William	Director, Office of Strategic Services
Dunn, Sgt. Thomas	Ranger Squad Leader
Hanson, Jack	Dunn's squad member
Hayes, Tommy	P-51 Mustang pilot
Kenton, Col., Mark	Commander, Special Operations
Langston, Dennis	C-47 jumpmaster
Lawson, Howard	OSS Officer
Miller, Captain Norman	P-51 Mustang pilot, Flight leader
Morris, Daniel	Dunn's squad member
Murphy, Bill	P-51 Mustang pilot
Nelson, David	Miller's commander
Oldham, Timothy	Dunn's squad member
Pierce, Captain, Vincent	C-47 pilot
Roosevelt, Franklin D.	President of the United States
Thompson, Chuck	P-51 Mustang pilot
Ward, Patrick	Dunn's squad member
Wickham, Stanley	Dunn's squad member
Young, Steve	Eisenhower's aide

British

Barltrop, Cpl. Steve	Saunders' squad member
Brisdon, Graham	Saunders' squad member
Churchill, Winston	Prime Minister of Great Britain
Coulter, Simon	Churchill's assistant
Finch, Alan	MI5 analyst
Hardwicke, Mrs.	Pamela's mom
Hardwicke, Pamela	British nurse
Jenkins, Col. Rupert	Commander, Commando Training
Lewis, Edward	MI6
Marston, Neil	British spy
Owens, Neville	Saunders' squad member
Saunders, Sgt. Malcom	Commando Squad Leader

French

Abrial/Helga	Küfer's house girl
Adrien	French Resistance
Briard, Dr.	Calais hospital
Dubois, Gaston	Saverne policeman
Gauvin, Louis	French Resistance
Gereaux, Anne	French farmer's wife
Gereaux, Claire	French farmer's daughter
Gereaux, Philipe	French farmer
Henri	French Resistance
Laurent, Remi	Saverne French Resistance Leader
Luc	French Resistance
Madeline	Calais French Resistance Leader
Rene	French Resistance

German

Adler, Meyer	Chief Gestapo agent in Saverne
Bauer, Dr. Volker	Physicist
Engel, Hans	Horten test pilot
Farber, Klaus	Old anti aircraft gunner
Gerber, Dr. Rudolph	Physicist
Göring, Hermann	Luftwaffe Commander
Herbert, Edwina	Dr. Herbert's wife
Herbert, Dr. Franz	Physicist, Director – Project Dante
Hitler, Adolf	Nazi Dictator
Horten, Reimar	Airplane manufacturer
Horten, Walter	Airplane manufacturer
Küfer, Leonard	Gestapo agent in Calais
Mauer, Hugo	Horten Engineer
Nagel, Carl	Horten Chief Mechanic
Ostermann, Lt.	Commander – patrol in Calais
Speer, Albert	Minister of Armaments
Winkel, Dr. Gunther	Physicist

1

Berlin
25 May 1944, 0407 Hours

Neil Marston feared for his nation's survival. A just-developed photo lying on his creaky desk revealed a top-secret German document, a memo addressed to Hitler from the German Minister of Armaments, Albert Speer. A small desk lamp threw a spotlight on the terrifying information.

Marston had labored three months to cultivate a friendship with Arne Dortmer, a pompous official who worked for Speer. Marston correctly guessed Dortmer could access the kind of secrets he was searching for. It didn't hurt that Dortmer was prone to bragging, especially after a few German dark ales and finally Marston worked out the location of the documents he wanted. After that, it was just a matter of breaking and entering. If he got caught doing the same thing back home in England, he would get five-to-ten, which was a far sight better than what the Germans would have in store for him if they ever caught him. They had an unsettling tendency to shoot spies.

During tonight's nerve-wracking expedition through the

darkened streets of Berlin, he'd ducked into a shadowy doorway twice to avoid detection by security patrols. Now safely back in his tiny, third floor apartment, he slid off his black stocking cap, revealing short-cropped blond hair. With brilliant blue eyes peering out from under fair eyebrows, Marston's hair-eye color combination was one of the two reasons he'd been recruited by the Security Service, otherwise known as MI5. The other, more important reason was his ability to speak German as though he'd lived in Germany his entire life. He hadn't, of course, growing up instead in London's West End.

As a gifted, natural linguist and professor of English at Oxford, he drew the attention of an MI5 recruiter when he gave a speech on medieval German's influence on modern English. Afterwards, the man invited Marston to a pub for a chat and a beer. Marston laughed out loud when the man offered him a job, saying he was just a professor and didn't know anything about the spy business. The man chuckled in return and said that was all right, he used to be just an accountant. Then he added, "Don't worry, we'll teach you everything you need to know." Marston was still waffling on the idea a week later when he heard the news that Germany had invaded Poland. He called the recruiter that day to say he wanted in.

Marston had completed many successful assignments while in Berlin over the past four years, but several times, like this morning, he'd barely evaded capture. He had learned to live with the daily fear, somehow pushing it down out of his consciousness, at least for short periods at a time. This mission, though, was one set above and apart from all the rest. When the ramifications of the information became clear, it frightened him beyond his own personal safety.

He reread the document. After wiping his suddenly damp palms on his trousers, he slid a one-time pad from a hidden slot in the desk. The message was short and required only a few minutes work. When decoded in London it would read:

Germans have uranium. Quantities sufficient for A-bomb.

2

Camp Barton Stacy
60 miles southwest of London
27 May, 1531 Hours

The U.S. Army's Camp Barton Stacy sat nestled in the rolling hills of the British countryside between Andover and Whitchurch. Home to a wide variety of American units ranging from armor to infantry to medical, Barton Stacy hogged land on several farms. The American government paid the farmers a more or less—depending on who you talked to—fair amount for the use of their land. Having the Yanks on their property upset some farmers, but others simply accepted the situation and, of course, the money.

A pair of armed soldiers guarded Barton Stacy's front gate. After showing his identification to the bored sentries and passing through the gate, Staff Sergeant Thomas Dunn parked his Willys jeep in front of the administration building. He shut off the engine, jumped out and took the stairs two at a time. Colonel Kenton's office was the first door on the right of the wide hallway. Dunn opened it without knocking and walked right into an argument.

Colonel Mark Kenton stood toe-to-toe with a British Colonel. Dunn grimaced in recognition. Colonel Rupert Jenkins was the no-nonsense commander of the Commando school where Dunn and his team had graduated with honors. Throughout the entire twelve weeks, Jenkins had reminded the American soldiers daily of two things: there was only one way to do things, the British way, and if they didn't like it, they knew where to find the gate.

Colonel Kenton was slight of build and barely five-nine, with black hair graying at the temples. Unaccountably, he had a deep, resonant voice which surprised most people the first time they heard it. Even though Colonel Jenkins towered over him, Kenton was doing the shouting. "Colonel, you Brits think you're the only ones who know how to do anything right and I'm sick and tired of hearing about how you'd do things. We've learned a few things and can do—"

Jenkins somehow managed to out-shout the little colonel, "Kenton, you can take your American can-do attitude and shove it up your collective arses as far as I'm concerned."

Kenton raised his hand and was about to poke the British Colonel in the chest when a soft cough caught his attention. He glanced over at his aide, Lieutenant Samuel Adams, who was shaking his head ever so slightly, more of a wiggle than anything. With a sigh, Kenton lowered his hand and took a step back. "Colonel, my apologies. Perhaps we can just focus on the mission and save our difference of opinion for the pub." He held out his hand.

Jenkins stared at it for a long moment, then grudgingly shook it. "Of course, Kenton."

Kenton suddenly noticed Dunn standing just inside the door and his face lit up with genuine pleasure. "Sergeant Dunn. It's good to see you."

Dunn stood six-two and topped out at 183 pounds. He wore the standard uniform of the day: khaki slacks and shirt, with an olive green waist-length jacket and black tie. His short-cropped, light brown hair was visible below the hat that was tilted just-so over his right eyebrow. A slim nose sat between dark brown eyes capable of flashing in anger or twinkling with laughter.

Stepping over to Dunn, Kenton shook hands. A frown

touched the Colonel's face. "How's the shoulder? All recovered, I hope."

"Yes, sir. The docs held me over an extra week to watch for infection. I'm fine now."

"No problems?"

"No sir. I've been running and doing calisthenics. I started on the firing range a couple of days ago. I'm getting my usual ten spots." Bulls eyes.

Kenton beamed as though Dunn was his own son bringing home an all-A's report card. The colonel was forty years old, had a son only six years younger than Dunn's twenty-four, and did think of Dunn as a son. Which made days like this difficult for him.

Dunn's first combat action took place during the ill-fated Battle of Kasserine Pass against Rommel's forces. Although the operation was a humiliating defeat for the Americans, there were flashes of individual bravery and success. Dunn was one such soldier. On 25 Feb 43, after his squad leader had taken a round through the face, Dunn took over and led his men in wiping out a German machine gun crew that was mowing down U.S. soldiers as they tried to retreat from the battlefield.

In recognition for his action, he was promoted to Sergeant and awarded the Bronze Star. He was also immediately reassigned to the Rangers school run by the British in Achnacarry House, Scotland. When Dunn graduated, he was promoted to Staff Sergeant and invited to join the school as a trainer. This was where he met and first worked for Kenton, then a Major, who commanded the Ranger Battalion. Then they got orders for the Italian Campaign and went ashore at Anzio in January. Delays and indecision at the highest command levels allowed the Germans to redirect forces and the attack fizzled. The Allies were literally mired down, and the battlefield looked more like something from World War I, including trenches and underground passages. The Ranger Battalion, still led by Kenton, newly promoted to Lieutenant Colonel, was in the thick of things and suffered the same heavy losses as did the regular army. The bulk of combat fatalities and wounds came from the Luftwaffe and artillery, including the infamous railway guns, Anzio Annie and Anzio Express, which both fired 280 millimeter shells miles onto the Allies.

Dunn admired Kenton and he learned to appreciate Kenton's tactical skills because he could make the most out of an impossible situation, and always instinctively knew where the murky line between recklessness and daring lay. Kenton learned he could depend on Dunn to always get the job done.

Kenton's skills were noted and passed upward. On 21 Feb, he was reassigned to Camp Barton Stacy to prepare elite teams for special operations.

On 2 Apr, Dunn and his squad, while on a mission to capture a small fortification just south of Cisterna, came under heavy artillery fire and Dunn lost two men but still managed to capture the target. Unknown to Dunn, Kenton had already requested that he and his squad be reassigned to him. It wasn't until a week after losing his men, something Dunn took hard, that he learned of the assignment.

Once at Barton Stacy, Dunn immediately began training his team along with the two replacements. On the fifth day, while undergoing a live-fire exercise, one of his men inexplicably stood up. Reacting immediately, Dunn dived at the soldier, knocking him out of harms way, but in the process took a bullet through the upper right shoulder. Lying on the ambulance litter with his team surrounding him, Dunn had told them he'd be all right soon and not to worry. Then he told the miserable kid who'd stood up that he was washed out and was going to be RTU (Returned to Unit). The team never heard from the kid again. Nor did they care to. Getting killed in combat was one thing, but getting someone else killed, well, that didn't cut it.

"We should get started." Kenton gestured toward the British officer standing ramrod straight with a soon to be permanently etched frown on his face. "You know Colonel Jenkins, of course."

"Yes, sir, I do." Dunn forced a smile. "Hello, Colonel."

Jenkins merely nodded in response, almost looking down his long nose at Dunn.

"Here, we have other company, too." Kenton gripped Dunn's arm and turned him toward another British soldier who had been standing quietly in the background. Dunn hadn't noticed him in all the commotion.

Dunn wondered how he could have so quickly fallen into his own personal hell. Standing before him was none other than Sergeant Malcolm Saunders. In October '43, he was the squad leader of a British team going through the rigors of training at Achnacarry House at the same time as Dunn was there preparing for Anzio. Saunders had taken glee in becoming Dunn's nemesis, doing everything possible to annoy, berate, and, just in general, make Dunn and his men look bad. In December, Saunders and two of his men managed to sneak into the armory in the middle of the night and doctor up the Americans' ammunition. They had painstakingly replaced every *other* round in the M-1 clips with blanks. On the firing range the next day, when Dunn's men fired their *second* round, they, to the man, did double-takes when they saw they hadn't hit the bulls eye, or for that matter, any part of the target.

The Saunders bunch might have gotten away with it if they hadn't all burst out laughing. The ensuing melee had cost both squads a weekend pass. Saunders was heard to say later it had been worth it just to see the Yanks' expressions.

Although he was six feet tall and heavily muscled, Saunders moved with an easy grace, seemingly gliding over to Dunn. He offered a hand. "'ello, Sergeant Dunn." He spoke with a thick cockney accent and when he grinned the tips of his red handlebar moustache twitched.

Dunn grasped the hand, "Good to see you, Sergeant Saunders."

"I'm sure 'tis."

In spite of himself, Dunn grinned back.

"What's it been? Five, six months, now?"

Dunn nodded. "Not long enough."

Saunders chuckled.

Saunders had followed the feisty General Montgomery since his unit first arrived in North Africa. He battled back and forth across the desert between El Alamein and Tobruk, then up the east coast of Sicily. He earned a commendation for bravery and his squad was instrumental in the destruction of a valuable German outpost. It was this action that put his name in front of Colonel Jenkins. In May '43, his commander told him he was headed back to England for some specialized training. When

Saunders asked what it was, the commander winked and said commando school. Then, like Dunn, he'd been called back from Italy with his team for special operations.

"Over here, gentlemen." Kenton swept his hand in the general direction of a hastily erected pine table standing against one wall. A large map of France was spread out, the curling edges held down by some heavy glass ashtrays. Coming through the windows, the afternoon sun cast bright light on the paper.

"We're on the brink of the invasion. Ike's supposed to make his decision on the date in the next few days. Your mission is to destroy a supply depot just southeast of Calais. This depot is for Rommel's 21st Panzer Division. The attack will act as yet another confirmation of the invasion's location. The Germans are convinced we're coming straight across the channel to take advantage of the shortest, most direct route. We want to encourage them to remain interested in that area."

Dunn leaned over to examine the map more closely, then asked, "What's the strength around it?"

"Infantry company, with one platoon right on top of it," answered Adams.

Dunn whistled lightly. "So you'll want us to waltz in there and turn it into a fireworks show, right, sir?"

Kenton smiled and said, "Something like that, Sergeant."

"Who's our local boy?" asked Dunn, referring to a resistance group leader.

Adams chuckled and said, "Actually, it's a woman. Madeline. She's been vetted and has a reputation as being tough and clever. Her group has reconned the depot and sent us detailed maps." He pulled some worn papers from a leather travel pouch and laid them on the table.

Dunn spread them out in front of himself and Saunders. The British Sergeant edged closer, bumping Jenkins, whose frown deepened, but the British Colonel stepped back out of the way. The drawings were excellent, showing the locations of the sentries, barracks and the two main storage buildings. Dunn and Saunders stared at them in silence for several minutes taking in the details.

Suddenly, Dunn poked the map with his finger. "This is where one team goes in . . . " he slid his finger a half-inch across the paper, "and here's where the other enters."

Saunders' moustache twitched. "I see you 'ave learned a few things, Sergeant Dunn."

"Most assuredly, Sergeant Saunders."

They turned their attention back to the maps. With Saunders writing and periodically erasing, they hashed out a detailed plan of attack and escape. The senior members in the room watched closely, but said nothing. Every now and then, Kenton or Jenkins would nod in agreement with a point of the plan. Not once did either raise a concern. Both knew it was better to let these two extraordinary men just do their job. Over managing Dunn and Saunders was not an option. They would just do it their own way, regardless.

After twenty minutes, Saunders dropped the pencil nub on the desk and stood up. "That should do it."

"It'll work," agreed Dunn. "We don't even need the Germans' cooperation."

Everyone laughed.

Dunn said, "So what's the timetable?"

Adams said, "You're due out the night of 1 June at 2230 hours. You'll be dropped about five miles due south of the city. Madeline and her resistance group will pick you up there." He handed a three-by-five note card and a sheet of paper to Dunn. "Here's the code word, the response and the mission orders."

Dunn read the note card once and dropped it back on the table. Then he gave the orders a cursory check, confirming that Kenton had signed them. He folded the paper and slid it into his jacket pocket.

Kenton looked at the two sergeants. "Get your teams together tomorrow morning to go over your plans." He paused and his eyes narrowed, "There will be no screwing around on this. Both of you will ensure that your teams put the bullshit antics aside and stay focused for the duration of this mission. Have I made myself perfectly clear on this?"

In unison, the sergeants responded, "Yes, Colonel."

"Good. That will be all, then, gentlemen."

Again together, "Yes, sir." Then Dunn and Saunders stepped back, saluted and left.

After the door closed behind the warriors and the sound of

their footsteps faded, Adams asked, "What odds do you give this mission, Colonel?"

Colonel Kenton looked at Adams with a worried expression. "I give it one in three, Sam."

Adams looked equally unhappy. "But Dunn and Saunders are leading it, sir."

"I know. That's what raises it to one in three."

"God help them," said Jenkins.

Dunn and Saunders, standing beside Dunn's jeep, eyed each other glumly. Neither wanted to be the first to say what was on his mind. Saunders lifted the flap on his shirt pocket and pulled out a pack of American Lucky Strike cigarettes, a white package with a large red dot, everybody's favorite. He gave the pack a quick flick, then held it out to Dunn. They lit up and puffed away contentedly.

"What was the argument about?"

Saunders shook his head and gave Dunn a wry smile. "Colonel Jenkins didn't want your team to go. He thought we should send two British teams."

"His usual point of view." Dunn took another puff and exhaled slowly. "What do you think?"

"The truth, Dunn?"

"Yes."

"You have the best team I've ever seen." Saunders grinned. "Next to mine, of course."

Dunn smiled. "Of course." He finished his cigarette, dropping the butt to the ground and smashing it with the toe of his boot. "This has the makings of a bad one, Saunders."

"Aye. I 'ave a bad feeling about this one."

"Ever have a bad feeling about a mission before?"

"Aye. A few times."

Dunn looked away, across the compound, at the PX. A soldier held the door open for a young woman, probably an officer's wife, who was coming out of the store. She carried a brown paper bag in one arm and a baby in the other. She smiled at the soldier and he tipped his hat. Dunn shook his head at the normalcy of it all. He faced Saunders and said, "And?"

"I was always right."

"Someone didn't come back."

"Correct."

Dunn held out his hand. "No fucking around this time, Malcolm."

Saunders grasped Dunn's hand firmly. "Not a chance, Thomas. Not a chance."

"Need a ride out to the barracks?"

The British Commando gave Dunn a sly smile, "No, thanks. Got to go spend my last free night with a sick friend."

Dunn grinned and turned away.

Dunn drove to the barracks and turned off the engine, but didn't get out. Sitting there, hands on the wheel, he worried about the mission and his uncharacteristic fears. He'd lost men before, but instead of getting used to it, he'd come to dread it more and more. He wondered whether it would begin to diminish his capability as a leader. As he dwelled on this, a sudden ugly thought struck him. Maybe it already had. If so, would he even know it? Worse, would his men? He knew he'd have to buck it up before he went inside or the men would sense something was wrong, like a dog smelling fear. As a leader, he just couldn't have that. He rubbed his face, took a deep breath, then let it out. Feeling no better, but at least under control, he got out of the jeep and went in.

Dunn's team members sat around a makeshift table playing poker. "Gentlemen, who's winning?"

"Hey, Sarge," was the response. They put down their cards and got up, forming a half circle around Dunn. They knew he'd be getting their next mission from the colonel and were curious.

Dunn looked at the six faces staring back at him, each with the same expectant expression. "The mission has the blessings of Colonel Kenton and our old friend Colonel Jenkins."

A groan passed around the group and Corporal Dave Cross, Dunn's second in command, originally from Maine and now from New York City, said, "Shit. That old bastard's still around?" He was tall and lanky, with sandy brown hair that fell over his forehead. His gray eyes searched Dunn's face for a moment, and seeing something there, said, "There's more isn't there? What is it?"

Dunn nodded and grinned. "Oh, it does get better, gentlemen. We have a British Commando unit going with us."

"Ah, not one of them combined jobs," said Timothy Oldham. Timothy was from rural Kentucky and his speech reflected a bit of less than perfect English now and then.

"Yes. A combined job and guess who's commanding."

Cross, who already had an inkling said, "Saunders. It's Saunders and his team isn't it?"

Dunn nodded.

"Jesus, Dunny, couldn't you talk Colonel Kenton out of it?" Jack Hanson had a high, squeaky voice that could grate on the ears. He was the only person alive who got away with calling Dunn 'Dunny.' Dunn had no idea why he permitted it, but he'd never asked the little tough guy to stop.

"When was the last time *anyone* talked the good Colonel out of anything? Besides, Saunders and Jenkins were both standing right there. I talked with Saunders and we both agree that we're all playing this one straight, no plans for revenge. Am I clear on that?"

Everyone nodded and, satisfied they meant it, Dunn continued, "We take off Thursday, the first, from the field down the road a piece. The target is near Calais. We're hitting a huge supply depot and we're working with the French underground."

A few wolf whistles pierced the barracks' stale air and Hanson said, "Ooh la la! Maybe I can score with one of those hairy Frenchie girls."

Cross poked Hanson hard in the ribs and said, "Is that all you ever think about."

"Ow. Yeah, what else is there?"

Laughter erupted and Dunn waited a few moments before continuing. "We have the night off, but mission planning, followed by firing range work, is scheduled for 0800 hours. I'm letting you sleep in one last time."

"Indeed. Thank you ever so much, Sergeant Dunn." Stanley Wickham had a deep Texan drawl, yet he had somehow picked up a slight British accent and had fallen into British word choice. He said he had English blood in him and that the accent must be coming out due to their surroundings. This odd combination drove the British girls crazy and he was constantly surrounded by them whenever he went into town.

Dunn looked at the two men who had remained silent, Patrick

Ward and Danny Morris. Both were quiet by nature, but that's where their similarity ended. Ward was a Yale graduate from New Hampshire and a brilliant mathematician with a future on Wall Street. Morris was a farmer's son from Kansas who loved and respected the land for its agricultural importance and beauty. One time, early on in their existence as a unit, Cross had made a crack about how boring it was to drive across Kansas. Morris had calmly remarked that it was a shame city folk couldn't appreciate the beauty of a single tree or a wheat field. Cross never thought about it the same way again.

"Do either of you have any questions?"

They both said no and Dunn nodded. "Okay, fellas, let's get out of here, 0800 is going to come mighty early."

Cross held his hand up. "Well now, just a minute, Sarge. Not so fast. We'll be heading on over to the pub in Andover and we expect you to join us."

Dunn looked embarrassed. "Ah, thanks, anyway, Cross, but I have plans."

"Uh huh. Would these plans have anything to do with a tall, slender and quite gorgeous blonde?"

"Yes."

"Gentlemen, it looks like our esteemed leader would rather spend the evening with a certain Miss Pamela Hardwicke than with us. I don't know about you, but I'm feeling neglected. Maybe even hurt." He looked at Dunn with sorrowful eyes, as if saying *How could you?*

Dunn laughed and said, "All right you win. We'll try, try, mind you, to stop by and have a brew with you after dinner. Satisfied?"

"Indeed we are, Sarge, and we look forward to seeing you and your bonnie lass," said Wickham in his Brit-Tex accent.

3

In flight over Germany
27 May, 1708 Hours

Captain Norman Miller hurtled through the crisp blue sky in his silver P-51D Mustang. As he looked around at the world at 25,000 feet, an unbidden, unwelcome thought burst its way forward: *This is too beautiful a place for men to die.*

Miller carried the burden of his own fear of dying as well as for the men in his squadron, but at least he and his men could maneuver and fight back, while regulations required the B-17s to stay in formation. Protecting them was difficult at best, impossible at worst. Although he knew he could count on his squadron to give its best, sometimes it just wasn't enough. When that happened, planes and crews were lost.

A natural flyer, if there ever was one, Miller knew from the age of ten he was born to fly. When a barnstormer's bright yellow biplane swooped overhead at the Howard County Fair, just outside Kokomo, Indiana, Norman was fascinated by the things the pilot could make the plane do. The rolls, loops and dazzling dives sparked a strange feeling deep in his chest, one he

RONN MUNSTERMAN

didn't recognize at first.

After the air show, he was first in line with one of the handbills from the grocery store. It said the first five people got free rides. The moment the pilot jerked the stick back and the little plane darted skyward, pushing his butt down on the leather seat, Norman understood the earlier feeling. He knew he was in love with flying.

Born and raised in a large German family in central Indiana, he'd grown up speaking German at home, church and school. In 1916, his grandfather had changed the family name from Mueller to Miller to sound more American. When Miller entered the Army in 1939, right after high school, they'd duly noted his second language skill, then promptly sent him off to flight school after he had proudly showed them his pilot's license. The school suited him very well and Miller finished first in his class. Years and thousands of flight hours later, he had become a talented pilot and a smart aerial tactician. His highly developed sixth sense had saved him many times. There were ten swastikas painted under his plane's canopy, making him a double ace. His squadron buddies made more of this badge of honor than he did. For him, he was just doing his job. Kill the other guy before he kills you.

The roar of the Mustang's powerful Merlin engine pounded his ears and he could feel the smooth vibration in his chest, like a good bass note during a Glenn Miller concert. He had grown accustomed to the sounds and vibrations long ago. You had to, otherwise you'd lose focus. Pilots who lost focus didn't come home. He intended to come home to his wife. As a reminder, his plane bore a likeness of her and the name *Sweet Mabel*.

He turned his head toward the flight of bombers on his right. The twenty-four B-17s flew in the standard box formation to present the best defense. Each Flying Fortress had a dozen .50 caliber machine guns, including the double-barreled turrets above, below, fore and aft. The bomber could cruise at close to 200 miles an hour while carrying three tons of bombs, the typical payload. The problem with the B-17 was, in spite of all the weaponry for self-defense against marauding Messerschmitts and Focke-Wolfes, it was still an albatross flying amongst the hawks.

Since the P-51s had been outfitted with drop fuel tanks in January, the Mustang squadrons could escort the big boys all the way deep into Germany and back. Prior to that, it had been heart wrenching for the escort pilots to leave the bombers on their own. Often the enemy fighters were visible, blatantly waiting just out of the Mustang's range, circling like hungry lions waiting for an especially juicy lunch.

Today's target had been the Gothaer airplane factory in Goetha, half way between Cologne and Berlin, where the B-17s unleashed a raining nightmare. Getting to the target unscathed was a rarity and Miller was pleasantly surprised, but now he was worried the Germans had something planned. He figured if he assumed the worst, he and his team wouldn't let their guard down. Speaking into his high-level mask, he said, "Stay awake, gents. We're not home yet." He prayed that just once they'd be lucky.

Which they weren't. Just minutes later, Tommy Hayes, a farm boy from Pennsylvania, shouted, "Bandits at twelve o'clock!"

A flight of Messerschmitt 109s, armed with machine guns and twenty-millimeter nose cannons, was coming straight at them at over three hundred miles an hour, using the Luftwaffe's favored tactic, the head-on attack. They would focus on the Plexiglas bubble and windshield at the front of the B-17 where the bombardier, pilot and copilot sat exposed like mannequins in a store window. Then they would loop back and come in from behind aiming for the bomber's weakest point, where the wings joined the fuselage. This back and forth process would continue until they were shot down or run off by the Mustangs.

Miller spotted the enemy fighters, pushed up the throttle control, and pulled back on the stick to increase his altitude. The Mustang bolted, shoving him back into the seat, a feeling he loved, but one he couldn't spare the time to relish right now. The rest of the squadron did the same as they quickly moved ahead and slightly above the bombers, so as to be able to come down into the pack of 109s. Picking his target, Miller advised the squadron which one it was. The radio chatter increased as each man did the same to avoid two pilots wasting rounds on the same enemy aircraft.

Miller knew his team of eight planes might get one or two on the first pass, but the others would break through to the bombers.

After that it would turn ugly. Air fights were never the same, except for one facet: they were always semi-controlled chaos.

He let the Mustang's nose dip toward a spot ahead of his target 109. At a closing speed of more than 600 miles an hour, the distance shrank in seconds. When the gap between the planes reached a mere five hundred yards, he pressed the trigger. Tracers sped toward the intercept point. The Messerschmitt flew right through them, the bullets striking the engine compartment. Oil and smoke spurted. Flames roared into the cockpit. The enemy plane keeled over, looking strangely graceful as it began its death dive that would end five miles down.

Miller pulled the Mustang up onto her back, then slapped the stick to the left, rolling her over smoothly in a textbook S-roll, the fastest way to reverse directions. He searched briefly to find another target and chose the last Messerschmitt in the V-formation's right leg. Jamming the throttle all the way to full, he bore down on the next victim.

He realized two other enemy fighters had been destroyed when he saw their trailing plumes of smoke, but when he glanced at the B-17 formation, some 109s were hitting their targets. The lead bomber seemed to stutter, then nosed over, smoke pouring from the port inboard engine. Miller's stomach lurched when the Fortress slipped into a flat spin from which there would be no escape. Ten men. Gone.

He closed on the Messerschmitt's tail, centering it in his circular gun sight. Once again, he squeezed the trigger and the tracers lined the sky. They were a bit high and went right over the enemy's cockpit. The pilot saw them, realized his predicament, rolled to the right and pointed his ship downward to escape, using gravity to help increase his speed.

Miller gave chase. He knew they weren't supposed to go below 18,000 feet, but he wasn't about to let one get away to come back tomorrow and kill someone. They continued earthward and every few moments Miller loosed off a few rounds, but they missed their mark. The Messerschmitt's pilot tried to shake the stubborn Mustang off his tail, but nothing worked. At 15,000 feet, they zipped into a puffy white cloud, the kind you saw shapes in from the ground when you were a kid. In the cloud's milky world, Miller completely lost all sensations except the one of falling. When they emerged seconds later, the bright blue sky and the rushing patchwork of earth returned.

Finally, at an altitude of 11,000 feet, after dropping nearly three miles, Miller fired another burst that clipped the Messerschmitt's right wingtip, which sheared off. Seconds later, the rest of the plane's wing snapped off from the enormous stress. As it fluttered away, like a leaf in the wind, a spark ignited the fuel spurting from an exposed hose and the plane exploded.

Miller yanked back on the stick, narrowly missing the Messerschmitt's fireball, and settled into level flight. He searched for the bombers' contrails so he could rejoin the group. After a moment, he spotted them a little ahead. He clicked his mike button and said, "Miller to Murphy. What's going on up there?"

"We've run 'em off, Boss. Where'd you go?"

"I'm at eleven. How many?"

"We lost one, two are damaged, but can make it home."

"Our guys okay?"

"That's affirmative."

Miller was relieved to hear that all of his men were okay. "I'll be back up soon."

"Roger."

Out of habit, Miller did a pilot's head roll to scan the blue sky around him. Off to his right, he spotted a large plane about two miles away. It was flying at a slightly lower altitude and paralleled his course. Above, and in front of it, was a smaller plane. Three Messerschmitts flew escort. Suddenly, the lead plane climbed and turned away. Miller puzzled over this maneuver for a moment, then it dawned on him that the larger plane was being towed and the cable had just been disengaged. He had never seen or heard of such a large glider. Curiosity got the better of him and he decided to go investigate. "Miller to Murphy."

"Go ahead, Boss."

"I just spotted something and I'm going to check it out."

"Be careful."

"Roger that, Murphy."

Miller edged the stick over and slid toward the unfamiliar plane and its escorts. He planned to come in directly from behind and above them. The sun was at his back, rendering him virtually invisible to the other pilots. As long as he didn't get too close or careless, he would stay invisible. Tangling with a single 109 was one thing, to take on three by yourself was just damn stupid.

He closed the distance cautiously. Soon, the large plane's features became more clearly defined. It had swept-back wings, but there was no tail. This plane was just one giant wing about the same size as a B-17. Miller idly wondered how you controlled a plane with no vertical surfaces. It would be an interesting problem to solve.

Slipping his powerful fighter in behind the flying wing and slowing to half throttle, so as not to zip past the enemy planes, Miller closed to two hundred yards. If he stayed in this relative position, the fighter pilots would never be able to spot him, even if he wasn't in line with the blinding sun, because their cockpits had airframe directly behind their heads.

Miller flipped the gun switch down to camera-and-sight only and pressed the trigger, thinking, the intelligence guys are going to lick their chops over this plane. He studied the plane as the camera ran. It was an elegant, yet simple, design resembling a boomerang that had been straightened out just a little. The color was the mottled gray the Germans favored. On the wings' trailing edges, six black openings stared at Miller, like a spider's eyes. Just rearward of the plane's pointed nose sat the cockpit and Miller could see the pilot's head through its bubble canopy. Both wings displayed the black German cross, trimmed in white, that Miller hated.

Letting the Mustang fall slightly, Miller eyed the undercarriage. The black eyes led up through the wing where Miller guessed they came out in front as engine cowlings. He was trying to fathom just what kind of engines fit there, when something in the plane's belly caught his attention. "Ah, shit," he muttered, for there he saw a set of bomb bay doors as big as the ones on a B-17. "What are the bastards up to now?" He hoped the doors showed up clearly on the film.

Deciding he had enough film, he released the trigger and pushed the gun switch back up to arm the six .50 caliber machine guns. With a flick of his wrist, Miller peeled off, turning away to rejoin his squadron.

4

Andover, England
2 miles southwest of Camp Barton Stacy
27 May, 1747 Hours

Dunn stomped on the brakes and the jeep skidded to a stop next to the curb. An elderly couple gave him a dirty look as they walked by in the opposite direction. He returned a small smile and an apologetic wave. In spite of herself, the woman waved back. Shutting off the engine, he stepped out. His rubber-soled jump boots made no noise as he strode toward the one and only flower shop in downtown Andover.

A flight of Spitfires roared over at better than 300 miles an hour and Dunn glanced up, fascinated by the beauty and power of modern fighters. He'd briefly considered applying for the army's flight training school following boot camp, and would have certainly gotten in, what with his education, intelligence and physical condition, but he'd fallen in love with the challenges of tactical problem solving. Quick on his feet, he frequently found solutions to training exercises that none of the instructors had ever seen. He once had an instructor tell the training class, and

RONN MUNSTERMAN

several other instructors, that Dunn was so good at thinking outside the box he was nowhere near the damn thing.

After the Spitfires roared out of sight, he glanced at the people on the street. Not one had looked up. Dunn thought this was remarkable considering that only a few years ago London was being devastated by German bombers day and night. He had just started his junior year at the University of Iowa in the fall of 1940, when news of the Blitz came out. Every week, he and his parents gathered around the RCA radio in the living room and listened to Edward R. Murrow's broadcast detailing the horrors of the attack. Dunn was amazed by Murrow's accounts of the British people and their will to fight and survive. At the time, he'd tried to imagine what it would be like living with the threat of death every day and night, but thought he would never truly understand it. Now he did, having faced it in Italy.

With three of his closest friends, he enlisted the day after Pearl Harbor. If the attack on Pearl hadn't been on a Sunday, they'd have gone down the moment they heard the terrible news. When he told his parents what he was going to do, his mother cried out, nearly fainting, and his father looked at him with a strange mix of pride and fear. Just one semester shy of graduation, Dunn was shocked neither parent tried to talk him out of joining. It was as though they already knew it would be a pointless plea and had reluctantly accepted his decision. He was, after all, twenty-one years old.

Dunn pushed open the shop door and a little warning bell tinkled his arrival. The proprietor, a plump, gray-haired woman, with wire-framed glasses situated near the end of her thick nose, glanced up from an arrangement she was putting together. She shot Dunn a wide smile. "Good afternoon, Sergeant."

"Afternoon, Ma'am." Dunn removed his hat and walked closer, eyeing the selection of roses displayed to the side of the woman's counter.

She followed his gaze and nodded. "Roses for your lass?"

"Yes, Ma'am."

"Oh, dear, you're not going to 'Ma'am' me to death, are you? Please, call me Margie."

"Okay, Margie. Yes, I'd like a dozen roses." When he reached the counter, he noticed a small collection of white glass vases. One caught his eye and he pointed. "Could you put them in that vase?"

Margie's eyes twinkled. "You have excellent taste, Sergeant. A dozen, you said. How about some nice baby's breath to go along?"

"Sure."

Margie moved over to the roses, selected twelve long stemmed flowers and slipped them carefully into the vase. "Tell me, what's your girl's name?" Margie smiled when Dunn's cheeks tinged red, and continued building the arrangement, tossing in the baby's breath in just the right places.

"Um, Pamela, but this is our first date."

"I'd venture to say you're off to a good start."

Dunn grinned sheepishly. "I sure hope so."

"Believe me, Sergeant, when you give these to Pamela, you'll get at least a kiss on the cheek."

Dunn looked doubtful.

Margie laughed. "I'll let you in on a florist's secret." She beckoned him closer with a wrinkly finger. As Dunn leaned toward her, she said, "All you have to do is remember these words: 'Beautiful flowers for a beautiful lady.'" She winked. "I hear it works every time."

Dunn shrugged.

"If it doesn't work, you come back here and I'll refund your money."

Dunn shook his head in wonder. "All right, if you say so."

"I say so." She told Dunn how much and he paid her. At the door, he turned to wave goodbye, but Margie was already back at work on the arrangement he'd interrupted.

Pamela Hardwicke stared at herself in an old walnut full-length mirror with a critical eye. She wore a dress borrowed from her roommate. It reached just past her knees, had puffy shoulders and was a robin egg blue, a color she knew would enhance her own sparkling blue eyes. Her breasts were well shaped, somewhere between perky and full. She thought her hips too wide, but they accented her narrow waist, around which Tom's hands would soon be resting as they danced. Smiling at that thought, she reached up and brushed back a wayward strand or two of fine blond hair. Then she ran a hand down the front of the dress to smooth it. Finally satisfied, she picked up her purse, turned, and walked out the door.

As a nurse, she'd had to do plenty of fending off the usually persistent men in the hospital ward by saying she had a rule of no dating the patients. That is, until one Thomas Dunn arrived. A quiet patient, he never asked for a solitary thing, even when it was clear the pain was severe. Pamela took one look at him and felt something new and delightful deep inside. She immediately told the other nurses she would be handling this particular soldier's case. This announcement was greeted with surprise and knowing smiles. The ice queen had succumbed.

She hinted at her interest and availability, subtly at first, then after two long weeks, in exasperation, bluntly. It was like whacking a stubborn, and none too bright, mule over the head with a two by four. When Dunn finally got it through his hard noggin he should ask her out, he phrased it in a remarkably stupid fashion, saying, "You wouldn't want to go out with me would you?" She forced herself to refrain from screaming, 'Yes! Yes! You big lunk.'

Pamela didn't have to wait on the front stoop of her building very long before a grinning Dunn arrived. He jumped nimbly out of the jeep, took one step toward Pamela, and stopped cold. His eyebrows seemed to be scrambling to climb under his hat and his mouth dropped open. He'd never seen her in anything except the plain white nurse's uniform and the transformation obviously caught him completely by surprise. He sucked in a breath and Pamela smiled, pleased by his reaction. He started around the jeep, then suddenly reversed directions, leaned over into the back seat and pulled out the white flower vase. He carried it gingerly and held it out to Pamela.

Pamela took the flowers, raised them to her nose and sniffed one of the roses. "Ah. Thank you, Thomas. These are gorgeous."

"You're welcome." Dunn hesitated, then thought, why not try it. "Beautiful flowers for a beautiful lady."

Pamela tilted her head and blinked. "Why, Thomas, that's just so sweet." She leaned close to Dunn and planted a soft kiss on his cheek.

Dunn blushed.

"I'm going to run them inside. Don't go away."

Before Dunn could say anything, she whirled and disappeared back into the apartment building. He rubbed his cheek thinking he should go back and pay Margie a second time for the flowers.

Two minutes later she returned, grinning like a schoolgirl. "Ready?" she asked brightly.

"Yep." Dunn held out his elbow and Pamela slid her hand into the crook. They walked to the jeep and she got in. He ran around to the driver's side, stopping long enough to pop up the jeep's windscreen for Pamela's protection from the wind. She smiled her thanks. He got in, started the engine, and said, "Where are we going for dinner?"

"The Star and Garter. We can get a nice little dinner there, nothing fancy mind you, but good food, nevertheless."

"Oh, yeah. Okay. I know where it is." He slipped the jeep into gear and pulled away from the curb.

The Star and Garter was a fifty-year-old hotel on High Street. A three-story Tudor building, it inexplicably had two, twelve-foot tall Doric columns supporting a second floor balcony, which was framed by an intricate wrought iron railing. Some say the first owner, long dead now, had visited Greece once and upon his return set to work replacing the balcony's support pillars with the out-of-place Greek columns.

Dunn escorted Pamela through the entrance, then to the right and into the restaurant. He stopped at the doorway and stared in wonder. A gorgeous long bar of dark walnut stretched the length of the restaurant. Behind it, in front of a mirror as long as the bar, heavy beer mugs were triple-stacked along with a large assortment of bottles; whiskeys and other liquors.

There wasn't much of a crowd, since not many people went out for dinner during the week, and they were able to get a table by the front window. A clean white tablecloth covered it and a small red vase with a single white gardenia perched near the window. After they sat down, Dunn drew back the white curtains, exposing the quiet High street.

Pink light from the setting sun streamed in, highlighting Pamela's hair and Dunn tried not to stare. It was just that she was so beautiful. He decided to risk a long glance. Her eyes were the bluest blue he had ever seen and when she laughed they wrinkled up at the edges in a way that melted his heart. Dunn was surprised to find himself feeling nervous in spite of the earlier peck on the cheek. He noticed Pamela was fiddling with her red and white checked napkin, folding it, smoothing it out, then unfolding it again. It suddenly hit him that she was nervous, too. *Good, I'm not alone.* He felt like he did on his first date ever, back when he was a junior in high school, and had no idea what to say. Mercifully, a welcome memory surfaced. His dad's advice before he left the house on that date: *"Tom, if you ever find yourself tongue tied with a girl, just remember two things and everything will work out just fine. First, she's as nervous as you are, and second, pay her a compliment, but don't go overboard. That'll get things rolling surprisingly well."*

Dunn smiled at the memory, and Pamela said, "You're smiling. What is it?"

"Oh, just something my dad once told me." He paused and deciding to follow his father's advice once more, leaned toward her. Pamela lifted one eyebrow expectantly and he said, "You look absolutely beautiful tonight, Pamela."

"Thank you, Thomas." Pamela smiled, pleased again by Dunn's attention.

Dunn grinned. "You're welcome." He started to say something else, but the waiter arrived.

A stocky man in his fifties with a wafer thin black mustache, the waiter wore a clean, crisply pressed black suit and a starched white shirt with a black bow tie. Instead of providing a menu, he just told them of their choices, very limited, you see, no beef, of course, but we have some fine liver and onions, or if you'd care to pay the price, we can cook up a bit of chicken. Dunn questioned Pamela with his eyes and they agreed on the chicken and an ale.

The waiter departed and Dunn asked his previously interrupted question, "How did you come to be a nurse?"

"I took my nursing training right out of school and started working in London during the blitz. Last winter, I heard they needed some extra help here at Barton Stacy, so I volunteered so I could be closer to my parents."

"The good daughter?" Dunn smiled.

Her gaze flicked away, just for a moment, then returned to Dunn. He thought something lay hidden behind her eyes as she said, "Yes, something like that."

Dunn hesitated, but then asked, "What's the real reason, Pamela?"

Pamela didn't answer immediately. She stared at her hands, which were folded on the table. Without looking up she said, "I thought my parents needed me. My older brother, Percy, was killed at Dunkirk. He was a member of the Royal Norfolk Regiment, 2nd Battalion."

"Oh, Pamela, I'm so sorry. I've heard of them. They were extraordinary men."

The Miracle of Dunkirk, as Churchill called it, began on May 26, 1940, and took ten days. The German Wehrmacht had trapped over 330,000 British and French soldiers against the English Channel. The Allied forces were outnumbered two to one, with no hope of surviving a head-to-head battle against the Wehrmacht. Quick thinking led to the Allies conducting the largest evacuation in military history. They used over 800 boats, including everything from Royal Navy destroyers to pleasure craft and fishing boats. However, the Royal Norfolk Regiment, 2nd Battalion defended the perimeter and suffered terrible losses while the mass of Allied soldiers escaped.

Pamela raised her head and looked at Dunn. "I miss him every day."

Dunn nodded. He understood the pain all too well and a terrible memory from his high school days flared. He quickly extinguished it and asked, "Any other brothers or sisters?"

"No, just me. Mother had a hard time with my birth, as she was older. The doctors said she shouldn't have any more children for her own safety, so they performed an operation on her. I think it broke her heart. And father's, too. You?"

"Two sisters. One older, Hazel. She's married to a sailor who's in the Pacific. And Gertrude." He rolled his eyes. "She's a senior in high school and thinks she knows everything." He paused, thinking. "I guess she's graduated now. I think maybe a week ago. Hopefully, I'll get a letter from home about it, maybe a picture or two."

"That'd be a nice thing," said Pamela. Then she laughed

lightly.

Dunn gave her a questioning look.

"I was just thinking I might have been a little like that. A miss know-it-all."

Dunn grinned and said, "But you've outgrown it, of course?"

"Oh, no. Not exactly. Just tempered it a bit." She smiled. "It makes it easier to 'fit in' as they say."

Dunn nodded.

Dinner arrived and they attacked their meals. After a few minutes, Pamela said, between bites, "Tell me about this Iowa you're from."

"I grew up in a rural area in the eastern part of the state. We have a lot of humongous corn fields everywhere and cattle, too. This time of year, the corn stalks are only about knee high, but soon they'll be taller than me. The people are a lot like those I've met around here, hardworking, friendly, always willing to help out a neighbor or a stranger."

"You lived on a farm?"

"No, in town. Dad's a teacher at the high school. Math."

"And your mother?"

A wistful, sad expression flashed across Dunn's face, then disappeared. "Ah. The best cook in Linn County." He grinned in an attempt to hide his feelings.

Pamela had seen the fleeting sadness and put her hand gently on top of his. "Tell me what's wrong."

"You'll think it's stupid."

"No, I won't. Tell me. Please."

He looked into her compassionate eyes and believed he could tell her anything. "You know how sometimes a little thing will remind you of something?"

"Yes, sure."

"This food, the way it looks and smells, reminded me of my mom's cooking and I realized I haven't seen my family in almost three years." He stopped abruptly to keep the lump in his throat from jumping out. "Lord, I miss them all so much."

Pamela gazed into Dunn's eyes steadily, comforting him with her own. She squeezed his hand gently. "I can't imagine what it's like being so far away from the people you love the most. It must be very hard."

"That is so true, Pamela." He turned his hand over and rubbed his thumb over the soft back of her hand. It suddenly dawned on him they were in a restaurant in a *hotel*. A hotel with lots of beds. The thought must have occurred to Pamela, too, because she blushed and gently withdrew her hand. A comfortable silence drifted over them and they resumed eating. A little later, the waiter stopped by just as they were taking their last bites. "Would you care for another draught?"

Dunn looked at Pamela and she shook her head. "No, thanks. I could really use some coffee, though."

"Coffee for you, too, sir?"

"Yes, please."

"Right away." The waiter cleared the table and was back quickly with the coffee. Pamela lifted hers in both hands and sipped carefully, the steam wafting in front of her face. She peered at Dunn through the cloud. "You were almost finished with your degree, right?"

Dunn nodded.

"What discipline?"

"History."

"What were your plans? Teach like your father?"

"I think so. I like kids, even the smart-assed ones in high school. I don't know why, exactly."

Pamela laughed. "Do you suppose it might have something to do with helping others?"

Dunn thought for a moment before answering. A trait he'd picked up from his father; think first, then speak. "You may be right. I've had it pretty good, really. Maybe that would have been my way of giving something back."

"You signed up the day after Pearl Harbor. Any regrets?"

Dunn's answer was an immediate, "No."

"Couldn't you have stayed in school, then used your degree to get a more meaningful job teaching?"

Dunn's face fell and his cheeks flared red. What the hell was this? She should know better. What the hell did she think we're doing in the first place? Dunn felt his anger getting away from him and fought to keep his voice even as he leaned over the table and said quietly, "What I do *is* meaningful, Pamela."

Pamela put a hand to her mouth, as if to keep it from blurting something else out that would hurt Dunn. "Oh, no, Thomas. I'm sorry, I didn't mean that. I just . . . " uncertain now, her voice trailed away, her eyes glistening.

Dunn clenched his jaw, frowned, then signaled to the waiter to bring the check.

5

Project Dante Lab
7 miles west of Stuttgart
29 May, 0833 Hours

Dr. Franz Herbert adjusted his gold-framed spectacles so they were more comfortable on his long, bulbous nose, then stared at himself in the common bathroom's mirror. His deep-set blue eyes were red rimmed from the building fatigue and he noted the puffy skin sagging under them. How did I come to be in this place, he wondered, not for the first time.

After a few moments, when it became apparent the figure in the mirror wasn't going to enlighten him, he answered himself, "Because Mister Doctor Herbert, when Einstein and his cronies fled the country, you became the leading physicist by default, being only the best of the fools who stayed behind."

The mirror image grinned crookedly, then the grin faded. Herbert quickly looked around to see if anyone heard his careless remark. Seeing no one, he sighed in relief. He decided he'd better be more careful in the future, if he hoped to have one at all.

He turned away from the mirror, grabbed his favorite,

threadbare white lab coat from a hook set in the wall tile, and started toward the lab, pulling the coat on.

The Project Dante lab lay buried deep underneath a thirty-meter tall hill. Here the scientists labored free from fear of the American and British bombers. Bombs could fall directly on top of them and the lab would be safe. Once, when an errant flight of B-24s accidentally dropped a few loads on them, the scientists believed it was just thunder until someone realized you couldn't hear thunder inside the lab. At that moment, the scientists finally felt safe and secure.

Early on, Herbert naively believed he'd been given the freedom of selecting his team for the project, but in reality, everyone he picked was subjected to intense Gestapo investigation. It was just a matter of luck that no one had anything in their past that kept them from being approved, like being related to a Jew, however far removed.

He reported to Albert Speer, who was a brilliant organizer. Speer had approached him in 1941, nine years after Heisenberg discovered and proved the principle of fission, the splitting of the atom. One thing Herbert appreciated about Speer was that whenever he needed something for the project, all he had to do was ask and it miraculously arrived; the advantage of Speer being a Hitler favorite.

Herbert hadn't been offered the job solely because of his qualifications, though, something that troubled him terribly. His wife, Edwina, was a true believer in Hitler's vision of a powerful, rebuilt Germany. She came from a moneyed family, the Meiers, and her father and grandfather had made their fortune on the back of war, running one of the chief armament companies in Germany. Now it specialized in large bore shell, which included the fantastically successful eighty-eight millimeter round used in both artillery and the terrifying Tiger tank.

A socialite by nature and upbringing, she had been one of the first in her circle to embrace the Nazi Party, carefully turning her head when confronted with the sinister side of Hitler's more or less legal rise to power. She had inserted herself quickly into the inner circle of Hitler's followers, especially among the powerful women, where she was soon regarded as the leader.

Herbert met her at a mid-summer rally in 1933, and they

officially began seeing each other soon after. When her father learned Herbert was a highly respected scientist at the university who followed the Nazi rules to the letter, he surprised both Edwina and Herbert by calling them into his sitting room and suggesting they marry. Even though both had been thinking along those same lines, it was a slightly embarrassing moment. However, they followed through and were married the following summer in a huge Berlin wedding. Hitler attended the reception, if only briefly. The new Mrs. Doctor Franz Herbert worked her way farther up the social power structure and her connections led to Herbert's name being dropped on Speer's desk in the first place. She never let him forget it.

In the beginning, Herbert had been excited and flattered to be considered for the top post of such an critical project. Now, three years later, all he wanted was for the war to end so he could return to a normal world and just do nuclear research.

As he walked down the brightly lit hallway toward the main conference room, his thoughts centered on the news he had gotten the night before. The Czechoslovakian uranium was nearing the end of the process of being enriched at the Auergesellschaft plant located in Oranienburg, twenty-five kilometers north of Berlin.

In physics circles, it was thought that U-238 made up 99.3% of all uranium on the planet, but is not fissile, and is therefore unable to sustain the nuclear chain reaction necessary for a massive release of energy in the form of an explosion. Through the use of centrifuges, U-235 isotopes are scooped from the uranium, and the result is enriched U-235, which is most definitely fissile.

Herbert pushed open the conference room's door and stepped in. This room was where the most lively debates took place. If there was anything scientists loved to do more than research or lab work, it was argue a point. Endlessly. Which is exactly what the three men at the front of the room were doing. They faced away from the door, standing in front of a rolling chalkboard, which was almost completely covered with mathematical formulas and schematic drawings. At the top of the board, scrawled in huge block letters and underlined, were the words:

The shortest man was doing the loudest talking, gesturing wildly with his hands. Dr. Volker Bauer, who at five-foot-two, liked to proclaim to anyone unsuspecting enough to listen, that while still a youth, he had suffered from a specific gravity problem that had stunted his growth. "Look, gentlemen, I think we agree that the only way available us to generate enough force to provoke fission is through an explosive meeting of two separate pieces of enriched uranium. Correct?"

"Yes, yes, we know all that. Move on, Bauer." Dr. Gunther Winkel was an impatient, balding hulk of a man, who towered over his colleagues, especially Bauer. He was known for both his brilliance and his complete lack of a sense of humor.

In his excitement, Bauer was oblivious to Winkel's attitude. "What method is available to us?" Without waiting for an answer, he continued, "Why a gun, of course! We just shoot one block of uranium, we'll call that the 'bullet' into another, which we'll call the 'target' and once crushed together they create critical mass, then boom. Success!" He waved his hands exuberantly and grinned.

Herbert joined the group, standing quietly behind them, curious to see who would respond first. Soon, he was rewarded for his patience.

Dr. Rudolph Gerber, a rumpled looking man, said in a surprisingly soft voice, "Volker, let me get this straight. You're suggesting we put equal quantities, equal, right?" He paused and raised an eyebrow at Bauer.

"I believe the bullet should be slightly larger than the target, so perhaps a 55/45 ratio," said the little scientist.

Volker turned to Herbert, who was still standing behind the group, and asked, "Dr. Herbert, how are the fast neutron calculations going?"

Before Herbert could answer, Winkel snapped, "You know we hate it when you sneak in on us like that."

"I didn't want to interrupt you."

"Humpf."

"I should have my calculations done in about two or three weeks." Fast neutrons were theorized to be released during U-235 nuclear fission. The calculation was horribly complex due to its many variables, but the end result was to determine the speed at which the neutrons would move during the chain reaction. The final fast neutron calculations would provide the quantity of U-235 needed to reach critical mass. "My first estimates are that we'll need a combined total twenty kilograms of U-235 enriched to at least eighty-five percent. That would be a sphere about 6.8 centimeters in diameter."

Winkel snorted, then said derisively, "And just how efficient is a bomb like this?"

Herbert knew Winkel well enough to know what was coming next, but answered calmly, "Again, this is a rough estimate, but we only need the fission of one percent of the total mass to achieve our goal of an explosion equal to thousands of tons of high explosive."

Winkel's face reddened in anger, "I formally protest, again, Dr. Herbert, to going down this path. I know," he placed a fingertip against his temple, "*know*, that if we obtain enough plutonium and use the implosion method, we'll have a much more efficient explosion and its power would be a minimum of ten times more destructive. We are wasting our time and should start on this method instead. Our nation, our *Führer,* deserve and require our best, and the gun method is not our best.

"I talked with Dr. Wolfgang Klein at the Auergesellschaft plant just yesterday and he promised me he and his team could produce enough plutonium within eight weeks. I am contacting Herr Speer today with my plan—"

Herbert drew himself to his full height of five-nine and moved close to Winkel, who at six-four had seven inches and seventy-five pounds on him. "You dare go over my head and have these kind of . . . conversations? No, you will not be talking to Minister Speer today on this topic, nor will you continue speaking with Dr. Klein at the Auergesellschaft plant! I am the Project Leader, not you. The decision has been made and approved at the highest level. The *highest* level, Winkel. This is the end of the discussion. If you do anything, *anything*, without my express approval, I will remove you from this project entirely, and you will go back to teaching. And we all know how much you like that," he finished sarcastically.

Winkel's red face drained and he stepped back. Without another word he turned and stormed out of the meeting room.

After a moment of quiet, when the only sound was the snick of the door closing behind Winkel, Bauer piped up, "That went well."

Gerber chuckled nervously. He and Bauer weren't used to Herbert's anger. Herbert was a strong manager, but used persuasion, humor, and kindness to inspire and lead rather than push his staff. This was a different side, and they assumed it was Winkel's attitude that generated such anger. They were wrong.

Berlin
29 May, 1128 Hours

Hermann Göring sat alone in the back seat of his long, black Mercedes. He'd unbuttoned his too-tight, pale blue uniform jacket for comfort. His matching officer's hat lay upside down on the leather seat next to him. Drumming his fat, dough-colored fingers on the leather satchel sitting on his knees, he stared out the window in disbelief. Every building the car passed was nothing but a rubble strewn skeleton, thanks to the Allied bombings, which had intensified of late.

On his way to the regular morning meeting with the *Führer*, Göring wondered what Hitler's mood would be today. One never knew which topic would set off another unbelievable display of rage in the form of a spittle-flinging tantrum. With a sigh, he opened the satchel and pulled out a sheaf of papers. As his chauffeur continued guiding the powerful car through the city streets, he began reading the reports on air group strengths, or weaknesses, to be precise. He'd already been forced to resize and reorganize his air groups, including shutting down some airfields, consolidating his forces. He had, so far, hidden this from Hitler, but would have to tell him soon. That would be an unpleasant meeting.

Still lost in concentration, Göring looked up in mild surprise when the car pulled to a stop. The driver bounded around the car and opened the door. The Field Marshal put his hat on and stepped out carefully. He nodded to the chauffeur, then lumbered up the long walkway to the Reich Chancellery and his meeting with the world's most dangerous, unpredictable man. Two Waffen-SS soldiers guarded the entrance and they saluted smartly as Göring walked past them. He acknowledged the salute with a wave of his right hand. Passing underneath an enormous golden eagle suspended above the door, he entered the building that spanned two blocks.

His heels clicked on the marble floor as he marched down the ten-meter-wide gallery. He walked by several large tapestries hanging on his right. When he knocked on one of the tall double doors guarding the entrance to Hitler's office, an aide in a crisp uniform swung them open and beckoned him inside.

Hitler stood facing a window opposite the doors with his hands clasped behind his back, a common pose. He seemed to be peering out at the destruction in the streets of Berlin, but he might not be. He could be lost in thought about Russia, perhaps, or the impending Allied invasion, or his beloved dog, Blondi.

Göring stopped a few meters from the *Führer* and waited. Hitler finally turned around and fixed Göring with a steely stare. A long moment passed, then he smiled. "Field Marshal Göring." He stepped closer and clapped the much larger man on the shoulder. "How good to see you."

Inwardly, Göring felt relief. It might be a good day. He smiled in return and raised his arm, giving the Nazi salute. "*Heil Hitler!*"

Hitler returned the salute with a quick flick of the wrist, then guided his number two man toward his desk and the awaiting chairs. He sat down behind the enormous oak desk and Göring seated himself in a beautiful beige winged chair. It was the only chair he trusted to support his girth. He removed the sheaf of papers from the satchel and looked at Hitler expectantly.

"So what are we to discuss today, my friend?" asked Hitler.

"I met with the Horten brothers about the new plane. As you know, *mein Führer*, Reimar and Walter began working on a dramatically new concept many years ago, long before the war. In essence, it is a flying wing, with no tail." Göring said this with excitement and pride.

Hitler nodded, but said nothing.

Göring continued, "This past Saturday, the Hortens flew the aircraft, proving the design's aerodynamics are sound and stable.

The plane has some exciting possibilities for us." He smiled hopefully. "I have two photographs, if you would care to see them, *mein Führer*."

"Of course." Hitler's expression gave away nothing.

This would be the moment of highest peril for Göring. He would have to sell the idea to Hitler. Slipping the black and white pictures from his satchel, he placed them on the desk in front of Hitler.

The *Führer* leaned forward and lowered his head to examine the photos. After a moment, he glanced up at Göring without raising his head. This gave him a particularly predatory appearance that unsettled most people, and although Göring was used to it, he knew what was coming was going to be bad. He took a deep breath in preparation.

"This is a bomber, Field Marshal."

"Yes, *mein Führer*. According to the Hortens' calculations, this plane, equipped with six Junkers 004B jet turbine engines, could cross the Atlantic ocean at an altitude of twelve kilometers and reach a speed of 1,000 kilometers per hour."

Hitler abruptly sat up and swept a hand across his forehead to brush the black hair back out of the way. He glared at Göring.

"It would provide us with a new, never heard of—"

"Stop!" Hitler jumped to his feet, his face red. He began waving his arms up and down, looking like an orchestra conductor on too much coffee. Suddenly, he pointed a shaking finger at Göring and shouted, "Bombers! You dare mention bombers again? Bombers, bombers, bombers! That's all I ever hear from you! I want rockets! I want rockets, do you hear? I want more resources at Peenemunde! Have you ordered the resources to Peenemunde yet? Have you?" Hitler was referring to an additional team of scientists and engineers that had been reassigned to speed up the development and delivery of Hitler's favorite toy, the V1 rocket.

"Yes, I have," answered Göring. He decided to wait and see if Hitler calmed down enough to allow him to present his plan for the bomber. If not, it would just have to wait until a later date.

"And are they there yet?"

Göring glanced at a heavy gold watch adorning his wrist and said, "They should arrive early this evening, in just a few hours."

"So you can do some things right, eh?" And with that, the tantrum was over. Hitler sat down as though nothing had happened, although he was breathing heavily, as if he'd just run 400 meters. Göring sometimes wondered whether it was just an act.

"How soon will the rockets be ready to launch?" Hitler leaned forward eagerly, hands clasped in front of him, resting on the green desk blotter.

"Ten days, *mein Führer.*"

Hitler clapped his hands in glee. "Oh, that is wonderful. I can't wait to hear from our sources in London how badly we hurt that English tyrant Churchill. He won't know what to do. Why, he can't do anything at all! He can't stop them from destroying that which he loves most. Ha! I have an idea. Maybe we can target the Parliament building. Isn't that a wonderful idea?"

"Yes." Göring smiled. Sometimes Hitler did hit upon a good idea. Of course, even a revolver with one bullet was bound to fire eventually. Giving Hitler good news was like giving a birthday present to a difficult child.

"You will keep me informed?"

"Yes, *mein Führer.*"

Hitler nodded and raised a hand to point at Göring's satchel. "What else have you for me in that bag of yours?"

"More good news." Göring pulled out another sheet of paper and held it up. "Speer's latest memo says they are on the verge of what may the final breakthrough. They'll be conducting a preliminary packing test of the Uranium 235 container in the next few days. It pleases me to tell you that I was instrumental in obtaining the last amounts of U-238 from which the 235 was extracted." He beamed.

Hitler picked up a pencil and leaned back in his high-backed leather chair. He grasped the pointed end and bounced the eraser on the blotter. "Does Speer think it will really work?" Hitler often needed to be reassured.

"He believes the theory is beyond reproach." He paused, stifling a little laugh.

Hitler's eyebrows went up and he asked, "What is so funny?"

"Oh, you know these scientists and how they love to debate everything."

Hitler merely nodded.

"Speer told me some of the scientists are worried about what might happen when the bomb explodes. They think it could ignite the atmosphere and set off some sort of chain reaction, destroying the world."

A frown settled on Hitler's face.

Göring quickly waved a hand dismissively and said, "It's utter nonsense, of course, Speer himself assures me that cannot happen."

The frown disappeared and Hitler asked, "Just how powerful will it be?"

"Speer reports the scientists' calculations suggest an equivalence to twenty kilotons of TNT."

How much of a city can be destroyed?"

"Perhaps ten square kilometers."

"Marvelous," said Hitler, beaming.

Göring decided this was the time to bring up the bomber again, however, he was more careful. "*Mein Führer*, if you would indulge me for a few moments, I would like to explain, in detail, my plan for the first bomb." He paused, waiting.

Hitler sighed and looked at Göring as though he was facing a wayward, stubborn child. "You're going to bring up the bomber yet again, aren't you?"

"Yes, but only if you're willing. I developed a plan I think you'll love."

"You have the airplane's specs there?"

"Yes." Another paper slid across the desk.

Hitler examined the airplane's specifications, then asked, "They're using wood for the primary surface?"

"Yes. It's a wood and carbon composite." Göring gave Hitler a conspiratorial smirk.

"What is it?"

"This surface makes the airplane invisible to radar," Göring replied proudly.

"We may have something valuable here, Field Marshal." Hitler sat back with an inviting expression on his face. "What's your plan?"

"As I mentioned earlier, this plane can cross the Atlantic Ocean."

"Yes, I heard you before. Go on."

"The payload is four thousand kilograms." He paused to let his leader think about that for a moment. Göring was giving the information to Hitler in small bites. Of late, it worked better.

Hitler was mouthing the words 'four thousand.'

Göring continued, "It is sufficient for the atomic bomb."

Hitler's eyes widened.

"We can deliver it to America."

Hitler's face became grotesquely animated, as though all of it was trying to express joy, but each part going in different directions. "Oh, that is beyond my wildest hopes!" Unable to contain himself any longer, he hopped out of his chair and danced around the desk to Göring.

"How soon can the Hortens deliver this marvelous machine?"

"Early July."

"So soon?"

"Yes."

At this news, Hitler said, "I can already picture Roosevelt's shocked expression when we drop an atomic bomb on New York. Or maybe we should drop it on Washington." He laughed. "That would be enough to sue for peace and keep Europe out of American and Russian hands. I would rule as no one before. My Reich would be preserved."

"Yes, *mein Führer*. It would be wonderful."

"Get me Albert Speer. I want to find out when the bomb will be ready. My, we have a lot of planning to do, don't we?"

"Yes, *mein Führer*."

The Horten Brothers Aeronautical Works
5 miles south of Göttingen, Germany
29 May, 1206 Hours

The Horten brothers, Reimar and Walter, were highly intelligent and inquisitive, a perfect combination for aeronautical engineers. They first began building planes as boys, creating innovative and beautiful model gliders. Their parents, indulging the boys' intelligence and interests, allowed the youngsters to turn the family home into a workshop. They were often spotted at the top of a hill launching one of their hand-built airplanes over and over again, laughing in delight as it soared high, then glided smoothly toward the bottom of the hill.

As they grew older, their planes became more sophisticated, and larger, some with wingspans of three meters. Since they could no longer be launched by hand, they constructed a catapult five meters long. They loaded the plane onto the long wooden rail and attached a spring to the plane's nose. With the release of a simple trigger, the plane would whoosh down the rail and rise gracefully into the sky. Usually.

There were the occasional set backs, like the time the spring release on the nose failed to let go. The plane did a not-so-graceful somersault right into the ground, shearing off the wings at the roots. The boys, young men really, who had matured beyond their years, simply picked up the pieces and headed back to the workshop. They learned early on that no matter how much you planned, how much care you put into design and construction, sometimes you had failures. It was what you did after the failure that counted. So they analyzed exactly what happened to cause the failure and took steps to prevent it from ever happening again.

Both young men were Luftwaffe pilots, as was their eldest brother, Wolfam, who had been shot down and killed near Dunkirk. They'd both been trained on the Me-109, but only Walter had seen action, and that for only six months. The brothers' design philosophy helped them attract Göring's attention. Göring loved new airplanes and he was eager to meet with the Hortens when he heard they had some swept wing designs for a jet propelled fighter and a bomber. The meeting had lasted less than an hour and Göring ordered them pulled off the flight line to complete construction of the bomber. He approved their design for the bomber with a promise to ensure they received the Junkers jet engines on time.

Since then, the brothers had worked long and hard hours. The team they assembled was made up of their best men. All were dedicated to completing the project on time. They were on schedule and the plane had performed perfectly during the gliding test two days ago. Their lead test pilot, Hans Engel, was grinning ear to ear when he'd climbed down from the three seat cockpit. He told the Hortens, and the rest of the team, it was like flying a Mercedes on an aerial Autobahn. Turn the wheel and the plane responded immediately and fluidly.

Reimar, pragmatic as usual, reminded everyone the test had been done with no engines and no power and the next test could be dramatically affected by the weight and performance of the engines. So, he warned, make no assumptions, make no mistakes.

The brothers walked side by side, as they had done since they were little, into their construction facility's hanger. A massive structure, its original purpose had been for building zeppelins. The ceiling, thirty meters above them, seemed more a part of the sky than the hanger. The doors at the opposite end were three hundred meters distant. Light filtered through opaque windows giving the cavern adequate brightness that was enhanced by hanging lights.

In the hanger's center stood their showpiece, the Horten XVIII, which they called the H18. Even parked in the hanger, the plane appeared to be in flight. Painted the standard German gray, its simplistic beauty still overpowered an observer even from a distance. The wingspan was forty meters and it sat on a tricycle set of landing gear, its nose up slightly, as if sniffing the air.

Two men huddled near the empty engine cowlings on the left wing. They were inspecting the interior of the outermost one and talking animatedly, not quite an argument, but certainly a disagreement. The Hortens stepped close and Reimar asked, "What seems to be the problem, gentlemen?"

Both workmen looked at the brothers. Carl Nagel, the Chief Mechanic, spoke first, "Mauer found some pitting on the front of number one's cowling. We are in disagreement, as usual, over how to repair it." Nagel wore surprisingly clean blue mechanic's coveralls. His blond hair was cut short and his rugged face had plenty of crinkles at the edges of his blue eyes, perhaps from a lifetime of laughter or squinting.

"Only on number one?" asked Walter.

Hugo Mauer, the trusted Chief Engineer, nodded. "We do agree it probably came from debris on the runway. Even though the pits are not deep, we can't allow them to throw particles into the jet." Mauer was a slender six footer and he also wore coveralls, but they were a light shade of green. Like Nagel, he had short blond hair over blue eyes.

"We'll leave it to you to resolve. Just keep us informed," said Walter. The Hortens were both hands-on types and knew everything about what each workman was doing. It had been difficult to relinquish some of their control, but they hired the best men they could find, stealing more than a few from the Messerschmitt Group, with Göring's approval, of course. Finally, over time, they learned to rely on their men.

"Yes, Walter. Any news on the engines?" Mauer asked, his expression hopeful.

Walter and Reimar exchanged glances, passing an unspoken message as was common among siblings. They explicitly trusted Nagel and Mauer and whenever possible gave them all the latest information. Reimar said, "Field Marshal Göring assured us we will have all six of the Junkers 004Bs in just a few days." A thrilled Nagel started to speak, but Reimar held up a hand. "Before you get all excited, I must tell you he said security and secrecy on these engines was of the highest national importance. He also emphasized that anyone caught dispensing any information about them outside this building would be shot immediately." He paused to let that sink in before continuing, "Any questions?"

Nagel and Mauer were both visibly alarmed by this news and neither could think of anything to say. They shook their heads.

"Good. As the delivery date grows closer, we will inform those who need to know at the proper time. Until then, you will keep this news to yourselves. You will not mention this to the men."

Mauer said, "Yes, Walter."

With that, the Hortens turned away and headed toward their office.

6

Leiston Air Base
100 miles northeast of London
31 May, 1330 Hours

Captain Norman Miller stopped in front of Colonel Nelson's office. He felt no particular concern to be called into the Colonel's office. It wasn't quite the same as being called to the principal's office. Not usually, anyway.

He'd gotten the message to see the Colonel from his flight chief who, in his typical crusty manner, said the Colonel wants to see you yesterday, then turned back to his beloved Mustang. According to the unwritten rules, once the plane was on the ground, it belonged to the chief, not the pilot. For that matter, the chief often told Miller he was only loaning the plane to him and he'd better take good care of her or he'd personally kick his ass, officer or not. Miller believed him.

Although the P-51 Mustang's beginning was less than stellar, quick design changes altered the plane, making it, by far, the world's best fighter. In 1940, the Royal Air Force approached North American Aviation with the intention of getting some of

RONN MUNSTERMAN

the P-40 Warhawk fighters made famous by the Flying Tigers in China. Instead, North American offered to build a completely new plane and the Mustang was born. When North American delivered the first P-51s, the British had been shocked to see it outperform their own treasured Spitfire. However, there was a serious flaw. The engine, the same Allison used in the P-40s, was severely underpowered for the P-51's extra weight. A forward thinking engineer convinced the team to install the British Rolls-Royce Merlin inline engine and the true Mustang came to be. The P-51D could reach 437 miles an hour and outpaced, outmaneuvered and outfought everything in Göring's flying arsenal. Every Mustang pilot was proud of his bird and most had experienced getting out of a jam due to its phenomenal performance. To say they loved their airplane was an understatement on the order of saying American servicemen loved baseball.

Miller rapped his knuckles on the open door, and entered the office when Nelson's voice carried out into the hallway, "Come."

Miller hadn't taken the time to change and was still wearing his flight gear. His blond hair was crinkled in places from the leather flying cap, and his face was nearly as weathered as the cap. At five-ten he was on the high end of being able to fit into the Mustang's cockpit.

A man wearing a rumpled black suit sat in one of the two old wooden chairs in front of Nelson's desk. He held a black leather briefcase protectively in his lap. His black hair was a little longer than most and was combed straight back from his forehead. Sharp brown eyes examined Miller. He nodded a greeting.

Miller nodded in return, then was surprised to see handcuffs leading from the man's wrist to the handle of the briefcase. The man gave him a wan smile that Miller couldn't bring himself to return. The stranger's presence and the top secret briefcase meant something big, very big, was going on. He thought back to the plane he'd filmed and was sure that was it.

Colonel Nelson said, "At ease, Captain." Which meant 'have a seat.'

Miller sat down, crossed his legs and looked at Nelson, waiting.

Nelson was a red-haired, freckle-faced man who looked years

younger than his twenty-eight. A West Point graduate, Nelson arrived in England in 1941 as a lieutenant volunteering to fly a Spitfire for the British. He quickly earned a reputation as a talented pilot and achieved the coveted ace status. Driving back from leave on a rainy night, he'd been hit, literally, by a truck. His car was flung off the road, slamming into a tree so hard his knee shattered. The damage was so bad he would never fly again.

He thereafter had only desk assignments. Instead of taking the pity route, he used the same drive that made him the pilot he had been and grew into a smart, demanding commander who cared for his men. He often drove his men nuts because he always insisted that pilot reports were in perfect order and confirmed before passing them on to those in the upper levels. He was a prudent man and he wasn't about to send something up the line that would later be proved wrong. If you gave him accurate information that turned out to be valuable, though, he made sure you got the proper recognition and reward, even if it was only a pass for a few extra days leave in London.

"I heard all the bombers came back today. Good job."

Miller wasn't surprised that Nelson already knew the mission's status. He had eyes and ears everywhere. He smiled at the compliment. "Thank you, sir. Yes, one with a bit of engine damage, but they nursed her all the way back."

"Good, good." Nelson leaned forward, clasped his hands on top of the desk and cleared his throat. "That report and film you gave me last Saturday have drawn quite a bit of attention."

"Yes, sir." It was clear whose attention it had attracted, since he was sitting right there beside him.

"This is Howard Lawson, with the Office of Strategic Services in Washington."

Lawson swung his hand, the one not attached to the briefcase, toward Miller. "I'm pleased to meet you, Captain."

Miller grasped Lawson's hand, surprised by both its roughness and strength. Lawson was accustomed to hard work. "You, too."

"I'd like to spend some time with you. View the film and go over your report. The Colonel has kindly offered to let us use his office." Lawson was clearly taking over now.

Miller glanced at Nelson and from the slight change in the

Colonel's expression, knew there had been no offer.

"Let's get started, shall we?" Lawson rose and headed toward a table by the windows. There, he laid his briefcase and withdrew a key from his suit jacket pocket.

Miller got up, stretched his aching back, then ambled over to join Lawson.

Lawson unlocked and removed the handcuff, then rubbed his wrist, grimacing. "That gets to be painful after awhile."

"I would think so."

Lawson unlocked and opened the briefcase, then pulled a reel of film and a file folder out. He reached under the table and lifted a projector to the table top. After a few minutes, Lawson had the film loaded into the projector. He turned to Miller. "Would you pull the shades and get the lights?"

"Yes, sir." Miller complied and returned to take a seat beside Lawson.

Lawson said, "While we watch the film, speak up if you think of something new, okay?"

"Yes, sir."

The OSS officer flipped on the projector and the grainy gun camera film showed the airplane that had drawn a lot of attention.

Colonel Nelson turned his chair so he could see the screen better.

They watched the short film, with Lawson asking only a few questions, primarily to confirm Miller's report here and there.

Afterwards, with the lights back on and the shades up, Lawson lit a cigarette and leaned back. He turned to Miller. "You did a remarkable job filming that aircraft."

"Thanks. "

"How did you keep the Germans from spotting you?"

"I put the sun behind me."

Lawson nodded. "Of course, why didn't I think of that?" He took a puff and blew the smoke out his nose, then frowned. "We're extremely concerned about this airplane of yours, Miller."

"We? Who exactly is 'we?'"

"That would be William Donovan, head of the OSS and me. He sent me here to get it from the horse's mouth, so to speak." Lawson's eyes flicked away, just for a moment, then returned to

Miller.

Miller raised his eyebrows at the name drop, but his bureaucrat alarm beeped away. *You didn't come all the way across the Atlantic for that. You have another reason. When are you going to tell me?* "So, Mr. Donovan's seen the film, huh?"

"Yes."

"Why are you guys so concerned? It's just a prototype for a new bomber."

Lawson bristled. "We know that, Captain. But we believe it's not just another bomber. We showed it to some people at Northrop and they all went bug-eyed at the sight of it. They thought that with the right kind of engines, this had the makings of being a long range bomber."

Miller shrugged. "Well, we have long range bombers, too, sir. I mean we're flying all the way to Berlin."

Lawson shook his head. "No, I mean *really* long range. Transatlantic."

Miller glanced over at Nelson who looked as surprised as he felt. *Ah, you didn't know either.* Miller mulled over the implications of this news. *A new German bomber that could reach the United States? For what purpose? We control the sky, both here and at home. It couldn't get close, even if it managed to get out of Europe. The B-17 had a range of about thirty-seven hundred miles and it was the top of the line in bombers. What were the Germans doing to exact that kind of performance?* Puzzled, he shook his head and said, "This is what your top guys at Northrop came up with?"

"Yes, but there's something else."

Miller waited, thinking, *isn't there always?*

"One of the engineers spent time in Germany back in 1931. He heard about two brothers, Reimar and Walter Horten, who were making a name for themselves in aeronautical engineering. Their specialty, if you will, was swept wing aircraft."

Miller raised his chin in understanding. "You believe these brothers are responsible for the plane I saw, right?"

Lawson nodded and said, "Northrop is looking into that design platform, too, and the engineer is part of that team." He pulled an eight-by-ten glossy photo from his folder and laid it on the desk. Miller leaned over to examine it. Nelson got up and came over to stand behind them. "I had the boys make some photos of the film so we could blow them up for detail. When our engineer looked at this he about went nuts."

"What? Why?" asked Nelson.

The picture was grainy, but clear enough for them to see the six engine exhaust ports and the German cross on the wings. A red circle marked a point on the leading edge of each wing between the wing tip and the outmost engine cowling.

"He's the one who marked these points. If you look close, you can see they're little rises, flares, almost, with unusual shapes. His conclusion was that these drastically change the airflow across the front of the wing and increase the aircraft's lift, without compromising control."

Although Miller wasn't an aeronautical engineer, he understood perfectly well the main principles of flight: power, lift, and its enemy, drag, or friction. Alter any one of the three and the flight characteristics of a plane changed dramatically, sometimes for the better, sometimes not. One thing was certain, though, increasing lift without increasing power made the plane more efficient and therefore able to fly longer distances. This was all well and good, Miller thought, but there's still one major problem for the Germans. "Just how do you expect the Germans to get that plane out of Europe, across the Atlantic and to the states without being shot down?"

A grimace shot across Lawson's face. "That's the worst part of what the engineer told us. He said the Hortens were experimenting with large body structures covered by a wood and carbon composite."

Miller sucked in his breath, then in a soft voice said, "Ah shit, invisible to radar."

Lawson looked unhappy. "Invisible to radar."

"You didn't come here just to interview me, did you?"

Lawson shook his head. "The engineer managed to meet them back then and they were happy to give him a tour of their facility."

"Then we know where to strike," said Colonel Nelson.

Lawson shook his head. "It wasn't anywhere near where Miller saw the plane." He looked embarrassed. "We don't know where it is."

Miller refrained from smiling. You don't like not knowing, do you?

"We have a top priority mission for you. Your flight will go back to the same area where you first spotted it and find the hanger."

Miller grimaced and, his voice heavy with sarcasm, said, "To do what, take more pictures?"

Lawson ignored the tone and said, "No, we must find this aircraft and destroy it before it's too late."

Puzzled, Miller said, "Too late? Too late for what?"

"I can't tell you. It's need to know only."

Miller's lips compressed, then he muttered, "Of course it is."

"Me either, Miller," piped in Colonel Nelson.

Miller looked worried and turned to Nelson.

Lawson, seeing the expression, felt a moment's panic. Please don't tell me you're afraid of the mission.

"Colonel, what about the escort flights? This is going to interfere with that."

Lawson was relieved that this was all that was bothering Miller. In a terse voice, he spoke up before Nelson could. "Even so, Captain, this is your mission and it will remain your top priority until we decide it's not."

"Mr. Lawson, I don't think you understand what you're asking. To take even one plane off escort duty increases the chance that a B-17 crew won't come back. To take away four, is, well, reckless."

"Captain, I sympathize with you and admire your dedication to the B-17 crews, but I'm not asking you, I'm telling you what your mission is. If we have to lose another B-17 crew, or more, because of your flight's absence, then we'll have to accept those losses, because," he held up a finger for emphasis, "believe me when I tell you this, there's more at stake than you know."

Miller jumped out of his chair, his face red and a vein throbbed on his forehead. He whirled on Nelson, "Come on, Colonel, you can't let this, this," he waved his hand toward Lawson, "*civilian*, do this."

Nelson shook his head. "It's a firm decision, Captain."

Defeated, Miller sat down, slumping in the chair. After a moment, he turned back to Lawson and said, "It would be helpful to know just what it is you are afraid of."

"I wish I could share that information with you, Captain, I really do, but I can't and that's all there is to it."

Miller shook his head. Fucking secrecy. "Fine. I understand. I hope to hell you have some sort of a plan."

Lawson nodded and pulled out some more documents and maps. He carefully spread them out on the table and began.

7

Whitehall
10 Downing Street, London
1 June, 2215 Hours

Light from a lone brass desk lamp was partially dampened by thick, curling smoke emanating from the huge cigar held in a pudgy hand. The hand belonged to Winston Churchill and his other was tipping a whiskey glass to waiting lips. He swallowed happily, then set the glass down and peered at yet another report, one of dozens he had read, with more yet to go. He would go through them all tonight.

As he read, he occasionally grunted in surprise or disgust depending on the news. It caused his assistant, Simon Coulter, a few false starts when he'd first started working for Churchill, thinking the grunt was a call for him. Now, he just ignored them. When Churchill really wanted something, he would bellow.

A light tapping on the open door caused Churchill to look up, annoyed at the interruption. "What is it?"

Simon stepped into the doorway and said, "Prime Minister, Alan Finch with MI5 has an urgent message for you."

Churchill waved a hand impatiently. "Yes, yes, send him in."

A man wearing a worried expression slid into the office. In his early thirties, he was tall and slender, wearing a black suit that looked like he'd slept in it, which he had, but for only a few hours the night before. The lack of sleep was evidenced by dark circles under his eyes. Under one arm was tucked a small brown leather satchel like the ones favored by barristers. This was Finch's first trip into the inner sanctum of Churchill's wartime office, buried deep in the lower levels of 10 Downing Street. He approached Churchill warily, like a man getting too close for comfort to an uncaged tiger. Opening the satchel, he removed a piece of paper and held it out for Churchill. His hand trembled and the paper rattled. Churchill snatched the message from Finch, who flinched at the sudden movement. The Prime Minister's attention was immediately and fully on the document. He didn't notice Finch's reaction.

Churchill frowned halfway through and by the time he finished, he was into one of his famous full-fledged scowls. He glanced up at Finch and said, "Son of a bitch. I knew it, I just knew it." He turned to the door and hollered, "Simon! Simon!"

Simon stuck his head in and said, "Yes, Prime Minister?"

"I need Lewis, Moore and Eisenhower's aide."

Simon replied, "Yes, Prime Minister." He departed to make the calls. He would be waking up a few people, and not for the first time. Churchill kept his own hours, ignoring his wife's pleading, his assistant's nagging, and his doctor's threats. Winston Churchill would go to bed when he damn well felt like it. He understood not everyone could keep the hours he did, but if he wanted to talk to someone, he wasn't beyond sending for him even past midnight. They always came, too. One simply did not say, 'No' to the Prime Minister of Great Britain.

Churchill looked at the MI5 officer still standing in front of his desk. "Mr. Finch, thank you for personally bringing this to my attention. I know the hour is late."

Finch said, "You're welcome, Prime Minister." He felt relieved not to have stammered.

"Have a seat."

Finch looked at Churchill in surprise, wondering why the Prime Minister didn't just dismiss him. What could he possibly want? I've already delivered the document. He sat down, putting the satchel on his lap, knees together, and tried to be inconspicuous as he watched Churchill.

Churchill began sifting through a gigantic pile of papers on his desk. After a short search, he shouted, "Simon!"

Even though Simon hadn't finished with the calls, he appeared quickly and unruffled at the doorway once again. "Yes, Prime Minister?"

"Find me that bloody message from Marston."

"Of course, sir." Simon turned to the huge bookshelves with drawers underneath that lined the wall across the room from Churchill's desk. He opened a top drawer, riffled through a folder, and withdrew the one-time pad Marston had used at 4:00 A.M., a week ago. He walked over and handed the slip to Churchill. "Here you are, sir."

"Thank you."

"Of course, sir," Simon replied, then departed again to complete the calls and wait for the soon to be arriving, and likely grumpy, trio.

Churchill read the message and looked over the top of his glasses at Finch, as though taking the measure of the man. Finch began to fidget under the intense scrutiny and had no idea what was going on. Finally, Churchill said, "Did you do the analysis for this document," he picked up the paper and waved it, "yourself, or are you just the messenger?"

Finch sensed that Churchill was testing him, perhaps even baiting him, and answered truthfully, "I did the analysis, sir, and my boss, Mr. Evans, thought it would be better for me to deliver it."

"You understand the implications of the information?"

Finch replied evenly, "I believe so, yes, sir."

Churchill nodded, seeming to make a decision. He plucked the Marston message off the desk and handed it to Finch. "Here, read this."

Finch took it, read it quickly and muttered, "Shit," causing Churchill to smile in spite of the circumstances. Finch read it again as if that would make the message change to some better news. His mouth plopped open and he looked up at Churchill, alarm written all over his face. "Sir, if you don't mind my asking,

RONN MUNSTERMAN

is the source reliable?"

Churchill nodded grimly. "One of the best we have. What do you make of it?"

Finch knew better than to just blurt out an answer. He needed to allow time for the logical part of his mind to snap and snarl at the topic like a terrier chasing a rat. "Give me a few minutes, sir?"

Churchill nodded and resumed reading his stack of reports.

Finch began to mull over what he knew about the Germans' work toward building an atomic bomb. They had the right scientists, and Albert Speer, on the project. They were thought to have a laboratory and testing ground somewhere in western Germany, the location of which was not yet determined by MI5. The problem they had run into was finding enough U-238, from which the needed U-235 could be extracted, or enriched. But now they had found a possibly sufficient supply. Therefore, they might be able to construct a bomb . . . sooner than we thought and . . .

He jumped to his feet with a gasp, knocking his satchel to the floor. He looked at Churchill, who was nodding solemnly. Finch fought off the lump that had leapt into his throat, threatening to constrict all sound. "Dear God, sir, this is terrible news."

Churchill grunted then said, "I have to say Mr. Evans was right to send you. You've caught on to it and, I must say, quicker than I did."

Instead of feeling proud of himself for receiving praise from the Prime Minister of Great Britain, Finch felt fear. Fear deeper than the fear he felt when he heard the report that German bombs had fallen in his neighborhood, miles from any worthy military target. Fear deeper than he felt when he finally scrabbled his way through the rubble of his house to find his dying wife . . .

"Sir, we have to find a way to stop them. If they complete this project, we are lost." to

"Yes. That's why I want you stay and join us in the meeting. You can shed some light on all this for my staff."

"Me, sir?" Finch's voice rose an octave.

Churchill nodded, suppressing a smile at Finch's discomfort. He opened a drawer and pulled out a clean glass, setting it on the desk. He poured some golden whiskey and held the glass out to

Finch. "Here. You'll need this. Drink that down and, for God's sake, try to relax."

Finch's legs felt like they had just turned to rubber and more or less fell into his chair. Relax. You are bloody joking, right? My God, what have I gotten myself into? He took a swallow of the whiskey, then grimaced and coughed.

Churchill took a drink from his glass, draining it.

Hampstead Air Base
3 miles north of Andover
1 June, 2230 Hours

Two teams of men from tremendously varied backgrounds had come together in just a few days of rigorous side-by-side training. They marched together, ate together and fought each other in hand-to-hand combat drills that would have spooked a Kung Fu master himself. If it was ever possible to please a sergeant, both Dunn and Saunders were pleased with the men's ability to put the past behind them and stay focused on their tasks.

The men stood around, not segregated into their own teams, but in one large group, intermingling. If not for the differences in the uniforms, you couldn't tell the teams apart. As they waited on the cool tarmac under the blanket of the English night, each handled his fear in his own way. Some talked non-stop, others spoke not at all. Some chain smoked, others fiddled with gear, checking again and again to ensure every piece and part was in the right place.

Dunn and Saunders stood off to the side, their attention split between watching the men and the doorway of the C-47 transport plane. They were waiting for the jumpmaster to beckon them on board. They said little, the time for talk was over, at least until they met up with Madeline's French Resistance group. Then they would get the latest scoop and reevaluate the plan to make sure it still would work as originally laid out.

Dunn looked at the plane thinking that in perhaps just a few days, this same plane would be carrying another group of frightened men to Europe. The difference between the two flights was that Dunn's men would be coming back to England in a few days, while the others would be staying for who knew how long. Without a doubt, he and his men would be going back into Europe, but they would specialize in hit-and-run sneak attacks on critical targets. As would Saunders' team.

Slipping his Thompson .45 caliber submachine gun's sling from his shoulder, Dunn checked to make sure the safety was on, even though he knew it was. Can't make a mistake with a gun capable of firing 700 rounds per minute. The weapon was the namesake of retired General John T. Thompson, who had always been interested in developing a hand-held machine gun. Eventually, the Auto Ordnance Company contracted with Savage Arms in Utica, New York to build the eleven pound Thompson. The weapon of choice for all U.S. Army Rangers, the machine gun was at once, reliable and powerful.

Dunn lifted the gun and checked to make sure the blade sight at the end of the barrel was blackened. Shiny things were, shall we say, bad for soldiers sneaking around the dark woods in occupied France. Satisfied the sight had no reflective spots, he put the Thompson's sling back over his shoulder. He turned away from the plane and thought back to his disastrous dinner with Pamela. He had gruffly paid the check, escorted her back to the jeep, then driven her home, saying little. She tried to get him to accept her apologies several times on the drive, but he rudely brushed them aside. Pamela finally gave up and when the jeep shuddered to a stop in front of her building, she had jumped out, no easy feat in a dress, and ran inside without even a glance over her shoulder.

Now in the dark, on his way to battle, maybe even death, he came to understand he had let something special slip away for no reason other than stupid pride. Twice, he had picked up the phone to call her and beg forgiveness and twice he'd put it back in the cradle in shame. Why would she even want to speak to an ass like him? Idiot!

A tap on the shoulder from Saunders brought Dunn out of his unpleasant reverie. He turned back to the plane and there in the red-lit doorway stood the bulky jumpmaster, who waved a hand.

Saunders trotted over to the plane. Standing at the bottom of the rickety looking aluminum ladder hanging from the doorway, he gave a sharp whistle and the men snapped into an organized line in front of him. He nodded at Dunn, who quickly took a place at the end of the line, then the British Commando turned and climbed the ladder. One by one, the men followed, ducking their heads as they passed through the door. Within minutes they were all seated, buckled in and ready to go.

The jumpmaster closed the door and locked it, then punched the button that told the pilots the men were ready. The engines coughed to life, then revved up. The noise pounded everyone's ears. It would make talking virtually impossible in flight. The plane rumbled down the runway. The Gooney Bird reached take-off speed and the bottom fell out as the nose lifted, pointing toward the black sky.

Their flight path was indirect to reduce, as much as was ever possible, the likelihood of discovery. They were heading southeast to the coast of France where the plane would turn east. Shortly after that, it would turn onto a short leg north so they could come in from due south. The drop zone was a field surrounded by trees, five miles south of Calais.

Each of the men tipped his helmet forward and slumped back to catch whatever sleep he could.

8

Whitehall Cabinet Room
10 Downing Street, London
1 June, 2302 Hours

Finch followed the Prime Minister down a long narrow
corridor and into a large conference room. This was the room
Churchill preferred to use because it held a table large enough for
twelve people. A map of Europe completely covered one wall
from floor to ceiling. Three men were already seated, waiting,
having been ushered straight there instead of Churchill's office.
They rose at the Prime Minister's arrival. Finch wondered where
Churchill would sit, then whether he would be invited to sit with
them, or just stand in the corner. He soon found out, for Churchill
stepped around the table and said, "Come along, Finch. You'll sit
next to me."

Churchill sat down and the rest followed suit. Finch placed
his satchel on the table, on the side away from Churchill to keep
it out of the way. As he settled in and tried to get comfortable, he
suddenly noticed that all three men were watching him, clearly
appraising him. He felt like a biology lab specimen, but returned

their gazes calmly. He hoped. Then he realized he was sitting at a table with the Prime Minister and some of the people he trusted and depended on the most. A sheen of sweat broke out on his forehead, but he curbed the impulse to wipe it away.

Churchill put his cigar into a heavy glass ashtray, folded his hands on the table and thanked everyone for coming at such a late hour, getting nods from all three men. Then he quickly made the introductions, although Finch recognized them. Sitting directly across from him was Eisenhower's aide, Colonel Steve Young, a slightly built man in his early forties. To the Colonel's left was the Secret Intelligence Service, MI6, representative. Edward Lewis was perhaps sixty, with a craggy face and wisps of gray hair that confounded all combs. To his left was Colonel Kenneth Moore, Montgomery's aide, who sat ramrod straight, peering at Finch over half glasses. Even at this time of night, Lewis wore a spotless suit, and Young and Moore crisp uniforms; all three wore freshly starched shirts and perfect ties.

Finch glanced down at his own disheveled jacket and felt, not quite ashamed, but certainly out of place. *If there's ever a next time for me to come here, I will not appear like this, no matter what.*

"Mr. Finch, if you'd please begin?" Churchill waved a hand in the general direction of the men around the table.

Finch rose unsteadily, cleared his throat, then said, "Gentlemen, earlier today I received a coded communiqué from an agent working in Peenemunde, located on the Baltic Sea. As you probably know, we have been trying to ascertain just exactly what the Germans are doing with their rocket program. We'd heard rumors that additional rocket scientists and engineers had been added to the program. That's been confirmed.

"The program is broken down into two efforts; both are called *Vergeltungswaffen*, which means 'vengeance weapon.' The V-1 is a flying bomb, an unpiloted craft designed along the lines of an airplane. The other weapon, the V-2, is a true rocket. It'll be able to carry two thousand pounds of explosives. After it's launched, instead of coming in on a low trajectory, it'll climb sixty miles into the stratosphere, traveling on a parabola, then descend onto its target. There will be no warning. The first sign of danger will be the explosion. The destructive power of this rocket will make the damage caused by the German bombers seem like—"

"Those bombers nearly destroyed London, young man," interrupted Moore. His lips curled into a feline grimace, a baring of the teeth seen in circus acts with snarling lions.

Finch bit back the reply that jumped to the tip of his tongue and said, "Yes, sir. I wasn't trying to demean the damage they did. I was—"

"Were you ever in London during one of those attacks?"

Finch glared at Moore and decided it was time to put a stop to this arrogant prick's attitude. "Yes, sir. I was." He swallowed, "I lost my wife and unborn child during one of them. That's why I do what I do. Sir."

Moore looked thunderstruck. He glanced at Churchill, saw no help there, and finally took a breath and said in a soft voice, "Mr. Finch, I do apologize. I had no right. We have all been affected by the attacks and many have suffered so much. Will you accept my apology?" He rose and extended a hand.

Finch grasped the hand and said, "Thank you, sir."

Moore nodded, released Finch's hand and sat down, his face flushed.

Churchill watched the exchange with more than a passing interest. *Young Finch did a fine job with Moore, perhaps I should keep an eye on him.*

Finch regained his thread of thought and continued, "The V-1's range is about two hundred miles, maybe a little more, so the Germans will have to launch fairly close to the Channel. That's the good news. They'll be in range of our bombers and we think their launch sites will be easy to spot. However," Finch paused, not to add to the tension—which it did anyway—but to make sure he got everything right, "we're pretty sure they're going to be able to start firing the V-1 within a matter of weeks."

A collective groan went around the table and Colonel Young was the first to speak. "Weeks? What about the other one?"

"We're not one hundred percent certain, but they may be as close as ninety days away, say the end of August on that one. We have agents working on getting more details for our own scientists to examine, but I'm sure you understand the difficulties."

Lewis suddenly noticed that Finch's satchel still lay on the table, unopened. Why this fellow isn't even using notes. "You know this stuff forwards and backwards don't you, Mr. Finch?" He smiled and pointed to the satchel. "You don't really need that do you?"

Churchill leaned around Finch to look at the satchel, his eyes sparkling in delight. Yes, I'm going to have to give Evans a call about his man.

Finch wanted to look unaffected by the unexpected compliment, but found himself smiling in return. "Sir, I just have been working on it for a long while."

Lewis gave him a knowing look and said, "Of course." His face grew somber and he continued, "Please tell us the rest. You haven't gotten to the bad part yet, have you?"

Surprised at the man's intuitiveness, Finch glanced at Churchill, who was busy studying his hands. He wants me to deliver the shock. He doesn't want to do it himself. I can't say I blame him.

Finch looked at each man and could see the fear in their eyes. He imagined they saw the same in his. He wished he could give them comfort. "You're correct, Mr. Lewis. Gentlemen, I'm afraid the bad news doesn't end there. We have also learned," he hoped Churchill wouldn't mind the royal 'we,' "from an agent in Berlin that the Germans now have sufficient supply of Uranium 238," he paused to gauge their knowledge, and seeing it would be helpful, continued with, "this is the plentiful ore from which you extract U-235, and which is the primary component for an atomic bomb. The Germans are much closer to completing their atomic bomb project than anyone realized. Although we don't think the bomb could be carried by either of the Vee weapons, we," he turned to Churchill, who nodded, "believe the bomb could be smuggled into London, say on a fishing boat traveling up the Thames."

The men looked aghast. Silence descended on the room. If sound were color, it would have been the blackest black.

In flight over France
1 June, 2317 Hours

The jumpmaster checked his watch. They were nearing the

62   RONN MUNSTERMAN

drop zone. He opened the door and the wind roared in. Then he moved rapidly down the narrow aisle, having to step over outstretched legs, to shake the men awake. Returning to the door, he made sure he had everyone's attention, then lifted his arms like a minister imploring the congregation to stand. The men got up and faced him. He raised his right hand, formed a hook with his forefinger and slapped it against the cable that ran to the door. Each man held up his heavy silver clasp and latched it onto the cable. The clasp was fastened to a fifteen-foot-long canvas strap which was, in turn, connected to the parachute's release ring. When the paratrooper stepped out the door, the chute would automatically open when he cleared the bottom of the plane. Each man checked the parachute of the man in front of him and hit him on the shoulder to indicate all was well.

The jumpmaster stuck out his hand to Dunn, who as last on would be first off, and Dunn shook it with a grim smile. The red light blinked off. The green one lit up. Dunn stepped into the doorway. And leaped into the nothingness.

Whitehall, The Transatlantic Telephone Room
10 Downing Street, London
1 June, 2347 Hours

When Finch laid out the awful prospects, the meeting had disintegrated quickly into pandemonium. Everyone had an idea or three on what must be done to save civilization. Finally, after half an hour, Churchill had had enough and told them all to go home to bed. And not a word to anyone. Then he'd traipsed down the hall to the phone room. It was about the size of a large broom closet, which is what it had been before the war. A bright ceiling light hung over Churchill as he hunched down in a chair next to a small table. A banker's brass lamp with a green shade perched near the edge of the table casting its unnecessary light over the black phone.

This was no ordinary kitchen phone, though. It connected to a scrambling device, code named 'Sigsaly,' designed and built by the American Bell Telephone Laboratories. From there, Churchill's words would travel down a cable to a monster piece of equipment called 'X-Ray,' which was buried in the basement of Selfridges' department store on Oxford Street. The last step would be to completely encipher the message and send it across the Atlantic by radio waves.

He stared at the phone as if willing it to prevent him from giving Roosevelt the news. Checking a brass clock high on the wall, he calculated it was just past dinner time in Washington, D.C. With a resigned sigh, he picked up the receiver.

9

Drop Zone
5 miles south of Calais
1 June, 2352 Hours

Dunn's legs folded as he ducked and rolled at the moment of impact. It always seemed to take the wind right out of you, no matter how good you were, and Dunn was very good. He scrambled to his feet, yanking on the parachute's quick release. The harness popped loose and he quickly gathered up the white silk. He shaped it into a not-so-neat ball, like a boy grudgingly rolling up his bed sheets on laundry day. Dunn glanced up, then around him. The rest of the men were either already on the ground or almost ready to land.

As soon as each soldier gathered his chute, he ran to the trees on the eastern edge of the clearing. This was the appointed meeting place. The darkness was pervasive, but the fingernail sliver of a waning moon gave just enough light to help the men get their bearings quickly. Within minutes, the men stood in a small circle, like a football huddle.

Dunn and Saunders checked quickly to make sure they had

everyone and that no one was injured in the jump.

Dunn glanced at his luminous watch and whispered, "Our French friends should be here any minute. Everybody sit tight. Cross, Ward, set up the perimeter."

Cross and Ward slithered into the forest and set up about twenty yards in and about the same distance apart.

Ten yards farther out, a black figure disengaged itself from the shadow of a tree and slid unseen through the gap between Cross and Ward. It pulled a pistol from a cloth holster under a sweater and advanced toward the rest of the team. One foot in front of the other, on black rubber-soled shoes, the intruder grew nearer. It raised the hand with the pistol. Suddenly the cold, hard barrel of a Webley .38 jammed into the figure's neck, while a hand snaked around and grabbed the pistol.

"That'll do, matey," snarled Saunders. He gave the figure a shove and said, "Keep walking."

The figure remained where it was and said sweetly, "Very nice work." A slim hand reached up to remove a stocking hat and long red hair fell out, covering the shoulders. Turning around slowly, Madeline said, "Now don't get all excited and shoot me by mistake, okay?"

Saunders stepped back and shook his head. "That was dumb. What if I'd shot you first?"

"You didn't, did you? I was just curious to see how good you are. I made it past the first two so easy, I must have let my own guard down, thinking they were the only ones. Pretty impressive. I'm the best there is, if you don't mind my saying so myself. How did you find me?" She was clearly puzzled.

Saunders tapped his nose with a forefinger and smiled. "Your soap."

Madeline's eyebrows shot up. "My . . . soap? You can't be serious."

"Yep. Come on. Let's get over to the team." He led the way and Madeline followed, shaking her head in chagrin, thinking that was the last time she would ever bathe just a few hours before a mission.

Saunders gave a low whistle just before he and Madeline stepped close to the circle of men. "We have company," he announced. He turned toward Madeline and held out her pistol to her. "Name's Saunders, Ma'am."

She took the pistol and, in a flash of motion, holstered it. "Madeline, please."

Dunn stepped forward with a frown on his face. He looked at Madeline, then Saunders with a quizzical expression. *How in the world?* His eyes narrowed and Saunders suppressed a smile at Dunn's obvious discomfort. He knew Dunn was mighty unhappy to find out Madeline had slipped right by his own two best sneakers.

Dunn recovered and stuck out his hand for Madeline to shake, which she did. "I'm Dunn, Madeline. Glad to see you." He studied her briefly. Tall for a woman, Dunn figured she was only a few inches under six feet. Her oval, fine-featured face was pale in the limited light, and clearly beautiful. Although he couldn't quite tell for sure, he had the distinct impression her eyes might be an emerald green.

They exchanged code words to each other's satisfaction and Madeline said, "We should hurry, the Germans are quite efficient. If they got a report on your plane or parachutes, they'll be in the area soon. I have a truck just through the woods, about two hundred meters."

Dunn nodded and turned to the men, "Let's not keep the lady waiting, gentlemen." And with that, they trooped off after Madeline as she quickly weaved the way to the waiting truck. Along the way, they picked up a surprised and crestfallen pair of sentries.

An old farm truck with a canvas-covered bed sat in the entrance to a farmer's access road. Its engine was off, to conserve precious fuel, and the lights were, too, for obvious reasons. Four heavily armed men crouched beside it, facing the road and the direction they expected Madeline to come from, hopefully with the British and American soldiers.

Madeline crept up to the road's edge and whistled lightly. An answer came immediately from the other side. She turned toward Dunn and Saunders, pointing to the truck. In a matter of seconds, everyone had scrambled into the truck. Two of the resistance members jumped in just as the truck pulled out onto the road. They sat on the bench seat across from Dunn and Saunders and stared in stony silence at the two commandos.

The trip was short, less than fifteen minutes by Dunn's watch, but there had been many sharp turns, some left, some right, so that by the time they arrived, Dunn had no idea where they were relative to the drop zone. This was a feeling he could have done without.

The truck slowed, then ground to a halt. Dunn heard the passenger door open, then snick shut. He glanced at one of the Frenchmen and tipped his head toward the back of the truck in a silent request to get out. The man held up a hand. A wooden door creaked as it was being pulled open, then the truck moved forward and settled inside a barn. The man nodded at Dunn, who gave the word to exit.

The barn was small and there was just enough room for the men to sidle past the right side of the truck. Two small electric bulbs shed dim light, casting muted shadows of the wood beams and posts. Dunn noticed three stalls to his left and could hear, but not see, something big moving around inside one of them. The rafters above leaked tiny bits of hay that fell like a peculiar yellow snow.

The barn's odor brought back a flood of memories for Dunn. Even though he hadn't grown up on a farm, plenty of his friends had. Some of his best memories stemmed from adventures in a barn and only some of them with a girl. But a barn also held his worst memory, his first waking nightmare.

It was a hot July day after his junior year of high school, when he was seventeen. He offered to help his best friend, Paul, toss hay. Paul's fifteen-year-old younger brother, Allen, completed the trio. They had a simple arrangement: one drove the tractor, one stood on the wagon and stacked the seventy-five pound bales that were tossed up by the third, who walked alongside the slow-moving wagon. They rotated positions, out of fairness, and it made the afternoon pass quickly. After they pulled up to the barn, Paul hooked up the big conveyor belt to the tractor for power. He stayed on the wagon while Dunn and Allen scooted up the ladder to the barn's loft. It was faster to have two above and one below since you had to carry the dusty bales farther in the hay loft.

Paul saw them in the doorway and hollered, "You guys

ready?"

"You bet your sweet ass we are!" shouted back Dunn, with a grin on his dirt-smeared face.

Paul flipped on the conveyor belt and started loading. The three worked fast and hard, but it was mind numbing work; grab a bale, toss it, go get the next. Later, Dunn believed that factor caused what happened next. Dunn was coming back to get his next bale, while Allen was grabbing one off the belt. Suddenly, Allen's foot slipped on the hay strewn floor. Over balanced, he pitched forward toward the gaping opening between the conveyor's frame and the barn wall. He stuck out a hand to grab something, anything, to stop himself from flying out into open space, but his fingers scrabbled ineffectively against the wood door frame. Dunn grabbed a fistful of Allen's sweaty tee shirt, but with a ripping noise, the shirt tore loose in Dunn's hand and Allen fell, screaming.

Paul heard the scream and looked up just in time to see the flash of his brother's body fly by and crash into the ground beside the wagon with a sickening thud. He saw Dunn standing in the doorway, his mouth open for a scream that never came and a piece of white cloth in his hand.

At home after the funeral, Dunn sat slumped on the porch swing with his head in his hands. His dad sat next to him, a hand draped over his son's shoulder. Dunn raised his head and turned to his dad with tears streaming down his cheeks. He swallowed the lump in his throat and said, "Dad, I had him in my hand. If I'd've been just a hair quicker, he'd still be alive."

Mr. Dunn sucked in a breath at the sight of so much pain in his son's face. "Tom, you don't know that. You did everything you could. You can't blame yourself."

Dunn shook his head and said, "Yes, I can, Dad. Yes, I can." He wiped away the tears and vowed, "I promise you one thing, though, I'll never let anyone around me die."

Dunn could have kept that vow, maybe, if it hadn't been for the war.

"Dunn. Hey, Dunn."

Dunn started, then said, "Yes, I'm coming."

Madeline and her four teammates waited around a makeshift

table of carpenter's horses and a weather-worn door. A single light bulb hung from the rafter just above the table. Dunn and Saunders joined them after giving instructions to the men to find a spot and rest. Madeline didn't bother to introduce the men around her. Instead she said, "Here's the latest information on the German defenses. My people scouted it out two days in a row, including yesterday, at the time sent by your commander, 0400 hours." She pointed to a spot on the map spread out on the table. "The main gate is approachable only by way of a narrow road and is guarded by machine gun towers on either side. The only weakness we see is this place," she pointed again, "here, to the east, where the fence comes up against the forest."

Dunn and Saunders glanced at each other and smiled. Madeline's finger had touched the exact spot they had decided on while in Colonel Kenton's office.

"The ground there is rough, with deep ravines and heavy underbrush. They obviously believe no one can make their way through without making a lot of noise. They do have periodic patrols that cover those areas, but they're not using dogs. Why, we don't know. The patrols follow a twenty minute pattern."

Saunders nodded and said, "That's more than enough time to cut the fence and slip through."

"I agree." She checked her watch and said, "We'll be leaving here at 0300 hours. We'll drop you at this place," she pointed, "which is a hard ten minutes from the fence. Your escape route is to come back the way you came. If you cannot make that route and have to depart in any other direction, you must get to this farm," another jab at the map, "where we will have a backup team waiting inside the barn." She paused, a frown creasing her forehead, "If you cannot make it to either location, you're on your own. Is that clear?"

"Yes," answered Dunn.

"Any questions?"

Dunn and Saunders looked at each other, then Dunn said, "No, we have it all."

"All right then, you should rest. Don't go outside and don't make any noise. We'll set up a perimeter and watch over you."

Dunn nodded and said, "Okay, thanks, Madeline."

After Madeline and her men left, Dunn whispered, "You still

have that feeling?"

Saunders nodded.

"Me, too. Did we miss something?"

"If we did, I have no idea what it is," a miserable expression flew across Saunders' face.

"Me either." With a flick of the wrist, Dunn turned out the lights and darkness settled over the men.

Minutes later, a dark form climbed furtively into the back of the truck and pulled the canvas cover tight. By feel and memory, the stealthy figure went right to the pack carrying the detonators. It picked up the pack and lowered the one with faulty detonators in its place. Carefully and quietly, the traitor descended from the truck and moved into the darkness.

10

French Resistance safe location
4 miles south of Calais
2 June, 0300 Hours

Madeline opened the barn door and slipped quietly inside. She switched on the small flashlight she was carrying and found the wall switch, turning it on. It wouldn't do to go stumbling around in a darkened barn full of armed and dangerous men. As she let her eyes adjust to the light, a few groans wafted toward her. "Sorry, fellows, but it's 0300. Time to go. Sergeant Dunn, where are you?"

Madeline heard a slight rustling sound to her left and she saw Dunn rise from the floor of one of the stalls, brushing hay off his clothes.

"Here, Madeline." Dunn said, as he stretched his arms and back.

Madeline got the impression he was uncoiling and sensed a suppressed power hidden beneath the combat tunic. Unexpectedly, her imagination painted an image of his rippling muscles as he lay atop her, their bodies entwined. She looked away quickly, feeling the heat rush to her cheeks. *Lord, what is wrong with me? I have no time for this.* But the sudden desire for this stranger wouldn't go away. She looked back at Dunn who was staring intently at her. He knows, she thought. Taking a breath she said, "We'd best get your men back in the truck. Make your equipment checks and load up. We're leaving in five minutes."

Dunn took a few steps toward her and said, "Yes Ma'am." He gave her a mock salute, but she turned away, giving no indication of having seen it. Dunn wondered what that was all about, but turned his attention to getting the men ready.

Saunders stood with Dunn at the tailgate of the truck. They had just swept the barn ensuring no evidence that heavily armed men had been there remained. "I think we're ready to go, Dunn."

Dunn lowered his chin in agreement and jumped into the truck, Saunders right behind. The two non-talkers joined them and one of them pounded on the back of the truck's cab. A moment later, it backed out of the barn.

After five minutes, the truck turned off onto a dirt road and the going got rough. It seemed as though the driver was purposely finding every single hole along the way. Every time the truck hit one, the men's teeth clattered together as they jostled against each other. They had to grab onto the sides of the truck to keep from getting tossed onto the floor.

"Fuck!" grunted Oldham, after one especially violent back-breaking jolt. He looked toward the two Frenchmen accusingly, "Don't you Frenchie's know how to make a decent fucking road?"

The one named Henri grinned and poked the other with an elbow. In heavily accented English, and loud enough for all to hear, he said, "See, Luc, the poor American has a soft ass." Ass came out as 'ahs.'

Luc grinned at Henri.

Oldham glared at Henri and flipped him the bird.

"Oh, *mon cherie*, you should be so lucky as to have the sex with a Frenchman."

Everyone burst out laughing. Even Oldham finally gave up his glare and smiled ruefully, shaking his head.

Mercifully, the ride along the road from hell was short and

soon the beaten truck stopped. The men practically stampeded over each other to get out the gate, most rubbing their behinds after exiting.

Hanson eased up next to Dunn and said, "You know, that ride makes jumping out of a perfectly good airplane seem like a walk in the park."

Dunn grinned and said, "I agree, Jack."

Madeline approached Saunders and Dunn, stopping in front of Dunn, staring into his dark eyes. *I could fall for this man. If only things were different.*

Dunn returned her gaze steadily, wondering what was going on behind those beautiful green eyes.

Finally, she broke the silence. "Sergeant Dunn, you must be sure to either make it back here or to the backup location. Do you have any questions or doubts about finding the other location?"

"Nope, we understand our options."

"You also understand that if you don't make it to either one in time, you're on your own in enemy territory?"

Dunn wanted to tell her to stop acting like a school marm. Instead, he smiled and said, "Yes, we understand, but we'll make it fine, to one or the other."

Madeline studied Dunn for a moment longer, then nodded. To Dunn, she seemed reluctant, like a mother agreeing to let her child go somewhere unsafe. She said, "Let's get you on your way." She turned and pointed, "Luc will guide you."

Luc took a step forward, extending his hand. Dunn shook it first, then Saunders. "Gentlemen, this way." He started off toward the northwest.

Dunn was about to follow, but Madeline suddenly slid over in front of him, grabbed him by the shoulders, and kissed him squarely on the mouth. She stepped back, more surprised than Dunn. "For good luck," she said sheepishly.

"Here now, don't I get one?" asked Saunders indignantly.

Madeline smiled and leaned over to peck him on the cheek. "Good luck."

Saunders touched his cheek and muttered, "Oh, that's swell, a sister's kiss. Now I see where I stand."

The men laughed lightly.

Dunn eyed Madeline for a long second, as though committing

her face to memory. With a sigh, he said, "Off we go, men. Follow that man."

Luc stopped at the edge of the forest, waiting patiently. He was in no hurry, he knew where they were going. As did the Germans.

Dunn and Saunders caught up with Luc, who said, "The depot's eastern perimeter fence is about ten minutes from here. We must work our way over a ridge, then down through a difficult ravine. Once we are through the ravine, we will go up again to reach the top of a small rise. The fence lies just beyond, so you'll have an excellent view through the trees."

"It sounds like you've done an excellent job of scouting for us. Thanks." Dunn said, then smiled.

"It is important, no?"

Dunn nodded.

"Then I am glad to have played a small part." Luc smiled for the first time, thinking, a smile costs so little when you know the man and his team will be captured or dead within the hour.

Luc was the product of a French father and a German mother who felt trapped in France and had grown to hate living there. She taught her son to appreciate Germany and hate France. When Luc was fifteen, his drunken father killed his mother in a fit of rage over the wrong meal being on the table. That same night, Luc killed his sleeping father, driving a butcher knife through the man's heart. Luc left town, circulating around France for five years until the war started. He had been found in a small town north of Paris by a Gestapo agent carefully recruiting French men to infiltrate the resistance groups.

He knew he played his part well, by leading missions against the Germans with a high degree of success. It had been painful killing men he viewed as his countrymen, but he knew their sacrifices would pay off eventually.

Luc also knew Madeline would kill him herself, in a split second, if she had any inkling of what he had done, and was doing. But this would be his last resistance mission. He would be rewarded with a place in the Gestapo where he could display his true loyalties. It would feel so good to be able to treat the French as the enemies they were.

Dunn and Saunders gave orders to the teams, then Dunn said

to Luc, "Lead the way."

Dunn and his team were first behind Luc, with Saunders and the rest of the British team following. They moved silently, carefully, but the forest was thick and it was indeed difficult travel. The path they followed was little more than an animal trail. They had to watch out for roots sticking up underfoot and thick branches hanging down in their faces. More than once, Dunn heard a swish of a branch, then a whack, followed by a muffled curse, causing him to inadvertently recall the Three Stooges hunting a black bear in the forest.

Dunn was amazed that Luc could find his way at all, but the Frenchman certainly did know where he was going. He exuded a quiet confidence that Dunn immediately took a liking to. He imagined that Luc would be fierce in a firefight. A good man to have on your side. With part of his mind watching his step, the other part began to mull over the insertion plan, searching for weaknesses. After a few minutes, he was still satisfied it was a sound plan. When the teams arrived, they would examine the depot to make sure the reality matched the drawings. Then Saunders' team would slide along the fence to the north about twenty yards. The insertion would be launched precisely at 0400 hours.

Luc stopped so suddenly that Dunn nearly ran into him. Luc turned and whispered, "We are at the top of the ravine, which is about twenty meters deep. We must be careful. Pass the word to move cautiously, or someone could misstep, tumble down and break a leg."

Dunn sent the message and waited for confirmation to come back from the end of the line. When it did, he turned to Luc and said softly, "Let's go."

Luc started down the steep embankment. The foliage was softer and not as dense, and he didn't have fight his way through it. Behind him, he could hear the sounds of the men as their feet slid now and then in the dirt. Upon reaching the bottom, he crossed the small ravine, perhaps ten yards wide, and waited for everyone to catch up. After they joined him, he started up the other side, feeling a deep disappointment that not one man had fallen and broken a leg or worse.

At last, they arrived at the top and Dunn squatted down,

sending word for Saunders to join him. While he waited, he examined the depot. The gap between the edge of woods and the fence was five or six feet and in that space, the brush had been cleared away to give the guards a good view of anything moving.

Saunders knelt beside Dunn and whispered, "Looks just like we expected. There's your target." He pointed to a large wooden building with a steep roof to their left. Then he turned and pointed at another building to their right. "And that's ours."

According to Madeline's intelligence, the two buildings housed the Panzer unit's 88-millimeter shells. Each team carried enough satchel explosives to send the buildings into outer space. Opposite the depot sat the barracks, as far away from the explosives as possible. Dunn and Saunders had viewed this as a plus.

Luc watched the two soldiers point and gesture, and smiled to himself. He stepped closer and knelt down. "Gentlemen, I would be honored if you would allow me to accompany one of your teams." He gave Dunn a sneering smile. "It would give me great pleasure to help kill as many Germans as possible."

Dunn said, "Luc, we appreciate your offer, but we can't allow you to go with us. We need you to stay here and help guide us back to the truck."

Luc feigned disappointment to cover the satisfaction he truly felt. Dunn had responded exactly as he had foreseen.

Dunn reacted to Luc's displeasure by putting a hand on the man's shoulder, saying, "Besides, Luc, Madeline would kill us if anything happened to you."

Luc managed to avoid flinching at the enemy's touch and nodded his understanding. "Yes, of course, you are correct." He stood up and shook hands with each leader, then said, "I'll just slip back into the woods and await your return." *Which will never come to pass.*

Dunn and Saunders checked their watches, synchronizing them. It was 0350 hours; ten minutes to go. Saunders patted Dunn on the back and said, "See you soon, Dunn. Good luck."

"You, too, Saunders."

Saunders moved away to gather his team and move north.

Madeline's stomach hurt and something niggled the back of

her mind, refusing to show itself fully. She had participated in many missions over the past three years and led many. Most were successful, but there had been failures due to unexpected German patrols popping up at the just the wrong time or communications breakdowns. The number of ways to fail was as large as the number of Germans occupying her country.

Since she couldn't identify the cause of her unease, she reached for the radio set in the truck and turned it on. Speaking softly, she sent out a call to her contact. Immediately, as if he was sitting on top of the radio, the contact's voice came across clearly, "I am here."

"How are our friends this morning?"

"They are fine, thank you, and sleeping well."

"Good. Give them my best, please."

"I will."

Madeline switched off the radio, feeling a little better.

Luc made his way over to a specific tree and knelt. He dug with his hands briefly, unearthing a small wooden box. Wiping the dirt off, he opened the lid and removed a radio. This will show them, all of them. He switched on the device. His call, too, was answered immediately. Speaking German, he said only two words, "It's time."

At precisely 0400 hours, Morris and Hanson pulled their wire cutters from their belts and began clipping the chain link fence. They worked fast, side-by-side, with Morris starting at the top of the opening, about waist high, and cutting downward, while Hanson worked his way up from the ground. In one minute, they were done and set to work on the horizontal top. Soon, they were able to peel the wire back, like a mini-door.

They stepped back as Dunn and the others crawled through. Morris followed, then Hanson, who pulled the makeshift door closed. He worked with it for a moment to make it appear normal, at least to a cursory glance by a passing guard. The team glided across the cleared area, staying in the shadows of the two-story building. Oldham, who was on point, went to the corner of the building and edged his head around for a quick look. The space between the building and its smaller neighbor to the south was about ten yards, ample room for two trucks to pass each other. There were no guards in sight, and more importantly, the nearest light pole was fifty yards away. Oldham pulled back and turned to Dunn, who was right behind him. He gave the team leader a thumbs up. Dunn patted him on the back and Oldham ran around the corner.

Dunn waited a few seconds, then peeked. Oldham made his way stealthily to the door, then stopped and put his hand out. Dunn held his breath, waiting to see if the door had been unlocked by Madeline's inside source. They had a backup plan just case, but it would take a few extra minutes to open the door with the small pry bar Oldham had in his pack. The more time a mission took over its plan, the more likely it was that Murphy's law would strike. Plus, using the pry bar could make unwanted noise. Oldham suddenly disappeared and Dunn let out his breath softly. Turning quickly, he signaled and the team swung around him to follow in Oldham's footsteps, sticking close to the building.

Within thirty seconds they all had entered the building. Dim light from the depot's security lamps trickled in through the windows. The air was filled with the smell of gunpowder and it reminded Dunn of a biology class sulfur experiment that had gone stinkingly wrong, sending the putrid smell throughout the school. To the right, stacks upon stacks of armor ammunition cases, reaching fifteen feet in height, covered the entire rear half of the building. To the left was a canvas-topped truck and beyond it, a garage door.

Dunn checked his watch and whispered, "Let's get started gents, five minutes."

Oldham stayed at the door, locking it with a twist of thumb and forefinger, while the others fanned out quickly.

Dunn eyed the truck. Curious, he jogged over to investigate. Lifting the canvas flap covering the back of the truck, he peered inside. The truck was fully loaded. Moving around to the driver's side of the truck, Dunn yanked open the door and climbed in. Pulling a penlight from his shirt pocket, he switched it on and played the light around. He quickly found what he wanted, the glint of the ignition key in the slot. Turning off the penlight, he hopped down, leaving the door open and walked over to the garage door. Leaning forward to look out a grime-covered window, he saw a narrow road leading straight ahead in the valley between various buildings. About a hundred yards away it turned left, presumably to get to the main gate and the highway. At the turn, a barracks faced the warehouse.

Moving quickly back to the truck, Dunn unbuckled his brass belt buckle, slipped the belt out of its loops, and threaded the canvas belt around the left side of the steering wheel. Cinching the buckle, he slipped the loop over the outside mirror's metal support and with a quick tug, he snapped it tight. He wiggled the steering wheel. It didn't budge. Satisfied, he turned away and made his way back to the men, who were busy sliding blocks of explosives between the stacks of German ammunition.

Dunn checked his watch again. So far, so good. Stepping over next to Oldham, he said, "There's a better view of the barracks from the garage door. Position yourself there."

Oldham gave a quick nod and trotted off.

Madeline's radio chirped to life, startling her and Henri. She grabbed for the handset and said, "Yes?"

An urgent voice said, "There's activity in the barracks."

Oh, no. Madeline took a breath and said, "What's happening?"

"I can hear them getting up and they haven't turned on any lights."

"Can you get word to our visitors?"

"Impossible."

"There must be something you can do!" hissed Madeline.

There was no reply for nearly a minute and she thought he had disconnected. "Are you still there?"

"Yes. I was thinking. Perhaps there is something I can do. I must go."

"Thank you. Good luck."

Dunn checked his watch one more time. The five minutes had passed. He was about to gather the men when Oldham came running up. "Sarge, there's lights on all over the place at the barracks!"

"Shit! Okay, go unlock the garage door."

Oldham hesitated. It was as if his boss had just told him to go to Mars. He blinked and stuttered, "What for?"

"Just do it. Unlock the door and get ready to raise it."

Oldham looked doubtful, but said, "Okay," and took off.

Dunn spun around and found Morris close by. He said, "Danny, I need a charge right now."

"I already planted my last one. Do you want it?"

"Yes, and quick."

Morris squeezed in between the wall and a stack of ammunition boxes and came back with the explosive device in his hands, wires sprouting like some kind of unlikely wild hairdo. He handed it to Dunn.

Dunn took the package carefully and said, "Tell Cross to get the men out now. Make your way back to Luc and get to the truck."

"Sarge? Shouldn't we wait for you?"

Dunn shook his head and said, "Absolutely not. Oldham and I'll catch up later."

"Okay." Morris turned away.

Dunn ran to Oldham and said, "Raise the door and get ready to lay down some suppressing fire if those Germans pop out of the barracks."

"Yes, Sarge." Oldham yanked on a dingy, greasy rope, pulling on it hand over hand. The door creaked and groaned all the way up, but it was open. Oldham dropped to one knee, taking cover behind the wall, and aimed his Thompson at the barracks.

Dunn ran back to the truck and hopped in. He put the bomb on the seat next to him and, stomping on the clutch, shoved the shifter into neutral. He turned the key to the on position and pressed the starter button on the dashboard. The powerful Mercedes engine coughed and turned over briefly, but sputtered to a stop. "Come on you son of a bitch! Start." He yanked on the choke handle and tried again. This time, the engine roared to life, coughed once more, then settled into a smooth idle. Dunn picked up the bomb, set the timer for sixty seconds, thinking, Lord, I hope this timer is accurate, and started it.

Dunn jumped out and pulled his foot-long commando knife from its scabbard. Reaching into the cab, he pushed the gas pedal half way down and stabbed his knife into the floorboard across the pedal to hold it in place. The engine's sound reverberated in the warehouse. He shoved the Thompson's barrel into the clutch pedal, while reaching over to the shifter to slip it into first gear. Okay, thought Dunn, this is the tricky part. Let go of the clutch and get out of the way in time.

Madeline's contact, Rene, closed the electrical room's door quietly, intending to make his way undetected to the kitchen, where he worked. Stepping into the common hallway between the barracks and the mess hall, he turned a corner and abruptly stopped. Not five feet away was Leonard Küfer, Calais' resident Gestapo agent. A humorless man, Küfer was nevertheless smiling broadly and pointing an ugly black Luger at Rene's chest.

Rene's legs turned to jelly.

"Rene. How nice to see you. Thank you for turning on the lights. Now we can both see better, no?" Küfer lowered the pistol slightly and pulled the trigger. The weapon jumped in his hand.

Rene collapsed to the floor in agony, his hands holding his shattered kneecap. He somehow rolled onto his side, so he was lying facing away from Küfer. Slipping a shaking, bloody hand into his shirt pocket, he grasped a small object with two fingers and inserted it into his mouth. With a crunching sound, he crushed the cyanide vial. By the time Küfer reached down to turn the Frenchman over, Rene was dead.

"Damn it, Rene! I shot you in the knee to keep you alive. Now you're no good to me!" Küfer stood up, then kicked Rene in the head as hard as he could. The sickening crunch made him smile again. He holstered his Luger, then calmly walked away.

The barracks door burst open and Oldham pressed the trigger. The first three soldiers fell as Oldham's rounds hit home, but the others reacted quickly and dived back inside. Moments later, Oldham heard the crash of breaking glass as rifle butts knocked out the windows. He ducked back as bullets peppered the side of the building. During the barrage, more Germans poured out the door, running full speed toward the ammo building. Suddenly, the firing stopped. The Germans apparently remembered what kind of building they were shooting into.

Dunn leaned out of the truck as far as he could, then yanked the Thompson off the clutch and, praying the engine wouldn't die, leaped away. The truck darted forward, straight toward the door. Dunn lost his balance and fell. The truck's crushing rear tires thundered by just inches from his head. He scrabbled away on all fours muttering, "Shit, shit, shit."

Most of the advancing German soldiers dived out of the truck's path as it barreled toward the barracks, but a few were flung aside or crushed under its relentless tires. A moment later, it crashed square into the barracks. Inside the cab, the timer hit zero. The electric spark from the timer ran down the wire into the faulty detonator and stopped.

Oldham was already on the move and grabbed Dunn by the collar, yanking him to his feet. "Come on, Sarge, let's get the hell out of here." Oldham gave Dunn a push and followed him out the door. They turned left and started toward the fence. The Germans spotted them outside the building and began firing again. Bullets snapped and whined just over their heads. Dunn heard a grunt behind him. Spinning around, he found Oldham staring down at blood gushing from a gaping hole in his chest. Oldham lifted his gaze to meet Dunn's. "Go," he whispered, then his eyes rolled up as he collapsed in a lifeless heap.

"Oh, no. Timothy." Dunn instinctively reached down. He heard a bullet snapping past his left ear, but not the one that turned his world black.

11

East of the German Ammunition Depot
Calais
2 June, 0420 Hours

The sound of gunfire shattered the early morning silence. Saunders and his team were just wrapping up their work and he gave the order to evacuate. Within minutes, the Brits made their way back to the fence and clambered through.

Luc grinned at the sounds of gunfire as he quickly packed up the radio. He stood up and slipped the radio over his shoulder, then started off to the north, so as to circle around the depot and come in the front door, as it were.

Dunn's men crawled through the fence, but didn't see Luc's shadowy form slinking away. Saunders and his team joined them. Morris frowned at Saunders. "Dunn and Oldham are still back there. He said to get the men back to the truck pronto and not to wait for them."

"He did, huh?"

"Yes." Morris noticed that Luc was nowhere in sight.

"Where's Luc?"

Saunders looked around in the gathering morning light. "I don't know, but we can't wait for him."

Morris said sadly, "I know. Sergeant, you're in charge now."

Saunders nodded. "All right, gentlemen. We have to leave right now."

One of Saunders' men took the point and the two teams headed back to the truck. A short time later, the teams burst into the clearing where Madeline and Henri waited, worry on their faces. Saunders joined them, as did a shaken Cross. Madeline looked at Cross. "What happened?"

"The Germans came charging out of their barracks. It's like they knew we were there."

Madeline looked around at the men who milled about in the clearing. "Where's Dunn?"

"I don't know. He's still back there with Oldham. He ordered us out."

Madeline's heart sank. It was all she could do to nod. She looked around at the men again. "Where's Luc?"

Cross shrugged. "He wasn't waiting for us at the fence."

That explained it. That bastard. Madeline shook her head in anger. Realizing that now wasn't the time to try and solve that particular problem, she said, "Load up the truck and let's get to the safe house."

Within minutes, the teams and the French Resistance members boarded and Henri gunned the engine. Madeline sat in the front seat beside Henri. She stared morosely out the window, furious over the obvious leak and betrayal, and worried about the handsome Dunn. Was he even still alive? What if he wasn't? What if he was? With that thought, she tried to ignore the growing pain in her heart. She had no idea why she felt this way. Until the war, she'd been a regular teenager growing up in Calais and had gone on a few dates. None of the boys she'd been with had been anything special. She'd never felt 'in love' and had always believed in true love, but not in love at first sight. She struggled to understand if what she felt was love or just attraction. She sighed deeply and tried to do what seemed impossible: put Dunn's handsome face and dark eyes out of her mind.

When the truck reached the main road, she didn't have to tell Henri to go to the right instead of the left. They were heading toward a different safe location. The one Dunn and Oldham would go to if they were still alive. They would have only twenty-four hours before the rest would have to depart for the coast and their escape back to England.

12

Andover, England
2 June, 0337 Hours, London time

Pamela's eyes popped open with a start. She immediately closed them again, hoping sleep would return. After a few minutes, she gave up and twisted around onto her side, opening her eyes again to look at the alarm clock. She couldn't see it clearly and reached over to turn it so the dim moonlight lit the face. Groaning, Pamela flopped onto her back. Two nights in a row she had awakened early and been unable to get back to sleep. Tonight, like the previous, a little voice kept asking, Why hadn't he called? Then the voice turned accusing, Why didn't you?

OSS Office Building
Washington D.C.
1 June, 2337 Hours, U.S. Eastern Daylight Time

General William Donovan, Director of the Office of Strategic Services, sat at his desk with his back to the office window to reduce distractions, although the special heavy, black blinds were currently closed, according to the east coast blackout rules. The desk was uncluttered, holding only a phone, a wooden reading lamp, a file folder and a round, black pen holder. When the pen was out, the holder looked like a bowling ball for a one fingered man.

A few years ago, Donovan, then a high-powered millionaire Wall Street lawyer, had recognized the need for a centralized intelligence force. He had President Roosevelt's ear and made the plea for such an organization several times. Finally, on Secretary of the Navy Frank Knox's recommendation, Roosevelt appointed him to the newly created job of Coordinator of Information in June of 1941. Now, just three years later, his agency was an effective intelligence gathering organization. Known as the OSS, this foundling government entity led America's espionage and sabotage efforts in Europe and Asia.

A handsome man of sixty-one, Donovan wore a gray suit, white shirt, and a blue and white striped tie. His silver hair, parted on the right side, was perfectly cut and combed neatly. Blue eyes looked out from underneath bushy dark eyebrows.

In front of the General sat an exhausted Howard Lawson, who had suffered through a fifteen-hour flight from England to carry his report personally. Donovan knew Lawson was a detail oriented person, but was blessed with the ability to cut through the bullshit quickly, getting to the crux of the matter in as few words as possible. This was a notable skill in a city where doublespeak and not taking any stance at all were commonplace. At the moment, Donovan was especially glad he had been able to talk his young Wall Street friend into coming aboard.

The lamp cast a circle of light across the folder Lawson had just delivered. Donovan pulled it closer with a gnarled hand and opened it. He read the cover page, the report's summary, which covered Lawson's interviews of the Northrop engineers and Captain Miller. After finishing it, his thoughts had turned darker than the blinds behind him. Donovan was a worried man. An old army man, he served as a regimental commander during World War I, where he'd received many awards including the Medal of Honor. He understood battlefield strategy and tactics and easily grasped the methods of modern air warfare, which were no longer constrained to shootouts between fighter pilots. The massive air raids had forever altered the airpower skyscape. He raised his gaze to Lawson, whose eyes were closed. "Howard."

Lawson immediately opened his bloodshot eyes, rubbing them with the heels of his hands. "Yes, sir?" He covered a massive yawn with the back of his hand.

"As usual, this is a perfectly done report."

"Thank you, sir."

"I wish, just once, you'd bring me a report with good news in it. This is getting hard on an old man." Donovan smiled grimly.

"Yes, sir. Sorry, sir."

"I need to go talk to the president about this, but I want to make sure I have it right, so I want to recap it for you. Okay?"

Lawson ran a hand through his hair, then squeezed the back of his neck. This seemed to help somewhat and he said, "Yes, sir. Go ahead."

Donovan rattled off the information he'd just read and Lawson nodded, indicating that the older man had it right. At the end, Donovan closed with, "And lastly, you've given Miller and his flight the assignment of searching for the most likely place for the airplane."

"Yes, sir. They're scheduled to begin in, uh," Lawson looked baffled. "What is today, sir?"

Donovan smiled at his friend's expression. "It's Thursday night, the first of June."

"Oh, yes. Thanks. In three days, on Sunday, the fourth. Their assignment is to find the plane or its hanger, but not to engage. I want to be able to send in a ground team to ensure the plane is in the hanger, then destroy it."

"Why didn't Miller shoot it down when he had the chance?"

"He could have, but three Me-109s escorted the plane. His odds would have been poor and then we'd have never seen the film. He did the prudent thing, sir."

Donovan nodded. "The thing is, if this is just a prototype, how many are they going to build and how soon? And another question is, if this plane has that kind of range, would they target England or us?"

"I don't know sir. It'd be a one-way trip to reach us, so I don't think we're the target. They're bound to be looking at resuming the bombing of London."

OPERATION DEVIL'S FIRE   89

"Thank you, Howard. Go home. Get some sleep. I'll probably need you tomorrow, fully rested."

"All right, sir, thank you." Lawson got up unsteadily and left.

Donovan stared at the report, his gut screaming. He always listened to his instincts because they had served him so well in the past. As he reached for the phone to call the president, it rang, making him jump. He snatched the receiver off the hook, "Donovan here."

"Mr. Donovan, the President asks that you come to his office right away," said the president's secretary.

"I'll be right there."

The Oval Office
Washington, D.C.
1 June, 2355 Hours, U.S. Eastern Daylight Time

Donovan marched into the waiting room outside the Oval Office. Betty Nichols, a woman of forty, and the President's secretary, looked up from her black Royal typewriter and said, "Good evening, General Donovan, he's ready for you."

Donovan nodded. "Thank you." He opened the door and stepped into the most powerful office in the world. President Roosevelt sat in his wheelchair, facing the darkened window, apparently deep in thought. Smoke curled toward the ceiling from a cigarette in a slim, shiny black holder. Without turning around, he said, "Good evening, Bill."

Since his college football days, Donovan had been called Wild Bill Donovan, a nickname he relished, especially to his face. However, in spite of the name he was a methodical thinker, careful and thorough. He had grown close to Roosevelt and was a trusted source of information for the President. In 1940 and '41, Roosevelt sent Donovan to Europe on a fact-finding mission. He had not returned with good news.

"Good evening, Mr. President." Donovan watched Roosevelt whirl his wheelchair around and pull up behind his desk. He thought the president looked even more tired than usual, the dark circles under the eyes had become a permanent symbol of the price of the presidency during wartime. But Donovan knew an almost superhuman strength lay beneath the worry-lined face and exhausted body of the president, who was in the last year of his unprecedented third term. Somehow, he was also campaigning for a fourth.

"Harry will be here soon, so you might as well sit down." Harry was Harry Stimson, who had been the Secretary of War since 1940.

"Certainly, sir." Donovan sat in one of the two leather chairs facing Roosevelt's desk.

The door opened and Stimson strode through, his white panama hat in his hand. "Hello, Mr. President."

"Evening, Harry."

Stimson sat down in the empty chair, then nodded to Donovan, smiling. "Hi, Bill."

"Mr. Secretary." Donovan returned the smile. He liked Stimson and respected him, too, and knew the feeling was mutual.

They both turned to the president expectantly.

"I received a phone call from our friend Winston. He had some terrible news and I want to share it with you so we can develop a plan to assist the British." He paused, frowning. "It seems the Brits have discovered the Germans are frighteningly close to completing their first generation of flying rocket bombs, perhaps just weeks away."

Stimson and Donovan both nodded, neither was surprised.

The President continued, "More importantly, the Brits found out that the Nazis have also acquired sufficient quantities of uranium for the development of their atomic weapon. Churchill and his staff believe the Germans could put the weapon on a fishing boat and slip it into the heart of London on the Thames. That's not far off what Einstein suggested in his letter, back in '39."

Stimson and Donovan nodded. They'd seen the letter. Einstein had sent the letter to the president in August 1939 stating that work being done by Fermi would lead to the creation of an atomic bomb. The famed physicist went on to suggest the Germans were also on their way toward the same goal.

"It's absolutely imperative that we assist the British in any way possible to destroy Hitler's atomic lab."

"Have you told Eisenhower, sir?" asked Stimson.

"No, there's nothing he can do and I don't want to burden him while he's trying to decide when the invasion is going to take place. The European weather is playing havoc with the air cover and airdrop plans, not to mention the terribly choppy waters in the Channel."

"Do you know what day he might be shooting for, Mr. President?" Donovan asked.

"This coming Monday, the fifth, but the meteorologist is only giving that date a fifty-fifty chance." Roosevelt looked glum. "Back to the damn Germans and their threats. How are we going to help?" He sat back and looked at the two men with raised eyebrows, "Hmm, gentlemen?"

Stimson put his hands together, forming a tent and said, "Mr. President, I'm not sure—"

"I'm sorry to interrupt, Mr. Secretary, but we have another problem." Donovan paused, got a nod from Stimson, then continued, "We have a report, based on visual and photo confirmation, and interviews, that the Germans are also developing a long range bomber. It will have jet engines and be capable of making a one-way trip to the United States."

"Oh, damn it," the president looked exasperated. "Give me the details."

Donovan spent a few minutes relaying Lawson's information and plan, then finished with, "We thought the Germans were going to use it to resume the bombing of London, but with this news about the German atomic bomb program, I think it's the United States."

"But you said it would be a one-way trip to send a plane across the Atlantic," said the President.

"It would be, but if they drop an atomic bomb on the United States, New York, maybe even Washington, D.C., Hitler could sue for peace and we'd have no choice. He'd happily sacrifice the plane and the crew to achieve that."

"You paint a horribly accurate picture," said Stimson, looking decidedly unhappy.

"I agree," said Roosevelt, with a pained expression. "What do you suggest we do?"

"In addition to Lawson's plan to find the airplane, I think we have to get a commando team on the ground for the atomic lab."

Roosevelt said, "Do it. Churchill mentioned a fellow by the name of Finch with MI5. He's the one who did the work on the rockets being constructed at Peenemunde. I want Lawson and Finch to work together to come up with a plan to destroy both the plane and lab. Lawson can contact Finch in London at the MI5 office."

Donovan was a little surprised by this. He'd envisioned an American only attack, but had no real problems in working with the Brits. He'd done that on many occasions and the men he'd met had proven themselves more than capable. He rose from his seat. "Yes, Mr. President. Good night." He turned to Stimson, "Good night, Mr. Secretary."

"Good night, Bill."

Outside, as Donovan slid into the back seat, his driver looked over his shoulder. "Home, sir?"

Donovan shook his head sadly. "No, Phil, the office, but then you can go home."

Phil gave his boss a disapproving look. "Again? You're going to sleep at the office, again?"

Donovan smiled at the concern in Phil's voice. "I should be so lucky, Phil."

"Yes, sir."

Donovan glanced out the window at the darkened Lincoln Memorial. *Sorry, Howard, but you're heading back across the pond.*

13

St. Mary's Hospital
Calais
2 June, 0515 Hours

Dunn's eyelids fluttered and he took a deep breath, his chest rising slowly. He opened his eyes and tried to make sense of things. Above him, instead of sky he saw a white ceiling. Confused, he started to turn his head to look around and was rewarded with a blast of pain just above his left ear. Instinctively, he tried to raise his left hand to touch the injury, but it stopped well short with a clanking sound. Ever so carefully, Dunn turned his head to look. His wrist was manacled to the side rail of his bed, a hospital bed. He lifted his right wrist and it, too, jangled.

"You shouldn't move around, Sergeant. The doctor thinks you have a concussion."

Dunn grimaced as he turned his head toward the grating voice. A pock-faced man wearing the common Gestapo uniform of a black suit and hat sneered at Dunn. He had been sitting in a chair waiting for Dunn to regain consciousness and now he jumped to his feet, trying to stare down the American Ranger.

Dunn fought back the pointless, not to mention impossible to accomplish, urge to throttle the pipsqueak. Instead, he turned away and said nothing.

Angered by Dunn's indifference, Küfer slammed his black riding crop against the bed rail near Dunn's right hand.

Dunn had steeled himself for some sort of demonstration and didn't flinch. "Go away. Get me a doctor. I want to find out when I can go home."

Küfer moved around to the foot of the bed into Dunn's field of vision and shouted, "You will never go home. When we are through with you, you'll be sent to a *Stalag*, if you're lucky." Küfer smiled, showing uneven, yellowed teeth, then pulled a gold case from his inside breast pocket, removed a thin cigarette and lit it with a matching lighter. Dunn noticed they were both adorned with an engraved black eagle atop a swastika. A Nazi party favor, thought Dunn, with no small amount of disdain.

Dunn eyed the cigarette, wanting one, but not about to ask. Plus, he figured it might be difficult to smoke it. Look, Ma, no hands.

"My name is Küfer. I am the Gestapo representative for this area. Who might you be?"

"Dunn, Thomas. Sergeant. Serial number 06088552."

Küfer gave an evil snicker and said, "Do you believe that's all you're going to tell me before I am through with you?"

Dunn simply stared back at the man.

Küfer leaned over the edge of the bed, impervious to the smoke swirling around his face and said, "You will tell me whatever I want by the time I am finished." He straightened up and said, "We'll be moving you soon to a place," he paused to look around the empty room, "more suitable for questioning."

"Torture, you mean."

The small shoulders shrugged. "If you wish. You and your men were conducting sabotage. I'll want to know who you were working with and how you came to be here." He didn't mention that he already knew the answers to both questions. "Too bad about your man dying."

In spite of himself, and his desire not to give the Gestapo agent anything, Dunn's jaw muscles twitched at the way the creep belittled a good man's brutal death.

Küfer saw the telltale sign and pushed harder, "My men told me you were shot trying to run away instead of helping your downed compatriot. Not honorable behavior if you ask me, especially for a leader."

Dunn could feel his heart rate jump at the ridiculous remark, but instead of rising to the bait, he snorted derisively and said, "You wouldn't recognize honor if someone served it to you on a silver platter."

Küfer's face flushed bright red. He took a few quick steps back around to the side of the bed and backhanded Dunn's right cheek. Dunn's head snapped to the left and he thought he was going to pass out. Through watery eyes, Dunn watched Küfer stomp away. Dunn sighed. Score one for the prisoner, he thought as he closed his eyes. Better get some sleep while I still can.

About an hour later, Dunn awoke to find a doctor checking his pulse. He was a tall man with a kind face.

"Hello, Doc."

The doctor glanced up from his watch and smiled. But the smile only touched the lips. After a few more seconds of counting, he let go of Dunn's wrist and said in a pleasant, rumbling voice, "Sergeant, good to see you awake. Sorry I couldn't be here earlier. Küfer wouldn't allow it. Damn swine." He grasped Dunn's hand and said, "Dr. Briard."

Dunn returned the grip without actually being able to shake hands. "Dunn. Thomas. He is quite a little something, isn't he?"

"Yes. But you be careful. He's smart, devious and totally devoid of any humanity. Anything done in the name of the Fatherland is acceptable.

Dunn nodded.

"How's the headache?"

Dunn rotated his head slowly in each direction, then said, "Seems to be better than before, still hurts though."

"Hmm. Yes, the improvement is a good sign."

"I assume I got grazed pretty good."

"You did. Just above your left temple. We've put a bandage on it and you'll have a nice streak through your hair for awhile." Dr. Briard reached over and lifted Dunn's eyelids one by one, shining a penlight into them to check the pupil's reaction to light. "I think you might have a slight concussion. Any nausea?"

"No. I'm actually hungry. What time is it?" He nodded toward his own empty wrist, "They took my watch."

"I hope that's all they take." The doctor glanced at his own watch. "It's about fifteen after six in the morning. I can get a small breakfast for you, probably just some toast and coffee, possibly an apple. They don't exactly allow us to give premier patient care in this wing. Even though it won't be much, I'd recommend you finish it all. Küfer has many tactics, and depriving prisoners of food and sleep are high on his list."

"Thanks, I will." Dunn raised his head a little and looked around the barracks style hospital room. "How come I got a private room? I'm pretty sure there were German casualties this morning."

Briard smiled and said, "Yes, there were about ten fatalities and another dozen injuries when the truck hit the German barracks."

Dunn's eyebrows lifted. It should have been worse than that. "That's all? That truck was loaded with ammunition and should have leveled the building and more in the explosion."

Briard shook his head. "There was no explosion, Sergeant."

"What? Damn it."

Briard shrugged. "I agree. Too bad there weren't more. To answer your question, this is the townspeople's wing. The Germans forbid mixing our people with the soldiers."

"You don't have any sick or injured people in town? That's why this room is empty?"

Dr. Briard shook his head and his face flushed in anger. "They will only allow the most serious cases to be admitted. If you aren't already dying, you can't come in here."

Dunn looked at Dr. Briard and, suddenly curious, asked, "Doc, how come you're here in this place?"

The doctor sighed and looked away for a long moment. When he turned back to Dunn, his eyes held so much despair and profound sadness that Dunn immediately knew the doctor had seen unspeakable things and lost much.

"My family is all gone. I tried to spirit my wife and two young sons out of the country, to England by boat, but it was sunk by the Germans before it even got a mile off shore. They had been lying in wait for it. How they knew, we never discovered. I watched from the safety of some woods, high on a hill overlooking the Channel. After the boat went down, I could hear the screams until the German machine guns opened up. Then it was silent again." Tears slid down the stricken man's face, but he made no effort to wipe them away.

"That night, I vowed I would do everything in my power to harm the Germans, which I do by supporting the resistance whenever possible." He paused, taking a breath. "I also try to save one person at a time, since that's what I do best."

"I'm very sorry about your family."

"Thank you." The doctor seemed to be on the verge of asking something, then stopped. Dunn waited patiently and Dr. Briard finally leaned closer and placed his stethoscope on Dunn's chest. Whispering, he asked, "When are the Americans and British going to invade?"

Dunn wanted to desperately to tell this poor man that it was coming soon, but had to say, "Doc, I'm sorry, but even if I knew, I couldn't tell you."

The doctor pulled back and said, "I thought as much, but we need your help so badly. You cannot imagine how horrible it is to have your country overrun like this. There has been so much suffering."

Dunn swallowed hard. The truth was, no, he couldn't imagine. Germans in Iowa seemed, . . . impossible. Dunn looked at Dr. Briard, who stared directly into his eyes, as if searching for something. Dunn didn't know what it could be.

Finally, Dr. Briard said, "You've killed Germans before today, many times." It was not a question.

"Yes, Doctor. In Italy."

"And if you are returned to your unit, you'll kill more Germans?"

Dunn didn't know where this was heading, but answered truthfully, "Yes, sir, if at all possible. It's my duty."

Dr. Briard quickly looked over his shoulder at the door. Satisfied no one was watching through the small windows in the door, he reached down and pulled up Dunn's long shirt sleeve, exposing the elbow. Then he pulled a small bottle of rubbing alcohol and a clean white cloth from his coat pocket. Using limited motion, he swiftly dabbed the alcohol onto the soft inside of Dunn's elbow. He returned the items to his pocket and withdrew a rubber strip. With another deft motion, he tied the rubber around Dunn's upper arm and said, "Make a fist." Soon, Dunn's vein appeared as a nice, thick blue snake. Dr. Briard carefully removed a syringe filled with clear liquid from his pocket and after pulling the safety cap off, slid it home and pressed the plunger. "This is going to knock you out for the rest of the day. Sorry, but you aren't going to get your breakfast, after all. Tonight you will be leaving this place." He smiled.

Dunn wanted to say thank you, but suddenly couldn't get his tongue to work. His eyelids fluttered and his breathing deepened as he fell into a deep unconscious state.

Dr. Briard smiled and gently brushed Dunn's hair back off his face. "Yes, one person at a time."

Safe House
1 mile southwest of Calais
2 June, 0740 Hours

The secluded, abandoned farmhouse was about a quarter mile back from the nearest road, which ran along the eastern edge of the property. The access road was overgrown and virtually invisible. Dense, lush woods kept prying eyes off the house. Henri and several other resistance members guarded the perimeter, just in case.

Inside the house, Cross sat at the kitchen table with Madeline and Saunders. He stared at the steaming cup of coffee in front of him. The discussion centered on Dunn and Oldham and whether there was any way to rescue them, assuming they were still among the living. The rest of the team was sacked out all over the house, some in the dining room, some in the living room. The sounds of snoring floated throughout the house.

"We have to at least try to get them back," Cross said, not looking up.

Saunders glanced at Madeline, then said, "It's too risky. We could end up losing more men. Dunn and Oldham wouldn't want that. They knew the risk when they signed on for the mission. Look, Cross, I know how you feel."

"Bullshit! Don't give me that." Cross's anger flared as he

looked up at Saunders. "If it was one of your men, you'd try, don't tell me you wouldn't."

"That's where you're wrong. I've left men behind before. I didn't like it then, I don't like it now. But I had to do it to save lives."

Cross understood full well the weight of command, even if only at the squad level. He still believed there was a way to save Dunn and Oldham. You just had to plan well and act fast. The longer they waited, the more difficult it would be. He put his hands on the table and folded them while looking from Saunders to Madeline. "Look, we can't give up. There has to be a way. If you don't want to help, I'll take my team and we'll do it ourselves."

Saunders snorted and said, "Matey, you'd get lost in the first five minutes if you go out there alone. Or worse, picked up by a German patrol." He felt bad for Cross and didn't want to make things worse than they already were, but he knew he had to up the reality ante. "Cross, here's the situation as I see it. First," he ticked fingers as he spoke, "we don't know if they're even alive. Second, if they are, we don't know where the hell the Germans have them. And third, we don't have the manpower."

Cross looked at Madeline and said, "You don't think we can rescue them, either?"

Madeline swallowed, then said, "If they are still alive, they will be held, not by the German Army, but by the Gestapo. They will be locked away and heavily guarded. I'm sorry, but it would take a full scale assault just to break in, even if we did know where they are. The Gestapo would likely kill them at the first sign of trouble."

"But we're assuming they were captured. What if they weren't? Maybe they escaped through the fence in the confusion, but we were already gone."

"Then they will make their way to the coast and we'll see them there." Madeline gave a small smile, one she didn't believe in.

Cross turned away to look out the window. A decrepit barn stood in the distance and the barnyard, which while unkempt, had a variety of tall wild flowers in blues and yellows. He thought back to Morris's comments on enjoying the beauty of things and shook his head, wondering how war could come to a place with such beauty.

He had become Dunn's and Oldham's teammate when they'd first met at commando school. Since then, they had also become good friends. Friends don't leave friends behind, he thought. But friends don't put friend's lives in danger, either. He didn't want to admit it, but Saunders and Madeline were right. They had to leave them behind and pray for the best. Damn it. Damn it to hell and back.

Turning his attention back to Madeline and Saunders, he said, "All right. I agree. What's the plan for us?"

Saunders sighed in relief. He'd been prepared to hogtie Cross.

Madeline nodded. "We wait until dark, then we get you to the shore where the boat will be waiting for you. In the meantime, you should both get some sleep while you can. We'll stand watch."

Calais
2 June, 1330 Hours

Küfer pushed his now empty plate away and sat back, completely satisfied with his chicken and dumpling lunch. Nothing like a home cooked meal. He tipped the wine glass up and finished off the fine Chardonnay. As soon as he set down the goblet, a homely young woman of about thirty stepped forward. Her dark brown hair was pulled back in a severe bun and she wore a loose fitting plain beige dress to hide her full breasts, which she kept tightly bound, and her flat belly. Most men would never give her a second glance. But Küfer had. He had spotted her in the mess hall and as soon as he sampled the warm truth under the dour clothing, given unwillingly, he'd had her quickly reassigned to be his personal cook and servant.

"How was your meal, sir?" Her voice was sweet and fluid, like a singer's. He never tired of hearing it.

"Wonderful, as always, Helga."

She turned away and frowned. Her name wasn't Helga, but every time she told him so, he slapped her. She'd learned to answer to the despicable German name each time. She hoped she wouldn't forget her own, which was Abrial. "Good, sir. I'm glad."

She had to stand next to him in order to clear his table and she felt his hand on her behind. A gruff hand squeezed a cheek, hard, then slid underneath the dress, rubbing her between her legs. She moaned, as was expected, and pushed against the hand. Suddenly, it was withdrawn and he said, "Not now, Helga. You'll just have to wait until tonight."

She turned to look at him over her shoulder and gave him her rendition of a sexy pout. "That's not fair."

He smiled in return and said, "No, but I have important work to do."

"Of course, sir. Dinner at seven, then?"

"Of course, Helga. Seven sharp. I want a roast. Get a Merlot from Mr. Devereux's cellar."

She stepped away and said, "Yes, sir."

He rose from the table, walked down the dark hallway and out the front door. The house he had commandeered was about a quarter-mile north of the hospital. He could have walked, but instead, headed for his Mercedes staff car and waiting driver. After entering the spacious back seat, he gave instructions and sat back.

The driver pulled the car to a smooth stop in front of the hospital and Küfer stepped out. He straightened his jacket and, with the brush of a hand, smoothed the lapels.

Facing the hospital, he just stood there for a moment, admiring the building's simple facade. He fancied himself a student of art and architecture, emulating the great *Führer*, and often spent time pursuing that interest during his travels. The building was new by European standards, being only fifty years old. It was a two-story, symmetrical affair constructed of regular hearth-fired red brick and trimmed in white. An arched portico extended a few feet out from the entrance. The hospital was on the east side of the street and Küfer admired the way the early afternoon sunlight threw the portico's shadow against the brick. Light and dark, the way of the new world. He thought he would come back another day and sketch it.

The hospital was on the corner of the intersection and had only one neighbor. A men's clothier shop, now rarely open, abutted against the hospital's northern wall. The owner, Louis

Gauvin, a man of fifty-seven, who was built like a wrestler, seemed out of place in a fine clothing store. He stood back in the shadows of his shop's recessed doorway watching Küfer as the detested German stood there like a pompous peacock who thought he owned the world.

As did most people in Calais and, for that matter, most places in France, Louis displayed for the Germans the expected outward fear and respect while inside burned hatred. Every time he nodded and deferred to a German, he was thinking about his plans for retribution and freedom. He had plans for Küfer, too. Oh, yes, he did. He stepped through his door silently and went back to his daily duties. His extra-curricular work wouldn't begin until darkness settled upon Calais and its inhabitants, the rightful ones as well as the occupiers.

Küfer entered the hospital and stormed past the nurse at the main desk. She watched him silently then, when he moved on down the hall, ran to the other wing to get Dr. Briard.

As Küfer made his way down the hall toward the wing where Dunn was being held, he was thinking about his captive and smiling. He had plans for this Sergeant Dunn. Of course, they always thought they could withstand his techniques, but he was a master. His favorites were the airmen falling from their precious B-17s and landing in German hands. He always told them he would love to stop giving them pain. All they had to do was just answer a few simple questions, nothing important, he'd say. At first they'd refuse and act defiant, but soon enough, they'd begin whimpering and drooling. They begged him to stop, then they either died or they talked. If they talked and recovered, they were sent to a POW camp. If they died later anyway, they were buried. He didn't much care which. Of course, dying would save the Fatherland the cost of feeding and housing them.

As he passed the guard outside the door, Küfer grabbed him by the arm and said, "Come with me." He flung the door open and it banged against the wall. Watching Dunn, who was half way down the row of six beds, he had hoped to startle him into flinching. He was disappointed to see no reaction whatsoever. Standing by the bed he looked down at Dunn for a moment then raised his hand to slap the unconscious man.

"Here, now! Don't do that!" Dr. Briard ran into the ward

room. He stopped at the head of Dunn's bed and looked down at the injured man with concern all over his face. Frowning, he looked at Küfer and said, "You can't treat my patient that way."

The Gestapo agent gave Briard a terrible smile and lowered his arm. "Doctor, he is not your patient, he is my prisoner." The smile disappeared. "You had better come to realize that distinction very soon, if you want to continue to practice medicine. I wanted to verify that he was unconscious and not faking it."

"Striking a man in the head who already has a concussion is most unwise. You might cause more damage."

Küfer dismissed the doctor's worry with a wave of a hand. "I expected him to be awake and ready for me."

"As you've already seen, he is not. He lost consciousness right after you left this morning. I've checked on him personally every hour since then, but there has been no change. I'm afraid he's slipped deeper into unconsciousness."

The Gestapo agent's face turned crimson. "That's not possible. I spoke to him this morning and he was fine."

Briard shook his head sadly, "I know, Mr. Küfer, but head trauma is such an uncertain thing. He could wake again in a few minutes, or it might be tomorrow, or," he shrugged, "it may be never."

Küfer gave Briard a glare that would have wilted a lesser man, "You'd better be telling me the truth, doctor, or this will be your last patient. Ever."

"Mr. Küfer, haven't I always been truthful with you before?"

"Doctor, there is always a first time for lies."

The doctor was deeply worried, uncertain where his earlier course of action would lead them. He had grown to expect the worst from the German military, the Gestapo, and this man in particular. He was never surprised. Küfer was an especially vicious and brutal man. Briard had treated many of this man's victims and, over time, had come to recognize the horrible wound patterns.

Küfer abruptly twisted around and grabbed the doctor by his suit's lapels. Briard gasped. Lifting and pushing in one fluid motion, the Gestapo agent slammed Briard against the wall so hard the doctor's head bounced, making his eyes swim. "You stay right here."

He turned to the guard and said, "If this man," he pointed toward Dunn, wakes up within the next few seconds, shoot the good doctor."

The soldier nodded and leveled his rifle at the doctor's chest.

Küfer walked to the foot of the bed, pulled back the covers over Dunn's feet. Then he removed a leather lead-filled sap from his pocket and struck the bottom of Dunn's right foot with so much force Dunn's leg rose off the bed.

The doctor winced at the sound as it reverberated around the room, but he was relieved to see no reaction from Dunn, thinking, thank God the drug was working.

Furious at the turn of events. Küfer wanted to tell the soldier to shoot the doctor anyway, but he knew he couldn't. He was still too useful. In spite of his own threats against the man, Küfer realized doctors were woefully in short supply and consequently valuable. He raised a hand and pointed at the doctor. "You call me the instant he regains consciousness."

Briard nodded in response. He stood frozen in place as the two Germans left him. Only after the door closed behind them did he move. Carefully, he checked Dunn's foot for broken bones and was relieved to find everything in the right place. He gently pulled the covers back over the exposed feet. Moving around the bed to get closer to Dunn's head, he brushed the injured man's hair back from his face again, thinking, You don't resemble my sons, but I'd like to think they could have grown up to be a man like you.

14

Berlin
3 June, 0248 Hours

The sentry held Marston's papers up and shone a light on them. His eyes traveled back and forth between the papers and Marston's face, along with the beam of light. He pointed the light into Marston's eyes and asked brusquely, "What are you doing out at this hour?"

Marston gave his prepared answer, "I had to work late to get an important document ready for Minister Fiedler. I just finished."

The soldier nodded and seemed about to hand back the papers when he suddenly said, "Empty your pockets."

Startled, Marston could only manage to say, "What?"

The soldier backhanded Marston's cheek. "Empty your pockets!"

That was something Marston could not do, since his mini-camera was in his trousers pocket. His one second hesitation was all it took.

The German dropped the papers, slid his rifle's sling off his shoulder, got a grip on the weapon, and took a half step back to bring the Mauser around to bear.

The British spy flicked his right wrist and a knife appeared in his hand. Lunging inside the rifle's arc, he swept the knife flashing toward the soldier's neck.

Surprised, but possessing excellent reflexes, the sentry twisted to his left just in time to avoid having his neck splayed open, but in doing so, exposed his right hand, which was holding the weapon around the trigger guard. Marston reversed the knife's direction and struck the hand, severing the thumb at the knuckle. The soldier shrieked in pain and the rifle clattered to the sidewalk. He grabbed for the knife with his good hand and somehow got a death grip on the spy's wrist.

Marston rammed the man with his shoulder and both lost their footing. They landed on the ground in a heap, each struggling to get control of the knife. Marston ended up atop the soldier and tried to shove the knife into the heaving chest. Suddenly, the soldier struck him in the head with the damaged hand and gave a lurch with his hips. He tumbled off and the soldier rolled with him, forcing the knife point deep into the agent's upper left arm.

Marston screamed and yanked the knife out. A surge of fear renewed his strength and he wrenched his hand free of the soldier's vice grip. A second later, the knife pierced the soldier's chest and he stopped fighting. A moment later, he lay dead.

His body shaking, Marston got to his feet, breathing hard. He looked around for his papers. They had fallen out of the way and, miraculously, didn't have any blood on them. He carefully picked up the papers, putting them in his coat pocket. Pulling a handkerchief from his trousers pocket, he pressed it against his left arm and groaned. He turned, avoiding looking down at the dead man on the ground, and began walking the remaining two blocks to his apartment. He paused in an alley long enough to bend over, hands on knees, and vomit.

Back in his apartment, Marston pulled the gauze tight around the bandage covering his punctured bicep, sealing the now cleansed wound. He grunted in pain as he inadvertently pressed down directly on the wound while fastening the gauze with a safety pin. Taking a deep breath, he struggled to his feet, then tottered over to the wash basin where he rinsed the blood from his hands. The German's and his own.

He couldn't believe he'd been so careless. Holding his hands out flat in front of him, he watched them tremble. Was it because he'd almost died or because he had just killed for the first time? Raising his head to stare at the reflection in the dingy mirror, he wondered forlornly if it would be his last. He poured some water into a glass. Taking a sip, he swished the water around and leaned over the basin, hands on either side of the bowl, and spit the water out hoping it would take the cotton balls taste with it.

He lurched unsteadily to his desk, turned out the white light, turned on the red one, removed the film from his camera, and began the development process. While the film marinated in the chemicals, he sat down and pulled out a one-time pad. He began composing his message. It was more bad news:

Scientists excited. Breakthrough imminent. Expect initial test in weeks.

15

St. Mary's Hospital
Calais
3 June, 0130 Hours

Dr. Briard got up from his desk and stepped into the dimly lit hallway. All was quiet. He turned left and walked toward the coffee room. Once there, he poured some hours-old coffee into two mismatched porcelain cups. Pulling a vial from his pocket, he opened it, then tipped it over. Two drops fell into the black liquid and Briard carefully noted which cup had the drug. Closing the vial, he returned it to his pocket. He picked up a spoon and stirred the coffee, then lifted the cup to his nose. Sniffing, all he could smell was the coffee. Satisfied, he picked up both cups and left.

He approached the guard carefully, speaking in German before he got too close, in case the man was jumpy at this time of night. "Hello. Care for a cup?" He held out the special cup and smiled. "I can't get enough of this when I'm working late."

The guard returned the smile gratefully and said, "*Dankeschön, Herr Doktor.*" He took the cup.

Briard held his cup out, as if in a toast, and the soldier clinked his against it. The soldier took a long drink. Then another. The doctor stood by, patiently waiting for the drug to take effect. After one more swallow, the soldier blinked a few times and swayed slightly.

"Are you all right? Perhaps you should sit down." Briard pulled a chair around, put it behind the German, and gently pushed down on the man's shoulder. The soldier sat down abruptly and the doctor grabbed the coffee cup before it fell to the floor. The rifle sling slid off the barely conscious man's shoulder. Quickly setting down both cups, the doctor reached over and pulled the rifle away from the man, whose eyes were now closed. The guard's breathing suddenly became slower and deeper and his head slipped back against the wall.

Briard checked his watch. He had one hour. Accurately timing everything had been a real challenge. He'd had to give Dunn another injection earlier in the evening when Dunn had begun waking. The guesswork was to know how much to give him to keep him out just long enough.

He put the rifle on the floor behind the sleeping soldier and went through the wardroom's door. The room was lit only by a lamp on a desk all the way at the other end, but it was sufficient for what Briard needed to do. He went to a sink along the wall on the right and dumped out the coffee cups, then rinsed them and put them in the cabinet underneath.

He walked toward Dunn, pausing by the American long enough to check whether he might be coming out of it. Dunn's respiration was up slightly, a good sign, so the doctor made his way to the desk. Briard moved to one side and began pushing. After it moved five feet, he knelt down and pressed against one of the floor boards with his palm. The board immediately popped up like a springboard. He pulled it out and set it aside. Gripping another board, he lifted until a three by five foot section of the floor came out as one unit. Leaning it against the wall, he pointed a penlight down into the darkness. The beam revealed a solid staircase. The dank smell of moist earth floated upwards. Unexpectedly, a vision of Bela Lugosi with a cape draped over one arm and partially covering his face popped into the doctor's mind. He shivered, then laughed at himself and started down the stairs.

The staircase led into a large area, not a true basement, but a secretly excavated room. Louis, the next door neighbor and owner of the men's store, and several other resistance members had dug out the room, as well as a tunnel leading to the shop's basement. Another tunnel, fifty yards long and shored up with timbers, led directly out from underneath the shop into woods behind the buildings.

After reaching the bottom of the stairs, the doctor knelt carefully and pulled back the burlap bag covering the tunnel opening. He stuck his flashlight into the tunnel's black maw and flicked it on and off twice. Answering light dots appeared at the other end. Soon, he could hear the muffled sounds of someone crawling across the dirt. He stepped back as Louis emerged, looking like a troll.

The doctor clapped him on the back and said, "Hello, Louie. Are you ready?"

Louis puffed out his chest and smacked it. "Louie is always ready!" Then he grinned and patted the doctor's arm. "Whenever you're ready, Doctor."

They made their way quietly back upstairs and Briard stepped over to Dunn's bed. He reached down and shook the American's shoulder. After a couple of more shakes, Dunn opened his eyes and blinked in surprise at seeing two men leaning over him with concern on their faces.

"Sergeant, are you up to moving around? It's time to get you out of here," said the doctor.

"What time is it?" Dunn slurred his words.

"It's about a quarter to two." Seeing confusion on Dunn's face, the doctor continued, "In the morning."

"Where are we going?"

"We're sending you back to England."

"Already? How?" Dunn was becoming more alert by the second.

"Don't worry about that. We need to get you on your feet and on the move quickly."

Dunn raised him arms and the manacles rattled. "What about these?"

Louis reached out, grabbed first one arm then the other, deftly unlocking the manacles, which fell back with a clink. Louis smiled and said, "How's that?"

Dunn rubbed his wrists gratefully and smiled back. "That's great, thanks. Who are you?"

"I am Louis Gauvin. You may call me Louie." He held out his hand and Dunn shook it.

Briard said, "Yes, Sergeant. Louie and I work together often to help others. Come now. Time for talking has ended. We must leave." He unlocked the bed rail on one side and lowered it. Then he helped Dunn sit up and swing his legs around to dangle off the side. Kneeling, he pulled Dunn's boots and socks out from underneath the bed and began putting them on Dunn.

Dunn thought it was weird to have someone else do something for him that he'd been doing for himself since he was three. "I can do that, Doc."

"No, I can do it faster than you. You'll need a little time to recover." Briard finished and stood up, holding his hands out to Dunn.

Dunn slid off the edge of bed and his boots hit the floor with a thunk. He stood still briefly, then let go of the doctor. "I think I'm okay now," he paused, looking puzzled, "but my right foot hurts."

Briard's expression soured. "Yes, that's courtesy of Küfer. He wanted to see if you were faking it."

Dunn shook his head. "Asshole."

"Yes. Let's go."

As they turned to go back to the escape hatch, light suddenly flooded the room. Küfer shouted, "Halt!" He stood in the doorway, surprisingly, by himself. His deadly Luger was pointed in their direction. He stomped over to the three men as they waited silently at the foot of Dunn's bed.

Dunn was in the middle, the doctor to his right and Louis to his left. Dunn was watching the way the arrogant little Gestapo agent was handling the weapon, trying to gauge whether he'd be able to disarm him before someone got shot.

Küfer carefully stopped a few feet away and focused his attention on Louis. "*Herr* Gauvin, I always knew you were a part of this. I just haven't had time to haul you in for questioning." He smiled smugly, failing to notice the doctor pulling a syringe from his pocket. "Of course, now that I have the Sergeant on his feet and looking well, and also the doctor here to question—"

The doctor's hand was a blur as he drove the needle home into Küfer's neck, piercing the carotid artery. He pushed the plunger and the poison shot straight into the surprised man's brain within a second. Briard yanked the needle out and threw it onto the floor. Küfer tried to bring his weapon to bear on the doctor, but Dunn simply reached out and plucked it from the dying man's hand.

Küfer began gasping for breath and, as his knees buckled, he tried to grab the doctor's coat for support. Briard stepped back and the Gestapo agent fell face first to the floor, dead.

The three men stared at the body for a moment, then Briard and Gauvin picked it up and dumped it onto the bed. They pulled the bed covers up enough to hide Küfer's bright red face. Gauvin slid the man's hat under the covers, then grabbed Dunn and pulled him toward the stairs. "Come on, Sergeant, you've a date with a boat."

Dunn put the Luger's safety on and slipped it into his belt, then followed Gauvin, who went down the stairs. When Dunn started down, he turned, expecting to see the doctor right behind him. Instead, Briard was standing by the desk. Dunn frowned and said, "Come on, Doc. What're you waiting for?"

Briard said, "I must stay behind," he waved a hand in the general direction of the dead man, "and take care of things."

"Won't they arrest you?"

Pointing at Dunn's former bed, Briard said, "There lies the arresting officer. I'll attend to things and, as for you, sadly your injuries were more serious than first thought and you expired in the middle of the night."

Dunn nodded, but then a thought struck him. "But if Küfer hadn't arrived when he did, how would you explain my disappearance to him?"

The doctor stared back at Dunn.

A corner of Dunn's mouth lifted. "You arranged for him to find out, didn't you?"

Briard shrugged. "Time to go, Sergeant, good luck."

"You, too. Thanks."

Dunn darted down the stairs and Gauvin handed him a small

flashlight tied to a thin rope. "Here, put this around your neck and turn it on when we get in the tunnel." Gauvin had one of his own and as he knelt down to enter the tunnel, he switched it on. It gave off enough light in the immediate vicinity of his hands that he could see where to put them.

Dunn waited until Gauvin had moved ahead a few feet, then turned on his light and followed. After about five minutes of shuffling his hands and feet across the tunnel's dirt floor, Dunn's head began to throb in earnest. He tried to ignore it, but finally whispered, "Louie, I need a rest."

Louie stopped and whispered back, "What's wrong?"

"My head's killing me. I need a minute."

"All right, but just for a minute. We can't waste any time."

Dunn lay down on his stomach and closed his eyes. It seemed to help.

Good to his word, after one minute, Gauvin said, "It's time, Sergeant."

Dunn groaned.

Crawling through the tunnel took a long time and Dunn had to stop twice more to rest. Finally, after almost thirty minutes, Gauvin stopped and Dunn nearly bumped into the older man's shoes.

"Turn out your light and wait here. Make no noise."

Dunn turned off his light and lay down again, grateful for the rest.

Gauvin turned off his own light and crawled the remaining ten feet in the cloying darkness. He carefully pulled back the tree-branch-covered flap of burlap covering the exit and stuck his head out. He listened for a few moments, then let the flap fall back in place. "Dunn, come on. It's clear."

Shortly, the two dust covered men crawled out of the tunnel and, kneeling on the damp grass, breathed in the clear, cool night air.

"It is about two kilometers to the beach. Are you ready?"

Dunn took a deep breath and said, "Lead the way, Louie."

The sound of crashing waves met the men's ears as they climbed out of the truck one last time. Overhead, a partly cloudy sky allowed sporadic starlight to break through, providing more light than the average person believed possible.

Cross walked over to the beach's ridgeline, the point where the grass surrendered to the encroaching sand. He put his head back and inhaled the fresh salt air. The smell reminded him of the wondrous times he and his dad, a Maine fisherman, had spent working together on the ocean. The last letter from home said his dad was still going out every day, even at the age of sixty-seven. Cross fervently hoped the war would end in time for him to get back home and go back out with his dad again.

Madeline and Saunders joined Cross, and Madeline said, "The boat will be here in a few minutes."

"Are they going to be able to find this spot?" Cross knew from experience that navigating at night was difficult under these conditions. Even with a compass, it could be tricky if you weren't careful enough with the current's effect on your craft.

"Yes, they're quite experienced. Don't worry."

Cross nodded.

"Come on, let's get the men down to water's edge."

Cross stared at Madeline and said, "No, we should wait here instead. We'd be exposed down on the beach."

Madeline shook her head. "There's nothing to worry about, Mr. Cross, we have men posted in either direction along the road. We, too, are experienced. There won't be any German patrols tonight."

"Madeline, I can appreciate your confidence, but if there's only one thing I learned from Sergeant Dunn, it's that, on a mission, there's always something to worry about. We just can't know what it is every time. We'll stay here along the ridgeline until you confirm that the boat is here."

Madeline was about to continue trying to make her point when Saunders said, "Madeline, I agree with Cross. We can't take any unnecessary risks this close to our escape."

"Very well, gentlemen." Madeline turned and walked back toward the truck.

Saunders looked at Cross and shrugged. "I don't think she appreciated our lack of confidence."

"I don't think so, either." Cross looked around the immediate area and said, "I'll set up my team along the ridge from here to the west. You take the east side?"

"Sure thing."

The teams quickly deployed, facing back toward the road and the woods on the other side. Madeline, her pique over, took Henri and Adrien down to the water's edge to scout for the soon-to-arrive rescue boat.

Oberleutant Gerry Ostermann was tired and feeling grumpy at having to take a truck full of a dozen also grumpy soldiers out on shore patrol in the middle of the night. Some idiot back at headquarters still had the asinine idea that the Allies would invade at Calais. Ostermann thought it too obvious a spot since it was the closest to England, only forty-two kilometers away. If he had known it was Hitler himself who believed it would be Calais, he would have been mortified to think he had insulted the great man, even if only in his own mind.

Near the Channel
Northeast of Calais
3 June, 0245 Hours

Dunn was getting tired again as they wound their way closer to the beach. Gauvin had set a punishing pace through the dense and difficult woods, but he seemed to have a built-in instinct for finding the best path. Dunn's head felt like it was going to explode and he thought whatever contents his stomach might still hold would be on their way up soon, but they couldn't stop for a rest. They were so close to the channel, he could hear the pounding of the surf and he thought he'd gotten a whiff of salty air.

Gauvin stopped so suddenly that Dunn ran into him, but the shopkeeper's spark plug build helped him hold his ground.

Dunn leaned close to Gauvin's ear and whispered, "What is

it, Louie?"

"Shhh. Listen."

Dunn cocked his head, then he heard it. A vehicle was coming toward them from their left. A German troop truck rounded the curve seconds later and as it rumbled past them, Gauvin and Dunn were close enough that they could make out the figures in the truck. It was a fully loaded patrol. Gauvin swore in French then said, "This is bad, Sergeant. If they stop anywhere nearby, they can't help but see the boat. Come we must hurry."

Madeline left Henri at the water and returned to the ridgeline with Adrien. She found Saunders and Cross crouched near each other. Suddenly, a bird whistle pierced the air and Madeline hissed to the Brit and American commanders, "Get ready. There's a German patrol truck coming." She whipped around to Adrien and said, "Get Henri off the beach."

Adrien took off at a dead run.

Cross's first reaction was to say, 'I told you so,' but he didn't. Instead, he sent instructions down the line to get ready in case the truck stopped.

Adrien was still about five meters away when Henri raised a small flashlight and winked it on and off toward the water. An answering double blink flashed across the choppy water.

Sliding to a stop beside Henri, Adrien said, "Henri, give the alarm signal. Quick, a patrol's coming."

Henri immediately flashed a different signal, then took off toward the ridgeline with Adrien right on his heels.

Ostermann noticed a twinkle of light to his left, out on the water, and said, "Slow down, I think I saw something." He lifted a pair of field glasses hanging from a strap around his neck and swept the area where he thought he'd seen the flash. Nothing. He lowered the glasses and said, "Stop the truck, I want to get out for a minute."

Before the truck had rolled to a complete stop, he opened the door and stepped out onto the running board, then hopped off. Ostermann walked around to the front of the truck and lifted the glasses again. After only a minute of careful searching, he found what he was hoping to find. A light shape floated in the channel about two hundred meters off shore. He could make out that it was a large fishing vessel and he could also tell which direction it was traveling. Lowering the glasses, he got his bearings and compared them to the boat's direction. Darting back around the truck, he jumped up into his seat.

The driver gunned the engine without being told. He turned off his black-out lights and guided the vehicle carefully down the center of the road, concentrating hard to make out the shiny blacktopped surface.

"Stop five hundred meters from here and we'll get out."

"*Ja, Oberleutant.*"

Ostermann began thinking about the accolades he would receive if they captured those trying to get on the boat. Forgotten were his previous complaints.

The driver began braking and pulled the truck to a smooth stop off to the side of the road. Ostermann's men were well trained and used to working with him. As soon as the truck stopped, the rear gate was lowered and, in seconds, the ten man squad was out on the road, crouched and ready.

In moments, Ostermann was leading his team down the road. After they traveled another fifty meters, he held up a hand. He checked his location against his memory, then waved at his second in command to join him. He gave him instructions and the man gathered half the squad and guided them toward a point farther down the beach. Ostermann took the other half with him to complete the trap.

Cross spotted the Germans, who appeared to be trying to flank them, but he didn't think the enemy knew they were there, and were just trying to cut off the beach. He figured there would be another group coming down the road they'd have to handle. Crawling over to Saunders, he whispered, "They've split their forces. One's headed to our right, toward the beach, and the other's going to come down the road's edge. I'm going to turn my team to the right and get the group coming down toward the beach. Can you take care of the other bunch?"

"You bet your sweet ass, we can."

"Wait for us to start it."

"Yes, sir."

Cross grinned at being called 'sir' and clapped Saunders on the shoulder, then crawled back to his men. He gave instructions and the team quickly got into position. Although the numbers were about even, the American and British soldiers held the advantage, since they knew where the enemy was and the Germans did not. However, the element of surprise would last only seconds against seasoned combat troops, which these men undoubtedly were. They couldn't afford to be impatient.

He took his position in the sand and propped his Thompson up on his left hand. Five seconds later, the first German appeared, less than twenty-five yards away. Cross waited patiently, as did his men. Cross squeezed the trigger when the fifth German popped into view, then everyone else joined in.

Gauvin and Dunn crossed the road after the truck disappeared from sight and picked their way carefully along the beach. Dunn pulled the Luger out and flipped off the safety. He carried it at the ready; raised at a forty-five degree angle, which would allow him to lower it onto a target, easier and faster than lifting it from a dangling arm.

Sounds of gunfire shattered the night's silence. Both men dropped to the sand as stray rounds snapped over their heads. Gauvin muttered more curses in French, while Dunn spewed a few in English. The difference was that while Gauvin's reaction was based on fear, Dunn's was caused by the happy surprise of recognizing the distinctive chatter of the Thompson. As abruptly as the shooting began, it stopped. The sound of the weapons discharging in the cool night air echoed across the water. Silence returned.

Dunn raised up on his knees slowly and peeked in the direction of the gunfire. The last thing he wanted to do was to just stand up in the dark right after a firefight, short though it had been.

At first, he couldn't see anything moving, then one, then another, black figure stood up and ran in a zigzag toward him. At first, he thought they'd seen him and he lowered himself just enough so he could still see the figures. Suddenly, they stopped and one kicked something lying on the ground. Dunn realized the man was checking a fallen body for signs of life. Suddenly, the other man spun to his right and fired a shot into a moving form on the ground. The German stopped moving.

Dunn whispered to Gauvin, "Stay put. Those are my men." Gauvin nodded his understanding. Dunn safed the Luger and put it back in his belt, took a breath and stood slowly with his hands raised. "Thomas Dunn, United States Army. Don't shoot!" he shouted.

The two men raised their weapons and he shouted again, "Thomas Dunn, United States Army. Please don't shoot!" The two men lowered their weapons and ran toward him. He dropped his hands and turned to Gauvin, "Let's go, Louie, my friends are here."

The two pairs of men met and Hanson and Cross pounded Dunn's back. Cross grinned, teeth flashing. "We're glad to see you again, Sarge. We thought the Germans captured you or worse." He looked at Gauvin in surprise. Frowning, he said, "Where's Timmy?"

Dunn shook his head. "He didn't make it. We lost him at the depot."

Cross's face fell. "Ah, shit."

Dunn put a hand on Cross's arm and said, "I know. Let's get going, though. We can talk more later, after we get on board."

Cross nodded and they headed back to join the rest of the team.

Madeline sent Henri back to the water to signal the all clear to the boat and was relieved to see a response from the water. She had seen the Americans take off at run toward two distant figures. Her heart did a flutter when the name "Dunn" floated across the sand to her. Could it be? She wanted to run across the beach and jump into his arms, but there was much work to do; cleanup work. The truck had to be hidden and the bodies, too, but not together. She issued instructions to her men and they immediately got to work. The sound of the boat's engine drifted in as it bobbed a mere ten yards off the beach.

There was a lot of semi-organized milling about as the British and Americans gathered together to welcome back Dunn. Madeline made her way to the center of the group and saw Dunn standing among his celebrating friends, the lost returned. She saw an older man with Dunn and knew he was responsible for Dunn's arrival. As she got closer, she recognized him. She stuck out her hand. "Thanks for getting him here in time, Louie."

Gauvin smiled and shook hands. "It was my pleasure, Madeline. It's good to see you."

"You, too." Madeline had lived her entire life near Calais, and had known him since she was a child.

Dunn said to Saunders, "Let's get the men on board right away, shall we, Sergeant?"

"Too right, we shall."

Dunn grinned and punched Saunders in the arm.

Saunders said, "All right, gentlemen, and I use the word loosely, what say we get on the boat?" The men laughed and started moving.

Dunn spotted Madeline talking with Gauvin and when she turned to look at him, he waved. She waved back and walked toward him, stopping a pace away. "I wasn't sure I'd ever see you again."

"It was a close one, to be sure. I owe it all to Dr. Briard and Louie."

Nodding, she said, "They're good men." Closing the distance, she raised her face, put a slim hand on the back of his neck, and pulled gently.

In a split second, Dunn decided and he resisted, ever so slightly. Madeline lowered her hand, her emerald-green eyes boring into Dunn's. Softly, she said, "You have someone back home, don't you?"

Dunn shook his head. "Not yet. I hope to, but I didn't do very well the last time I saw her."

"No room for me," she touched his chest, "in here?"

"I need to know if she'll find room for me in hers."

Madeline's lips compressed, then she said, "Don't forget me." She spun away and ran toward the road.

Dunn watched her diminishing form, knowing he'd made the right choice. But could he win Pamela back? He knew he had to try. Could he summon the courage? Sighing deeply, he turned and walked slowly to the water, where he boarded the boat.

16

Camp Barton Stacy
3 June, 1800 Hours

The worst of Dunn's headache had finally gone away about half way across the Channel, which surprised him since the water had been so rough. By the time they'd ridden in the awaiting truck back to camp, it was just giving him reminders now and then. As soon as they got to camp, Dunn and Saunders told the men to head to their barracks and get some catch up sack time. No one argued.

Dunn and Saunders checked in briefly with Kenton to give him the bad news about Oldham and the mission failure. Kenton was sympathetic about Oldham and more than a little upset. He told the leaders to go get some sleep and report back for dinner in his office.

Entering Kenton's office, Dunn and Saunders were delighted to see a hot meal spread out waiting for them. Kenton, Lieutenant Adams and a man wearing a dark suit were already seated at the table. The room smelled of fried chicken and fresh cut wood, an odd combination it seemed to Dunn. The building was only a few

RONN MUNSTERMAN

months old, he remembered, so it figured that the wood's fragrance would still be fresh in the air.

Kenton smiled and said, "Gentlemen. Feeling better after some rest?"

"Much improved, sir, thanks," replied Dunn.

"What'd the doctors say about your noggin?"

Dunn's head still had a stripe of bandage around it. "I don't get dizzy or have a headache, so I should be good to go tomorrow or Monday."

"Good, good." Kenton turned slightly and lifted a hand toward the visitor. "I'd like to introduce Howard Lawson of the OSS. He'll be joining us for dinner."

Lawson stood up, wobbled a bit, and put a hand out on the table to steady himself. Kenton, sitting to Lawson's right, immediately put a hand on the man's arm and said, "Mr. Lawson, why don't you sit down?"

Lawson gave Kenton a combination embarrassed and grateful look, and sat down hard.

Kenton turned to Dunn and Saunders, "This is Mr. Lawson's second trip from the states *this week.*"

Saunders whistled, then said, "No wonder you look a bit peaked, old chap. What's so damn important you did that?"

Lawson gave Saunders a weak smile and Kenton said, "That'll be our after-dinner discussion, gentlemen. For now, let's just enjoy this meal."

"Yes, sir. I'm all for that," said Dunn with a grin.

The men dug into the meal and, after a few minutes, Dunn asked, "Colonel, is it all right to discuss the mission?" He tilted his head slightly in Lawson's direction. "No offense, Mr. Lawson."

"None taken, Sergeant."

Kenton nodded and said, "Mr. Lawson has all the clearance he needs, so feel free."

Dunn wiped his hands on his napkin, then took a drink of his contraband beer. Looking at Kenton, he said, "Colonel, I'm sorry about the whole thing. I feel as though I let you down. I've never had a mission failure quite this bad before."

Kenton looked at his most trusted non-com thinking that Dunn was being overly hard on himself. "Sergeant, I think you've forgotten the mission's purpose."

"Sir?"

"It doesn't matter that you didn't destroy the depot."

"What? Why not?"

"Your mission was to decoy the Germans, to convince them where the invasion was going to be. Your presence alone did that. The mission was successful in that vein and that's how I'm writing it up."

"Well, sir, I appreciate your point, but it still doesn't seem right. I lost a man, I got my ass captured and I didn't double-check the detonators. I just can't believe all of them were tampered with. That would have taken hours to do, so it was clearly done before we even arrived in France."

Saunders cleared his throat, then said, "Dunn, no one would have thought to check those damn things, I know I wouldn't have, I mean, they came from a trusted source."

Kenton leaned forward and said, "I agree with Sergeant Saunders, Dunn, you did what anyone would have done. No one here is blaming you for anything and I just told you how I'm writing it up."

Dunn nodded slowly, finally beginning to accept the Colonel's words.

"You're just damn lucky to have landed in the 'right' hospital. I'd hate to think of you languishing in some prisoner of war camp or worse," said Kenton.

Dunn laid down his napkin and pushed back from the table, feeling comfortably full. He smiled ruefully and said, "That's certainly what I thought was going to happen when that little prick of a Gestapo agent showed up."

"What was his name?" asked Adams.

"Keifer, Kofur, I don't know exactly, but something like that. Why? What does it matter, he's dead."

Adams smiled and said, "I know, but you never know when some little detail might be important. Maybe someone'll recognize the name from somewhere and we can piece together information that's useful."

Dunn gave Kenton an admonishing look and said, "Sir, you've been letting the good Lieutenant spend too much time with the intelligence pukes, haven't you?" He looked at Lawson suddenly, as though he'd forgotten the intelligence officer was there. "Oops, sorry again, Mr. Lawson."

Lawson grinned. The wonderful hot meal made him feel better. "And again, none taken."

Everyone laughed and Dunn felt reasonably human for the first time in a long while. His expression darkened as he said to Saunders, "If I ever cross paths with our old friend Luc, he'll be dead before he hits the floor."

"You and me both," said Saunders.

"I can only hope that Madeline and her team can get away from the area before that bastard turns them in."

Saunders nodded, "They're a good team. I wonder how Luc wormed his way in so deep."

"He must have been planning this for a long time, is the only thing I can think of." Dunn turned to Kenton. "Colonel, have you got a new assignment for us?"

Kenton and Adams shared a look that neither sergeant missed.

Dunn reached over and poked Saunders, "Uh oh."

Kenton said, "As a matter of fact we do."

Dunn and Saunders waited.

"Both of you, and your teams, will remain together. Sergeant Saunders, I've already gotten agreement from Colonel Jenkins. You and your teams will take a one week leave beginning tomorrow."

Dunn's eyebrows lifted. "What about the invasion, sir? I thought we'd be involved."

Kenton shook his head and said, "No, Dunn, your assignments have nothing to do with the invasion."

A surprised, even hurt, look crossed Dunn's face. He glanced at Saunders and saw the same expression on the British sergeant's face. Dunn was accustomed to being in the thick of it and now he wouldn't be? "I see. Yes, sir."

Colonel Kenton noticed Dunn's cool tone and said soothingly, "Tom, believe me when I tell you, your upcoming assignment is critical to the war effort. You know how much I trust and respect you. And rely on you."

Dunn's face reddened, "Sir, I apologize, I should have known better."

Kenton smiled and said, "No apology necessary. Mr. Lawson has the details of your assignments."

Dunn glanced at Lawson, whose expression turned grim.

Lawson pushed aside his dinner plate and lifted his black briefcase from the floor, putting it on the table in front of him. He popped the two silver clasps and opened the case, withdrawing several stapled sets of papers. He passed them carefully around the table. He turned to Dunn and Saunders. "Gentlemen, Colonel Kenton and Lieutenant Adams have already been briefed. I'm required to remind you that these are top secret documents. You will not discuss them with anyone outside this room. Is that perfectly clear?"

Dunn and Saunders nodded.

"This is a preliminary plan. We're still waiting for one of MI5's agents to find one of the targets outlined in the attack plan before you. Once that's accomplished, I will update the plan and finalize the timetable with my MI5 counterpart. Following that, we'll be ready to present the plan to you and your teams.

"We're hopeful that we'll get the information we need within the next few days, but you know how it is in the intelligence business."

"Murphy's Law," said Dunn.

Lawson nodded. "Exactly, except in war, Murphy is always working overtime." He flipped his document open to the first page. "Let's begin."

Dunn examined the cover sheet. The OSS stamp was in the upper left-hand corner. At the bottom was the angled TOP SECRET stamp in red. The title sat in big bold letters in the middle of the page: OPERATION DEVIL'S FIRE.

17

The Reich Chancellery
Berlin
3 June, 2000 Hours

Armament Minister Albert Speer waited outside the *Führer*'s office doors. A handsome man with a high forehead and brown hair, Speer wore the gray German Army uniform and black, knee-high boots. He'd been having a late dinner when the call came to meet with Hitler. Speer, the son of an architect, also became one himself in 1927, which might explain the *Führer*'s original interest in him, Hitler being a failed architect and artist himself, although no one dared mention this these days. Speer joined the Nazi Party in 1932, then in 1933, when he was only twenty-eight, met Hitler. The *Führer* gave him the monumental assignment of organizing the Nuremberg Rally scheduled for the next year. Speer did such a spectacular job that Hitler commissioned three projects: the German exhibit at the Paris Exhibition in 1937, the Party Palace in Nuremberg, and finally, the Reich Chancellery. The doors, outside of which he was waiting, were his design.

Speer was pretty sure the reason Hitler had called the meeting was to find out when the atomic bomb would be ready. Speer knew from his meetings with Dr. Herbert that they'd reached the point of not if, but when.

Footsteps floated to Speer and he turned toward them. His face immediately displayed intense displeasure because strutting down the one-hundred-fifty meter long entrance gallery was the fat and lazy Göring. He was wearing his favorite blue uniform; he was the only person Hitler allowed to wear anything but the standard black or gray uniforms. Speer despised Göring for his constant maneuvering. Like the time in 1942, following the airplane crash that killed the Minister of Armaments, Fritz Todt. The *Führer* had already appointed Speer to replace Todt, as Göring was rushing to the Chancellery to ask for the job he'd coveted for years. Göring was furious, but smart enough to hide it from Hitler. But not from the new Minister. Even though Speer immediately improved production levels, Göring let little remarks 'slip' now and again, always out of the *Führer*'s earshot, like a sniveling little bully trying to get even with someone who'd bested him fair and square.

Speer sighed deeply. When Göring drew to a stop in front of him, Speer said, "Good evening, Field Marshal."

"Mr. Speer." Göring never called Speer by the stolen title in private, yet another childish tactic.

One of the doors opened and Hitler's secretary stuck his head out, sparing Speer any more time alone with Göring. "Gentlemen, the *Führer* will see you." The man stepped back and swept his arm toward the interior of Hitler's office.

Speer gestured for Göring to go first, but Göring had already moved past him and didn't notice. Speer's face was a mask of courtesy, hiding his feelings. The two men walked to Hitler's desk, where the dictator sat calmly, at least for the moment, thought Speer.

As soon as Speer and Göring were seated in front of him, Hitler's calm disappeared. A scowl settled on his face and he said, "I've called you both here for one reason. I want a status update on your respective projects." He turned to Göring first. "Well?"

Göring knew very well that Hitler didn't mean what he was

doing with the Hortens' airplane. That was not for anyone else's ears, especially Speer's. "Yes, *mein Führer*. My scientists and engineers assure me that a working rocket will be ready by mid-August. After only a few test firings of the engines, they will be ready to launch the first 738 kilogram Amatol warhead by 1 September."

Hitler smiled and clapped his hands in glee. "Well done, Field Marshal. I look forward to that test and the first delivery of our new weapon on London." Turning to Speer, Hitler asked, "Minister Speer, how goes the building of my atomic bomb? Do you have as welcome of news as our friend here?"

Speer smiled. Even if he had bad news for the *Führer*, he wouldn't admit it in front of the blue-festooned buffoon sitting next to him. Fortunately, the truth would do nicely tonight. "Yes, *mein Führer*. I'm proud to report good news, too. Dr. Herbert's team has been doing a wonderful job with the conversion of the raw uranium into the requisite U-235. The gun mechanism is nearly complete and the first test is expected on 16 June."

Hitler was beside himself with happiness. "Oh, what a joyful evening this turned out to be! You have both done well. Thank you. Your *Führer* is proud of you." He slapped the palms of his hands on the desk and stood up. "Have you eaten your dinners yet?"

Both Göring and Speer replied, "No, *mein Führer*," even though Speer was thinking of his soon to be disappointed family awaiting his return to the table.

"Excellent. You'll join me, then. We'll have a good time, won't we?"

In unison, once more, "Yes, *mein Führer*."

18

West of Stuttgart
6 June, 2034 Hours

Following someone in a dilapidated car was much more difficult than Neil Marston ever expected. First, there was the problem of keeping up once they'd reached the outskirts of the city and were on the open road. As they wound their way up and down the rolling terrain, he lost sight of the big Mercedes several times, making his heart jump into his throat until he caught a view of the brake lights as the heavy car slowed for yet another curve. Then there was the problem of keeping the Mercedes in sight while not looking like he was keeping the car in sight.

Marston had followed Doctors Herbert and Bauer when they'd left Speer's office in Berlin. He would have loved to have heard the conversation, but would settle for getting a copy of the meeting minutes later. They were likely giving Speer an update on their progress. Marston had sifted through a ton of paper over a week's time to find their names and schedules. He hadn't had any more close calls on his forays into places where his mere presence meant death. He'd gotten over killing the German sentry somewhat, meaning he no longer woke up in a cold sweat while holding his hands in front of his face checking for blood. He understood it was either him or the German and that his job was reaching a crucial stage in helping the war effort, still . . . could he do it again? Or would he hesitate just long enough to get himself killed? He hoped he'd never have to find out.

He had stayed close as the scientists boarded the Berlin-Stuttgart train, taking a seat two rows behind them and on the opposite side of the aisle. He'd been relieved when they had walked to Herbert's apartment from the station instead of taking a car. He knew from the schedule they wouldn't be going out to the lab until later, so he did the next thing on his list.

Getting a car hadn't proven to be the problem he'd anticipated. Not far from the train station, as he was sneaking along behind the doctors, he'd noticed the piece of junk in front of a rundown house. After making sure of where the two men were going, he ran back to the house. He took a quick test drive, surprised the thing had actually started, and following a quick negotiation with the owner, a one-handed, grumpy old man, the car was his. Not exactly a pride and joy, but it would do. He hoped.

As they moved farther from Stuttgart, Marston couldn't help but be awestruck by the beauty of the landscape. The week of bad weather had broken and the blue sky breathtakingly framed the green trees and farmland. It suddenly made him homesick for England.

He guided his sad-sack car through a curve and when he came out of it, the roadway straightened out for almost a mile in front of him. The Mercedes was roaring away and the gap between them grew to a quarter mile. They were headed north and a sizable hill rose on their left. The Mercedes' brake lights blinked on, then the heavy car made a left turn.

Marston couldn't see any buildings along the road the doctors were now driving on, which puzzled him. He slowed as he approached the turn off and took a quick glance. All he could see was a newly paved road leading off toward the hill. He checked his mirror so he'd able to recognize the entrance later, after dark. He then eyed the odometer and memorized the number. He drove a little farther, looking for a spot to pull off the road and wait.

Two miles down, he slowed. A farmer's track led off to his left, winding through a hay field and bordered by tall hedges. There were no cars coming toward him and when he checked the mirror, none behind, either. Marston stopped the car, then backed onto the dirt road. He read the odometer again and calculated the distance, 4.2 kilometers. Sliding his arm over the passenger seat, he turned his head and carefully began backing the little car down the narrow strip. After covering about twenty yards, he stopped, turned off the engine and got out. Stepping up onto the running board, he scanned his surroundings carefully. Satisfied he wasn't visible to anyone on the highway and that there were no farmhouses in sight, he got back in. He checked his watch; 8:47 P.M. He estimated the sun would set around nine-thirty and complete darkness would take over about ten. He settled back to wait.

Even though the time passed slowly, Marston had grown accustomed to waiting for long periods of time. He often resorted to playing mental word games to pass the time, tracing the etymology of a word through several different languages. Tonight, though, he was thinking about going home. His last message included a recall to London. He was both shocked and relieved. Four years was a long time to be away from home. More to the point, it was a long time to be undercover in Berlin.

Finally, it grew dark and he started the car. A three-quarter moon was rising, which turned the narrow road into a pale white stripe. He eased the car ahead and drove back to the highway. Checking the odometer again, he guided the car out onto the highway and headed toward the atomic lab.

When he neared the turnoff, he pulled onto the shoulder and shut off the engine. He got out, stretched and started walking. Before he reached the road leading to the lab, he looked around. It wouldn't be prudent to just wander down the middle of the road. Hedges bordered both sides of the paved road and he opted to walk along them on the north side, out of sight. He hoped. Climbing through a barbed-wire fence, he found himself in a pasture. As he walked, thistle plants tried to prick their way through his pants; he was glad he had on long sleeves and boots. Marston tried to keep his hands out of the way of the stinging thorns, but got jabbed once. The pain was immediate, not quite like a wasp sting, but enough to teach you not to do that again. The grass was tall, maybe calf deep, so cattle hadn't been here for a while and he wouldn't have to worry about stepping in any stinky surprises.

After walking about a quarter mile, he ran into an impediment. A ten-foot tall chain link fence blocked his way. Marston stopped about two steps from the fence and stood perfectly still. As he examined it, moonlight glinted off the steel wire. He was grateful to discover it wasn't electrified, but it did have razor wire across the top. About to kneel, he noticed something shiny just in front of his right boot. Holding his breath, he slid his boot back, then let out his breath softly. Now he understood why the pasture grass was so tall. There wouldn't be any cattle roaming around where tripwires were set. He'd come within a cat's whisker of setting off an alarm.

Safely away from the wire, he knelt and eyed the compound. He estimated the distance at two hundred yards. Pulling a small pair of binoculars from his pocket, he lifted them to his eyes and could clearly see the compound's details in the bright moonlight. A red and white guard shack stood where the road met the fence. A rolling gate controlled the entrance. He kept his eyes on the shack for a few minutes. Before long, he was rewarded with a cigarette's sudden red glow just inside the doorway. The soldier certainly wasn't worried about being seen. Why would he, here in Germany?

A lone building, the barracks, sat to the right of the road, which continued on through to . . . a door in the side of the hill? Marston blinked in surprise. They were working underground. Then he realized he shouldn't be surprised, the Germans had already moved many of their manufacturing facilities underground to avoid the massive Allied bombing runs. He studied the door for a few moments and decided it was most certainly solid metal, heavy iron.

A single guard leaned against the door frame, which appeared to be concrete. Turning his attention back to the barracks, Marston tried to picture how many bunks could fit in there. He guessed fifty, which would make the garrison about the size of a platoon. He put the binoculars away and got out his camera. He wasn't sure how good the pictures would be, but it was worth a try. He snapped two each of the gate and the guard shack, then two of the barracks, with the hillside entrance in the background. He slid the camera back into his pocket and was about to stand up, when the barracks door opened and light poured out. Marston froze.

Two soldiers stepped out and the door closed behind them. One of them walked nonchalantly toward the guard shack and the other headed toward the hillside door. Marston waited while the shift change took place. After the two off-going soldiers went into the barracks, he rose and headed back to his car. Once there, he got in, started it, and pulled out onto the highway. He drove toward Stuttgart's relative safety as fast as the little car could go.

19

Dunn stared at the black phone on the wall as though it might jump off and attack him. He'd already reached for it three times, pulling his hand back each time just before it was bitten. He fought a mental battle:

For Christ's sake, you sissy! If you can jump out of airplanes, you can call a girl.

Yes, but airplanes aren't pretty and smart and don't have tempers.

Coward.

Yes. No. I just need a jumpmaster to kick me in the ass and boot me out the door.

What's the worst that can happen?

Are you fucking kidding me? She could say 'no.' Or hang up on me.

Ooh, and you're scared of that?

Shitless, thank you very much.

Dunn took a deep breath, the kind you needed to calm the

muscles and steady the body just before firing a rifle at a distant target. The receiver settled into his hand, didn't bite, and he dialed the number. Three rings and a voice. A sweet voice that nearly made him have to lean against the wall.

"Hello?"

"Pamela. Hi, this is Tom Dunn." He couldn't say anything more. His throat started closing up, as if he'd just eaten an entire box of saltine crackers with nothing to wash them down. Besides, what else was there to say? She was either going to yell at him and slam the phone down in his ear, or say something.

"Tom! How are you? Are you all right? Where are you?"

Relief washed over Dunn and he looked around for a chair, wishing he'd dragged one closer. He felt like he needed to sit down before he fell down. The nearest one was just out of reach. "I'm fine, Pamela. I'm back in camp."

"Well, my goodness, I'm glad to hear your voice. When did you get back?" To Dunn, her voice sounded light and interested and most importantly, not angry.

"Uh, last Saturday."

A pause lingered, long enough to make Dunn wonder whether he'd lost the connection. Just as he reached for the lever to pump it a few times, Pamela spoke. "Oh. I see." The warmth in her voice fell about twenty degrees.

"Pamela, it's not that I didn't want to call you."

"Oh?" A few more degrees disappeared.

"Yes. Honest. I've tried every day since last Sunday."

"Is that right? I didn't hear the phone ring and I don't have any messages from my roommate and she's usually so good about these things, you know."

Dunn's brow began to gather a sheen. *God, how do I get out of this?* "No, no, Pamela. I meant I reached for the phone, but couldn't bring myself to make the call. I—"

"You couldn't call me?" A bit shrill, now, he thought. "Why ever not?"

"Pamela, I'm trying to apologize. You're not going to help me with this are you?"

"No." Was there a wicked smile at the other end of the line?

"You're having me on aren't you? You're smiling. I can hear it."

Girlish laughter raced down the line to his ear. Several seconds passed and he realized she must be doubled over with mirth. That's a good sign, at least. "Any time now, Pamela. Are you done yet?"

Some not very girlish snorting sounds told him she was getting close. Another moment passed, then she said, "Yes. Tom. I'm quite finished. So, tell me about this apology you're trying to make."

Oh, Lord, give me strength. "When we had dinner the other night, I guess it's been a couple of weeks, my mom would have told me I behaved like a boor."

"She would, huh?"

"Yes. I realized, too late, that you didn't mean anything and I took things the wrong way and so, I, uh, I'm very sorry. I'd like to start again."

Another long pause, not quite as long as before. "Tom, I'm sorry, too. I spoke without thinking and, you were right, what you do *is* important. I'd like to start again, too."

Dunn thought his heart was going to pop out of his chest. If he'd had a mirror in front of him, he'd seen the ear-to-ear grin on his face. His grip tightened on the receiver, which gave no complaint. "Pamela, would you like to join me for dinner?"

Without a pause this time, Pamela answered, "I'll do you one better. Come with me to my parents for Sunday dinner tomorrow. My mom's the world's best cook."

Dunn didn't know which he looked forward to more: seeing Pamela again or having an honest-to-goodness home cooked meal. He had enough sense not to mention this particular thought. "I'd love to, Pamela. When should I pick you up?"

"Eleven-thirty. That'll give us plenty of time. They live only ten minutes away. Down toward Winchester."

"I'll see you then." They said their goodbyes and Dunn slipped the receiver back into its cradle. Amazingly, it no longer looked like it might bite him. As he walked away, a tuneless whistle floated in the air behind him.

20

Captain Miller and three members of his squadron sat in their P-51 Mustangs at the end of the runway, engines running, brakes on, waiting for clearance from the tower. Miller was first in line, then Murphy, his wingman, was five plane lengths behind. Tommy Hayes, the Pennsylvania farm boy was next, then Chuck Thompson, a short, skinny man from Detroit. There had been talk of scrubbing the mission due to possible overcast conditions in Germany, but the airbase's meteorologist was "pretty sure" they'd have clear skies long enough to complete the mission. Miller, like all pilots, hated to have a mission canceled. You always got yourself worked up into such a prepared state of mind, that coming down from it without combat was like spoiling for an argument, then getting none.

The planes carried a full load of just over two thousand rounds of .50 caliber ammunition for their six machine guns, and two external full tanks they would drop shortly after entering German airspace. Their target was the area around Göttingen where Miller had filmed the German plane two weeks ago.

Howard Lawson's plan was elegant in its simplicity: the four planes would diverge twenty miles from Göttingen and fly a predetermined grid pattern that, unbeknownst to the pilots, was drawn from the successful patterns Navy destroyers used when depth charging Jap subs. The pattern required them to fly five miles apart at an altitude of only 10,000 feet. They would pass over Göttingen and continue for another twenty miles. Their goal was to find a hanger large enough to house a plane as big as the B-17.

"Flight 23, you are cleared for takeoff. Good hunting."

"Roger, Tower. Thank you." Miller pushed the throttle up and the Merlin power plant roared its excitement. He let off the brakes and the Mustang started rolling, slowly at first, then with rising speed. When she reached 100 MPH, the tail lifted and the nose dipped, affording Miller his first complete view of the runway. The reverse tricycle gear made it impossible to see straight ahead over the plane's snout, and pilots always had to look out one side or the other of their canopy. Miller's silver beauty reached 120 MPH and he pulled back on the stick. The plane lifted smoothly into the sky.

After his team got airborne, Miller did a quick radio check and brought his speed up to 300 MPH. He set his course for eighty degrees magnetic and sat back for the almost two hour ride.

In flight
25 miles west of Göttingen, Germany
11 June, 0754 Hours

At 10,000 feet, the sky was relatively clear, with some clouds, but nothing that would obstruct visibility. They'd made the flight with no problems, encountering no enemy planes or ground fire. That was always a good sign.

Miller knew the odds of finding the swept-back flying wing in the air again were slim, but there was always a small chance. This time, he'd shoot it to pieces and watch it go in. "All right, men. Here's where we separate. Maintain current speed and altitude. We should pass the Göttingen line in four minutes and reach the end of our first pass in eight. Then we'll make our slide and head back on a reverse heading. Any questions?" He paused, listening, and when no one responded he said, "Very good, then. Good hunting, and for God's sake be careful."

Miller watched as each man banked his plane away from him. Moments later, they were mere specks, then they disappeared completely. By his reckoning, they would pass the twenty mile mark in five, four . . .

Miller flew in the right center of the group of four, with Murphy five miles to his right, Hayes, five to his left, and Thompson ten miles. His flight path would take him directly over the heart of Göttingen, then the slide, which was a big banking turn to the right, would line him up on a path running about two miles to the south of the city, running back through the empty space that currently existed between them. Miller had one major worry. Lawson's orders had been specific and heartless: if any one of them got jumped while running the pattern, the others were forbidden to leave their route to come to his aid. They were on their own until the pattern was completed and they were heading back to England. Court-martial awaited the pilot or pilots who failed in this regard. Taking a deep breath, Miller prayed for a free run today.

Looking down at the brown and green earth, Miller admired the beauty. There were no borders from the air. He could have just as easily been flying over the heart of Indiana. He saw the city approaching and knew he'd be over it right on schedule. He loved the laws of physics; the speed, distance and time formula's relationship and pureness always fascinated him. There were plenty of laws you could break, but none were of physics.

He rocketed over the city a minute later and saw some early morning activity, but still no enemy planes. He was about two minutes from making the turn, about ten miles east of Göttingen, when he saw an airfield. His heart jumped. Maybe. Just maybe. He flipped on his gun cameras and bore straight toward it. It was a little offline to the left and he made a mental note of exactly how far over he'd moved so as to be able to get back on line for the turn. As he got closer, and the field began to resolve into a clearer picture, disappointment draped over him. Not only was the runway too short, it was covered with pockmarks from bombs. He swooped away and got back on line. Another minute later, he slid the stick over to the right and began his turn.

Suddenly, a shout of alarm from Thompson crackled on the radio. "Shit fire, boys, I've got three Fuckers coming up to me." He meant Focke-Wolfes. "I'm going to try and take one out on the first pass, then run back and pick off the others."

Miller said, "Chuck, you are supposed to turn and run. Do not, I repeat, do not engage by yourself. Do you read?"

"Sorry, sir, It's too late for that. I'm already inside their circle." Meaning range of their guns. He'd never make a turn quick enough to get away.

Miller's grip tightened on his stick.

"I'm aiming for the one in the middle." Thompson kept his mike open so Miller could get the play-by-play. In the background, Miller could hear the sudden chatter of the Mustang's guns, then the sound of someone hammering, as though a blacksmith had gotten loose in the cockpit and was whaling away. A horrible whooshing sound came through the radio. "Ah, shit, that didn't work out so well. I'm on fire. I'm heading lower. I think I can—"

Miller had lost men before, but it always hurt. Always. *Oh, damn it, Chuck. Jesus. All right, Norman. Stay with us.* He had to remain focused on the task at hand. He'd deal with the emotions later. "Men, I assume you heard. Stay alert. We can't afford to lose anyone else. Understand?"

"Yes, sir," replied Murphy and Hayes.

"You should be into your turn. Keep your eyes open."

Miller let his attention drift back earthward. In another few minutes, he'd be crossing south of Göttingen.

"Captain Miller!" A shout from his wingman, Murphy.

"What is it, Bill?" Miller didn't like the sound of Murphy's voice.

"Sir, I've run into a flak field. I'm trying to jink and turn and get out of it, but it's really dense." A long pause settled in and just as Miller was about say something, Murphy said, "Okay, I dropped down to four thousand and they can't seem to get adjusted for the alt—"

Miller couldn't believe it. He'd just lost two of his best men in a matter of two minutes. *Damn. What have we gotten into?*

What did Bill find over there? There were no major targets around this small city. The conclusion was obvious though, wasn't it? The Germans don't put flak cannons around nothing and spend the money on the shells if it's not important. Right? This was a no-brainer. "Tommy?" Miller was afraid his voice would give away his shock, but what could he do about that?

"Yes, Captain." Tommy didn't sound so good himself.

"I'm going to take up station two miles south of the city. You meet me there. We're going to go take a look at what Bill found."

"Yes, sir. Right away, sir."

Miller figured Hayes was likely thinking about that court-martial, but was loyal enough to simply do what he was asked. Miller tipped his right wing down slightly and started a wide circle. Besides, fuck that Lawson. He ain't here.

A couple of minutes later Hayes said, "I've got you, sir."

Miller was flying in a southerly direction and had to crane his neck to see Hayes' bird coming from his seven o'clock. "Okay, Tommy. Pull in on my left. We're going in together, but at treetop and at four cees. Got it?" Four cees referred to the hundred dollar bill being a C-note, and meant four hundred miles an hour. Almost the maximum. And at less than one hundred feet from the ground. Not for the faint of heart.

"Yes, sir. I'll be on your wing at treetop at four cees."

Their field of vision would be severely reduced, but Miller had one of those feelings. If he headed southeast of the city, he was sure they'd find something worthwhile. When Hayes was in the correct position, Miller shoved the throttle up hard and the plane shot forward. Hayes kept pace. Miller calculated they'd be into the flak area within two minutes.

As they flew over a small hill, a little valley opened up in front of them. Miller couldn't believe his eyes. He switched on his camera and hollered, "Tommy! Camera."

"Yes, sir."

A monstrous hanger sat nestled up against the wooded hill, on the opposite side of the valley. It was big enough for ten B-17s and the still intact runway was long enough for them, too. He lined up on the hanger and bore straight in. He flipped his guns on and at four hundred yards pressed the trigger. The tracers walked right up to the hanger door and through. Hayes had taken his commander's lead and his tracers zipped into the side of the building to the left of the doors. They screamed over the hanger and Miller banked sharply to the right.

Hayes matched Miller's every move and they sped out of the valley on a two-sixty degree heading to get back home. After another few minutes of tree topping, Miller said, "Excellent work, Tommy. Now let's get back up to 10,000 and get the hell out of here."

"Yes, sir. A good idea, I must say."

Miller smiled for the first and last time of the day. The elation of a successful mission was quashed by the knowledge he would be writing two letters to the families of two men he'd grown to love.

21

Andover, England
11 June, 1130 Hours

When Dunn turned the corner onto Pamela's street, he spotted her from a block away. She wore a yellow dress and matching hat. As he got closer, she turned in his direction and sent him a smile he was sure he could have seen a mile away. He waved and slowed the jeep, pulling in next to her. She was on the passenger side and instead of waiting for him to come around and help her in, she gracefully slid into the seat next to him.

"Hi, Pamela." Dunn stared into her blue eyes, then noted her skin and how flawless it was. She appeared to have only put on red lipstick. Her dress bore a flowered print and the neckline, which was all the way up to the base of her throat, had a small band of white lace. "You look beautiful."

Pamela smiled again. "Thanks, Tom. You look nice, too."

Dunn was wearing his dress uniform, the class-A's, with an olive-drab waist coat over a khaki long-sleeved shirt. He had tucked his khaki pants into his ultra-shined boots and bloused them perfectly, as did all good Rangers. "Thanks. How do we get to your parents' house?"

"Follow this street until it curves right, then on our left we'll see Winchester Road. We'll follow that and I'll give you directions as we get closer."

Dunn grinned. "Tally Ho!"

Pamela grinned back and Dunn floored it. He already had the windscreen up, so Pamela's hat was safe as the jeep leapt away. A few minutes later, they were out in the countryside flying down the road at a romping forty miles an hour.

Pamela turned her head toward Dunn and asked, "Did you ever get that letter and pictures of Gertrude's graduation?"

Dunn glanced at Pamela in surprise. She'd remembered an off-hand comment from two weeks ago, plus she'd recalled his sister's name. This ability reminded him of his mom. She could remember some innocuous thing you'd said two years ago and bring it back to haunt you. More than once, he'd heard his dad just say, "Yes, dear," when Mrs. Dunn said he'd said something or other. "Yes. I got several pictures. Gertrude looked beautiful and mom and dad seemed real happy."

"Did you bring them with you?"

Dunn expression turned sheepish. "No. I didn't think of it."

"That's too bad. I wanted to see what a Dunn woman looked like."

"I'm sorry."

"What *does* she look like?"

"We all have the same brown eyes, though hers aren't as dark as mine. Light brown hair, in those long curls the kids like these days, fair complexion. She's kind of short."

"She sounds lovely." I'm sure everyone's short to you, though, you tall handsome fellow.

"Thanks. I'll remember the pictures the next time." He glanced quickly over at Pamela to see if his assumption bothered her. Her eyes were closed and she had her head tilted back to bask in the sun's warmth. Some loose strands of her wispy blond hair floated underneath the hat's brim.

"Please do," she said, her eyes still closed. "There'll be a weird right, then a left in the road soon, just stay on it and we'll be fine."

"Okay."

A few minutes later, Dunn maneuvered through the strange crook in the road. It was built that way to go around a little knob of a grass-covered hill poking up on his left. The thing looked more like a slice of key lime pie, without the meringue topping, than anything else. "How much farther?"

Pamela opened her eyes and blinked in the bright sunlight. A pleasant and welcome change from the over two weeks of overcast and cold. She lifted her left hand and pointed. "See that rise in the road about quarter mile down?"

"Yes."

"Just after we go over the rise, there'll be a turnoff on the left. Take that. It's the farm road to our house."

"Got it." Dunn looked off to his left and a wooded hill of moderate size extended from the end of the key lime pie ahead as far as he could see. To his right, a valley opened up and he thought he could see about five miles off to the south. They weren't high enough to see the patchwork of the different sections, but he could tell they were there by the changes of colors from dark to light green to the yellows of flowered fields. Farmhouses and outbuildings dotted the landscape here and there, and cattle and sheep grazed or moseyed along in the pastures.

He turned onto the farm road which seemed to go straight uphill. Shifting down to first helped the jeep's tires get purchase on the dirt and gravel. A few moments later, the road emptied out into a large farmyard between the house and barn, both made of stone. Two dogs, a black and white Border Collie and a black Labrador, bounded up to the jeep when it came to a stop, happily barking and wagging their tails at the sight of Pamela. Dunn looked at her dress and worried they'd get dirt and who knows what else on it from their barnyard paws, but Pamela raised her right hand, flat with the palm down and lowered it slowly. Both dogs promptly sat on their butts and licked their lips with a smacking sound.

Pamela stepped out of the jeep, after first carefully examining the ground just in case a little fragrant surprise awaited an unsuspecting foot. She bent over and while speaking softly, petted both dogs, each with a different hand. They remained perfectly still, no jumping.

Dunn got out and moved close to the dogs, who looked at him

with friendly faces. He reached down and stroked their ears and muzzles. "Pamela, I've never seen dogs quite that well behaved. Did you train them yourself?"

"Yes. They're about six years old. I was sixteen when we started."

Dunn suddenly wished he could have known her then. To see what she was like as a teenager.

Pamela said, "Let's go in. Dinner should be ready soon." She held out her hand expectantly and a pleased Dunn slipped his big hand around her slim one. They started for the house, the two dogs bounding after.

22

Leiston Air Base
11 June, 1230 Hours

A weary and heart-sick Miller joined Colonel Nelson and Howard Lawson in the commander's office. Nelson and Lawson stood by the lone window that opened out onto the runway. Miller drew to stop a few feet from them and Nelson turned. Miller saluted, which Nelson returned. "Reporting in, sir."

Even if Nelson hadn't been able to read Miller's face, he already knew, from his vantage point at the window, that two pilots hadn't returned. "Who went down?"

"Thompson and Murphy. I'll write up the report, but Chuck got jumped by three Focke-Wolfes and Bill ran into extremely heavy flak near the airfield where we found a likely target."

"Captain, I'm sorry about your men," said Lawson.

From his expression, Miller thought Lawson meant it sincerely and said simply, "Thank you, sir." He knew Lawson must be chomping at the bit to see the film, which he figured should be ready in a few minutes. He decided to try and work with Lawson rather than resent him for causing the loss of two men. He was, after all, like them, only doing his job. "Sir, if you've got a map, I can show you where the field is, while we wait for the film."

Lawson looked relieved and said, "I do, Captain. It's over there on the table."

The three men moved to the table and leaned over. Miller put a finger on top of Göttingen, then drew his finger down to a point just south of the city. "This is where the airfield is. The hanger was gigantic, probably used for the zeppelins, way back. Damn thing must be three hundred yards long. The runway was plenty long enough; a B-17 could use it easily. This has to be where that plane of theirs is stored. "We fired into the building, who knows, maybe we hit it. I sure hope so."

A light knock on the door interrupted Miller. It was the film processor, a corporal. Nelson said, "Put it on the projector table, please."

The corporal did as he was asked and departed.

Lawson immediately started setting things up and a few minutes later they were watching the tracers walk into the door. "That's got to be it," said Lawson in an excited voice. "It's just got to be. This is fantastic work, Captain." He stood up and flipped the lights back on. He stuck his hand out for Miller, who shook it. "You know, I can't tell you much of anything, but I can say my boss, General Donovan, will be pleased by this and so will the President." His expression turned somber and he put a hand on Miller's shoulder. "In your letters to those men's families, please tell them they helped the war effort far more than you can say."

"Yes, sir, I will."

Lawson packed up the film and the map on which he'd made a notation where Miller's finger had come to a rest. "Gentlemen, thank you very much. I've got to get over to London right away." And with that, he turned and left.

Miller turned to Nelson with a quizzical expression. "I wonder why that plane's so damn important."

23

Dunn drove the jeep back down the hill toward Winchester Road. He had more than a full stomach of home-made sausage, potatoes and beans. Mrs. Hardwicke had kept telling him to refill his plate until he begged for mercy. Then she brought out the bread and butter pudding. When the cinnamon wafted to his nose, he had raised his hands in surrender and dug in with relish. At the moment, he was quite sorry he'd had the *second* helping.

"My parents like you."

Dunn smiled. He thought so, too. They had been friendly and warm toward him. "Did they tell you that?"

"No, I can just tell."

"I like them, too."

"Good." Pamela started to say something, but stopped, biting her lower lip.

Dunn glanced at her. She seemed worried, nervous maybe. Had her parents said something about him she didn't want to tell him, like maybe, stay away from American soldiers? No, he didn't think so, they seemed too genuine, no apparent hidden agenda. "Pamela, what's bothering you?"

She stopped biting her lip so quickly Dunn guessed it must be an old habit, one her mom probably kept after her about while growing up. She laid a hand on his arm and said, "Tom, I usually go visit my brother on Sundays. Would you mind going with me?"

"No, of course not."

She let out a breath, as if she'd been holding it in fear of his answer. She squeezed his arm. "Thank you."

"You're welcome."

"If you just go back to my flat, I'll guide you from there."

The cemetery was a short drive northeast of her apartment building. Walking across the neatly trimmed grass, Dunn reached down and grasped Pamela's hand. She smiled and moved close.

"Tell me about Percy."

"He had a wonderful sense of humor, a bit of a prankster, actually, especially at school. Got quite a reputation for causing grief for the teachers."

"What, tacks in their chairs?"

"Oh, no. Much more sophisticated." Pamela paused, smiling at the memory. "You know those pull down world maps that all the classrooms have?"

"Yeah, sure."

"One time, he painstakingly cut up another map and overlaid the one in his eighth year social studies class, then rolled it up. He had America in China, China in South America and so forth. When the teacher pulled the map down, he was trying to point to America and, as it happens, he was quite nearsighted. He had his pointer on the map and when the giggles started he whipped around to look at the map and dropped the pointer in shock. When he turned back around, his face was paler than usual. He mumbled something about seeing the head of the department and scurried out of the room. So naturally, Percy ran up to the map, snatched off the replacement map pieces and hid them in his desk. When the teacher returned with the department head, he did a double-take and said he needed the rest of the day off."

Dunn chuckled. "That's excellent."

"Just one of many, over the years. That one pretty much

established Percy's reputation." She pointed a little to their right. "He's right over there."

They stood together beside his tombstone, a simple gray stone with his name and dates engraved on it, and below that was: Beloved Son and Brother. Pamela knelt and closed her eyes. Dunn thought she might be saying a prayer and bowed his head and closed his eyes. Almost immediately, the sight of Timothy Oldham's bloody chest charged into his mind. He opened his eyes to escape Timothy's haunting last expression.

Pamela wept silently. She was the first civilian he'd met who had lost someone in the war. He looked at the headstone again. Percy Hardwicke was born in 1920, so he was just twenty years old when he was killed, the same age as Timothy. *Oh Lord. Timothy's family will never get to kneel over his grave.* Suddenly, that seemed such a dreadful thing for anyone to suffer through. Overcome by all the death he'd seen and caused, his eyes filled with tears and a sob lurched out. He tried to turn away from Pamela, but her reaction was too swift and she saw the tears running down his face. She jumped to her feet and embraced him. He folded into her, arms hanging by his side. Pamela put a hand behind his head and pulled it down to her shoulder. She held tight as he wept. His body began to shake and she uttered soothing words. A few minutes passed, the guttural sobs subsided, and Dunn raised his head. Pamela wiped the tears from his cheeks with her fingers in cool, gentle caresses. They felt like a butterfly's wings fluttering against Dunn's hot skin.

He realized, to his surprise, he felt no embarrassment, no shame in breaking down in front of Pamela. In front of a woman. He wondered whether a part of loving someone was just being comfortable enough with them to let the inner fears and doubts out, as if the sharing somehow lessened their impact.

Dunn looked into Pamela's eyes and she gazed steadily back. Something unspoken transpired between them. In a soft voice, she said, "Take me home, Tom."

Pamela pulled back from the long kiss and stared into Dunn's brown eyes. She gave a deep satisfied sigh, then walked over to the lone window in the small bedroom and drew the curtains. Moving back in front of Dunn, she began undoing his tie. After dropping it on the floor, she unbuttoned his jacket and shirt and got those off, then unbuckled his belt. Soon, Dunn stood naked in front of her and she put her arms around his neck and kissed him again. It was gentle at first, then with rising heat and immediacy. She slid one hand down his chest, then it slithered below his waist. He groaned as her cool hand grasped him.

She put both hands on his chest and pushed. Dunn fell back onto her bed, put his hands behind his head and waited. Pamela unzipped her flowered yellow dress and let it fall to the floor, where it covered his pile of clothes. She unhooked her bra and slid the straps off her shoulders. Dunn's gaze slid down her throat to her newly released breasts. Pamela smiled, reached up and removed her hat, tossing it aside. Lifting her hands again, she removed the bobby pins holding her long hair in place. Dunn thought it was such a profoundly beautiful feminine movement, her breasts lifting with the motion, countered by the falling tresses. He could only whisper, "Oh. My." As his gaze slid farther down, sweeping over her flat belly and slim waist, Pamela hooked her thumbs in her panties and pushed, revealing tufts of blond hair.

Dunn raised his hands, beckoning.

Pamela fairly leapt into bed and straddled Dunn. He caressed her breasts. She arched her back. A moan escaped her lips. She raised her hips slightly, then lowered them. In spite of the wondrous sight in front of him, Dunn closed his eyes.

Dunn ran his fingertips lazily across Pamela's back as she lay with her head on his left shoulder.

"Tom?"

"Hmm?"

Pamela lifted her head and looked at him. "What are you going to do after the war?"

"I don't know. I mean I planned to teach, but that seems like a different world. Hell, it was a different world. I don't know if that's what I want. I've seen too much death and destruction. Maybe I'll opt for the quiet life. Go back to Iowa, be a farmer."

Pamela drummed her fingers on Dunn's shoulder absently. He wondered if that was her way of working things out. She bit her lower lip again and he was sure now she was holding back a thought. He put a finger on her lip and pushed down, laughing. "What are you afraid to say?"

"Think you've got me figured out, do you?" She formed a pout and batted her eyelashes at him.

Dunn chuckled and said, "No, just your little lip thing. You do that when you're debating something."

"So true. Habit. Can't break it. Tried." She sat up, crossed her legs and ran a hand through her hair, trying to get it under control.

Dunn admired the sight. "Pamela, you are a gorgeous woman."

"Thank you, Tom."

"But you haven't answered my question."

"I was hoping to distract you and make you forget." She smiled seductively.

"Nice try."

"Humpf. Here it is. I can only imagine what you've been through, so it's easy for me to give advice." She paused, "Promise you won't get mad at me?"

"Pamela, I won't do that again. I already apologized, you know." Dunn tried to keep his voice even, not defensive.

It must have worked, because Pamela nodded. "I think you'd be selling yourself short if you turn to farming. You said you liked teaching. Who better than you to teach history to a bunch of high school kids? You would bring history into the classroom with you every day. When you cover one of the too-many wars, you can bring it to life for those kids in a way no one else can. You can talk about its horrors, as well as the honor and pride that goes with being a soldier. You've lived it and survived to talk about it."

Dunn shook his head. "Pamela. I have a new assignment. It's going to be dangerous and there's no way to know whether I'll survive the mission, or any others in the future."

Pamela placed a hand on Dunn's cheek as tears rolled down her own. "Yes, you will, Thomas Dunn. You have to survive. For me. For us."

24

Luc Breton, now a full-fledged Gestapo agent, was known by his mother's maiden name, Vogel, thus ridding himself of the last vestige of his hated French father's memory and all that tied him to France.

He couldn't have picked a better town in which to be assigned. Saverne was in northern Alsace and everyone knew that the only people the Alsatians hated more than French politicians were the Germans. He'd been brought in to help squelch the rising resistance activities.

The region's Gestapo offices were situated in the massive Castle of Rohan, built in 1779 on the site of a twelfth century fortress. Commissioned by Prince-Bishop de Rohan, architect Salins of Monfort constructed the castle from red sandstone and surrounded it with a floral filled park. It faced the canal that joined the Marne and Rhine rivers. If you stood opposite the castle on the far side of the canal, the castle's edifice would be perfectly mirrored in the still water.

When the Chief Gestapo agent took the castle's keys from the mayor of Saverne, the elderly, gray-haired Alsatian had tears streaming down his face. He died a week later in the middle of the night. The townsfolk believed a broken heart killed him.

Luc arrived in Saverne only two days earlier, having received his orders not from Küfer in Calais, but from his replacement. Küfer had been found dead in his sitting room chair and his woman, Helga, or Abrial, was nowhere to be found. Since violence was clearly not the cause of death, his assistant had, naturally, asked Dr. Briard to examine the body. After a lengthy autopsy, which consisted only of a Y-incision and three cigarettes, Dr. Briard's report cited death by heart attack. It failed to mention the puncture mark in Küfer's neck.

Gestapo Agent Vogel tightened the knot of his tie, buttoned the black suit jacket, then picked up a black fedora and placed it on his head. He ran a thumb and finger around the front of the bill, giving it a downward pull. The house he had drawn for quarters was finely appointed and he stood in front of a large wall mirror in the second floor master bedroom. Satisfied that he looked exactly right, he left the house and headed toward the Castle Rohan for his meeting with the Chief Agent, Meyer Adler.

"So, tell me, Vogel, how do you find our fair city of Saverne?" Adler smiled. A cigarette dangled from his thin lips. He, too, wore a black suit. His hat hung on a rack by the door.

"It's a beautiful city, Mr. Adler."

Adler nodded. "Yes, some of it reminds me of Berlin. Don't you agree?"

Vogel was temporarily nonplused. Didn't Adler know he wasn't from Germany? Of course he did! It was a test. "I don't know, Mr. Adler, I've never had the pleasure of being in Berlin, although I hope to see it with my own eyes someday."

Adler pulled the dying cigarette from his mouth and stubbed it out in a marble ashtray. A tiny lift of one corner of his mouth told Vogel he had been right to tell the truth.

"Yes, Vogel. You'll enjoy the beauty very much." Adler looked down at the file folder on his desk, Vogel's. He didn't open it; he'd already read it three times. He tapped it with a stubby finger. "You have quite a little dossier here, Vogel. Your work in Calais was excellent. I'm depending on you to continue with that level of competence here, working for me."

"Thank you, sir. You can count on me." Vogel was pleased, but careful not to show it. "Do you have my first assignment?"

Adler regarded Vogel silently for a moment. This was going to be the true test, whether Vogel recognized it or not. "As you no doubt know, we had an incident yesterday out on the main rail line. The local resistance group blew up three sections of track just as a munitions train passed over it. Luckily, they were slightly premature and it caught the engine and the first car behind it, which didn't have any explosives in it. None of the munitions went off. The derailment was bad, though, and it'll take us a week to get the track re-laid. Then we have to get the cars back on the track and wait for another engine.

"Your first assignment is to round up ten men at random and conduct a public execution." Adler paused to check Vogel's reaction.

Vogel merely nodded. This wouldn't trouble him.

Satisfied, Adler continued, "It's important, no, critical, that you make sure the citizens witness the execution and that the reason is clear. Anything else you might think of saying or doing, is solely up to you."

Vogel nodded once more and checked his watch. "Would within the hour be satisfactory, Mr. Adler?"

Adler smiled. I think I'm going to like this young man. "Yes, Vogel, that would be just fine." He opened a desk drawer and slid the folder into it. "You've drawn your weapon from the armory?" He was referring to the personal hand gun carried by all Gestapo agents, the Luger.

"Yes, sir."

"Good. Now go see Sergeant Neumann to get your men."

Vogel got up. "Thank you, sir. *Heil* Hitler!" He gave Adler a perfect Nazi salute, which Adler returned sharply, repeating Hitler's praise.

Walking down the hall in search of Neumann, Vogel's thoughts centered on one thing: "your men." He'd never had his own men and he relished the prospects of making a name for himself by using *his* men.

Vogel tracked down Sergeant Neumann at the end of the hall, sitting in a coat-closet sized office. He gave the sergeant a quick rundown and a few minutes later, Vogel stood beside a truck as the sergeant bellowed at the men to get their asses going. As soon as the men got in, Vogel climbed into the passenger seat and said to the driver, "Go to the church down by the city square. Make it quick."

The heavy truck ground to a halt outside the church. The parishioners, heading to the 3:00 P.M. mass, recoiled in fear, clustering into a circle like a herd of animals faced with the sudden appearance of deadly predators. Mothers grabbed children and pulled them behind their skirts. Men stepped in front of their families. The hated soldiers jumped from the truck. Women screamed. Men grit their teeth. The soldiers' jackboots clattered on the pavement.

The soldiers quickly pruned all of the men, about one hundred, from the pack. One man was too slow and a soldier whipped his rifle butt into the side of the hapless man. The unlucky man dropped to the ground, bleeding. The soldier grabbed him by the back of his suit jacket and jerked him to his feet, pushing him along.

Vogel stepped down from the truck and looked around the neighborhood, pleased to see people with fearful faces watching from the safety of their windows, standing back, but not far enough. Good. He moved to the group of men, who had been expertly lined up. Walking down the line, he yanked ten men out of the line, enjoying the dread he saw in their faces. Soldiers grabbed each victim and pushed the condemned men into a smaller line, in front of the others. Gasps and shrieks emitted from the women and children, now twenty yards behind the lines of men, as they looked on in horror.

Vogel jumped up into the truck bed, then climbed up onto the wooden seat closest to the crowd. He surveyed the terrified people in front of him as a priest might his worshipers. Except Vogel's message would be quite different. "Citizens of Saverne, give me your attention." Vogel suppressed a smile when he saw the confusion on the faces staring up at him. A Gestapo agent who spoke unaccented French? What is this? Then, here and there, an expression flashed anger as realization set in. Traitor!

Vogel didn't wait. His voice was, at once, loud enough for everyone to hear and soft in manner, as if he was scolding a recalcitrant schoolchild. "Yesterday, a defenseless German passenger train was attacked. Twenty-four helpless, innocent women and children were killed, murdered, by the disgusting French Resistance forces holed up like rats in this city."

Mouths dropped open at the blatant lie; everyone knew what kind of train it was.

His voice rising in anger, Vogel continued, "This was an outrageous, horrible act by those who wish to do harm to the German Reich. This will not be tolerated! You must be punished for the actions of others. For every day that passes until one brave soul among you has the courage to step forward and identify the traitors to the German Reich, this city will lose ten men, beginning with this group," Vogel waved a hand toward the doomed men, "unless that brave soul is here today, perhaps?" He paused thirty seconds, then continued, "No? Very well. Sergeant, do your duty."

A typical firing squad execution amounted to one soldier and rifle for each victim, but today, the sergeant would employ a new tactic, Vogel's tactic. He and three other soldiers herded the ten men around the line of the reprieved and led them straight to the church's front stone wall. Here the soldiers lined the men up, not abreast of each other, but in front of each other, as though waiting in line for communion. They pushed the men close together until backs touched chests. Vogel followed close behind and the remaining soldiers kept their weapons ready, pointed at the crowd.

As was customary in German executions, there were no blindfolds. The sergeant unslung his Mauser rifle, one of the most powerful weapons on the battlefield, chambered a round and faced the line of men. He jammed the muzzle into the chest of the first man and squeezed the trigger. The bullet passed through all ten men and lodged in the wall. The men toppled over. Anguished screams echoed across the church yard.

Vogel walked the line and examined each man. He found one who wasn't dead yet. Drawing his new Luger from its holster, he shot the man in the forehead. After holstering his weapon, he strode purposefully past the stricken crowd and got in the truck's cab. Moments later, the soldiers were in the back of the truck and the driver pulled away.

At a rap on the window in the back of the cab, Vogel turned to see a smiling sergeant regarding him. He slid the window open.

"That was an excellent idea, Mr. Vogel. Simply amazing. Well done, sir."

Vogel nodded, careful not to show too much pleasure. "Thank you, Sergeant. You and your men performed well today, too. My congratulations. I'll be sure to mention it to your superiors."

The sergeant beamed.

Vogel wanted to look back at the crowd, to savor their stunned reaction, but knew it was more powerful to simply show no more interest. If he had, perhaps he'd have seen the face he would have recognized. The one with fury and recognition in its own eyes.

25

The Horten Brothers Hanger
5 miles south of Göttingen
11 June, 1522 Hours

"How in God's name did this happen?" shouted Reimar Horten. He was shaking with rage at the sight of his precious airplane listing to one side on flat tires. Several of the Mustangs' bullets found their way into the left wing, punching through it and into the landing gear.

The Hortens were in Berlin when Chief Engineer Mauer tracked them down at their parents' house, preparing for a leisurely Sunday dinner and afternoon of relaxation. Reimar and Walter had excused themselves and ran to their car, then drove at breakneck speed to the small landing strip nearby. Once airborne, they flew as fast as their little Heinkel He 46 reconnaissance biplane could go without rattling apart. They'd bought it from the Luftwaffe and used it often for their business travels.

"Two Mustangs strafed us. It was bad luck they hit her at all. We're fortunate it's not worse," said Mauer, a nervous tremor in his voice.

"Fortunate? *Fortunate*? Are you crazy, Mauer? Look at her." Reimar ran over to the H18 and, after sliding a step ladder over to the wing, scrambled up the stairs. He peered at the surface of the wing and counted four, no, five puncture wounds between the number two and number three engine nacelles. The plane was facing away from the hanger door and the direction of the attackers, so the bullets had ripped through at a low angle from back to front. He climbed down and looked under the wing. The first or second bullet had zipped into the tire. He hated to admit it, but Mauer was correct; they had been lucky. Reimar turned to his brother, who had walked over to examine the plane, too.

Walter's hands hung limply by his side as he stared at the damage. The analytical side of his brain was already shoving the emotional part aside, calculating work effort and time. He ducked and slid under the wing. Raising a hand, he lovingly trailed his fingers along the smooth, cool surface. He found the first puncture and put his forefinger carefully inside, feeling gingerly around the jagged edges of metal and splintered wood compound. Pulling a penlight from his shirt pocket, he switched it on and pointed it up into the wing's innards. After a few moments of peering in, he moved farther under the wing and repeated the process on the remaining holes. Finally, he stepped out from under the plane. He gave Reimar and Mauer a small smile. "We are unbelievably lucky. Not one of the bullets hit anything important, not even a strut or cable. All we have to do is repair the punctures themselves."

"Oh, excellent." Reimar smiled in relief. "How long do you think it'll take?"

"About two hours per hole, plus eight hours for the rosin and glue to set properly." Walter was referring to the thin wooden skin that layered the wing's outer surface.

Reimar nodded and clapped Mauer on the shoulder, "You'll begin right away, yes?"

"Of course, Reimar. You may leave it to me. By this time tomorrow, you won't be able to find where any of the damn holes were."

Reimar grinned at Mauer's cockiness. Unlike most braggarts, Mauer could actually back it up. Reimar glanced at Walter, who gave the slightest nod toward the office. They started off in that direction.

"What do you think happened, Walter?"

Walter shrugged. "A couple of loose enemy pilots, I guess. Saw an airfield and a hanger. Decided to have a shoot out at the All Right corral."

Reimar snickered. "You mean the OK corral, Walter." They'd seen a few American westerns along the way.

"Yes, of course."

Reimar shook his head. "I can't believe those pilots made it through the flak fields, though. That's a pretty amazing bit of flying, don't you think?"

"Either that or just dumb luck."

"Hm, I suppose." Reimar looked doubtful, but his mind was already moving ahead to the next pressing task: getting those six Junkers 004B jet turbine engines installed and ready to fire up. "Are we still projecting a test flight for the end of the week?"

"Yes. I had some buffer time built in, so the wing repair won't affect the timing."

Reimar smiled. This was no surprise. "Excellent."

They reached the office and stepped though the open door. The room was large, but plain, after all, it was in a hanger, not a downtown Berlin office building. Two steel desks faced each other. Opposite the door, two windows provided a pleasant view of a wooded hillside. It was the one Miller and Hayes had disappeared over after attacking the hanger.

The brothers each sat down at a desk and stared at another. Walter said, "The run-up time for the engines is going to be two hours." This was the amount of time the engines had to be run after they were installed in the cowling to check for vibrations. Even though Junkers would do their own run-up on each engine to ensure it wouldn't shake itself apart or blow up, the Hortens also had to make sure the engines wouldn't shake the plane to pieces. First, one at a time, then in pairs, always on opposite wings. Finally, all would run at the same time. A very critical step that, if ignored, could lead to disaster.

Reimar nodded absently and Walter said, "Reimar? What is it?"

"I think we should increase security. We have what, two soldiers on guard each shift?"

"Yes, that's right."

"I want to increase it to ten men per shift."

"Where do you expect to get that many men?"

Reimar smiled grimly. "Göring. He loves this airplane. He'll give us whatever we want."

"I don't think he'll do it, but go ahead, call him." Walter nodded toward the black phone between them.

Picking up the receiver, Reimar got through, surprisingly, and after a brief conversation, finished with, "Thank you, Field Marshall Göring. We'll expect the men to start tonight." With a relieved sigh, he hung up the phone.

"He gave us enough men for ten each shift?"

"He did. Not even an argument. I told you he loves the plane."

"Where are they coming from?"

"Some garrison in Berlin. They'll stay in Göttingen." Satisfied now, Reimar got up and walked over to a bank of file cabinets. After opening the top drawer of the one closest to the desks, he removed a thick blue notebook in which everything to do with the building of the H18 resided. Sitting back down, he said, "Let's go over the powered-flight plan . . ."

26

MI5 Building
London
11 June, 1643 Hours

Howard Lawson's rumpled suit looked like he felt. He was pretty certain if he hadn't written everything in his notebook, he'd have no idea whatsoever what he was supposed to do or where he was supposed to be. He had struggled to stay awake during the train ride from Leiston to London, but after ten minutes, was out cold. If the conductor hadn't been efficient and responsible, waking him as they arrived, he'd probably still be riding the train, which went all the way out to Sutton, ten miles southwest of London

Instead, thanks to the conductor's alertness, he was sluggishly walking up the steps to the MI5 building. He showed his ID badge to the guard inside the door, who, after checking a crinkled paper on a clipboard, let him pass on to the receptionist. She was a pretty woman of about twenty-five, with long curly brown hair and twinkling eyes. Smiling pleasantly she said, "How can I help you, sir?"

Lawson smiled in return, or at least thought he did, and said, "Howard Lawson, from the OSS. I'm here to see Alan Finch."

Miss Curly Hair nodded and said, "I'll ring him for you."

"Thanks."

She spoke quietly into her phone, as if Lawson wasn't to be privy to his own announcement, then hung up and looked at Lawson brightly. "Mr. Finch said he'd be right out, sir."

"Thanks."

"Surely."

True to his word, one minute later, Finch stepped through an open doorway off to the right. He had on a black suit that, this time, didn't look like he'd slept in it. He held out his hand. "Mr. Lawson, Alan Finch. It's nice to meet you."

They shook hands and Lawson said, "You, too."

"Let's go to my office and visit. Please follow me."

They went back through the door and wound their way through an obstacle course of desks, each occupied by a female clerk furiously typing away. The constant dinging of the carriage return bells made Lawson think of a demented Santa standing in front of New York's Macy's department store.

Finch reached his office and waved a hand for Lawson to proceed. Lawson peeked in at a small windowless space. There was a battered metal desk with its chair shoved back against the wall. Little black marks streaked the wall from inadvertent collisions. A guest chair sat in front of the desk, so Lawson maneuvered himself to it and sat down. He placed his briefcase, without the handcuffs this trip, on the floor beside him and waited.

Finch closed the door, then sat down carefully. Lawson figured some previous occupant created the black marks.

"Mr. Lawson, welcome to London. Your first trip here?"

"Yes. It seems like I've been all around it, but never made it in to the city."

"I understand perfectly. Let's get started shall we? The Prime Minister gave me specific instructions to work the attack plans out with you, since you've some military experience, and I, to be honest, am just an analyst."

Lawson smiled. "Mr. Finch, if Mr. Churchill selected you to work on this, I doubt you're just an everyday sort of analyst."

Finch shrugged his shoulders and tipped his head slightly at the compliment. Opening a drawer, he pulled out a map and laid it on the desk. Lawson scooted his chair closer and leaned over to see better. Finch situated the map sideways, so they could both read it, rather than one viewing it upside down.

Lawson scanned it quickly and pointed at a spot just south of Göttingen. "This is where we believe the bomber's hanger is located. The hanger is huge, probably used for building zeppelins, but as far as we could tell from the gun camera film, there's no additional security around it."

"The German atomic lab is located here." Finch pointed at a place west of Stuttgart. "It's heavily wooded and the lab is underground. There's a barracks large enough for a platoon and a fence with razor wire around the entire perimeter. No guard towers, just a shack at the main gate."

"Uh huh, that's good. Our resources are two commando teams, one U.S. and one British."

"One team per target."

"Yeah. I'm not worried about getting them in, but I am about the extraction." Lawson frowned. He'd been involved in a few planning sessions where casualties were expected, but he'd never been one of the primary designers.

Finch nodded. "If they were in France, we could count on some help from the resistance. In Germany, they're going to be completely on their own. Do any of the men speak German well?"

"I read their files. Not one of them can speak German, so a cross-country excursion is out of the question."

"When you send the men in, would it be in one of those Gooney Birds?" Finch couldn't help but smile, the name struck him as hilarious. Only the Americans.

"Yep. The C-47's our best transport. Not terribly fast, but reliable."

"How do you know the planes will arrive safely? Couldn't they be shot down?"

"That's always a possibility, but a lone plane might not attract much attention. I've been thinking about sending a fighter escort with them, just as a precaution. Plus, we know where the flak fields are around Göttingen because our pilot's team ran into it."

Finch turned his attention to the ceiling and pursed his lips. Lawson smiled. He often did the same sort of thing when thinking. He waited. After a few moments, Finch opened the drawer again and rummaged around, found what he was looking for, and produced a stack of eight by ten photos. He dropped them onto the map and spread them out like a deck of cards, searching. He spotted the one he wanted and moved it to the top of the bunch.

Curious, Lawson glanced down. It was an aerial photo of a city, but he knew it wasn't Göttingen, therefore it must be Stuttgart.

Finch pointed to a location west of the city, in heavy woods, and said, "Here's where the lab is." He slid his finger across the picture, south. "And here's an airstrip. Notice anything missing?"

Lawson examined the airfield. The daylight photo was of good quality, and he could see a couple of small buildings and one hangar. He studied it for several minutes, then sat back with a frustrated expression. "I give up, what's missing?"

"Aircraft."

"What?" Lawson couldn't believe it, but when he stared at the picture again, he saw that Finch was right. There were no planes anywhere, not one. Why would that be? The runway seemed to be intact, no obvious bomb craters, and it was certainly long enough for modern planes.

He looked up at Finch. "Why would the Germans abandon a perfectly good airfield?"

"It's not as mysterious as it seems. They're just consolidating their forces. Their losses have been so great this year they've had no choice. There are airfields like this all over the place."

"Okay, what's your point?"

"What's the casualty rate for airborne ops?"

Puzzled, but interested in where Finch was going, Lawson replied, "About ten percent." He pulled a pack of cigarettes from his shirt pocket and offered it to Finch, who shook his head and absently slid an ashtray over. Lawson lit one and took a deep puff, blowing the smoke straight up over their heads. "All right, Finch, where are you headed with this?"

"I've been thinking about this. Both our targets are near airfields, so why not have the Gooney Birds use them instead of the men jumping?"

Lawson jerked upright, aghast. "Land an airplane in Germany? Are you fucking crazy?"

"You already said you'd be sending an escort with them. Why not land the plane, egress the men, then take off again. The planes can leave the area, then return when the mission is accomplished and pick up the men."

"You want to land, not one, but two, American airplanes on German runways, fucking twice?"

"Why not?" Finch was calm in the face of an ally practically screaming at him.

"Because it's never been done."

Finch smiled at this.

Lawson was confused and angry. "What the hell are you smiling at?"

"That's the reason we should do it."

Lawson started to retort again, but thought better of it and tossed Finch's idea around in his head. If he doubled the fighter escort, they could fly cover while the plane was exposed on the ground . . . then what? After a few more minutes of picking apart the idea, he looked at the MI5 analyst. "I think you have something here, Finch."

Finch smiled, opened the magic drawer again and pulled out a legal pad. "Where do we start, Mr. Lawson?"

27

The Oval Office
Washington, D.C.
14 June, 2355 Hours

Donovan looked at the tired old man behind the desk and shook his head. Late night meetings were the way of life in Washington and Donovan had long ago resigned himself to that fate. The thing was, though, he, like virtually everyone in Roosevelt's inner circle, was worried about the President's health. The stress of office was bad enough in peacetime, but with the United States' involvement in the war reaching nearly three years, well, it was taking its toll. He hated to see his friend in this state, but the only thing he could do to help, was do his job well and keep things off the president's plate. Which was what he was going to do tonight.

Roosevelt signed the last piece of paper in front of him and slipped his pen into its holder. Then he picked up his gold cigarette case, removed one, carefully inserted it into his slim holder, and lit it. He took a satisfied drag, then said, "Bill, what do you have for me? I could sure use some good news, although I am encouraged by the invasion's outcome."

Donovan nodded. He'd read the reports. Eisenhower's troops had gained the beachhead after fierce fighting and thousands of casualties. They'd established a firm beachhead and at the end of eight days had disembarked over a half million men, but no doubt vicious fighting still lay ahead. "I'm hopeful we can liberate Paris by fall, Mr. President. And, yes, I do have some good news for you."

Roosevelt smiled and raised his hand, beckoning Donovan to tell him.

"I have a team assembled and a plan to destroy the Hortens' plane as well as the German atomic bomb lab."

Roosevelt's cigarette holder drooped as his mouth dropped open slightly. "Are you telling me you know where they both are?"

"Yes, sir. Lawson's pilot, Captain Miller, went out with three others in his squadron and they found a promising hanger and airfield not far from where the pilot originally spotted the plane. Two planes went down, but the other two strafed the hanger and escaped with gun camera footage.

"The only question is, is whether the Germans will panic and move the plane. I'm banking on them believing it was just a couple of dumb lucky pilots wandering the countryside who stumbled onto a target of opportunity, rather than the attack being a coordinated attempt to find them."

Roosevelt nodded.

Donovan leaned forward. "A British agent, who's been deep in Germany for several years now, the same one who got the intelligence on the uranium, managed to find the lab and not get caught."

"That's just fantastic. Where is it?"

"About seven miles west of Stuttgart."

"Can't we send a flight of B-17s and just bomb the hell out of it?"

Donovan shook his head. "Remember what the Germans did after the Brits tried that on Peenemunde last year?"

"Oh, I see. Damn it." The Germans had simply moved their production underground. "What's your plan? And who's involved?"

Donovan knew the President wasn't trying to micro-manage him. He just liked to know everything. "I have a joint team, ours and British, who've worked together before. They launched an attack on an ammo dump in Calais a few days before D-Day to continue the charade that we were going to come straight across the channel. The attack fizzled because they were betrayed by a member of the French Resistance group they were working with, but it didn't matter. The attack caused the Germans to divert yet another armored division."

"Who's our guy in charge?"

Donovan had pulled Dunn's service record before coming over and read it through twice, enough to get the details down. "Staff Sergeant Thomas Dunn. From eastern Iowa. Enlisted the day after Pearl. Took Ranger training in '43 under Colonel Jenkins, who I hear is real true blue British ass. But he turns out the best men anywhere. Dunn was then assigned to Italy where he conducted himself over and above. This past April at the Commando training school at Achnacarry, he saved a trainee's life during a live fire exercise, but got shot himself for his efforts. During the attack in Calais, he was wounded again and captured, but a local doctor helped him escape the clutches of the Gestapo agent in charge of the area and got him back with his team on the beach just in time to get back to England.

"Dunn's team makes up half of the group, the other half is a British commando unit headed by a tough sergeant named Malcom Saunders. He and his team took commando training with Dunn and his team. From what I hear, they have quite a running rivalry, which keeps them on their toes."

"You're just going to send these boys into the heart of Germany to blow up the lab and the Horten airplane?" Roosevelt raised an eyebrow.

Donovan shrugged. "Pretty much, Mr. President. There's no other way."

Roosevelt looked worried as a thought struck him. "How are they going to get back home?"

"Don't worry, Mr. President, we've got that in the plan. We'll take care of our boys." I hope.

"When do they go in?"

"A couple of days yet. Tomorrow, Lawson is going to meet

with them and go over the British agent's information and the pilot's film. He and the MI5 man have worked out an excellent plan and I have every confidence in them and it."

"All right, then, Bill. I know you'll keep me up to date." Roosevelt stubbed out his cigarette and pushed his wheelchair back from the desk. Moving around the side of the desk, he held his hand out to Donovan, who rose and shook it gently.

"Yes, Mr. President. I'll let you know as soon as we hear back."

"Thanks. Good night, Bill."

"Good night, sir." Donovan watched the president roll away. Before he even got to the door, Roosevelt's aide opened it and stepped quickly behind the president, then took control of the wheelchair, deftly maneuvering it through the opening. Donovan was always amazed when the aide did this. How he knew the president needed help was beyond him, but he always managed to suddenly appear out of thin air at just the right time.

As Donovan left the Oval Office, he was thinking about the extraction plan. He shook his head and said a little prayer.

28

Project Dante Lab
7 miles west of Stuttgart
15 June, 1435 Hours

Gunther Winkel was unhappy. He sat by himself in the cafeteria nursing a cup of black coffee. His day's work was not going well and while that wasn't the reason he was unhappy, it did nothing to improve his mood, which was dark most of the time. Winkel was unhappy because his status with the other physicists was not what he had expected when he joined the project. His career at the university had been going splendidly, doing more research than teaching, then the war came and he got sucked in on Project Dante. Speer had recruited him and gave him all sorts of promises, none of which had come anywhere close to being fulfilled.

The others always seemed to discount his opinions, no matter how well thought out they were. And that damn Dr. Herbert. He was supposed to lead the project, but all he did was show up in the middle of a discussion and make senseless suggestions.

Over one thousand men and women worked on the project,

and Bauer and Gerber each managed half. They displayed some semblance of control, but not Herbert. During the morning meeting, the one where the day's upcoming work was discussed, he just sat there the entire time, letting the pipsqueak, Bauer, run things. Why not me? I'm more committed to this project, this country, than any of the others.

"There you are, Gunther! I've been looking all over for you."

A hand slapped Winkel on the back, startling him. His head whipped around and when he saw who it was, he said in an icy tone, "Oh. Herbert. What do you want?"

Herbert either missed the tone or was ignoring it as he grinned. "I called a meeting at 2:45 in the main conference room. I'd like you to be there."

"What for?"

"I completed the fast neutron calculations. I am announcing the results."

Winkel sat still, thinking, *Terrific. Dr. Moron and his calculations.* To anyone else, Herbert's gesture of friendliness would have been taken as genuine, but Winkel's mistrust made that impossible for him. He sighed, knowing he couldn't say no. He didn't want to be removed from the project. He thought if that happened he'd be taken away in the night, never to be seen again.

Winkel's hesitation caused Herbert to prod the hulking man, "You'll be there, of course?"

A small nod was his only reply. Then Winkel stood up and walked away, leaving his coffee cup on the table.

Herbert stood there for a moment wondering when would it be time to get rid of Winkel.

Herbert stopped by his office to pick up his papers, lumped together in a large file holder, then made his way to the conference room. He expected to see Bauer and Gerber there early, and they were, but he was surprised to see Winkel sitting impassively at the table. He took a seat at the head of the table and opened the large file folder. After removing the papers, he straightened them, aligning the edges. The stack was an inch thick.

"I have done the calculations many times over the past few weeks and after plugging in the different variables, I am ready to state that the amount of eighty-five percent enriched U-235 we need is 35 kilograms. We currently have just over 110 kilograms ready for our use. Based on my calculations, we have enough for three devices, rather than one or two. This—"

Bauer and Gerber's applause stopped him, and he held up a hand.

"Thank you. We need to focus now on preparing the 'bullet' and 'target' portions of the sphere, which should measure 11.9 centimeters. Dr. Bauer's expectation of a 55/45 breakdown of the bullet to target was almost exactly correct; I determined it should be 53/47." He nodded at Bauer who smiled broadly in return.

Patting the papers, Herbert continued, "Which of you will volunteer to check my work?"

Bauer looked at Gerber, who nodded slightly; they'd previously discussed this. Bauer said, "No need, Franz, we have faith in your mathematical abilities, which far out shadow ours. Don't you agree, Gunther?"

"As you wish," was all Winkel said.

Herbert nodded. "These will be in my office, should you wish to view them. Just stop by anytime and I'll get them out for you."

"Volker, is the first gun ready for testing?"

"Yes, I will schedule it for tomorrow morning at 10:00." He stopped to remove a slide rule from its holster on his right hip. He deftly manipulated the slide, then said, "We'll need 18.55 kilograms of test weight in the bullet to take the place of the uranium plug. Now that we know the size of the bullet, we can work tonight to create the tamper and calculate the amount of high explosive we'll need to propel the target."

"Very good. Gentlemen, thank you for all your hard work. That's all."

The Herbert Apartment
Stuttgart
15 June, 1934 Hours

Dr. Herbert's apartment building sat two blocks from Stuttgart's utilitarian city hall. To his surprise, he liked Stuttgart. A true Berliner, he had always believed no city could compare, but Stuttgart was a definitely a close second. He and his wife lived in a spacious first floor apartment with a view of a small park across from their dining room window. In a past time, the park would have been filled with children playing and screaming in delight, but now, with the Allied air raids, only silence draped the park as the sun slid toward the horizon.

Edwina sat down at the intricately carved oak dining room table, large enough for eight, carefully unfolded her linen napkin, and placed it in her lap primly. She looked at her husband with delight.

Herbert knew it wasn't for him.

"Oh, Franz, I wish you could have been there! It was so wonderful, I got to hear the *Führer* speak again." She fanned herself with a hand, as if the excitement was too much to bear, and her diamond bracelet rattled.

Herbert gave his wife a smile he didn't feel and said, "That's wonderful, dear, I wish I could have been there, too. Who was there?"

"Oh, the usual group." Which meant those with money. Those in the power circle of a dying nation. At first, moving from Berlin had been a challenge for her—she'd almost refused—but she started traveling to Berlin on a weekly basis so as to keep her status intact.

Herbert had missed her presence at first, then as the work days grew longer and longer, he took to sleeping at the lab, in the barracks deep underground, and she began spending more and more time in Berlin, where the fun was. Now their time together was about three or four days a month. Herbert was glad because, this way, he didn't have to work so hard to conceal his inner thoughts. "Did the *Führer* make any new announcements?" he asked, wanting to show some interest.

Edwina waved her hand, "No, not really. He just reminded us that our support was helping the Reich win the war. He talked about how our brave men are driving the American and British invaders back into the sea and soon, Europe would be safe once again."

"Excellent. So all the money we've donated *is* making a difference."

"Oh my, yes. I wrote a check for another ten thousand." Edwina wasn't asking permission, it was her money, after all.

Inwardly, Herbert cringed. That was five years' salary.

"Good, I'm glad you did. Thank you."

Edwina beamed and started in on her roast dinner.

The evening passed quietly. Herbert read various daily reports and Edwina went to the bedroom to see what clothes to pack for her next trip to Berlin, on Saturday, two days away.

At 10:30, Herbert found himself re-reading paragraphs because he didn't remember what they said, so he gave up and got ready for bed. By 10:45, he was in bed next to his wife, who was already asleep. He lay there for a moment reflecting on his work this day. He was pleased with his accomplishment. And relieved Bauer, Gerber, and Winkel had decided not to check his work. He had inserted the slight error about half-way through the calculation counting on the fact that anyone following through would miss it, so subtle it was, and as Bauer had said, he did far out shadow all three men in mathematics. The real number was 50 kilograms, not the 35 or the original 20 he'd told them weeks ago. With only 35 kilograms of enriched U-235, the atomic bomb would do nothing more than create an explosion equal to that of a normal high-explosive bomb.

There was no way in heaven or earth that Herbert was going to let that madman get his hands on a weapon capable of destroying most of a city.

Herbert closed his eyes and fell asleep proud of his work.

29

The Horten Brothers Airfield
5 miles south of Göttingen
16 June, 0712 Hours

Hans Engel's stomach was queasy, a normal feeling when he was preparing for a test flight. He relished the mild misery because, deep down in his gut, he knew the day he didn't have this feeling would be the day he'd die. The nervousness helped keep him alert and gave him the sharp edge he needed to make split-second and life-saving decisions. At thirty-eight, Engel had worked for the Hortens for nearly five years as a test pilot, then became their chief test pilot two years ago. His predecessor had pushed the envelope a shade too far and augured his plane into the ground at nearly six hundred kilometers an hour creating a rather spectacular fireball. This was a debt test pilots sometimes paid for the thrill of riding in the newest, fastest planes in Germany; an obligation they understood could be called at anytime, even though none believed it ever would be.

Engel had survived his share of close ones because he always did the one right thing that allowed him to go home to his wife and three daughters that night. Whenever his wife complained about the risks he was taking with his life, he simply reminded her that as long as he was flying for the Hortens, he wouldn't have to fly for the Luftwaffe, where the chance of quick death was over fifty percent.

Today was the day. The day he would light up the six Junkers jet engines and lift the H18 into the blue sky for the first time under her own power. Even when on the gliding tests, he knew he was blessed to be sitting in the cockpit of a truly marvelous machine. He smiled in anticipation of how she would feel under her own power.

He flipped his silver and black striped silk flying scarf around his neck and looped it under his chin. After tucking the scarf's tails inside the front of his brown leather flying jacket, he zipped it up part way. It was an affectation in the spirit of the World War I aces like Baron Von Richthoffen. He gripped the jacket's front edges at his waist and pulled down with a snap. Perfect. He strode out of the ready room looking and feeling like the proud German flyer he was.

"Here he comes now, Field Marshal." Reimar Horten pointed toward Engel, who stepped through the hanger's door.

Göring turned toward Engel expectantly. On his arrival, Göring told the Hortens he wanted to say a few words to the pilot before he climbed into the cockpit. It was, after all, a historic moment for the Fatherland.

Mauer and Nagel stood on the runway with the H18, going over the pre-flight mechanical checklist. The repairs to the wings had gone perfectly and one last gliding test proved to be one hundred percent successful; Engel reported she felt exactly the same, no problems, no deviations.

The test firing of the installed engines had gone well, but they'd only been able to fire all of the engines at the same time once because of fuel restrictions. Today was the true test. Would the plane shake apart from some hidden vibration? Or would one or more of the engines ignite, then promptly explode; not an unknown occurrence with jets.

Mauer glanced over at Göring standing with the Hortens. He

snorted and said, "God, he's a fat one, isn't he?"

Nagel took a look. "Good Lord, I swear he looks bigger every time I see him."

"Shit, it must be nice to be able to eat that much."

Few people knew the truth behind Göring's weight gain. It was a side-effect of the morphine he took for an injury sustained in the 1923 Munich Beer Hall Putsch. Göring felt it better to let people believe he overate, rather than announce any health problems. That would make him appear weak. And unable to take over for the *Führer* when the time came, his one true wish.

"Are you nervous?" Nagel needed a net to catch the butterflies in his stomach.

"You're kidding, right? Of course, I'm nervous. If she doesn't perform perfectly today, we're going to end up on some damn flight line in France working on Messerschmitts and getting our asses bombed by the Americans."

Nagel noticed one of the mechanics kneeling by the nose landing gear. The man was fiddling with something and Nagel called out, "Is anything wrong?"

The mechanic looked up from the gear and shook his head. "Just double-checking the air pressure. It's fine."

Nagel nodded, relieved, then checked his watch for the tenth time. They should be getting the pilot in the cockpit in a few minutes, then take off about ten minutes after that, following Engel's rundown of his own pre-flight checklist.

Engel approached his superiors and Göring. He'd never met Göring, but knew the man could talk your ears off using nothing but bullshit. He stopped a few paces away and snapped a sharp stiff-arm salute. "*Heil* Hitler!"

As one, the Hortens and Göring returned the salute and phrase with smiles.

Göring held out his hand, "Mr. Engel, I've heard great things about you. It's a pleasure to meet you at last."

Engel was surprised by Göring's friendliness. Engel had heard that before his rise to power, Göring was a pilot's pilot. He could talk the language and other World War I pilots respected him. Maybe Göring missed that camaraderie in some way and being here on the flight line brought back those pleasant memories. Engel smiled and shook the big man's hand. "Thank you, Field Marshal Göring. It's a pleasure to meet you, too."

Göring faced the H18 and said, "She's a beautiful craft, is she not? I envy you and your maiden flight. You are a fortunate man, Mr. Engel."

"I feel the same way, sir."

"Good. I cannot overstate to you the importance the airplane represents to the Luftwaffe and the Reich." Göring put a meaty hand on Engel's shoulder. "I've spoken to the *Führer* about her. He is most anxious to receive the news of a successful flight today. He even asked me to wish you 'good flight' on his behalf." This was a lie, but Engel would never know and it often helped men to believe their *Führer* was interested in their work. It was an unparalleled motivator. Göring was rewarded by Engel's and the Hortens' surprised expressions.

"Thank you, Field Marshal, for the kind words. I won't let the *Führer*, or you, down."

"No, of course you won't, Mr. Engel. We have every confidence in you and the Hortens."

Walter checked his watch, hoping Göring would stop talking.

Fortunately, the Field Marshal seemed to sense the need to get the pilot into the plane and the plane into the air. He stuck out his hand once more. "Good flight, Mr. Engel. See you back on the ground."

"Thank you, sir." Engel smiled and headed off toward the H18.

"He's a fine man."

"Yes, he is, Field Marshal. We're lucky to have him," replied Reimar. "We should be ready for take off in ten minutes. Shall we take our seats?" He waved a hand in the direction of three chairs set up just outside the hanger, at a safe distance from the fervently prayed against explosion.

Engel ran the checklist and said, "Checklist complete, tower."

The engineer in the tower said, "You are cleared for engine start sequence."

"Affirmative. Starting engine start sequence." The sequence was preplanned: first the two inboard engines, then the next pair and finally the outboard pair. He flipped down the toggle switches for engines three and four. The spinning turbines' whine filled the cockpit. After a moment, the engines ignited and began to run smoothly at idle speed. Good, thought Engel. He went through the next two pairs with the same success, but now the engine noise was tremendous.

"Tower, engine sequence complete. Ready for takeoff."

"H18, you are cleared for takeoff. Good flight, sir."

"Thank you, tower."

Engel released the parking brake and the H18 rolled to the end of the runway, facing south, into the summer breeze. All engines were hooked to one throttle control, but could be operated separately, if necessary. For today, Engel hoped that wouldn't be required. He pushed the silver handle forward and removed his foot from the brake pedal.

Thunder rattled the hanger windows behind the Hortens and Göring. Reimar turned to Walter and smiled. Walter grinned.

The H18 reacted immediately to the freedom and shot forward. She streaked down the runway. Engel gently pulled the wheel back and the nose lifted, then the wing gear was free of the earth. Engel guided her up to 5,000 feet and banked right, the flame and smoke from her powerful jets clearly visible to the amazed audience. The flight plan called for a sweeping quarter circle to the west, then straight back over the hanger at three quarters speed, 750 kilometers per hour, all the more to impress the Field Marshall.

Göring lost sight of the H18 within two minutes. He waited. There. A black dot growing bigger, impossibly fast. As she rocketed overhead, his chest thrummed to her deep rumbling. He jumped up out his chair, knocking it flying against the hanger wall. "Dear God, what a magnificent machine."

The Hortens looked at each other, surprised by the Field Marshal's reference to God, but they shared smiles of delight.

30

Camp Barton Stacy
16 June, 0614 Hours, London time

Dunn stuck his head in the barracks door. He wanted to make sure his team was up and at 'em. Satisfied with what he saw, Dunn turned and headed toward the mess hall; his stomach was growling. As he walked through the early morning sunshine, he was feeling particularly pleased with himself and the way things were going with Pamela. After surviving the first family visit, evidently passing muster, and with Pamela's words of encouragement about a life after the war, he began to think that perhaps he might actually have a future.

He'd spent the night at Pamela's on Sunday and Monday; her roommate was fortuitously on leave in London. Each time they made love, they fit together better and learned to please each other in new ways. He had to force himself to come back to the camp Tuesday morning for drills. Each night since, though, he'd managed to get away in the evenings to spend some time with her.

As he rounded the corner of the administration building, next

RONN MUNSTERMAN

door to the mess hall, he saw Saunders and Corporal Steve Barltrop coming from the other direction. They saw him, too, and he raised a hand. They returned the welcome. After a few more steps, they merged and continued toward breakfast.

"Morning, fellas."

"Morning, Dunn."

Saunders lifted his face toward the sky. "Beautiful day to plan a battle, wouldn't you know."

Dunn nodded. "Yep. That it is. Do you know anything about the MI5 guy who's coming with Lawson? What's his name?" They'd gotten word two days ago that Lawson was bringing someone else.

"Finch. No. Never heard of the chap. Didn't bother asking around. Figured we'd find out soon enough."

"Yeah, I suppose so."

They made their way into the hall, got breakfast and found a table away from the rest of the troops. They ate in silence for a few minutes, then Saunders and Barltrop began chatting about nothing. Dunn didn't join in, instead, as he ate he thought of Pamela again.

Saunders noticed Dunn's withdrawal and stopped talking. He pointed at Dunn with a partial piece of burnt toast. Barltrop glanced at the American, who was staring off into space.

Saunders grinned and waved the toast in front of Dunn. "Hello? Hello?"

Dunn blinked and turned to Saunders. "What?"

"Got your mind on something, have you?"

"Oh. Just thinking."

Another grin. "Just don't use it all up too soon, my friend. What's on your mind?"

Dunn didn't answer and Saunders winked at Barltrop. "I noticed you've been off base a lot the past few days. Anyone we know?"

Should have known, thought Dunn. Can't hide anything around army types. Dunn shrugged.

"Oh come on. You can tell us. Can't he, Barltrop?"

"Yes, indeed, Sergeant."

Dunn's expression changed subtly, taking on perhaps a wistful look, then back to neutral so quickly that Saunders almost missed it. But in that split second Saunders understood.

"Corporal, would you get me another coffee?" Saunders pushed his still half-full cup toward Barltrop.

Barltrop raised his eyebrows, but said, "Of course, Sergeant. Be back in awhile."

Saunders waited until the corporal was out of earshot, then said, "Tom, thinking about your girl is fine while you're here, you know. But it'll get you killed in the middle of action. You want to talk about her?"

Dunn was surprised. First, that Saunders had figured it out so fast and, secondly, that he cared enough to even ask. Dunn stared at the big British sergeant with the red hair and handlebar moustache. He knew he could trust his life with this man; he already had. So why not trust him with his feelings? Because men don't talk about stuff like this with each other, that's why. But that was at home. War changed you in ways you never expected. The fear of dying was always there, but you learned to push it to the back at least a little. The ones who couldn't do that froze and ended up in the hospital or the morgue. What combat soldiers talked about was what they were going to do after the war; that was their way of believing they could return to a normal life, just like Dunn was doing with Pamela.

Dunn tilted his head slightly and took a deep breath. "It's like this, Malcolm, I never meant to fall for this girl. She just, . . ." Dunn frowned, trying to think of the best way to explain things. Saunders waited patiently. "She made me see myself through someone else's eyes and realize how I affect other people," he tapped his sergeant stripes, "in ways that have nothing to do with these." Dunn clasped his hands on the table and glanced down at them. "She gave me hope, Malcolm, but now I'm suddenly more afraid than ever I won't come back. To her." Dunn swallowed hard, avoiding a sudden catch that had risen in his throat. He raised his eyes to Saunders, half expecting to see a smartass grin, but Saunders' expression was just one of concern for a friend in pain.

"Tom, I have a girl back home and I haven't seen her for a few months. Can I tell you what I do? Maybe it'll help you."

"Sure."

"Now don't laugh, or I'll break your bloody neck."

Dunn grinned and held his hands up in surrender. "I wouldn't think of it."

Saunders grinned back, but said, "Sure you wouldn't. Anyway. The night before a mission, at bedtime, you know, the time when a man's thoughts can get away from him?"

Dunn nodded.

"Those quiet moments can tear you up with the things you start thinking about. So I began having a little conversation with Sadie. At the end, I'd say good bye and tell her I'd see her when I got back. Then I tucked her away in a safe place in my head and went on about my business."

Looking away, Dunn considered what Saunders had said. He knew he'd have to compartmentalize his brain. He knew a lot of married and engaged soldiers and they somehow seemed to be able to do something like Saunders was suggesting. It was just that he'd never needed to before. Maybe it got easier over time. He prayed it would. Turning back to Saunders with a grateful expression, he said, "Thanks, Malcolm."

Saunders nodded. "You're welcome." He pointed at Dunn's almost empty plate and said, "You done?"

"Yeah."

"Let's round up Barltrop and get on over there. I can't hardly wait to see what Intel has in store for us."

Dunn, Saunders and Barltrop walked into the administration building's briefing room. Dunn's and Saunders' teams stood around in separate pods. Standing in a cluster off to the right, four pilots sipped steaming coffee. Multiple conversations drifted towards Dunn and he spotted Kenton, Lawson, and a thin man wearing a crisp black suit, presumably the MI5 man, Finch, standing behind a long table at the front of the room. Lieutenant Adams was next to Kenton, as always.

Dunn headed in their direction. Saunders followed and Corporal Barltrop wandered over to where the rest of the British team was gathered.

"Morning, Colonel."

"Good morning, Sergeant. You remember Mr. Lawson. And this is Alan Finch from MI5."

Dunn shook hands with both men, as did Saunders.

Kenton leaned around Dunn and said to Lawson and Finch, "Are we ready to start, gentlemen?"

"Yes, sir," said Lawson.

Kenton said, "Be seated."

Even though he hadn't raised his voice, the men heard him and settled into the rickety folding chairs across the front row; no one sat in the back of the room during a mission briefing. Dunn and Saunders joined their teams. The pilots seated themselves inconspicuously in the row behind everyone else.

Colonel Kenton introduced Lawson and Finch, then said, "Gentlemen, Intelligence has learned that the Germans are working on a new weapon called the atomic bomb. This bomb, a *single* bomb, if dropped on a city like New York or London, would be capable of destroying as much as four square miles, leveling everything."

Gasps and shocked faces spread around the briefing room. After a moment, Cross raised a hand and said, "Sir, how would the Germans get the bomb over there? I didn't think they had a bomber that could reach the states."

"You're right, they didn't, now they do. A new plane was spotted by one of our Mustang pilots from the 357th Squadron. Captain Miller, would you stand?" Miller rose, then dipped his head as the soldiers all turned around to look.

Kenton continued, "This plane is capable of making a one way trip to our east coast and delivering the bomb." Kenton eyed the dozen soldiers in front of him for a moment. "Men, our job is to destroy the atomic bomb lab and that airplane. At all costs." The men gave no outward reaction, but Kenton knew the effect his last sentence would have on these warriors. It meant they must successfully complete the mission, even if it was the last man who threw the switch on the explosives. They were expendable and failure was not acceptable. Too much was riding on this one. The tide of the war would change against the allies if they failed. "Mr. Lawson and Mr. Finch have drawn up a plan. Lieutenant Adams and I have examined the plan and can say it's a sound one. There're plenty of risks, but you already knew that."

The men nodded.

"I'm going to turn things over to these gentlemen now. Mr. Lawson."

"Thank you, Colonel. Good morning, men. I want to tell you that this mission has been ordered from the highest levels. President Roosevelt and Prime Minister Churchill asked us to convey their best wishes for a successful mission and to tell you that this one is more important than any other ever conducted by the Allies," he paused, "including the Normandy invasion."

A few 'ah shits' escaped.

Lawson picked up a wooden pointer with a torn rubber tip and turned to the map of Europe behind him. He tapped Stuttgart's location and said, "The atomic bomb lab is west of Stuttgart and," he slid the pointer up and to the right, "the airplane's hanger is south of Göttingen."

"Each team will be flown to a target at night. Each of your planes will be escorted by a flight of P-51s and land on an airfield near the target."

"Are you fucking crazy? Land a plane in Germany?" Daniel Morris's expression was incredulous. Sympathetic murmurs rose around the room.

Lawson refrained from giving Finch an I-told-you-so look. "The Mustangs will provide ample protection."

"From other fighters, you mean."

"Well, yes, that's the biggest danger."

"What about ground fire?"

"That's certainly a risk, also, but the darkness should protect you from that."

Morris shook his head, but stopped talking.

Lawson was surprised to get involved in a debate over the plan. He was used to just giving orders with the expectation the men would simply follow them, no questions asked. He thought about asking Kenton about it later, but then recalled he wasn't dealing with just any soldiers. They were rangers and commandos, the toughest and most successful fighters the U.S. and England could put on the ground. He decided they deserved a more straightforward approach. "Mr. Finch and I argued about this at first, but keep in mind you'll have the advantage of surprise. Plus, your extraction will be more immediate with the plane available to you. You won't have to go cross-country to get home." Lawson could see expressions change as this bit of information settled in.

"Sergeant Saunders and his team will destroy the airplane and hanger—"

"Sir?" Neville Owens, who was on Saunders' team, held up his hand.

"Yes?"

"Why not just assign the plane's hanger to a bombing run? They could pulverize the target."

"You're right, but we need someone on the ground to see the plane and physically put explosives in it. We cannot assume anything."

Owens tipped his head at the sound reasoning.

Lawson continued, "The plane was designed and built by the Horten brothers. My sources at Northrop said these two men are the most advanced aeronautical designers anywhere in the world. When I showed a picture of the plane to the boys at Northrop, they just about shit their pants because the Hortens are building what American aircraft designers have only been thinking about: a plane with no vertical surfaces. It's just a giant flying wing.

"They also suspect that, to accomplish what they have, the Hortens are probably using a wood and resin mixture on the surfaces, which would mean the plane would be invisible to radar." Lawson paused again. Sure enough, eyebrows lifted. "We cannot allow this plane to take off with an atomic bomb because we'd never know it was coming."

"Christ Almighty," muttered Stan Wickham.

Lawson glanced at the flyers and said, "I'd like to introduce your pilots; the C-47 drivers and the fighter escort commanders."

"Sir?"

Lawson turned toward Dunn. "Yes, Sergeant?"

"How does the atomic bomb work?"

"Sorry, it's need to know and I don't need to know." Lawson happened to glance over Dunn's shoulder and spotted Miller with a small smile on his face. Lawson nodded slightly to acknowledge the irony of the situation and Miller nodded back.

Lawson turned his attention back to the group and said, "You've already met Captain Miller and he'll be leading the escorts for Sergeant Saunders' plane." Lawson introduced the other three pilots in turn, then opened his briefcase. He removed a stack of photos and handed them to Finch. "We have gun camera photos, taken by Captain Miller, of the airplane and the hanger to help you. Mr. Finch, if you please." Finch passed the pictures out to Sergeant Saunders' team. Lawson gave the men a minute to examine them, then said, "Your flight path will be up the channel to the northern tip of Holland, then across to Göttingen. The C-47 will land on the Hortens' own runway and the team will disembark.

"While we don't believe the Germans have any sizable ground forces in the vicinity of the Horten hanger—it is only 130 miles from Berlin—there is almost certainly a small force, perhaps two or three guards, on site to prevent sabotage. As to whether any workmen will be present, assume there is and act accordingly. Just remember your first responsibility is the destruction of that airplane.

"You'll be using standard plastic explosives. You're to make sure the plane is completely destroyed as well as the hanger and office."

Miller stopped listening to Lawson as an idea niggled the back of his mind. He mulled it over for a few minutes, then decided it might be possible. The problem is, he thought, I might just get court-martialed. He turned his attention back to Lawson, who was wrapping up.

"Sergeant, when you've completed the mission, you'll board the plane and get out of there. Any questions?" Lawson asked the room. No one said anything. "I'm going to turn this over to Mr. Finch now. He has the information on the atomic lab attack."

Finch moved over to the map and took the proffered pointer. "The lab is buried underground, in the side of a hill. Here." He tapped the area just west of Stuttgart. "Sergeant Dunn, your flight path will be down the border of France and Belgium, to Saverne, France, then straight into Germany. There's an airfield seven miles from the lab, but instead of traveling on foot, I've arranged for you to get a ride." Finch smiled at the men's reaction to this good news. "The entrance to the lab is approached through heavy woods over a paved road. We have an agent in Stuttgart, Neil Marston, who will meet you at the airfield with a German troop truck." Finch turned to Dunn. "Sergeant Dunn, Mr. Marston has been recalled to London for his own safety. He's been in Germany four years and we're afraid his luck will soon run out.

We'd truly appreciate it if you would bring him back home."

"Be glad to, Mr. Finch."

Finch nodded, then handed the American team a sheaf of papers. "These are his drawings and pictures of the compound."

After Lawson distributed the papers and photos to Dunn's team, Finch held a drawing up so it faced the men, and pointed. "You can see there's a fence all the way around, it's not electrified, but does have razor wire on top. The gate has a guard shack that is manned by one soldier. The barracks is large enough for a platoon and over here is the actual entrance to the lab, which is also manned by one soldier.

"The shift goes home at 2300, and your attack will be between midnight and 0300 hours. You should plan to be back to the airfield within two hours. You'll have to eliminate the two guards silently and as for the barracks, we recommend setting charges underneath and just be done with it." Finch surprised himself by his almost cavalier manner when talking about the death of perhaps fifty Germans. He shrugged mentally. "We don't have any knowledge of the interior of the lab, so that'll be the highest risk to you. For all we know, there could be another whole platoon in there. But the main thing is, you have to find the location of the device itself, the atomic bomb. It will likely be held in what will seem to be the most secure place in the lab. We believe the device may be as long as nine feet and as big around as two fifty-five gallon drums and of course, it'll look like a bomb, just the biggest damn one you've ever seen. We believe most of the scientists leave in the evening, but some may still be present. If they are, you're to kill them, no questions asked. Their knowledge of building an atomic bomb is another of your targets, if possible.

"You must plant your charges in a way you think will collapse the hillside onto the lab's entrance. Once that's done, we'll be able to keep an eye on the Germans. If they try to dig out a new entrance to the lab, then we'll begin dropping five hundred pounders on them, daily if we have to, to keep them out of the ruins of the lab.

"If you can, try to grab as many papers as you can carry. Don't try to figure out which ones are important, just take everything. We have people who can sift through the papers for valuable information." Finch took a deep breath. "Questions?"

"When's departure, sir?" asked Dunn.

"All planes will take off at 2300 hours this Sunday night. We need the full moon for the pilots to see the runways."

"What's the matter, sir? Can't get the locals to turn on the lights for us?" asked Morris, with a snicker.

Finch just smiled and turned to Kenton. "That covers it, sir."

"Thank you. Sergeants Dunn and Saunders, dismiss your men, then join us in my office. We'll be going over the minute details with Mr. Lawson and Mr. Finch."

After the men departed, Saunders turned to Dunn and said, "Well?"

"Well, what?"

"Do you have that feeling this time?"

Dunn paused, searching. "No, I don't. Hopefully it won't show up. I don't want to lose another man so soon."

Saunders clapped Dunn on the back. "Me neither, Tom, me neither."

31

The Reich Chancellery
Berlin
16 June, 1542 Hours

"*Mein Führer*, I wish you could have been there! The Hortens' H18 was magnificent. When she flew over us, her powerful sound was astonishing. She was so graceful. She will be our salvation against the Allies."

Göring had flown back to Berlin after he'd finished enjoying himself at the Hortens' hanger. He'd spent more time chatting with Engel, pilot to pilot, pumping the man with questions about the way the H18 handled, how she felt under power, what it was like to go that fast. On the flight home, Göring imagined being in the H18's cockpit and wished he could still fly a plane on his own, but those days were gone. The number two man in the Third Reich didn't go flying for pleasure.

Hitler regarded Göring with his piercing, unblinking gaze. "You still believe this plane will be able to reach America with an atomic bomb?"

"Yes, there's no doubt she will. The Hortens are asking for a crew of three from our Luftwaffe to begin training and then practice dropping dummy ordnance of the same size and weight as the bomb. We estimate the crew will be ready by July 20th. How are Speer's scientists doing?" Göring had to work hard to keep his dislike of Speer out of his voice.

"They successfully tested the gun mechanism this morning. Speer promised me they would be able to conduct a test of a bomb by the end of July."

"Where are we going to explode the test bomb?"

"I ordered Speer to select a spot in Poland."

Göring nodded. "That seems like a perfect place. How long will it take to complete the bomb we can drop on America."

"Four weeks after that."

"Four weeks?" Göring's expression turned thoughtful, then he smiled, "*Mein Führer*, that would be wonderful timing."

Hitler looked puzzled for a moment, then his eyes lit up. "Oh, of course. It would be the fifth anniversary of our march to victory in Poland, September first. That would be so fitting." Hitler was all animation now, his hands and arms began gesturing to the sky. "I have to call Göbbels. He can start working on the announcement we'll broadcast after we take care of Roosevelt. I want to drop the bomb on Washington, D.C., not New York. If they want to bomb our capitol, we'll destroy theirs. That'll give them plenty of incentive to bargain with us and give us what we want, which is their complete withdrawal from Europe. My Reich will continue to prosper and Germany will hold her rightful place as Europe's master." Hitler grabbed the phone receiver and when his secretary answered, gave instructions to get Göbbels.

Göring sat quietly, a small, pleased smile on his lips as he thought of the riches he would add to his already bulging coffers when Europe was once again solidly German.

32

German Army Motor Pool
Stuttgart
18 June, 2014 Hours

The setting sun glinted off the motor pool's entrance sign turning the white background a light shade of orange. It was about the only color around as all the buildings and vehicles were gray or brown. Neil Marston, wearing a black Waffen-SS Colonel's uniform, strode purposefully toward the office, his calf-high boots clattering on the pavement. He'd specifically selected the Waffen-SS uniform because he knew precisely what reaction it would provoke from anyone in the regular German army. Pure, deep fear. The kind you feel when you know your life expectancy could suddenly fall far short of the national average.

The Waffen-SS's original purpose, dating back to 1933, was to act as special purpose troops bound to do Hitler's bidding. The SS abbreviation stood for *Schutzstaffel* (protection squad) which was an armed escort for Hitler early on. However, they hadn't been trained in military tactics and methods, but once the war began, it was clear they would need that training as well as equipment. Heinrich Himmler, the bespectacled head of the SS, decided his troops would rival the German army and ensured they received the best weapons and equipment. The SS was elite in nature, primarily because the entrance requirements were much higher than for the regular army. However, this made it more difficult to find suitable recruits, but in spite of that problem, Himmler led over a half million Waffen-SS soldiers. The SS was often deployed side-by-side with the army and earned a reputation for brutality, a reputation fostered by the SS leaders, like the one whose uniform Marston had stolen.

The office was in a ramshackle one-story building. Marston yanked the door open and stepped through, slamming it shut as hard as he could. The wall rattled. A grizzled sergeant sitting behind a rickety desk, looked up at the noise with an angry expression. When he saw who was marching his way, he jumped to his feet. Anger immediately gave way to fear.

Marston had been prepared to fire off some bluster and threats, but the man's reaction told him it wasn't needed. "Sergeant, I'm here to pick up my truck. Where is it?" Marston held out an authorization paper, 'signed' by Himmler.

The sergeant took the paper and his face paled when he saw the signature. Things could go badly for a lot of people, including simple sergeants when the Waffen-SS arrived. He wondered what the SS had going on in Stuttgart, but certainly knew better than to ask any questions. The paper looked to be in order and was dated the fourteenth, only a few days ago, so who was he to get all official with this Colonel.

"I'll go get it myself, Colonel. I'll pull it up right outside the door, if that's all right with you."

Marston sniffed derisively and said, "Fine. Just make it quick. I have a timetable to keep for the *Führer*."

The sergeant's eyes widened at the invocation of Hitler's title and he threw a Nazi salute. "*Heil* Hitler. Yes, Colonel. Right away, Colonel."

As the sergeant reached the door, Marston called out, "Oh, Sergeant?"

The man spun around in his tracks. "Yes, sir?"

"Make sure the truck is fully fueled."

The sergeant bobbed his head. "Yes, Colonel, of course."

After the door closed, Marston let out a bubble of air in relief. Only a little longer, then he'd be safely away from here. He went out the door to wait. True to his word, the sergeant had the truck in front of him in just a few minutes. He hopped out of the cab with the engine running and the parking brake on. He saluted once more, as the Waffen-SS Colonel got into the driver's seat. Only hours later did he wonder why a colonel was driving the truck himself instead of a lowly private. He shrugged it off and went to bed with the thought that there was no explaining officers.

Marston drove the truck through the western part of the city and out into the countryside. The highway wound its way through heavily wooded terrain and he guided the heavy vehicle along carefully. After about five minutes, he spotted the dirt road he was looking for and slowed the truck. Turning onto the deserted farm's driveway, he downshifted, continuing to drive slowly. He'd found out about the farm by visiting with the man behind the counter at the meat market. The owner was a recent widower and childless. One day he just up and disappeared, no one knew where he went. Most thought he left to commit suicide due to his wife's death.

The sun was sinking fast and in the middle of the woods, it was getting dark, so Marston switched on the headlights. The little sliver of light helped him see the road emptying into a barnyard. He steered the truck toward a big, vacant machine shed and parked it inside. Turning off the engine, he jumped out, closed the shed's heavy wooden doors behind him, and dropped the wooden bar into place to keep them shut.

Marston walked the fifty yards from the shed to the old, two-story farmhouse, his boots grating on the barnyard's gravel and dirt. Stepping up onto the small porch, he went through the door into the living room, where a dingy sofa and two soft chairs formed a U shape. He pulled the curtains closed tight and lit a kerosene lamp on a table next to the sofa. Plopping down on the sofa, he took off his peaked officer's hat and lay it beside him. Leaning back, he rested his head on the soft sofa back, closed his eyes and breathed deeply to reduce the stress-induced adrenaline rush. After a few minutes, he felt calmer. He opened his eyes and checked his watch. Only four hours to go.

33

Hampstead Air Base
3 miles north of Andover
18 June, 2248 Hours

Dunn walked among his team feeling the loss of Timothy Oldham more than ever. He hadn't had time to replace Oldham, so the team was going out one man short. He assured Colonel Kenton they'd be okay, but Oldham's presence was missed by each man. Dunn didn't feel like talking much and it appeared everyone else felt the same way; the group was unusually quiet. Dunn patted the men on the shoulder or upper arm as he passed and got a few smiles, but most just nodded. He spied Saunders talking to his team down the flight line and started in their direction.

About half way there, Saunders turned around, saw Dunn and walked toward him. When they met, he said. "Tom, your guys ready?"

"As close as we can get. Nobody feels like talking tonight, though. We're feeling Oldham's absence something fierce tonight."

Saunders shook his head. "I understand, Tom. I'm sorry."

Dunn shrugged. "Yeah, well." He looked around the flight line noticing, for the first time, the row of eight silver P-51 Mustangs. Just sitting on the tarmac, they looked graceful, yet deadly. "I'm glad those guys are coming with us." He tilted his head in their direction and Saunders turned to look.

"Aye, me, too. Gives a bloke a warm and fuzzy feeling, don't it?"

"Ha ha," answered Dunn dryly.

"Finch and Lawson knew what they were doing, though, huh?"

"About the first time I ever worked with an intelligence puke who got things right." The details meeting between the men in Colonel Kenton's office had gone better than either sergeant had expected or even hoped for. The OSS and MI5 officers had broken down each mission into clear and manageable pieces with timetables that were, for once, probably accurate.

"You still feeling okay about the whole thing, then?"

"Yeah. So far."

"Tom, safe landing to you."

"You, too, Malcolm. See you tomorrow night."

Dunn glanced up. The full moon was rising over the hanger and he stared at its beauty as he walked back to his team. It wasn't the right time of year for a harvest moon back home, that wouldn't be until late August, six weeks away. He'd always loved watching the orange globe come up over the seven-foot corn. With a pang of regret, he suddenly realized he and Pamela had never gone out late at night. He wished she was here with him, or maybe he with her at her parents' farm, to enjoy the view. He was reluctant to allow his feeling for Pamela take their head, but he knew deep down he was hooked.

On more than one occasion, his dad, who'd married Mrs. Dunn when he was only twenty, and she eighteen, said he must have been extremely smart at such a young age, to have recognized this woman as the one for him. The marriage had obviously taken, since their thirtieth anniversary was coming up soon. Dunn pictured himself at the age of fifty-four, along with Pamela, and smiled.

"What are you grinning about, Sergeant?" asked a voice near

by.

Dunn jerked in surprise and stopped walking. Colonel Kenton had evidently been waiting for him and Dunn nearly wandered right into him. They exchanged salutes.

"Sorry, Colonel. Just thinking."

"Quite all right. Everything all set?"

"Yes, sir."

"I just wanted to stop by and wish you and your men good luck."

"Thanks. I appreciate that."

"This one has the makings of a rough one, you know."

Dunn nodded. "We'll do our best, sir."

"That goes without saying in my book. I just worry."

Dunn gave the Colonel a slight smile. "Got a little mother hen in you, these days, sir?"

Kenton sighed. "I suppose so. I've discovered that staying behind is a lot harder than I ever thought it would be." He looked out at the airplanes for a long moment, then faced Dunn. "In a way, I wish I was going with you. Did you know I used to coach my son's baseball teams?"

"No, sir, I didn't."

"Until he was about fourteen, I did. Loved it. Love the game, love the kids. Great time of my life. But the difference between coaching baseball and watching you guys from the sidelines is, at least in baseball, I could give signs during the game, make key decisions, that sort of thing, but with you, once that plane takes off, I can't do anything for you." Kenton frowned. "It's a helpless feeling."

Dunn saw the deep pain written on Kenton's face and felt sorry for the man. It *would* be a helpless feeling. "I understand, sir. I hope it helps for you to know that we appreciate everything you do for us."

"I know you do. Hey, do you remember me talking about my son going to West Point?" asked Kenton.

Dunn nodded. "Sure. He got the appointment?"

Kenton gave Dunn the smile only proud fathers wear. "Yes, he reports in the fall."

"Following in your footsteps."

"And his grandfather's. We're enormously proud of him. Of

course, my wife is scared to death." He paused, his gaze flicking away briefly, before returning to Dunn's face. "Truth is, so am I. Just between us, I pray every day that this war is long over before he ever sees active duty."

Dunn put his hand on his superior officer's shoulder. "Sir, I'd say the same prayer if I was in your shoes. I don't blame you a bit. Let's hope we're in Berlin for Christmas."

Kenton smiled and stuck out his hand. "Thanks."

Dunn grasped the hand. "You're welcome, sir."

"I'll be off. See you soon."

Kenton started to turn away, to go back to the main building, but Dunn said, "Colonel?"

Kenton stopped. "Yes?"

"I wonder if you'd do something for me if, um, if anything should happen to me."

Kenton frowned. "Tom, you shouldn't talk like that."

"I wouldn't normally, you know I wouldn't, but I've met a girl."

The Colonel lifted his chin, acknowledging this disclosure. "Go on."

"Her name's Pamela. Pamela Hardwicke, with an 'e,' and she's a nurse over at the base hospital. Her parents live south of Andover. If things look . . . bad, could you just keep her informed?"

Kenton examined Dunn's face and saw pain. "Of course, I'll do that for you, if you're sure."

Dunn's lips compressed as he reined in his emotions, then he said, "I'm sure. Thanks, Colonel."

"You're welcome." Kenton turned and walked away.

Dunn took a couple of deep breaths, then rejoined his teammates, who remained as quiet as before.

Captain Miller stepped into the pilot's ready room and headed for the front. The seven men waiting for him clustered together in a semi-circle of wooden folding chairs, talking casually.

After the terrible loss of Murphy and Thompson over Göttingen, Miller had drawn two replacement pilots from the 363rd squadron. Both were highly rated and one was just one enemy plane shy of the ace status. Miller had more confidence in them than was usual for new pilots.

The men stopped talking when Miller reached them. Each had a lot of respect for their commander. He was tough, but fair and their safety was always his number one concern. He also acted as a buffer whenever the brass got their collective noses in a twit.

"Let's go over the mission one more time, men." Even though Miller had already gone over it twice, earlier in the day, he was a creature of habit and that habit was to go over the mission with his men just before they took off. He pointed to the map of Europe hanging on the wall. "We're escorting two C-47's into Germany. They're going to land at German airfields. The men will exit the planes, conduct their top secret mission, then get back on the planes, which will be staying on the ground. We escort them back here before daylight.

"Flight B, that's my group will escort the plane going to Göttingen. We'll be traveling up the Channel to the border of Holland and Germany, then across to the target. But there will have to be a jog in the flight path to go around the flak fields, the ones that got Murphy." He traced the route with a finger as he spoke.

The men nodded their understanding.

"Does anyone need to see the photos of the airfield?"

"No, Cap, we've got it," said Tommy Hayes.

"Good. It's a long airstrip and should be clearly visible in the moonlight. By the way, we have confirmation of clear skies over both targets.

"Flight A is going to Stuttgart. You'll be following a path that'll take you along the border between France and Belgium, then France and Germany, then over to the target."

"Our primary role while the Gooneys are in the air is to keep them safe from German night fighters. We haven't had many reports of the little bastards being up there lately, but we'll have to stay sharp. It's unlikely the Germans would bother sending up any 109s or 190s for a single flight. Not since they've started losing so many just trying to keep the big boys out.

"But, once the planes are on the ground, our role changes to one of pure air cover and it's going to be harder than hell. We can't possibly see any German soldiers on the ground unless a firefight develops, so we'll have to be extra vigilant. The

Gooneys will be monitoring the frequency and they will have the freedom to take off without their passengers if they believe their plane is in danger of being captured or destroyed.

"That will, of course, put the commandos at terrible risk. Gentlemen, we will not permit that, so we're going to be the best we've ever been tonight. Is that perfectly clear?"

A chorus of 'yes, sirs' filled the room.

Satisfied, Miller said, "Let's go then." He checked his watch. "Wheels up in twenty minutes." As he watched his men leave the room, Miller ran over his idea one more time and prayed it would work.

The C-47 carrying Dunn's team trundled down the tarmac, its twin engines roaring. When she reached the proper speed, Captain Pierce pulled back on the yoke and she lifted into the air. The plane yawed to the left, akin to an automobile's skid on a slick road, and Pierce feathered the rudder pedals to get her back on a straight line. The C-47 continued to rise smoothly and he banked left to come around in a half circle to head east. As they came back alongside the runway he glanced down. The Mustangs were taking off in single line, instead of in pairs, for night safety, and he knew they'd be on his wing tips in a matter of minutes. The C-47 flew at less than half the speed of the bullet-nosed P-51. Pierce thought their pilots probably felt like a jockey riding the fastest race horse in the world.

Sure enough, two minutes later, the leader's silver plane slid up into position just off the port wing. Pierce flipped on the cockpit's lights and saluted the other pilot. Immediately, the wings waggled twice in return. Pierce turned off the lights and settled in for the long ride.

34

The Horten Brothers Airfield
South of Göttingen
19 June, 0232 Hours

The British team's pilot and copilot scanned the ground 10,000 feet below. In the bright moonlight, the runway would appear as a thin white pencil and according to the Mustang pilot, Miller, it ran north-south. A few minutes and another six or so miles later, the copilot said, "There it is." He pointed. Sure enough, the little ribbon of white was just coming into view a bit to the starboard, his side of the plane.

The pilot turned to the jumpmaster, who was crouching behind and between the two cockpit seats. Even though the team would not be jumping, it seemed prudent to bring the man along. Just in case. "Tell the men we should be landing in a few minutes. Make sure they're buckled in."

The jumpmaster patted the pilot on the shoulder to acknowledge the request and headed into the back of the plane.

The pilot glanced out his sliding window and was comforted to see the two Mustangs trailing his left wing. He knew the other two would be on the other side. To his copilot, he said, "Make sure the little friends on your side see the signal."

"Okay." The copilot turned his head to watch the pair of planes on his side.

Since they were under radio silence and he couldn't just pick up the radio to tell them he was landing, the pilot used the pre-arranged signal of the old standby, wing waggles. A moment later all of the Mustangs returned the signal. You couldn't just prepare for landing and not tell your escorts. The moment you lowered your landing gear and flaps, and your airspeed dropped forty knots, the escorts would zip ahead of you.

The lumbering C-47 floated downward, somehow looking graceful. The big wheels touched the runway at exactly the spot the pilot had selected. A small screech echoed as the rubber hit the pavement. The plane rolled down the concrete strip and came to a stop at about three quarters the way down the runway. She turned slowly to the left, wheeling around to face the way she had come from, and her propellers stopped turning.

The Mustangs, staying at a thousand feet, flew past. Miller was satisfied that the Gooney had landed safely. They would circle like parent eagles, keeping close watch over their eaglets.

Even before the plane came to a complete stop, the jumpmaster unlocked the door and the men unbuckled and got to their feet. They loaded their gear on their backs and when the door flew open, Saunders jumped out onto German soil for the first time. He took off, running as fast he could to get off the bright runway, then he squatted down in the nice dark grass, his weapon at the ready. His men jumped onto the ground and ran, their rubber soled boots silent. They caught up to Saunders and fanned out, putting him in the middle.

Saunders peered at the dark hanger, still a hundred yards away. No light seeped out; the Germans would be using blackout curtains. There was no way to know what awaited them inside. In the moonlight, he could make out the shape of the hanger door, which was huge, and a smaller door for people to its right.

He was about to give the advance signal when the smaller door opened and a soldier stepped out. Dim light from inside threw him in shadow. Soon he was followed by three more. It was clear they'd heard the plane's engines. The first soldier leaned back into the doorway and six more men came out. At the leader's command, the Germans fanned out and knelt, weapons up. The leader lifted a pair of binoculars and trained them on the C-47 at the end of the runway. At another signal, five men rose to a crouch and started running toward the plane. They were moving left-to-right from Saunders' perspective.

When the group made it about thirty yards they knelt and trained their weapons on the C-47, while the second group rose and started to move so as to leapfrog the first team's position. Standard cover and move tactics.

Saunders waited until the moving group was almost on a direct line with Saunders' men and the first group, then called out, "Fire!"

Two Germans fell in the onslaught, but the rest dove into the ground for cover and began firing back. After about thirty seconds it became obvious to both sides that nothing good was coming from the exchange of fire and a kind of status quo developed and firing ceased.

Saunders thought furiously, searching for an advantage. The two units were close in size, Saunders' seven to the Germans' eight. Both were outside with no cover. Now it would become a matter of who blinked first, the German or British squad leader.

Suddenly, a flare shot into the sky. Saunders looked to his right and saw it had originated from where the C-47 sat, engines idling. The scream of Merlin engines pierced the air. Then came the unmistakable deadly chatter of .50 caliber machine guns. Tracers darted earthward. The Germans had no chance, caught in the open and illuminated. The sounds of the four Merlins faded and the night grew silent. The flare burned out. Saunders rose carefully and signaled his men on the right to advance on the Germans. He fired a shot in the Germans' direction, but there was no answer. Turning to his left, Saunders called out, "Fire." Three more machine guns opened up as the other half of the squad, led by Corporal Barltrop, crouch-ran the remaining distance.

They quickly determined all the enemy soldiers were dead, chewed to pieces by the Mustangs' half-inch shells. Barltrop gave a sharp whistle. Saunders rose and led the remaining members of the team to the hanger.

Even after seeing the pictures, Saunders was astonished by

the hanger's size. It was like standing next to the Parliament Building. He shoved the people door open and stepped inside, followed by his three men. Barltrop had his team spread out near the door. They were to wait until they got the all clear before going in.

Saunders and his men quickly checked the office, then found the door leading into the hanger. Saunders turned the knob, opened the door and slid through. And saw . . . nothing.

35

Project Dante Lab
19 June, 0233 Hours

The lab was deserted, a night off arranged by Dr. Herbert who had told everyone they deserved a break before the final push to completion. There had been no argument; all were exhausted. The physicist walked the dimly lit hallway from the conference room to his office, shoulders hunched from fatigue. It had been quite some time since he last stayed this late. He struggled to remember when that was, then realized it was during the before time. The time when he believed in the project, no questions, no doubts, just follow the *Führer*, literally.

His sabotage of the fast neutron calculations had gone undetected, as he was certain it would, since no one had expressed any interest in checking his work. He knew he was committing treason and Hitler's preferred punishment for traitors was hanging by wire. This meant strangling and kicking for five minutes while being filmed for the madman to watch later for his own pleasure.

He reached his office and pulled a keychain from his pants pocket. The keychain was from the before time, a token gift from the physics department head at the university. It was a gold eagle grasping a silver swastika in its talons. Herbert rummaged through the keys, found the one he wanted and inserted it in the lock. As he turned the key, he thought he heard a noise from somewhere farther down the hall and glanced that way, but saw no one. He shrugged, thinking, I'm tired, that's all.

Opening the door, he stepped through, pausing to flip on the light switch. Unlike most scientists, Herbert kept his office in an immaculate state. The heavy metal desk, which faced the door, was clear of papers and the floor was uncluttered. Some wooden file cabinets filled the wall on the doctor's left and a long table sat against the opposite side.

Herbert walked around his desk and plopped down in the chair, tossing the heavy keychain onto the desk, where it landed with a clunk. Leaning forward, he put his elbows on the desk, his head in his hands, and closed his eyes, rubbing them with the heels of his hands. It felt as though someone had poured sand in his eyes. He sat still, resting, and after a short catnap, he swept his hands through his hair and took a deep breath.

What was he doing here? What was he trying to accomplish? These were questions he asked himself now and often in recent weeks. The thing that had, years ago, drawn him to physics was the beauty of science, the sheer perfection and order it offered. It was comforting, reliable, predictable. As the years passed, he also grew to love the problem solving aspects of science, of starting with a premise and setting out, not to prove it, but to disprove it; the scientific method. Then, when one couldn't disprove the theory, one had the makings of a discovery. Discovery was his goal when he joined the project, even though he'd known what it would lead to. Death and destruction.

But he'd accepted it. He understood his nation's survival was in his team's hands and that made it possible for him to push the nightmarish thoughts into the recesses of his consciousness. But now, with the invasion of Europe and the failure of the bastard Göring's Luftwaffe to protect the cities of Germany and her mothers and children, the war was already lost, but no one was doing anything to end it. He could end it. All he had to do was correct his fast neutron calculations, let the bomb be finished and sent on its way to America. It would all be over. But at what price? No. He would not be the cause of the deaths of millions. He would stick to the plan and ensure the bomb would never work.

Satisfied with his decision, he picked up the keychain and selected a small brass key. He leaned over to slide the key into the top-right drawer's lock, and froze. The keyhole was already turned to the unlocked position. He grabbed the drawer's handle and yanked it open. As he looked inside, he gave a sigh of relief. The folder was there. He must have forgotten to lock the drawer. As he lifted the folder out and placed it on the desktop, a sudden, slight noise just outside the door startled him. It sounded like the scrape of a shoe on the tile. Jumping out of his chair, he ran to the door and put a trembling hand on the knob. What's the matter with me? There's no one here. He turned the knob and pushed the door open a crack. He couldn't see anyone down the hallway on the half that was visible from his vantage point. He opened the door a little farther and poked his head out to look down the opposite way. Nothing. He chuckled at his nervousness, and shut the door, then returned to his chair.

He opened the folder and his heart stopped. Lying on top of the first page was a folded piece of yellow paper. His hands shook as he unfolded the paper. He read the note written in big block letters. His hands went numb and the paper slipped from them, falling onto the desk.

In the bright office light, the words stared up at Herbert accusingly:

YOUR TOMBSTONE WILL READ: HERE LIES A TRAITOR TO THE FATHERLAND.

LONG LIVE THE *FÜHRER. HEIL* HITLER!

36

Abandoned German Airfield
6 miles south of Project Dante Lab
19 June, 0234 Hours

Like Saunders, Dunn was first out of the plane and onto the deserted runway. Moments later, a pair of masked lights flashed twice, as expected. Dunn fought the urge to remain concealed and flashed his penlight twice in reply, praying it was the British agent in the vehicle. The sound of the powerful truck engine starting wafted across the dark distance. Slivers of lights appeared and began to creep toward the Americans. The truck stopped ten feet from Dunn and his team, facing the same way as the plane. The driver turned off the engine and silence settled over them.

A decidedly English accent drifted out of the truck's darkened cab. "I've never understood baseball."

"We'd love to take you to a game."

Marston jumped down out of the truck and, even though he'd given the password, it startled the Americans to see a Waffen-SS Colonel striding toward them. A few weapon barrels were lifted.

"Marston?"

"Aye. Are you Dunn?"

"Yes, sir."

The men shook hands.

"Let's get you all into the truck. Sergeant, why don't you ride up front with me so we can make sure we're in agreement on the plan."

"Yes, sir." Dunn turned to the team and said softly, "Load up, boys."

Cross took the lead and the men went to the back of the truck. Ward pulled open the canvas flap and dropped the tailgate. They spent the next five minutes loading the crates of explosives, then finally they tossed their personal gear in, and climbed in. Cross pushed the gate up. A hand reached down out of the cave-like darkness and Cross grabbed it, put one foot on the steel bumper, then jumped up and in.

Marston and Dunn were already in the truck's cab when someone pounded the back of the cab, signaling okay. The fake Colonel started the truck, switched on the lights, and pulled away from the C-47. He guided the truck off the runway and onto the service road that wrapped around the hangers, barracks and the administration building. A hundred yards farther on, the road led into the forest and the moon disappeared from view under the canopy of trees. Marston kept his eyes on the road as he spoke, "Sergeant, I trust you had an uneventful flight."

"Yes, we did. It was a little weird landing in an airplane for once, though. Can't say I liked the feeling."

Marston chuckled. "Yes, I see your point."

"Hope your wait wasn't too unbearable."

"Oh, you know, sitting around after midnight at a deserted German airfield, alone with the night sounds. Makes for an interesting evening for someone who's afraid of the dark."

It was Dunn's turn to laugh. "Yes, indeed."

"We're about ten minutes from the lab's entrance road. The main compound area isn't well lit. Here's my suggestion . . ."

37

The Horten Brothers Airfield
5 miles south of Göttingen
19 June, 0236 Hours

Miller lined up over the runway and pointed his ship's nose down. He would be coming in right over the top of the parked C-47, flying the opposite way to make sure he had plenty of room and wouldn't collide with the Gooney Bird. As he roared over the C-47, he could imagine the expressions of the two pilots on board. He doubted they would be happy. Thankfully they'd fired the flare on his request. After seeing the firefight from a thousand feet, he knew he needed to get his flight involved in the fight.

Saunders couldn't believe it. No wait, there at the far end. A black shape. Some moonlight seeped in through windows in the roof and his eyes made out the swept-back wings. He ran to it, relieved to see the German airplane's familiar form. He darted back to the office where Brisdon was waiting. "Get the—" The sound of a P-51 flying at low level and low speed interrupted him. "What the hell? Get out there and see what the fuck's going on."

Brisdon nodded. Several minutes passed, then he returned with Miller in tow. Miller stepped around the British soldier to face a bewildered Saunders.

"What the hell are you doing on the ground?" Saunders eyed Miller, then belatedly realizing it must have been Miller who had led the attack on the Germans, held up a hand. "First, thanks for lending a hand, sir. We were pretty jammed up at the moment."

Miller nodded, "I sure thought so. Glad it worked out right."

Saunders stuck out his big paw and Miller shook it.

The big Brit said, "What *are* you doing on the ground, sir?"

"I have an idea and I'd appreciate it if you'd hear me out."

Saunders' lips tightened for a moment, then he said, "Uh, oh." He sighed. "Okay. What is it? We're on a short timetable, you know."

Miller nodded. "I know. Look, we have an unprecedented opportunity here. Just think what it would mean to the Allied Air Forces if, instead of blowing up the plane, we uh, well, we took it home with us."

Saunders didn't say anything for a long moment and Miller wondered whether the man had actually heard what he said. He started to repeat himself when the sergeant said, "You're kidding, right? Dunn put you up to this, didn't he?"

Miller stared at Saunders. "What? What? No, I . . . no, Dunn didn't. This is my idea. All we have to do is fly the Hortens' plane out of here and let our guys take a look at her. Come on, it's a jet bomber and we don't have anything like it."

"You mean steal it?"

"Well, yeah, of course I mean steal it, what the hell else would it be?"

"You think you can fly this thing?"

"It's worth a try."

Saunders shook his head. "No. We can't do that. We have our orders. We'll all end up in the brig."

"No you won't. I might, but you won't."

"How do you mean?"

"I'm the ranking person here. I can order you to assist me in my plan. Besides, I'm not too shy to play the 'You owe me card.'" Miller smiled.

A snort jumped out of Saunders' mouth. "Of course. You're

nuts. Sir. You're not even in the chain of command. You have no authority here and you're wasting my time." He turned away, but Miller grabbed his muscular shoulder, spinning him around, and stepped close.

Miller whispered, "Saunders, I'm serious. If we get this baby back home and figure out how to build our own, we could shorten the war. The Luftwaffe fighters wouldn't be able to catch the planes and that would save countless airmen's lives. What's there to lose? If we can't get her in the air, we'll blow her up. If I can't fly her and crash, it'll be the same result as setting those charges right here." Miller shrugged. "Any way you look at it, we have to at least try."

Saunders peered at Miller for a moment. "Why didn't you bring this up at the briefing?"

Miller chuckled wryly. "Are you crazy? They'd have grounded me for sure and probably sent me to the company psychologist."

Saunders laughed lightly. "Maybe that've been better for you. What makes you think you can fly it?"

"There's probably a checklist in the cockpit. All we have to do is use that, fuel her up and pull her out to the runway."

"I hate to remind you, mate, but we're in Germany and that checklist is going to be in German."

"That's okay, I can read German." Miller went on to explain his heritage.

Saunders nodded. "Jesus Christ, I can't believe I'm agreeing with you." He checked his watch. "We have to get started. It'll be daylight in about two hours and we'd better be out of here before that."

Miller breathed a sigh of relief. The hard part was done, now all he had to do was do what he said he could do. He pulled a piece of paper and a pencil from his jacket pocket. "Shine your light on this for me." Saunders pointed his penlight at the paper. Miller hurriedly scribbled something, then handed the paper to Saunders. "Have your men look around at the fuel trucks and find the one with this word on it."

Saunders look at the paper and said, "*Strahl?*"

"Yes, that's 'jet.'"

Saunders nodded. "Got it."

38

Project Dante Lab
19 June, 0243 Hours

Dr. Herbert fought to control his panic. As he rummaged through his top desk drawer, he regretted his directive of a couple of years ago that no firearms would be allowed within the lab itself. God, I need some protection. He slammed the drawer closed in disgust, then his gaze settled on a gold letter opener, a gift from his wife some years ago. Snatching the opener, he gripped it like a sword, thrusting the point out in front of himself. He yanked his brown briefcase off the desktop and it almost dragged him down; he'd shoved as many important papers into it as possible.

Herbert ran to the door, flipping the lights off, before slowly opening it. He peered into the hallway, checking both directions. Seeing no one, he skittered through the door, not bothering to close and lock it. He wasn't coming back. His mind raced as he ran down the hallway toward the lab's main elevator. If he could just somehow make it out of Stuttgart and head west. Maybe he could make contact with the French Resistance once he reached

France. He spoke excellent French, finding a similar pleasure in learning it that science provided, another challenge. Unfortunately, he did speak French with a German accent. Would they help him escape the clutches of his own countrymen, who occupied their country, or just kill him? He didn't even know whether it was safe to go back to his apartment. He tried to determine if there was anything there he truly needed. He had some money on him, maybe it would be enough, he didn't know. What a mess. He reached the elevator and punched the up call button. Please. Hurry, just this once.

Marston stopped the truck after he turned onto the lab's paved road. Dunn hopped out and ran around to the back, climbing in with a helping hand. Another pat on the cab and Marston eased the truck into gear and it lumbered down the road.

Marston spotted the sentry standing in a circle of light by the gate. The soldier seemed alert, facing the truck as it neared his position. His rifle was slung over his shoulder. Perhaps that was a good sign. Taking a deep breath, Marston stopped the truck, leaving the engine idling.

The guard, a boy of maybe seventeen, stared up with what he must have thought was a tough expression. Holding his hand out, thinking he was talking to a lowly driver, he snapped, "Give me your papers. Why the hell are you arriving at this time of night?"

Marston leaned closer to the window so the light touched him, especially his officer's hat. "I'm here now because I'm supposed to be here now, private."

The boy's reaction was the same as the grizzled sergeant at the motor pool. Marston thought for a minute the boy was going to faint.

"I, I'm sorry, Colonel. I didn't know." The private gave the papers a cursory glance and handed them back. He made a motion as though getting ready to move toward the gate and open it.

Marston knew that just wouldn't do. "Private!"

The boy stopped. "Yes, sir?" His fear of the Waffen-SS Colonel was still etched on his face.

"Aren't you going to inspect the back of the truck?"

The private was stuck. He was required to inspect every

vehicle coming in and going out, but he'd assumed the colonel would become furious if he asked to do that. He was worried the colonel would report his lapse. He couldn't afford another bad mark on his record; he might end up fighting the Americans instead of being safe, here in Germany. "Yes, sir, of course, sir."

In the outside mirror, Marston watched the boy walk to his death feeling no guilt. The truck suddenly swayed slightly, then moments later, Patrick Ward stood outside the driver's door wearing the poor boy's hat and jacket. "Okay, Colonel, I'm going to open the gate."

Marston nodded.

Ward pushed the heavy gate open and stood aside as the truck rumbled through, heading for the lab entrance, a hundred yards away. He closed the gate and glanced at the barracks for any signs of activity, but it remained dark.

At the next sentry's station, events unfolded the same way as before and now all that remained was neutralizing the barracks. Marston backed the truck around so it faced the gate. After shutting off the engine, he got out, walked around to the back, and lowered the gate. Cross and Wickham jumped down and the others began handing down the crates of explosives. When that task was done, Daniel Morris and Jack Hanson leaped out and Morris opened one of the crates. He pulled out two satchel charges, some detonators and two timers. He handed over what Hanson needed and they took off at a run toward the barracks. When they got close, they slowed to a walk, praying their footsteps on the hard packed dirt were quiet enough.

The barracks looked like a box on stilts with a convenient two foot crawl space underneath. The men split up, each going to a corner of the building. Morris inserted a detonator into the compound explosives, set the timer and connected the wires, then started the clock. He glanced down the building's front and could make out Hanson's kneeling shape at the far corner.

Morris slid under the corner of the barracks and pushed the satchel as far as he could. When he got out from underneath, he knelt, waiting for Hanson, who had also disappeared. Hanson suddenly popped out and trotted over to him. They made their way back to the truck, where Dunn clapped them on the shoulders.

"All set, then?"

"Yes, Sarge."

"Good. Let's get on the other side of the truck." When they got around to relative safety, Dunn opened the door and pulled the light switch on and off twice. In the distance, he could see Ward get down behind the small guard shack. Dunn checked his watch. "Two minutes, men, better get down."

Dunn peeked around the around truck bumper. What he saw made his knees go weak. A soldier had opened the door. The light behind him turned his shape black. He saw the truck, then disappeared from view for a moment. He returned to the door carrying a rifle. The German went down the stairs and headed toward the waiting invaders.

Dr. Herbert thought the elevator would never get there and kept glancing over his shoulder while waiting. Finally, the doors opened. He fairly jumped in and pushed the button to go to the ground floor, three levels above him. He wiped the sweat off his face with the sleeve of his white lab coat. He was glad his wife was in Berlin. At least she would be spared the ignominy of witnessing his arrest. Life would be different for her after word of his arrest spread. Then he thought about her fawning over Hitler and her socialite attitude. He decided he didn't care. It would serve her right. A self-satisfying smile touched his otherwise terrified features.

The elevator doors opened again and as he stepped out, the floor shook and the sound of thunder reached his ears. Except he knew you couldn't hear thunder in the lab.

39

Outside Project Dante Lab
19 June, 0248 Hours

The world brightened and rumbled. The German soldier flung himself to the ground as pieces of burning wood shards began crashing around him. He rolled over and stared back at where the barracks used to be, mouth agape. Now it was a flaming hole, no sign of a building remained except for a couple of the stilts that looked like giant toothpicks stabbed into the ground. His instincts took over and his rifle barrel swung toward the truck.

Dunn was ready and fired a short burst. The German collapsed, the rifle falling from his lifeless hands.

Ward was on his feet and running full tilt toward the rest of his team.

Dunn turned to his men, "Everyone okay?"

The men jumped to their feet and nodded in response.

Marston walked to the lab's door, a large steel monstrosity with a wheel instead of a knob. The thing looks more like a bank vault than a door, thought the British agent, as he put his hand on the wheel. He looked over his shoulder at Dunn and said, "Ready,

Sergeant?"

Dunn, who was right behind said, "Let's go."

Marston spun the wheel and when it stopped, pulled the handle. A thunking sound came from inside the steel and the door started moving. Marston knew to stand aside, lest he be caught and perhaps crushed as the door's mass continued swinging toward the wall on their left. Light flared out from the interior. Marston twisted to peer inside. A white shape launched itself at him with a terrifying cry. Marston felt something pierce deep into his upper chest. A shriek of pain escaped his lips and he fell backwards, landing hard on his right side.

A shocked Herbert dropped his briefcase and stared open-mouthed at Marston. Cross, the closest to Dunn and Marston, raised his Thompson, but seeing the shaking man had no other weapon and didn't seem to be a threat any longer, lowered the machine gun.

Dunn was already working fast. He knelt by Marston and pulled the letter opener out, but only after checking for bubbling froth around the wound to make sure it hadn't gone into the left lung. He opened Marston's uniform jacket and shirt to expose the wound. Pulling a sulfur packet from his first aid kit, he snapped it open, then poured the contents onto the wound. Next was a four-square bandage, which he opened and slapped in place, pushing hard to stop the bleeding. Marston groaned.

As Dunn glanced up at Herbert, the German scientist's eyes widened. "Americans? Oh, God, thank you." Herbert stared down at Dunn, then swallowed. "Why are you bothering with that scum? Let him die." His tone dripped with hatred.

Dunn was surprised by the expression on the man's face, which matched the tone. This German scientist wanted Marston to die. What the hell? But he didn't have time for whatever was troubling the white-coated, white-haired old man. "Wickham, Ward, finish up with Marston and get him into the truck. Wickham, you stay with him and keep your eyes open for company."

Dunn got up and grabbed Herbert by the lapels. "Who are you?"

"I'm Dr. Franz Herbert. I work in the lab. What are you doing here?"

Dunn gave the smaller man a steely look. "What do you think we're here for?"

Even though Herbert was frightened, he was no idiot. He noted the crates on the ground, the heavily armed men in front of him, the German Army truck a few feet away, the injured German officer. It clicked in a matter of seconds. "Oh dear, what have I done? I'm so sorry. He's on your side, isn't he? You're here to destroy the bomb."

Dunn let go of Herbert, but didn't answer right away.

His silence was answer enough. Herbert plucked at Dunn's sleeve and turned to go back in the lab. "Come. I can you show the best places to plant your explosives. What kind do you have?"

Dunn and Cross exchanged glances. Cross's right eyebrow lifted slightly and he tilted his head as if to say, why not?

"Dr. Herbert, why should we trust you?"

Herbert lifted the heavy brown leather satchel. "Because I have all of our plans for the atomic bomb in here. And I've been sabotaging the project for the last few months." A terrified look came over his face. "Someone found me out and left me a threatening note. I was running for my life when I ran into," he glanced over at Marston, who was breathing heavily and sweating, "this poor man." He looked at Dunn, his eyes pleading. "Please, we must hurry."

Dunn examined the doctor's face for a long time. Either he's the best actor around or he's truly scared to death. Dunn knew the place was huge and haphazard placement might not destroy everything. They planned to size things up carefully, then make the best guess, being sure to heavily load the entrance to bring the hillside down. "Mark, how long do you think we have before company arrives? Or will it?"

"There're no flames left, the building's gone. The Germans would have to have been paying close attention to identify the location. Chances are they'll just think it's another night air raid."

"Perhaps. All right, gentlemen, we're going to follow the doctor's suggestion." Dunn looked at the small group of men around him and suddenly wished he had twice as many. Counting himself, there were now only five men to carry and place all of the explosives. Jesus Christ, what was he thinking? He suddenly realized he'd never answered Herbert's question. "Dr. Herbert, you asked what kind of explosives we're using. Why?"

Herbert gave Dunn a professorial look as if saying, don't you know? "That'll help us determine the best place to put them."

Dunn understood, but thought most explosives were created equal. "We're using the British Nobel 808."

Herbert's eyebrows rose approvingly. "Ach. Excellent." Nobel 808 was made by the Nobel Chemical Company, which Alfred Nobel, the inventor of dynamite, created. "That will do nicely. You see, that has an extremely high detonation velocity. Let me see, now," Herbert paused, thinking. "Yes, it's almost 9,000 meters per second. That's two thousand meters per second faster than dynamite and that means . . ." Dr. Herbert stopped his dissertation and gave Dunn an apologetic look. "Sorry, you probably don't care about the physics associated with an explosive, provided it does explode. No?" Before Dunn could answer, the doctor grasped Dunn's sleeve and pulled. Hard. "Come, we must get started."

Dunn turned to Ward and Wickham. "You guys ready to move Marston?"

"Yes, Sarge," said Wickham. Then he and Ward lifted Marston and carried him to the back of the truck. They slid Marston in headfirst, then Wickham climbed in and knelt beside the injured man. He put a hand on Marston's good shoulder, "Sir, you're going to be all right. I know it hurts, but the blade missed all the important stuff."

"I guess that's the good news, huh?" Marston said weakly.

"Yes, sir. I'm going to give you an ampoule of morphine to lessen the pain. It should help real quick."

"You're the doctor."

"I am, indeed."

Marston blinked slowly as the drug began circulating through his veins. "You have . . . an interest . . . ing accent."

"So I've been told. Texas and British."

"Yes, that's what I would . . . have . . ." Marston's eyes closed.

After leaving Wickham to stand guard and also keep an eye on Marston, Dunn led his team of Ward, Morris, Hanson, and Cross into the depths of the German facility. They all struggled to keep up with the excited German scientist as he sped down the corridor. Dunn was surprised by how fast the older man was moving. They passed a crossroads of another perpendicular hallway. Dunn glanced down both ways. The end of the hallways were at least a hundred feet in either direction.

Herbert kept up a running commentary. "It's not important that we destroy the whole place, although that might happen. Let's see, now if I just had the time to do some calculations, but no, we'd better not stop that long. I'll take you to the most critical places."

Dunn tapped Herbert on the shoulder. "Doc, can't you just tell us how to get to the places? We're on a short time table here."

"No, you need keys to get in."

"Doc, we've got our own keys." Dunn held up his Thompson.

Sudden understanding crossed Herbert's face. "Of course, how stupid of me. You understand that this complex is vast, don't you?"

Dunn nodded. "We guessed it would be."

"How were you going to place your charges if we hadn't met?"

Dunn mulled over whether to give a straight answer for a moment, then decided it couldn't hurt anything. "We had some intelligence that gave us some things to look for."

It was Herbert's turn to nod. "Yes, I see. That makes sense, except that would have taken you hours, maybe until morning and that's too long. The folks start arriving at 5:00 A.M. With my help, you'll be able to set them in less than an hour and then we can be on our way."

Dunn stopped walking and Herbert turned to see where his new partner had gone. "Dr. Herbert, you said 'we'." Herbert's expression turned sad for a fleeting moment and Dunn thought perhaps he'd imagined it.

"I want you, I need you to take me out of here. Take me back to England. If you don't, I'll be dead in a week or less."

Oh, sweet Jesus. First, I have a seriously injured man to take care of and now we'd have to baby-sit an old man. It wasn't a matter of room, the C-47 could hold three times their number. But civilians had a tendency to create problems even when they meant well. A hand touched Dunn on the shoulder.

"Please. I have nothing to stay for anymore."

"Okay, Doc. You're coming with us." I hope to God I don't regret this.

Herbert gave Dunn a hug and a single tear slipped down his cheek. "Thank you, Sergeant. Thank you."

Dunn patted the man on the back and the men behind him, who had stopped walking during the little exchange, looked on in surprise. Cross and Morris glanced at each other and Morris shrugged.

Herbert let go of Dunn and said, "The complex has three main levels. We're on the top level. All of the important research and the bomb itself is on the third level." They turned a corner and he pointed. "We can take the elevator down."

Dunn eyed the elevator door, twenty feet distant. An alarm was dinging in his head. "Doc? How about some stairs, instead?"

"You want to walk down, carrying those things?" Herbert pointed at the crates.

"Elevators have a bad habit of not working at just the wrong moment."

"Oh. I didn't think of that. Yes, of course, this way." He led them past the silver sliding doors and stopped at a recess in the corridor wall. He opened the large green door and entered the stairwell.

They made their way to the third level and exited into another corridor, that, to Dunn's eyes looked exactly like the one they'd just left. No, the walls are a different color. These were light blue and the first level had been a pale green. Leave it to the Germans to color code their floors.

Herbert opened the conference room door and turned on the lights. He grabbed a small stack of white paper off the top of a gray metal file cabinet and put it on a gray metal table. He leaned over the paper and began drawing with a stubby pencil. Dunn and the others formed a circle around the lab-coated man. Herbert's hand moved quickly; it was obvious he had the layout of the entire complex committed to memory.

After five minutes, Herbert leaned back. Dunn examined the drawing. It looked like an architect had drawn it. Herbert had circled and labeled two "Xs" with the numbers one and two.

Dunn glanced up at the doctor with a smile.

Herbert chuckled. "X marks the spot, eh?"

"The numbers are for priority?"

"Very good, Sergeant." Herbert nodded enthusiastically. "Number one is where we keep the bomb and the enriched uranium. It's U-235, which we get from the painstaking process of taking U-238—"

Dunn held up a hand. "Doc. Not now, okay?"

Herbert shook his head. "Sorry. Once a teacher, always a teacher." He looked down at the drawing, then back at Dunn. "Can your men find number two while I go with you to number one?"

Dunn frowned. "Well, sure, but why do you need to go with me?"

The physicist slapped his forehead. "Ach, of course, you don't know. The uranium gives off an invisible poison, radiation, like an X-Ray, but lethal. A large enough dose creates radiation poisoning and it can kill a man in days. It's a horrible, agonizing death. We had an accident and lost one man early on in the project. It was awful. We call it Project Dante, by the way."

Dunn lifted one eyebrow and his lip twitched.

"What is it?"

"Our mission has a similar name."

"Oh. The main thing is, you must be protected when near the uranium. I plan for you to plant an explosive in the room where it's stored. I want to make sure it's sealed in its lead containers before you go in there." Herbert saw confusion on Dunn's face and explained, "Lead stops the radiation.

"The second X is where all of the project documents are kept, except for some that I stuffed into my briefcase."

"Okay." Dunn quickly gave his orders. Hanson and Ward would go with Cross to "X" number two, and Morris would accompany Dunn and the doctor. He checked his watch: 0257 hours. "No time to waste, gentlemen. Set the timers for 0400 hours." He gave each man a look in turn. "Don't dawdle, fellas. You hear me?"

Dunn got a chorus of, "Yes, Sarge."

"Let's go."

The bomb and the uranium storage location were both at the

end of the complex farthest from the exit, meaning it was the deepest underground, under the hill overhead. Which also meant Dunn and Morris had to lug the crates of explosives the farthest. Herbert set a furious pace and with the extra load, Dunn and Morris again struggled to keep up.

It took several minutes to reach the end of the corridor, which had two offshoots. Dunn glanced down each one of these, expecting them to be long like the others, but they were only about twenty feet in length.

Herbert turned left and they reached a single black steel door. In bright red paint on a yellow background were the words: *EINTRITT VERBOTEN!* Herbert pulled his keychain from his pocket. He stopped and stared at the gold swastika, as if angry to find the despicable thing in his hand. He selected a key, inserted it into the heavy lock and twisted. He lifted and pulled on the horizontal lever, and the door swung open. Cool air gushed into the corridor. "This way, gentlemen."

Two massive bombs sat in the middle of the room. Dunn was awed by their size, almost ten feet long, four in diameter, with enormous fins. Painted gray, they had black swastikas on their noses. "Lord Almighty. Those are huge."

"Yes, we need the length to properly start the chain reaction."

"Chain reaction? Dr. Herbert, how does an atomic bomb work? And, please, just a short version."

Herbert smiled for the first time. "The basic idea is to strike one block of enriched uranium with another and with sufficient speed that the uranium molecules are crushed and go into an excited state. If there's enough uranium, the combined loads reach what we call critical mass and the uranium expands through a chain reaction of the excited molecules, probably at the speed of light, we're not sure. That's the explosion. Of course we don't know what that will look like. We think the bomb could destroy a small city, or at least a large portion of it."

Dunn shook his head. Who would want to create that kind of weapon? A sudden thought crossed his mind. He tried to push it aside, but it stuck there like an embedded tick. "Doc. Who else is trying to make a bomb like this?"

Herbert gave Dunn a wan smile. "Oh, some of our best physicists are in your country, Sergeant. I'd wager they are busy doing the same thing somewhere."

Dismayed by this news, Dunn shook his head again. "Come on, Morris, let's load this room up." It only took five minutes to plant the charges and set the timers. Morris and Dunn double-checked each other's work to ensure no mistakes.

Dunn straightened up from the last charge he was checking, and turned to Herbert. "Lead the way, Doc."

They went out the way they came in and started down the hallway. Soon, they stood outside another black door with the same red and yellow warning sign. Herbert unlocked the door and they entered a small room, ten feet by fifteen. Herbert turned on the lights and moved toward the next door in their path. He passed by a small recess in the wall on his right, fumbling with his keys. With a guttural roar, Gunther Winkel charged into the smaller man.

40

Miller borrowed a flashlight from Corporal Barltrop and climbed to the top of the ladder. He played the light around the H18's cockpit and was surprised to find more room than he expected. The three seats were arranged with two in front with the third behind and in the middle. The rear seat was for the bombardier, who likely doubled as the navigator. He slid a leg up and over the edge of the cockpit, and dropped into the pilot's seat on the left.

The seat felt good to Miller. It would be comfortable for a long transatlantic flight. Looking around quickly for the main item of interest, his heart nearly stopped when he didn't see the checklist in plain sight. Running a hand under the front of the seat yielded nothing, then he reached into the gap between the seat and the cockpit wall. There! His fingers grasped a hard, flat object and he withdrew the key to success.

As Miller read, his admiration for German attention to detail grew. It was all here in the simple, easy to follow, step-by-step checklist. Leave it to the Germans to be so precise and concise. Whenever the list referred to a setting, he searched the instrument panel, found the dial, and memorized its location. He did the same thing for the myriad of switches that could be toggled from one position to another. Time passed swiftly and Miller's concentration on his task was so great he didn't hear the footsteps growing closer.

"Captain, are you getting anywhere?"

Completely startled, Miller snapped his head around to face Saunders. "Damn. Don't do that." He wiped his face.

"You've been in here half an hour. Are you getting close to figuring that shit out?" Saunders gestured toward the checklist.

"Yes, I'm nearly finished. Did you find the fuel truck?"

"Yes, sir. It was parked in a garage not far from here."

"Here's what we have to do." Miller gave his instructions quickly, but double-checked periodically to ensure the British sergeant understood completely. "According to what I see here," Miller tapped the checklist, "It'll take me ten minutes to run through this and get the bird fired up and ready for take off. That's about how long it'll take to fuel her up, too, so we're going to have to get a move on."

Saunders nodded and took a step down the ladder, but stopped. "What about your plane? How're you planning to get it back to England?"

"I'm not. You have to plant some explosives in her so the Germans don't get her."

Saunders frowned. "What about our copilot? Couldn't he fly it back for you?"

"No. Absolutely not. He's there in case something happens to your pilot. I won't risk your men for my plane."

Saunders' eyebrows shot up, as did his respect for the Mustang pilot. "I understand. We'll get you hooked up to the towing tractor and out on the runway in a few minutes." He eyed the pilot closely, then asked, "Are you sure you can fly this thing?"

"Yes."

"What about landing it?"

Miller chuckled lightly. "That may be an entirely different story, Sergeant. Off you go."

Miller was pleased by Saunders and his men. They had worked quickly and smoothly to get the plane out of the hanger and lined up on the runway. The H18 sat at the end of the runway looking like a black hawk poised to leap into the air. Miller was amazed by the sheer beauty of the cockpit. Now that he'd spent a little time there, it felt comfortable, familiar, like a favorite pair of jeans. He had started all six engines with no problems, and the plane rumbled as the turbines settled into a smooth idle. He double-checked all of the engine gauges. So far, so good. Now he just needed the plane in front of him to take off. He glanced down the runway where he could make out the dark figures of Saunders' men lugging one more of the heavy, important objects to the C-47 and manhandling it up and in. Then the men climbed in and the door closed behind them.

He'd ordered Saunders to also drop a satchel of explosive in the hanger office to cover up the other larceny they'd committed against the Horten brothers. Instead of trying to break open the file cabinets in the office, Miller decided they should just take all five of them, each with four drawers. If they truly contained what he thought they did, all of the design papers related to the H18, it would be much easier to replicate the Hortens' work.

The C-47 began to move, picking up speed. Miller had insisted that it take off first, then he would follow. He'd broken radio silence to send a cryptic message to his wingman Hayes, letting him know he'd be flying a different plane home and to make sure no one got excited and shot him down when they saw the Horten go airborne. He'd thought about all of the things that could go wrong, then forced himself to set those thoughts aside. No sense making things worse. He'd told Saunders that if he couldn't get the plane off the ground and didn't crash on takeoff, he'd stop the plane, run to his Mustang and get the timed charges. Then he'd place them in the Horten and take off in his own plane. If much else went wrong, he was just plain fucked.

The C-47 lifted off the runway. Miller took his foot off the brakes and shoved the throttles forward. The thrust surprised him, but he grinned at the feeling it gave him. The memory of that first ride in the yellow biplane flitted through his head. He was already halfway down the strip and his speed was 200 kilometers per hour, about 125 miles per hour. He'd done some quick math before running the checklist to make sure he knew his airspeed in miles per hour at each 100 kilometers per hour. Shit, what's take off speed? I'd already be in the air with *Sweet Mabel*. He pulled back on the wheel but the nose remained firmly on the ground. Miller suddenly realized he was riding in the world's fastest tricycle and knew the darkness rushing toward him was the dense woods of the German forest.

41

Inside Project Dante Lab
19 June, 0318 Hours

Winkel and Herbert crashed to the floor. The massive man rolled Herbert over onto his back. He clamped his hands around the terrified man's neck and squeezed, then glanced up, seeing the two Americans for the first time. Dunn and Morris started to set the boxes down, but Winkel shouted, "*Nein!*" In a show of tremendous strength, he got to his feet, dragging Herbert with him and making a human shield out of his fellow physicist, wrapping a forearm under Herbert's chin. Herbert struggled to get loose, but Winkel just tightened his grip, like a python waiting patiently for its victim to exhale. Herbert stopped struggling. Winkel took a step toward the Americans.

Dunn and Morris glanced at each other, backed up one step and separated themselves by several steps, in effect, fanning out.

Winkel smiled. It was a chilling smile. Into Herbert's ear he said, "So, Franz, you worthless traitor. You've brought the enemy right into the fatherland? Did you think I'd let you destroy man's greatest achievement? I knew you were up to something.

You fool, I found your "mistake" in only one hour. Did you really think your mathematic skill was greater than mine? That's why I stayed tonight. I was right in thinking you'd come here." Winkel switched to English, which was thickly accented, but clear enough, "And you, you filthy Americans. Do you think I'm going to let you past me?" Dunn and Morris moved another few steps apart and a wary expression crossed Winkel's face. "Stop moving or I'll kill him."

Dunn stared at the man, thinking fast. Winkel must want to turn Herbert over to the Nazis, not kill him. Maybe for a reward from Hitler himself. In a split second, he decided. "Go ahead. You'll be dead one second after he is and we'll still set the charges."

Herbert's eyes widened at the remark.

Winkel's lips tightened and Dunn knew he'd called the bluff correctly.

"Why did you do it, Franz? Why did you sabotage the calculations?" Winkel hissed.

"It's wrong, Gunther. The *Führer* would order this bomb dropped on innocents—"

"What about the Allied bombing and ruination of our cities?" Winkel shook Herbert for emphasis. "Don't you ever think about our own suffering? This is our one chance to stop it. We can make the enemy retreat from Europe. Just the threat of the bomb is enough for that. Who cares if some innocent Americans die? Their deaths would represent justice for what the enemy has done to us."

"Hitler is mad, Gunther, don't you see that? Ever since he came to power, our country has suffered loss of innocent life. Germans are killing Germans. Where is the justice in that? No, we must stop this madness. Let me go and I'll help you escape to America with me."

"You'd leave the Fatherland? How could you? Of course, you are a traitor. You deserve only death. I just regret it must come quick for you."

Winkel shifted his weight to get a better position on Herbert's head to snap the man's neck. Herbert felt the movement and with strength born of terror, suddenly twisted to his right, in spite of the pain. As big as he was, Winkel was still caught off balance just enough that he had to lean and twist with the little man or risk losing his grip. Dunn dropped his crate on the floor, and with a crashing sound, the wood splintered, spilling some of the green Nobel 808 bricks out of their satchels. He snatched his Colt .45 from its holster in a draw quick enough to shock an old west gunfighter, flipped the safety off with his thumb and fired once. The round's explosion was deafening in the confined space.

The blood and brains of a formerly living and quite intelligent bulk of a man sprayed across the room, some of it landing on Herbert. He slipped out of the slack grasp as Winkel's body fell to the floor with a thud. The doctor dropped to his knees gasping for breath. He lifted a hand and wiped some of the slimy mess off his face and stared at it. Then he threw up.

Dunn moved to help the doctor get up and pulled a handkerchief from his back pocket. He handed the cloth to Herbert, who took it gratefully. Herbert wiped his face and hands, and threw the cloth on Winkel's body. He got to his feet unsteadily and stared down at his almost murderer. Suddenly, he started kicking Winkel, careful not to hit the bloody remains of the man's head, shouting something in German. Dunn grabbed Herbert and pulled him away. "It's okay, Doc. You're okay. Come on, we still have work to do."

Herbert's chest was heaving and tears ran down his face. He got control quickly and said, "I'm sorry, I've never felt such fury."

"It's okay. It's a normal reaction to almost being killed. Come on, let's get these charges set and get the hell out of here before something else happens."

Herbert smiled weakly and wiped his face with the clean right arm sleeve. He glanced at the left side of his lab coat, saw the mess there and gagged, but managed to suppress the reflex. Yanking off the coat, he threw it on the body, too.

"Are you okay, now, Doc?" Herbert lifted his chin slightly and Dunn took that for a nod. "Okay, let's go. Morris, let's use the packs in this crate first, since it's useless for carrying anything now."

"Okay." Morris had already put his box down and now he moved over to start picking up the exposed packs of explosives, which made the small room smell of almonds.

Herbert walked to the small window in the next door. He reached out, turned on a switch and light filtered through the glass. Then he peered inside. Backing away, he unlocked and opened the door. "It's safe. Everything is in the protective containers."

They went into the brightly lit room and Dunn was surprised by its simplicity. A long metal table, that looked to weigh about five hundred pounds, was bolted to the floor. Who could move that anyway, wondered Dunn. Five gray containers huddled in the middle of the table. Based on the doctor's earlier comments, Dunn guessed they were made of lead. Which meant the radioactive uranium lay hidden inside. His stomach suddenly fluttered at the thought of dying a horrible death from radiation sickness. The quicker they set these, the better.

Morris and Dunn went about the job of placing the charges around the containers. Dunn stopped for a moment, staring at the containers. Morris noticed and said, "Sarge, what's the matter?"

Dunn ignored the question and turned to Herbert. "Doc, can we place these charges so they'll create your chain reaction?"

Herbert frowned. All of their calculations were based on known speeds of the explosive charge in the launch tube, the length, the mass. It was impossible to know. What did it matter? He shrugged. "There's no way to know."

"But if it did, it would destroy the entire lab, nothing left?"

"Yes."

"Help us."

"We need two containers. Don't touch anything, I'll be right back." Herbert went back out the door and they heard him open something, then came a rustling sound. A moment later, a man stepped through the door looking like something neither Dunn nor Morris had ever seen, except maybe in the comic books with aliens from space. Herbert was wearing a yellow lead suit complete with a helmet that looked like a remodeled welder's face shield. Herbert moved deliberately and slowly, like a man who'd had too much to drink and had to work at not looking like he'd had too much to drink.

He motioned for them to move back, so Dunn and Morris stepped aside to make room. Herbert picked the two containers closest to the middle of the table and slid them, not together, but apart, making a larger space between them. Without turning, he spoke. His voice was muffled by the gear, but easily understandable. "Build a circle of explosives here about this size." He leaned carefully over the table and spread his hands out about a foot apart. "And this high." He raised a hand to a foot over the table. "Make it so the charges will explode toward the center of the circle."

"All right, Doc. Morris, I'll do it." Dunn moved around to the other side of the table so he wouldn't have to reach around the doctor. It's like using a kid's building blocks, only this is a bunch of un-building blocks. He almost laughed at himself. After a few minutes, he was done and he stepped back. "Now what?"

"You and your friend must leave the room and close and latch the door behind you. Then you must also go out in the hallway and close that door, too. I'm going to lift two uranium blocks out of the containers and put them in the circle. I'll tighten the pack of charges as best I can. When I'm done, I'll have to get out of this protective clothing and then I'll join you."

"Okay, Doc. Be careful not to dislodge any of the wires."

"I will be careful, to be sure, Sergeant."

The wait was dragging on to ten minutes and Dunn began to worry, fearing that something had happened to the doctor. He was contemplating opening the door and checking on him, when the latch suddenly moved and the door swung open.

Herbert emerged, smiling. "All done, boys. Let's get the fuck out of here." He grinned at a surprised Dunn, and asked, "Did I say the idiom correctly?"

Dunn grinned back. "Yes, sir, Dr. Herbert. You got it just right." They began trotting down the hallway, then turned at the corner and headed for the stairwell.

A few minutes, later they ran out into the cool night air. Dunn was relieved to see that Cross and the others already standing outside beside the truck. Cross's expression turned from worried to relieved. "Christ. What took you so long? We've been out here for over ten minutes." He glanced at the doctor and said, "I thought maybe . . ."

Dunn patted Cross on the shoulder. "No. We ran into a crazed scientist who created a tense moment before we got it handled."

His tone told Cross how it was handled. "Into the truck, men. Now." He grinned at Herbert. "Want to give us that idiom again, doctor?"

"All done, boys. Let's get the fuck out of here."

The seasoned soldiers started laughing and were still chuckling as Dunn closed the truck's gate. He got in the cab, started the engine and pulled off into the night. It was a good thing he'd been paying attention to the route, since Marston had fallen asleep.

42

The Horten Brothers Airfield
19 June, 0337 Hours

The Horten streaked toward the darkness. Miller yanked on the wheel, praying at the same time. Suddenly, the nose lifted and the plane soared skyward. He sensed the trees pass below. He raised the landing gear and the plane's speed immediately increased. Checking the climb rate, he was astonished to see it was 5,000 feet per minute, nearly twice his Mustang's ability.

At 10,000 feet, he pulled back on the throttle and started looking around for his wingman, Hayes. A moment later, a sliver of moonlight reflected off something to his right. The Mustang glided close enough for the two American pilots to see each other through the canopies. Miller raised a hand and got a wave in return. He checked his airspeed and converted the value. The C-47's usual cruising speed was 175, but if the she could stay at 200 MPH, they'd be fine. He wouldn't over fly the formation and lose protection. Miller switched on his radio and dialed the frequency. "Devil's Fire Bravo Two to Devil's Fire Bravo."

"Devil's Fire Bravo to Devil's Fire Bravo Two, go ahead."

"Will you be able to sustain 200 MPH?"

A long moment passed, then, "Affirmative. We can maintain two hundred."

"Roger. Out."

Miller glanced over his shoulder and saw *Sweet Mabel* disappear in an orange fireball. His looked away with a heavy heart. He didn't look forward to the conversation with his Flight Chief.

Miller wiggled in the seat and prepared for the long flight home, completely unaware that in one of the file cabinets aboard the C-47 was a mechanic's inspection report. It detailed the need to tighten three bolts securing the main fuel line feeding engine number three, the inboard starboard engine. It said these must be tightened *prior* to the next flight or the line would work loose and fuel would pour all over the engine. The superheated engine.

43

Baden-Baden, Germany
19 June, 0354 Hours

Moonlight streamed into the barracks. Klaus Farber opened his eyes and groaned, not because of the light in his eyes, but because he had to take a piss. And he was still exhausted from yesterday's training. Farber was fifty-three years old and felt ninety. He'd started having to get up in the middle of the night to piss when he'd turned fifty and he was sick of it. At least it's not winter, he thought, when it's cold enough to shrivel your dick to the size of a green bean and your balls sucked up into the body cavity to stay warm. Shit. That thought brought a grateful lift to his lips. Thank goodness, I don't have to take a dump, too.

Farber was a reluctant member of the 46th Anti-aircraft Group based in Baden-Baden. He'd been "inducted" a year ago when his name came up on the list of able-bodied men younger than seventy. Hitler was getting desperate. Farber had been relieved when he was told he would join the 46th. He'd dreaded being sent to fight the Cossacks on the eastern front. This assignment wasn't all that bad. The physical training probably saved his life as he was twenty-five kilos overweight on his entry. Now he weighed a decent eighty-one. Still the training run yesterday had been exhausting.

He slid his legs off the edge of the thin straw-filled mattress, slipping his bare feet into his boots, not bothering to tie them, and got up slowly. He wore tan boxer shorts and an athletic undershirt. Running a tired hand through his thinning hair, he shuffled to the door, which he opened quietly. No sense punishing his friends for his pee problem.

As he went down the steps, the night sounds met him. An owl hooted. A cool breeze rustled the trees. Instead of going all the way to the latrine, fifty yards from the barracks, he walked at an angle about ten paces from the stairs. Even though it felt as though his bladder was going to burst, it still took a few minutes for things to get started. He sighed blissfully as the sound of splashing water joined that of the night creatures. Being quite full, it took a long time to rid his body of everything. Finally, as he was shaking the last clinging drops loose, another night sound reached Farber's ears. He strained to determine which direction the sound was coming from, and as he put things away, he turned to look east, over the barracks. It was definitely coming from that direction. What was a plane doing flying here at night? They were off the nighttime raid path typically used by the British.

Farber glanced at the barracks, hesitating, debating. The engine sounds grew louder. No time. He ran to his gun and, with the moonlight, had no trouble getting it loaded and ready to fire. Swinging the forty millimeter weapon around to the east, he was prepared. Would he be able to see it? He waited. Yes, there. A glint off a wing. Now that he had it in his sight, he knew he'd be able to track it; nothing was wrong with his eyesight. He made out the distinctive shape of the American C-47's bulbous nose. It was going to go right over him. A smile touched his lips, then disappeared as he caught a glimpse of something near the target. Several other slivers of light revealed four of the dreaded P-51s. He knew they'd easily follow the tracers back to him. If they did and decided to come after him . . . well, he'd better just make damn sure he hit the target early enough, before they could react. Then he'd disappear into the darkness. After taking a deep breath and letting it out slowly, he picked his lead point and pulled the trigger.

The tracers flew away, looking like deranged fireflies. Their path was on the exact lead distance he'd selected, just ahead of the plane and he held the weapon steady, letting the plane come to the bullets. He saw a flash of light as the port engine caught fire. He swept the barrel left to go after the starboard nacelle, but was disappointed when there wasn't another flash. As the planes roared over him, he swiveled around, not taking his eyes off the target. He continued firing until he saw the trailing Mustang roll over and head back toward him in a steep dive. As soon as he stopped firing, the Mustang did a big sweeping turn, then disappeared. Soon, the sounds of the planes dissipated and the night noises returned.

Farber unhooked himself from the gun and started back toward the barracks. His friends ran toward him. His first thought, as they encircled him asking if he got the bastard, was that he may be the first German to shoot down a plane wearing only his underwear. Suddenly, he was grateful for his piss problem.

44

Whitehall Cabinet Room
10 Downing Street, London
19 June, 0254 Hours, London time

Winston Churchill stood by the floor-to-ceiling map of Europe with a glass of his favorite amber liquid. He took a sip and jabbed a stubby finger at a point on the map west of Stuttgart. "So this is where the damned Germans have their atomic lab?"

"Yes, Prime Minister," answered Alan Finch. He and Howard Lawson had been asked to join the Prime Minister for the duration of the missions. The three men stood together, Churchill in the middle. Across the room, an RAF signalman manned a radio.

Finch continued, "It's buried under a large hill, not big enough to be called a mountain, but probably about one hundred feet above the rest of the terrain and it's heavily wooded."

"Any chance there'll be visible evidence after the demolitions go off?"

Finch lifted a hand, palm up and shrugged slightly. "We're just not sure, sir. The complex is likely pretty deep under that

RONN MUNSTERMAN

hill, which could simply absorb the shockwaves. We do have a recon flight scheduled to be over the target at daybreak." He checked his silver wristwatch and continued, "It should be taking off in a few minutes. We should be able to see the destruction of the German barracks outside the lab, but I don't know about the other."

"I see. Let's sit down, fellows." Churchill looked and felt tired, but refused to sleep until they heard something. He sat down to rest his feet and legs. Putting the glass on the table, he sat back, folding his hands over his ample belly. Finch and Lawson returned to their chairs and looked at Churchill expectantly. "When will we hear from the teams?" he asked.

Lawson replied, "They're under strict orders to maintain radio silence until they've reached the Channel." He glanced at his watch. "Saunders' team should get there in about an hour, Dunn's team, another hour after that." He seemed to hesitate.

"What is it, man?"

"They can also break radio silence if there's an emergency."

"You think there might be some kind of emergency? Even with the fighter escort?"

"You never know, sir."

Churchill understood. Fortunes of war and all that. Moments when things go desperately and tragically wrong for no apparent reason. Bad timing, bad luck, whatever you want to call it. Sometimes fortune favored you and sometimes the enemy. He had seen plenty of both, from Dunkirk to the Battle of Britain. The successes of D-Day were fresh in his mind, but the worries of the future were, too. If this plan failed . . . "So we wait."

"Yes, sir."

"I hate the waiting."

"Yes, sir."

"We should eat something. Do you boys want something to eat? I'm starving."

Finch and Lawson both replied, "No, sir."

Churchill frowned. "How can you not be hungry? Come on, have a bite."

"As you wish, Prime Minister," Finch said.

"Yes, sir," Lawson said.

"Simon!"

Churchill's secretary immediately poked his head in the door. "Yes, Prime Minister?"

"Have the cooks rustle up breakfast for us and some fresh tea. We're going to be here awhile."

Simon nodded. "Right away, sir."

Churchill closed his eyes and Finch and Lawson, not knowing what else to do, just sat quietly.

About fifteen minutes later, Simon reappeared with the early breakfast feast, putting the huge platters on the table, close to the Prime Minister. He put place settings in front of the men, starting with Churchill, who had opened his eyes at the smell of the hot food.

"Ah, here we are." Churchill dug in as Finch and Lawson stared at the fixings. The platters held at least a loaf of bread's worth of toast, scrambled *and* fried eggs, sausage, bacon, mushrooms, and a pile of breakfast tators that must have cost six potatoes their lives.

Churchill smiled at the men's expressions and held up a speared sausage. "Come on, boys, I can't eat this all by myself. Dig in." Churchill glanced over at the signalman. "Corporal. You, too. Come on over, there's plenty."

The man turned in his seat so he could see Churchill. "Sir, if it's all the same to you, I'd rather stay here."

"You can hear the radio over here."

The signalman shrugged, ever so slightly, and Churchill nodded. "Good man."

About half way through breakfast, the radio came to life. Churchill gave Lawson a questioning look that said, this can't be good.

"Golden Guard, this is Devil's Fire Alpha, come in." There was static on the line and fear in the voice.

The signalman answered promptly, his voice calm, "Devil's Fire Alpha, this is Golden Guard. Go ahead."

The three men at the table shoved their chairs back and rushed to the side of the signalman, who was leaning toward the radio the way people do when they're trying to make sure they hear everything.

" . . . 've lost the pilot and one engine to anti-aircraft fire—" Static erased the rest.

"Devil's Fire Alpha, do you read?"

Silence was the response.

"Devil's Fire Alpha, do you read?"

". . . situation bad . . . may have to . . . oh, God, there goes the other—"

"Devil's Fire Alpha, do you read?"

Static filled the room. Finch and Lawson exchanged looks. Both thought the same thing: Please, God. Let them at least to have set the charges and be on the way back.

"Golden Guard, this Devil's Fire Alpha Two."

The signalman turned slightly to face Churchill. "That's the escort flight leader, sir."

Churchill nodded.

"Devil's Fire Alpha Two, this is Golden Guard, go ahead."

"Alpha received enemy ground fire. Port engine on fire. Starboard engine smoking. Air speed dropping. Doubtful Alpha will make secondary target." The secondary target was Leiston. "Do you read, Golden Guard?"

The signalman had written down the words and read them back verbatim, then added, "Did I copy correct, Alpha Two?"

"Affirmative."

"Ask him if they reached Stuttgart," Lawson's face was pale.

"Alpha Two, did Alpha team reach primary target?"

Lawson seemed to hold his breath.

"Affirmative, Golden Guard. Alpha team reached primary target."

"Oh, thank God." Lawson went to the table and collapsed into his chair.

The signalman asked, "Any other questions, gentlemen?"

"Tell him to advise us if Alpha goes down." Churchill wore a frown and had spoken slowly, as if it pained him to say each word.

The signalman repeated the order and got confirmation.

Churchill looked at Finch. "When will we hear from that recon flight?"

"Three hours," Finch replied.

Churchill grimaced. "I hate the waiting," he repeated.

45

In Flight
Just over the German-French border
19 June, 0356 Hours

Copilot Bob Clark desperately tried to keep the bird in the air. He also tried to keep the gruesome sight in the seat to his left out of his mind. An anti-aircraft round had pierced the cockpit floor and caught his friend under the chin. Clark was as near to panic as he'd ever felt in his life. He knew he couldn't give in to it, though, too many lives depended on his staying focused.

As soon as the port engine caught fire, Clark triggered the built-in fire extinguishers placed around the engine inside the cowling. It took three discharges, but the fire went out. Of course, now the engine was a useless lump of twisted, deformed metal. Clark frantically worked to keep the starboard engine running by feathering the propeller to bite as much air as possible. The plane was tough and designed to be flown in a straight line with one engine, but he had to keep his right foot jammed against the rudder pedal to compensate for the one-sided pull of the working engine. He watched the oil pressure and the airspeed gauges drop.

The Gooney Bird was dying.

Clark looked over his shoulder at the jumpmaster, Sergeant Dennis Langston, who'd been standing behind the pilot and copilot during the attack. A round had snapped by his nose so close he had felt the heat. He was still shaking at the near miss, his first. The two men made eye contact. Neither spoke. Clark saw understanding touch Langston's face and he nodded. "Better get the men ready. We're going to have to jump."

"Yes, sir." Langston left to go aft and break the news.

Lieutenant Clark stared at the radio, wishing he could make a call, but the thing had sparked and caught fire in mid-transmission. The jumpmaster had grabbed the extinguisher and taken care of it, but it was a complete loss. He tried to think of a way to tell the escort leader what they were going to do, but there was no way. Well, they'd figure it out when the parachutes started popping open. Clark stared out the windshield, feeling very alone.

Dunn reacted quickly to the jumpmaster's news. His initial worry was whether there would be extra chutes for Dr. Herbert and Marston and felt relief when Langston said there would be plenty. Marston had regained consciousness shortly after takeoff and, although in pain, seemed lucid. Dunn assigned Cross to look after Marston while he himself would work with the doctor. He thought about the problems of teaching an old man how to survive falling two miles in the dark on his virgin jump.

Carrying on a conversation in a C-47 in pristine condition was hard enough, but when the plane was damaged, with numerous holes along the airframe leaking roaring air, it was almost impossible. Dunn sat on the bench next to Herbert and grabbed the older man's arm. He leaned close to Herbert's ear and began shouting. "Dr. Herbert, we have to parachute out of this airplane. I assume you've never jumped before, right?"

The doctor's expression turned stoic and he shook his head. Dunn hadn't expected hysterics, but the doctor's calm demeanor made Dunn's respect for the man move up a few notches.

"Okay." Dunn got up holding the parachute he'd carried over with him, "Stand up, Doc."

Herbert stood up and Dunn slipped behind him, instructing him to step through the leg straps. After that, Dunn pulled up the shoulder straps and helped him slide his arms through. In a few moments, Dunn finished cinching everything, making sure it was all tight. He turned the doctor around and showed him the dangling clasp hooked by a strip of canvas to the chute. "Doc, hook this on that wire." Dunn pointed. "All you have to do his step out the door. Are you afraid of heights?"

"Not until this moment."

Dunn tilted his head and lifted an eyebrow at the remark. "For the landing, you have to bend your knees just before impact and keep your feet close together. The moment your feet hit the ground, try to tuck in and roll over onto your side to absorb the shock. Can you do that?"

Herbert shrugged. "Does it matter? I have to jump, no?"

Dunn stared in to Herbert's eyes, thinking, this is a pragmatic man. "Yes. Two more things. If your chute doesn't open right away," he lifted a silver handle on Herbert's left shoulder strap, "Pull this. Hard. Do *not* hesitate. Do you understand?"

Herbert's expression flickered for a moment, as though imagining falling two miles. "How often does that happen?"

Dunn gave what he hoped was a convincing smile, "It's very rare, Doc. Don't worry. Okay?"

A nod.

"Last thing. After the chute opens, you can control your flight a little by pulling on the straps. If you want to go right, pull down on the right strap and left for left. You'll want to watch for a pasture or some large grassy field and try to guide yourself to it. Avoid the trees at all costs. Okay?"

"Yes. How soon?"

Dunn glanced around at the other men, "Two minutes, Doc. You'll jump right after me. Try to keep me in sight."

"I will."

Dunn moved over to see how Marston was holding up and was relieved that the British spy seemed to be alert. His biggest fear was that Marston wouldn't be able to stay awake for the jump, but somehow he was managing to joke with Cross, using the old line of jumping out of a perfectly good airplane, then with an expansive sweep of his hand, finished with, ". . . of course, *this* one might be an exception."

The jumpmaster went back to the cockpit to check on

Lieutenant Clark. Seconds later, he came running back, motioning for them to get hooked up. "Gotta go! Now!"

Dunn gave the order and walked over to the jumpmaster.

Before opening the door Langston shouted, "The copilot can't hold her much longer."

"He's going to get out, right?"

"He'll be right behind us." Langston turned away and opened the door. The roaring sound of rushing air stopped all talk. The jumpmaster maneuvered himself down the line of men and hooked himself onto the wire. He leaned around the men and waved.

Dunn waved back and grabbed Herbert by the straps to get his attention. Dunn poked two fingers toward his own eyes, then pointed one finger at himself.

Herbert nodded, eyes on you.

Dunn gave a thumbs up sign and stepped through the door.

46

Whitehall Cabinet Room
10 Downing Street, London
19 June, 0256 Hours, London time

The radio crackled to life, startling everyone except the signalman. "Golden Guard, this is Devil's Fire Alpha Two. Come in."

Churchill and the two intelligence men moved over to stand behind the radioman again.

"This is Golden Guard, go ahead, Devil's Fire Alpha Two."

"Alpha's cargo has departed. Counted nine white flags."

"Copy, Devil's Fire Alpha Two. Nine white flags."

"Wait, there's one more. Must be the boss. Total of ten now."

"Copy. Ten."

"Do you have location for discussion later?"

"Affirmative, Golden Guard, have location noted. Devil's Fire Alpha Two, out."

"Roger, Devil's Fire Alpha Two. Golden Guard out."

Lawson glanced at Finch and frowned. "Ten? Is that the right number?"

"Yes, including Marston."

Lawson nodded, satisfied. He started to say something when the radio crackled again.

"Golden Guard, this is Devil's Fire Alpha Two. Come in."

Baden-Baden, Germany
19 June, 0400 Hours

Klaus Farber hadn't bothered trying to go back to sleep. The sun would be rising soon anyway and he was still on his adrenaline rush from hitting the American C-47. The men had pulled him along to the mess hall and someone made a pot of potent coffee. They chatted amiably, as soldiers do, and Farber took a sip of his steaming dark liquid, then set the mug on the table.

Blinding light suddenly shot through the mess hall's east windows. The men reflexively turned to look. Immediately they closed and covered their eyes. Light brighter than the sun burned through and the men could see the bones of their hands through their closed eyelids. The light faded and they lowered their hands. All blinked rapidly, seeing spots.

After his vision cleared somewhat, Farber looked around at his friends and wondered if his face wore the same fearful expression. "What the hell was that?"

At that moment, the trees visible through the eastern windows began to sway as though a storm was brewing. Seconds after, there came a rolling thunder that the men recognized as being from a tremendous explosion. The floor shook under their feet and the walls seemed to bulge outward, as though a giant pair of hands was pushing down on the roof. A few more seconds passed, and it was gone. The men stared at each other, then as one, ran for the door. Once outside, they all faced east and, to a man, their eyes widened.

Farber raised a shaking hand and pointed. In a whisper he said, "What in God's name is that?"

No one answered.

In the distance, a gigantic cloud of smoke was racing to the top of the sky, looking like a tall, skinny mushroom waving in front of the pink sun.

Whitehall Cabinet Room
10 Downing Street, London
19 June, 0300 Hours, local

"This is Golden Guard, go ahead, Devil's Fire Alpha Two."

"There was a massive explosion behind us, on or near the primary target. The light was so bright I thought the sun had risen in two seconds. I'm seeing an unusually shaped cloud that is still climbing. I'd estimate its height at 40,000 feet. Do you copy, Golden Guard?"

The signalman was writing furiously. "Copy, Devil's Fire Alpha Two. Any more info you can share over the air?"

"Negative."

"Understood, Devil's Fire Alpha Two. Golden Guard out."

"Devil's Fire Alpha Two out."

Lawson clapped Finch on the shoulder and was about to do the same to Churchill, then thought that might not be a good idea. He smiled at the two men. "Sounds like we have success."

Churchill and Finch smiled back, relief on their faces. Then Churchill's doughboy face frowned. "We just have to hope our heroes can get home safely."

"We'd better notify Colonel Kenton, sir."

Churchill nodded and gestured with his cigar toward the phone sitting on a nearby table. He rose and said, "I'm going to go call President Roosevelt. Be back shortly."

"Thank you, sir." Lawson picked up the receiver and prepared himself to give Kenton the good and bad news.

47

East of Saverne, France
19 June, 0405 Hours

Three miles due east of Saverne lay a strip of farmland. It ran north to south and was one mile wide by three long. If the men in the doomed C-47 had waited another forty-five seconds to jump, they would have landed smack in the middle of downtown Saverne. Another thirty seconds after that and they would have landed in the dense forest growing atop a one thousand foot hill.

As it was, Dunn landed safely in a wheat field, grateful for the nearly waist high crop. He rolled his chute into a tight bundle and wrapped the cords around it, tying it tight. Looking around in the growing light for his men, he was especially worried about Dr. Herbert. He scanned the field and several heads popped up. Dunn held up two hands and the men began rallying toward him as he continued searching. With growing concern, he began walking toward the west, expecting the older man to have landed farther down flight from his position. He had walked about twenty yards, cutting a swath through the yellow strands, when motion off to his right caught his attention. A white-haired form rose not ten feet from him.

Dunn ran three steps and grabbed the shaky doctor by the upper arms. "Doc! You okay?"

Herbert gave an anemic smile. "I think so. The landing knocked the wind out of me. Haven't had that happen since my football days at university, when I took a ball in the stomach in front of the goal."

"Ah, yes, it does. Come on, we have to get out of the open. Can you walk?"

Herbert took a few tentative steps, to make sure everything was still in working order. Dunn walked alongside with an iron grip on the man's arm, just in case.

"I'm fine, Sergeant. Thank you."

The men formed a circle around Dunn and Herbert. Dunn counted faces quickly and relaxed when the number came out right, including Clark, Langston and Marston. The British spy was somehow managing to stand on his own two feet, although Cross stayed close. Dunn moved over to Marston and asked, "How're you holding up?"

The agent gave a small smile. "I think I'll make it."

"Good. All right, men, I know it's obvious, but we need to find shelter, damn quick." Dunn surveyed their surroundings. He spotted several farm houses and the nearest looked to be about a half mile away. It was closer to the town, but that might not be all bad. He turned to Clark, "Are we in Germany or France?" Dunn thought France, but needed to know for sure.

"France," answered Clark promptly. "I'd say thirty, maybe forty miles."

"Fellas, that's the good news. But we're still in occupied territory. We're going to make our way to that farm over there." He raised a hand and pointed. Then he swept the hand around, gesturing at the paths and flattened wheat they'd all made while trampling about. "But we can't go straight there. It'd be like making tracks in the snow. We have to go the opposite way." He glanced over the men's shoulders in the direction they would need to go. He estimated the distance to the field's eastern edge to be a few hundred yards and just beyond, a grove of trees poked into the blue-black sky. His eyes swept the terrain and he decided they would then go south, then back to the west.

"Everyone got their chute?" After replies of "yes, Sarge," Dunn said, "Off we go, boys." He took the lead, with Herbert right behind him. The rest fell in line and Cross took up the rear. They quickly reached the edge of the field and climbed carefully over the fence. In front of them was the grove. Dunn instructed everyone to drop their rolled-up chutes in front of a giant blue spruce. The blue-green fronds lay across the ground like a kneeling woman's skirt. Morris wriggled under the skirt and disappeared. A moment later, a beckoning hand poked out. Ward began handing the chutes to the hand, which promptly disappeared, then quickly returned. They could hear some rustling under the skirt. Morris must have put a hand down on some sharp needles because he let loose a choice series of words, just loud enough for the men to hear. A few men smiled. In no time, Morris slithered out and stood up, brushing the dead needles from his clothes. "All set."

Dunn said, "Let's go. There's a barn a-waiting for us and the sun is rising soon. We need to move fast, farmers'll be up soon."

Fifty yards separated the farmhouse from the barn. A chest-high stone wall ran the length of the barnyard from the house to the back of the barn. Dunn chose this hidden-from-sight path and the men followed him in a running crouch. At the end of the wall, Dunn peered around the corner. The way was clear, no dogs running about to send off a barking frenzy.

A ten-foot-long wooden gate extended from the wall and connected to a wooden fence that wound ahead several hundred yards. All they had to do was cross the short distance from the gate to the barn, twenty yards. A wire on the gate looped over a small stone mortared into the top of the wall, a simple latch. Dunn reached up, slipped the loop off the post and pushed, praying the gate would swing quietly. It did, and he created a gap of a few feet, then turned to look at Morris, who was behind Dr. Herbert. Dunn whispered, "Pass the word for Cross to close the gate and put the wire back in place."

Morris complied and Cross leaned around the line of kneeling soldiers to give Dunn a thumbs-up once he received the message. One by one, the men rose and darted through the gate, then ran to the back side of the barn. Cross took care of the gate and joined the group. Dunn tapped Morris and pointed to the door as he put his other hand on the piece of wood acting as a latch. Attached to the barn wall by a screw in its center, all you had to do was turn it. Morris moved around Dunn to stand off to the left of the door and out of its way, as it would swing toward him. He lifted his Thompson and nodded.

Dunn swiveled the latch and nudged the door open an inch. He slid his hand into the narrow slot and gave the door a big push. It swung open and he peered in. Nothing was amiss, so he nodded to Morris who jumped through the door, then went right. Dunn ran through the opening and went left. In the barn's dim interior, Dunn and Morris could see well enough to make out stalls running down both sides of the barn's main walkway, which was about ten feet wide. The door facing the farmhouse was at the other end. The loft was overhead, but the stairs leading up to it were also at the opposite end. Dunn walked down the left side with Morris on the right. They checked each stall as they passed. At the end, Dunn found two light tan Guernsey dairy cows standing quietly in separate, neighboring stalls; all the rest had been empty.

Standing at the foot of the loft's stairs, Dunn said, "I'm going up. Be ready." Although he didn't believe an enemy soldier would be lurking in the loft, it paid to be cautious.

"Yes, Sarge," replied Morris.

Dunn climbed the stairs and when his head neared the loft's floor level, he raised up on tiptoe to take peek. Hay bales covered his side of the barn, but the other side was clear. Straw lay scattered all over the floor. A crisscross of heavy oak support beams in a high vaulted ceiling looked like a giant wooden spider web. He continued up the ladder and made short work of checking the area around and on top of the bales. Satisfied, he moved quickly back to the top of the ladder and hissed, "Morris. This'll do fine. Get the rest of the men in here."

"Will do." Morris took off at a jog down the aisle.

Dunn knelt and peered at the barnyard and farmhouse through a quarter inch slit between two barn wall slats. He was thankful there was no activity. The sound of pounding boots reached him, then Cross's head popped into view. Soon, everyone was milling about in the loft.

"So how do we hide up here?" Cross, the city boy, wanted to know.

Dunn had plenty of experience playing in lofts with his friend, Paul, and his brother, Allen. Hide and seek was a favorite and he had become quite adept at hiding. "It's simple, we just create a kind of open-topped room in the hay bales, like an igloo without the dome. Then once we're all inside, we pull the last bales back in."

Cross lifted an eyebrow. "Okay . . . whatever you say, Sarge."

With Dunn giving instructions, the men began rearranging the hay bales, making an opening big enough for all of them to stretch out comfortably. This meant the bales formerly in the middle were now stacked farther out, making the size of the stack larger. Dunn made sure all the extras were placed away from the ladder in the hopes the farmer, should he come up, wouldn't notice a change right away. He'd thought about just going up to the farmhouse and introducing himself, hoping maybe the farmer was a true French patriot and not a German sympathizer, but the risks were too great. They needed some rest anyway, and he had to have a clear head before deciding what to do next.

After everyone was safely inside, Dunn and Ward began plugging the doorway, with Dunn outside, while everyone else was inside. They stacked the bales on top of each other until the opening disappeared.

Dunn called out, "Everyone get some rest. I'll take first watch. Cross, check on Marston would you? Make sure he's doing all right."

"Yes, Sarge."

Dunn walked over by the ladder and looked out through the gap in the slats again. Good, no movement. He sat down cross-legged, his weapon across his lap and his thoughts began to wander. First, worry about the team's safety caromed around his head. Then the question of how they were going to get back to England from so far behind enemy lines popped up. He realized he didn't have any idea. They needed help from someone. Who that might be, he wasn't sure. Maybe a resistance group existed here, as there had been in Calais. One thought ran to another and he recalled his farewell to Madeline. He wondered how she was doing. Was she alive? And Luc, the treacherous bastard that had gotten Timothy killed. Dunn knew if he ever ran across the man again, he'd kill him on the spot, no questions asked.

Dunn's breathing slowed and his eyelids grew heavy. He caught himself just in time. Jesus Christ. He checked his watch. Only ten minutes had passed and he'd have to stay awake nearly another hour before rousing Cross. By then, the sun would be bright yellow and moving fast toward mid-morning.

Pamela's beautiful face and sparkling blue eyes entered his mind and he smiled at the memories of the things they'd shared: the feel of her skin, her lilting laugh nearly brought tears to his eyes. He glanced upward and prayed silently, Lord, please help me get back to my Pamela. Amen.

48

In flight
53 miles northeast of Hampstead Airbase
19 June, 0315 Hours

Flying the Horten across the continent of Europe made Miller feel as though he was the guy on the block with the newest and fastest car. Several times, he'd had to fight the urge to cut loose on the throttles just to see what she could do. Twice though, he'd pushed the handles forward a tiny bit and the six jet engines responded immediately, pushing him back in the seat. After shooting ahead of the group, he'd had to slow down and let them catch up.

He'd quickly developed a love for the way the plane felt and behaved. The instrument panel told him everything he needed to know. As he scanned it again, all was normal. Then he checked the planes around him to make sure his distance was still good. He'd radioed as they approached London to make sure no one got trigger happy and decided to shoot his prize down just fifteen minutes from home. It would be good to get the bird on the ground. Lord, he'd love to see Hitler's expression when he found out his plane was gone.

Suddenly, the plane bucked. It felt like someone tapping the brakes of a car speeding down the highway. Miller immediately looked at the RPM gauges for the engines. There. The trouble was with number three. Its turbine was turning at less than half that of the other five. He looked out the cockpit toward the starboard side. Smoke was pouring out of the rear cowling. The handles for the built-in engine fire extinguishers dangled on his right and he quickly grabbed the third one and yanked hard. He glanced out at the wing. The smoke changed color briefly, from black to white, then turned black again.

Pausing to think for a few seconds, although it seemed much longer, Miller reasoned there must be a fuel leak on the engine and switched off the fuel going to number three. Nothing changed. He had no way of knowing that when the last of the loose bolts had fallen off, the fuel line had flopped around and jammed itself in the worse possible place: up against the fuel cutoff valve. There was no way to stop the flow of fuel.

Miller jumped on the radio. "Hampstead Tower, this is Devil's Fire Bravo Two declaring an emergency. I have an out of control engine fire on the starboard wing. Do you copy?"

"Devil's Fire Bravo Two, we copy. Do you need to evacuate the ship?"

"Negative. I think I can get her down."

"We'll have emergency equipment ready for you."

"Be advised I'm flying a German aircraft powered by jet engines."

"Copy, Bravo Two. Good luck."

Miller noticed that the escort Mustangs and the C-47 had reacted to his emergency call by climbing and falling behind him to provide ample room for maneuvering. *Oh, damn it. So close.* He glanced out at the wing and it seemed to him that the smoke was getting thicker and he thought he saw a flicker of red and yellow flame. Now his chief worry was that the fire would spread inside the wing and find its way to engine number two, or worse, the fuel tanks. Nothing for it now, but to get on the ground as soon as possible, which might or might not work.

As he prepared to get into a landing path, something occurred to him. What had he read in the checklist? He fought to find the answer as he reached for the landing gear switch. Just as he yanked down on the silver knob, it hit him. The Horten fuel system was set up with duel pumps. One for each side of the plane. If he switched off the pump for the starboard side, the fuel would stop flowing to all three engines. The negative to this idea was that he would only have one wing's worth of engines. He knew multi-engine planes could fly with only one side running, but the bomber pilots all said it was rough. But then, what else could he do? If he waited too long, he might end up turning into a bright orange fireball, a false sunrise.

Looking around the cockpit, he searched for the pump switches. In the excitement, he'd forgotten where to find them. Ah! There they are. Placing a hand on the starboard switch, he was about to throw it, when he remembered one other thing the pilots had mentioned: you had to increase engine power on the remaining wing or you'd lose altitude so fast you might not recover before gouging a path through some farmer's pasture. Shit. I need three hands, one for the wheel, one for the throttle and one for the damn switch. I'll just have to be damn quick.

With his left hand on the wheel and his right on the pump switch he took a moment to say, "Mabel, I sure hope this works." Then he flipped the switch and flicked his right hand against the port engine throttles boosting power. At the same time, he jammed his left foot down on the left rudder pedal to counteract the twisting motion of the now power-unbalanced plane. The Horten's nose slid back in line with the direction of travel and Miller spotted the airfield straight ahead.

He checked the wing again. The smoke was dwindling. Maybe. Just maybe. Checking his airspeed, Miller decided it was time to let the plane fall, so he backed off the throttles gently. At five miles out, the radio chirped to life. "Hampstead Tower to Bravo Two. There's no need to respond, we know you're busy." Miller nodded appreciatively and the voice continued, "We have emergency equipment ready at the far end of the runway. Please prepare yourself for a quick exit after you shut down all engines. Good Luck, Bravo Two."

Miller lowered the flaps and landing gear. The plane bucked and tried to twist to the right again, but the Horten seemed to want to help him by being immediately responsive to his turn of the wheel and he got her lined up again. As he passed over the tree line bordering the airfield, he imagined the tires brushing the top leaves. Then the tarmac was right under the nose and he let off the throttle a little more. The flying wing settled onto the pavement without even a single bounce. He yanked the throttle back all the way and stomped on the brake pedal. The speed dropped steadily and it was clear he had plenty of runway.

Miller stopped the Horten right next to the red fire trucks and shut off the port engines. He quickly got the harness buckles open and popped the canopy. Four seconds later, he scrambled out of the cockpit and slid down the port wing, then jumped to the ground and ran.

Behind him, the firemen sprayed the smoldering number three. After a few minutes, it was obvious the Horten wasn't going to go up in flames or explode. Miller made his way back to her. He walked around to the starboard side and examined the damage. The burned-out engine was a complete loss, but the airframe still seemed to be solidly intact. Good enough for anyone trying to repeat the Hortens' work. He glanced over his shoulder, pleased at the sight of the C-47 touching down with three silver dots coming in right behind it.

As the other planes made their way down and came to a stop, Miller lovingly patted the Horten's skin, then jogged off toward the others.

Hampstead Air Base
19 June, 0436 Hours

Saunders walked with Miller toward the building housing the ready room where Colonel Kenton was waiting for their report. "You realize there's an even chance we're fucked over this, right?"

"Yeah. I'll just have to talk fast and point out the window toward the Horten. It's always better to ask forgiveness rather than permission."

"Huh. I don't think that applies to the military, Captain." They reached the stairs and Saunders stepped to the side and swept his hand with a flourish. "After you, Captain, sir."

"Thanks, oh so very much, Sergeant."

"My pleasure, sir."

Colonel Kenton, Lieutenant Adams, and Lawson sat at the only table in the room. Saunders tried to read Kenton's expression, but it was neutral, as were the others. A mess cook rattled things around on a cart not far from the table. He brought over cups of steaming coffee for Saunders and Miller, and set down a ceramic pitcher of cream and a bowl of sugar lumps.

Saunders picked up his cup, no cream or sugar, thank you, and held it under his nose, breathing in the wonderful aroma. Then he took a sip, letting the satisfying warmth run down his throat. A deep sigh slipped from his lips. He took another sip and put the cup down. Fortified now, he gave his attention to Kenton and started to speak when the Colonel held up a hand.

Kenton's expression was no longer neutral and his eyes bored in on Miller. "Captain Miller, you have a hell of a lot of explaining to do. You deliberately disobeyed the mission orders. If it were up to me, I'd have you court-martialed. But it's not up to me. It's up to your commanding officer, Colonel Nelson. What do you have to say for yourself?"

"Colonel, I take full responsibility. I ordered Sergeant Saunders and his team to assist me in my plan to, uh, bring the Horten home. I figured it was well worth the risk and as I explained to the good sergeant, if I couldn't get her off the ground, we could still destroy her. And if I did get her airborne, but, uh, ran into trouble of some sort, then the plane would likely have been destroyed anyway."

"And you along with it. Do you have any idea how valuable you are to us?"

"Well, not exactly, no, sir. I didn't consider that. I thought the risk was minimal."

"I can only wonder why you didn't bring this up during the mission briefing."

"As I mentioned to someone recently, sir, I believe it's always better to ask forgiveness rather than permission."

Kenton sputtered and his face reddened. "I'm going to call Colonel Nelson after this meeting and recommend a court-martial for disobeying orders."

"Sir?" Lawson leaned around Adams to see Kenton better.

"What?" snapped the furious Colonel.

"Perhaps if we consider the positives of Captain Miller's actions, we might be able to see this as a terrific opportunity."

Kenton shook his head. "I suppose you want me to see the 'big picture,' huh?" He slapped a hand on the table. "Orders are orders!"

In placating voice, Lawson replied, "Colonel, under most circumstances, I would agree. But please keep in mind that Captain Miller isn't a private on the front line where following orders to the letter often means the difference between life and death. He's been a fighter pilot for a long, long time. He's an ace, sir, and his job is to think and plan and execute that plan on the spur of the moment. Often in split seconds. Don't forget, sir, that if it weren't for his innate ability to do what's right, we wouldn't even be here discussing his fate. The Horten would have never been discovered until it was much too late. I think it's prudent to commend him instead of court-martialing him. And that's what I'll put in my report. We should give him a medal, too."

Kenton's jaw muscles were working overtime, but he seemed to be considering Lawson's points. After a few more seconds, he visibly relaxed. "All right, you've sold me." He turned his attention back to Miller. "Captain, I imagine Colonel Nelson is more accustomed to your style and I'll leave it to him to decide what to do. After all, my own man, Dunn, is a lot like you and I trust him completely, so I guess it's only fair to give you that same treatment."

"Thank you, sir."

Saunders noticed something in Kenton's voice when he mentioned Dunn. "Colonel, is there something you need to tell us about Dunn?"

Kenton cleared his throat, mad at himself for somehow giving his emotions away. He'd wanted to give the good news he'd received from Lawson first. Leaning forward, he clasped his hands on the table. "On the return flight, Sergeant Dunn and his team had to bail out over eastern France."

"Oh bugger all, Colonel. What the hell happened?"

"First of all, we think the lab was completely destroyed. We got a report from the escort leader that a tremendous explosion cloud was climbing over 40,000 feet at the lab's location."

Saunders whistled his appreciation of that news.

Kenton continued, "However, Dunn's plane took anti-aircraft fire somewhere in Germany, killing the pilot and knocking out one engine right away and damaging the other."

"Did everyone get out?"

"Yes."

Saunders shook his head, as though trying to clear the cobwebs. "What's the plan to get them home, sir?'

Kenton fidgeted in his seat and glanced away. "We don't have a plan, Sergeant." He raised a hand to forestall Saunders, who had opened his mouth to speak. "Not yet, anyway. We have to find out where they are and what their condition is. Until then, making any plans would be a waste of time. You know that."

Saunders did know that. He just didn't like it. Judging from the faces of each man at the table, they didn't much like it either.

"Damn it to hell, sir, that's shitty."

"Yes, it is." Kenton nodded, then glanced at his watch. "Men, we'll do a complete debrief at noon. Go get some sleep. Saunders, I'll let you know if I hear anything about Dunn."

"Thank you, sir." Saunders pushed his chair back, then picked up the coffee cup and drained it.

"Captain Miller, could I have a minute before you go?" asked Lawson.

"Sure." Miller turned to Saunders. "Go ahead without me, Sergeant. You need your rest."

"All right, sir." Saunders put the cup back on the table and left.

Kenton nudged Adams and they both got up and followed the British sergeant out the door.

Lawson rubbed his face with his hands. He'd hightailed it from Downing street to Hampstead as soon as he'd heard about the Horten landing. He'd urged his driver to go as fast as possible. A smile creased his weary face. "You did an amazing thing here, Norman. To steal the plane right out from underneath the Germans' noses, my God, what a feat. As soon as I get over to the admin building, I'm going to call the guys over at Northrop. They're gonna drop everything to get over here and start digging into the plane."

"I'd love to see their faces." Miller grinned wide.

"I think you will."

"Sir?" Miller was perplexed.

"I want you to work with them. You're the only man in England who knows how to fly this beauty."

Miller frowned. "Mr. Lawson, I'm a fighter pilot and I'm needed with my squadron, not handholding a bunch of engineers. They've got their own pilots, don't they?" Lawson nodded. "Then bring them over. They can figure it out without me."

"It'd just be a short time. We could work it out so you wouldn't miss any missions. Would that satisfy you?"

Miller looked dubious, but said, "If we can do that and stick to it, then yes, provided Colonel Nelson says okay." He raised a finger, "But if you try to get me to spend time with these guys and I miss a mission, there'll be hell to pay. Sir."

Lawson grinned and stuck his hand out. "Deal, Captain."

Miller shook Lawson's hand, then got up. "Sir, thanks for standing up for me, back there."

"Glad to do it. You deserved it."

"Well, thank you." Miller yawned. "I'm exhausted. See you around, Mr. Lawson."

Lawson stood up, too. "Sure thing." He picked up his ever present briefcase. "I'm going to go make some plane builders damn happy."

Miller turned to leave, but Lawson said, "Oh, by the way. Good thinking on getting those file cabinets. I peeked. They're full of schematics and design papers."

Miller nodded. "Good. I'd hoped so."

49

The Philippe Gereaux Farm
2 miles east of Saverne
19 June, 0546 Hours

Twenty-year-old Claire Gereaux was typically the first up in the family and today was no exception. She slipped out of bed, grabbed a brush from her dresser and ran it through her long, light brown hair. Watching herself in the dresser's mirror, Claire's hazel eyes gazed back calmly. Putting the brush down, she dabbed her flawless skin with a linen handkerchief. Finishing that, she dressed quickly, then padded into the kitchen. It still bore the early morning chill, so she opened the wood-burning stove and threw in two split logs, then some kindling. Striking a red-tipped match on the stove top, she tossed it inside. The kindling caught immediately. The heavy door clanked when she closed it.

Claire opened the front door, letting the brisk morning air in. She breathed deeply and forced herself to forget they were in a war. A war that had taken her fiancé from her. A gentle and loving young man he had been, until the war befell their nation.

The war had changed Antoine into a zealous resistance fighter. He had become good at it, but not quite good enough. The Nazis had captured and tortured him, then strung him up in Saverne's town square a year ago.

Claire's dreams shattered with his fall on the makeshift gallows. For a month after, she refused to come out of her room. Her mother brought meals in and almost had to force feed Claire. Then, one Sunday afternoon, Antoine's mother came to visit. She brought a letter written in Antoine's hand. Claire's mother gave it to her unopened and left the room. Claire stared at the envelope for ten minutes, afraid to open it, terrified of what reading Antoine's words would do to her. Finally, she drew courage from the depth of her soul and tore open the letter. She made it all the way through before the tears came. To her surprise, they weren't tears of grief, but of joy and wonder that his words could fill her heart's desperate need for comfort.

It was, of course, a death letter, and his mother found it only after she'd summoned enough courage to go into his room to pack his things. In the letter, he counseled Claire to understand he'd died doing what he thought was important, that he was sorry to have left her behind, but had no choice. He then begged her not to follow in his footsteps.

Do not join the fight to conduct revenge, for there can be none. You must survive. There are many others who can do the fighting. But if you can provide help in other ways, you must do so. I pray you will find comfort in our love. I will love you forever, but you must live your life. It is my fervent wish for you to survive the horrible tragedies of the war and to marry and have children. May happiness find you and keep you safe.

My love,

Antoine

Vive La France!

Claire wiped her eyes and got up from the bed. When she opened her door and stepped into the kitchen, her mother saw her expression and burst into tears of relief. Her daughter was back.

Time for the chores. Slipping her feet into a pair of brown work shoes, Claire grabbed a faded blue jacket from a hook on the wall. Putting it on, she stepped onto the porch then flew down the stairs. Her thumping woke up the dog sleeping to the side of the stairs. Beaux was a mostly brown, collie-shepherd-something else mix. He got up slowly and shook himself, his tail wagging furiously at the sight of his beloved master. White hair framed his muzzle, giving away his age, almost thirteen. Claire's father had brought him home as a surprise. The six-week-old pup and Claire were instantly inseparable. The only place Beaux was not allowed was the house, a mother's firm rule, never broken unless Claire was sick. Then Beaux would climb into her bed and keep her company until she recovered. On more than one occasion, as a young girl, Claire had declared herself 'sick.' It worked most of the time.

"Good morning, old boy." Claire knelt beside her furry companion and scratched him behind the ears. She planted a big kiss on his nose and he licked her cheek in return. Patting him on top of the head, she said, "Let's go say 'Hi' to the girls shall we?"

Beaux gave a dog nod and Claire set out toward the barn. She walked briskly across the barnyard, her best friend right beside her.

Cross, who'd taken over for Dunn, heard crunching sounds outside and put his eye to the opening. Oh, shit! He jumped to his feet and scrambled over to the hay bales. Climbing over the top, he dropped into the hidey-hole and shook Dunn. When the exhausted man opened his eyes, Cross whispered, "Sarge, someone's coming. A farm girl and a damn dog."

Dunn was instantly alert and he whispered back, "Wake up everyone, but keep 'em quiet." Couldn't have the sounds of snoring drift down to the girl or the dog.

Claire unlatched the barn door and stepped inside, leaving the door open for extra light. A metal three-gallon bucket hung on the wall to her left. She grabbed it and moved on down the barn's walkway. She was about to open the first stall's gate, when she noticed Beaux hanging back by the door. His nose was buried in the straw on the floor and she could hear him snuffling. He lifted his nose and sniffed some more. After a few more sniffs, he moved over to the base of the stairs.

"Come on, Beaux. We've got work to do." Claire felt no

alarm. He probably found the scent of some animal that had made its way into the barn, a cat or a raccoon, perhaps. She raised her hand again to open the gate, but Beaux suddenly growled, a low rumbling that made Claire's heart jump. Like most dogs, Beaux only growled when necessary, when something was wrong and possibly dangerous. Maybe it was a big animal.

The dog put a paw on the stairs and she whispered, "Beaux! Stop."

He looked at her and put his paw back on the floor, but growled again.

Claire looked around. She spotted a pitchfork and grabbed it with both hands, her knuckles turning white. She advanced on the stairs with the weapon held out in front of her, looking over her head at the ceiling, the loft's floor. What could be up there? It couldn't be a small animal, Beaux wouldn't growl at something like that. It had to be a German soldier. But why would he be hiding in the barn? That didn't make any sense. In spite of her fear, Claire put a foot on the first step. Going to get her father didn't occur to her.

She climbed the steps carefully, her shoes quiet on the wood. Beaux followed.

Claire, like Dunn had a few hours earlier, peeked over the edge of the floor when she was high enough. She searched the loft and, after finding nothing untoward, finished climbing. Still holding the pitchfork out in front of her, she walked slowly around the loft. She started toward the far end and Beaux growled again. His nose was in the straw on the floor near the hay bales. She looked at the stack. Whatever was troubling her old friend was in the hay.

Instead of telling Beaux to be quiet, she let him continue to make noise while she climbed up the hay bales. She made it to the top and her eyes widened. There was a hole in the hay! Claire got down on her knees, crawled to the edge and peered over.

50

The Hardwicke Farm
South of Andover
19 June, 0454 Hours, London time

Pamela put the black phone on its cradle, choked back a sob, and collapsed into a chair.

Mrs. Hardwicke, who'd answered the phone, was standing by her daughter and put a comforting hand on Pamela's shoulder. "What is it, dear? What happened? Who was that?"

"That was Thomas's commander, Colonel Kenton. He said Dunn was on a mission and the plane he was in was shot down."

"Oh, dear!"

"The colonel said it looked like everyone got out all right, but it was likely they were in occupied France. I asked if he'd heard from Thomas and he said no, there wouldn't be any communication, they're cut off. Oh. Mom, he might not come back!" The sobs took over. Mrs. Hardwicke pulled up another chair and put an arm around Pamela, rocking her like she did when Pamela was a little girl.

Pamela cried for a few minutes, then wiped her eyes with her hands and wiped her hands on her nightgown. She turned so she could see her mother's face. Although Mrs. Hardwicke was forty-four, Pamela thought she was still beautiful. She'd inherited her mother's eyes and cheekbones, as well as her even temperament. Over the years, she'd learned her mother was a good listener and relied heavily on her advice. Now she needed it more than ever. "Mom, what am I going to do? What if he doesn't come back to me?"

Mrs. Hardwicke grasped her daughter's hand and said, "Come with me." Pamela rose and allowed herself to be pulled along into the hallway leading to the bedrooms. A few steps more and Mrs. Hardwicke pushed open the door to her own bedroom. Mr. Hardwicke's bulky form lay under the covers. He was on his back and snoring lightly.

"See those hands?" she asked Pamela quietly. Mr. Hardwicke's hands were visible on top of the covers. They were clasped together under his chin, as though saying a sleeping prayer.

Pamela whispered, "Yes, Mom, I've seen that before."

"He's done that as long as I've shared his bed." She pulled the door closed and turned Pamela around. They went back into the kitchen and sat down again.

Pamela eyed her mother expectantly.

"Do you know what he said when I asked him what he was doing when he was like that?"

Pamela shrugged.

"We'd been married about a week, I think, and he said, 'I'm pretty sure I'm thanking God for you.' Then he took my hands and said, 'I also do it when I'm awake, in case you're wondering.'"

Pamela smiled.

"He was always corny like that, but I swear that's when I knew for certain I'd made the right decision to marry your father. Oh, it's not that I was a-doubting it any, mind you, but it did seal it for me."

Pamela frowned slightly.

Mrs. Hardwicke noticed and said, "You're wondering just what this has to do with your Thomas."

"Yes."

"During the Great War, your dad turned eighteen in the last year. We'd only been married a few months when he got it in his head that he had to join the army and do his part. I begged and pleaded, but you know your dad."

"Stubborn as a mule."

Mrs. Hardwicke nodded, a smile on her lips. "Stubborn. He calls it persistent, don't you know. Anyway, even crying didn't work, blast his soul, and he joined up. We were down to the train station in town and I was all over him and hugging and couldn't stop crying. He took my hands and folded them up in his big ones and held them under his chin, the way he's doing back there," she nodded in the bedroom's direction, "and said, 'Darling, every night, I'll be sleeping like this, as though your hands are in mine. I'll be saying a prayer to come home safe, and you do the same for me.' Then he said, 'If it's meant to be, I'll be home and I promise I'll never leave again.'"

Pamela sat up straight. "Dad said that?"

"Surprised the dickens out of me, too. So I said I would. Months later, after his training was over, his ship was set to sail the next day. November 11th. The war ended and he came back home soon after that."

Pamela nodded. "So that's why he's never gone farther than town without you."

Mrs. Hardwicke nodded and had to pause a moment to wipe her own eyes. "He kept his promise." She grasped Pamela's hands again. "Dear, say your prayers. Judging from what I saw of your young man and the way he looked at you, he's saying his." She got up and pulled Pamela into an embrace. Then she whispered in her daughter's ear, "If it's meant to be, he'll come home to you, too."

51

The Philippe Gereaux Farm
19 June, 0557 Hours

In the dim light inside the room made of hay, Dunn made out Claire's face just above him. He'd heard the scratching sounds as someone moved across the bales and handed his weapon to Cross.

At the sight of armed men in her hay loft, Claire's mouth opened to scream.

Dunn raised his hands, as though surrendering to her, and said, "Americans. We're Americans."

Claire closed her mouth and her eyes opened wide. *"Tu es Américain?"*

Dunn nodded vigorously and dug out an old phrase from Ranger school, *"Parlez-vous anglais?"*

Claire shook her head. *"Non."*

Uh, oh, thought, Dunn. This could be a problem.

"On est amis, mademoiselle," said a helpful voice behind Dunn.

Dunn moved to see who had spoken. He knew none of his

men did, so it was—

Claire jumped down and started pummeling Marston, who was sitting up against the hay. She yelled things that Dunn didn't have to speak French to understand. Marston took a good clop to the chin and his head snapped back. Dunn and Cross grabbed Claire and pulled her off the agent and sat her down.

Claire flipped her hair out of her eyes and folded her arms across a heaving chest.

"Stop it! Just stop it." Dunn saw the fury in Claire's eyes and pointed to a shaken Marston. *"Bon Ami!"*

In French, another voice piped up, "Ma'am, we're all friends. The colonel is not really a German colonel, he's our friend from England."

"You're German! Why should I trust you." Dunn thought the young woman was going to spit on Herbert.

"I am German, yes, but we're trying to get back to England. Our plane was shot down a few hours ago. We used parachutes to escape the plane."

Dunn and the others, except for Marston, watched the exchange with the expressions of someone who has no idea what's going on. Which they didn't. Dunn glanced at Marston, who seemed to have recovered from the attack. "What are they saying?"

Marston translated for Dunn.

Dunn nodded. "Will she talk to you?"

"Ma'am, may I translate now?"

Claire turned from Herbert to Marston and the ingrained fear of a German officer returned. She squelched it somehow. "Yes. I'm sorry. I didn't know."

Marston held up a hand, as though waving it all off. "My name is Neil and this is Thomas." Marston tipped his head toward Dunn.

"Claire."

Dunn asked, "Where are we?"

"We're two miles from Saverne." Claire pointed to the west. "It's that way."

"How far are we from the German border?"

Claire shrugged. "Maybe forty kilometers?"

Dunn frowned. They were deep in occupied France, farther

inland than any other American troops. Lifting the flap on his jacket, he removed a map, which he flipped open. He found Stuttgart and drew his eye west across the map. There. Saverne. Checking the map's scale and using his fingers, he gauged the distance to Calais. He suppressed a groan; it was nearly three hundred miles. How in the hell were they going to cross three hundred miles through German lines? They had no extraction or escape plan and were cutoff from any help. Unless . . . Dunn lifted his gaze to meet Claire's curious eyes. "Do you know of a resistance group around here?"

Claire heard the word 'resistance' and was already nodding when Marston translated.

"Yes, there's a group here."

"Can you get in touch with them? We're going to need help."

"I can contact them, or rather my father can. They're in Saverne."

"Please do that as soon as possible."

"I will." Claire got up and moved toward Marston. He involuntarily flinched away. Claire giggled. "No, no. I see you are hurt." She pointed to Marston's chest. "Can I help?"

"No, Sergeant Dunn bandaged me. I think I'll be fine."

"Have you food?"

"No."

"I'll bring you all something to eat, then." She paused and turned to look around at the American soldiers. With wonder on her face she said softly, *"Américains."* She stepped over to Dunn and brushed her lips on his cheek.

"What is it with you and French women?" demanded Ward.

Dunn ignored him and stared at Claire. Something was buried in her expression, a sadness lying close to the surface. Claire burst into tears and leaned against Dunn, who wrapped his arms around her to hold her steady. After a moment, she pulled back and began speaking quietly.

Marston translated as she told the story of Antoine's work and death. At the end he repeated her words, finishing with, "I wish you had come in time to save Antoine."

"We do, too."

Claire wiped her eyes and said, "I'll go now. I'll be back as soon as I can."

Dunn nodded, "Thank you."

"Everyone try to get some rest." Dunn retrieved his weapon from Cross and climbed back out to stand watch again. *If we can get help, maybe there's a real chance of getting home.* He'd heard stories about flyers making it home using the French rail system, then to a boat. They'd had forged documents, but how they managed to communicate safely was beyond him. Glancing out, he saw Claire bound up the stairs to her house and go inside. He didn't like relying on others and was accustomed to solving problems on his own. Shaking his head at their circumstances, he tried to relax.

Claire went inside the house and found her mother cooking breakfast, and her father sitting at the table nursing his first cup of coffee.

"Good morning, Mama. Good morning, Papa."

"Morning, Claire," replied Philippe Gereaux. Philippe was sixty, wide of shoulder with a monk's fringe of graying hair. He was a third generation farmer, inheriting the land from his father twenty-four years ago. Before that, he had worked the farm side by side with his father, as his father had done before him. The farm covered 148 acres and until the war came, had a herd of fifty Guernseys, now shrunken to the two in the barn. The Germans were big eaters and even though the Guernseys were dairy cattle, they evidently tasted pretty good anyway. The Germans hadn't paid for them, of course, so it was a complete loss. Just making it from one growing season to the next was a serious challenge. They could barely grow enough vegetables and wheat to pay for the next year's crop and cover expenses.

Philippe raised his mug, "Want some?"

"Not yet, Papa."

Anne Gereaux smiled at her daughter. "Were the girls good this morning?" Anne was a slim woman of fifty-five. Her hair was still light brown and she had pulled it back in a bun. As a farmer's wife she never wore makeup, not that she needed it. She still held her beauty and it was no mystery where Claire's classic looks came from.

"I didn't milk them yet, Mama."

Both parents glanced at her in surprise. *Not milk the cows?*

Claire moved over to stand next to her mother, her backside against the counter by the stove. She folded her arms and said, "Mama, Papa, I have something to tell you."

The Gereauxs exchanged glances. What could Claire be up to now? As a girl she'd often start a conversation this same way. Just as often, they became heated discussions because she wanted to do something her parents opposed.

"What is it, Claire?" Anne successfully fought to keep impatience and exasperation out of her voice only because of Antoine's death and its lasting effect on Claire.

Claire thought her parents would be willing to help the Americans, but having seen what happened to Antoine, opposing the Germans was clearly dangerous. Helping the Americans wouldn't be healthy for any of them if the Germans found out. She took a deep breath. "There are American soldiers in our barn."

Anne and Philippe stared at their daughter with the same disconnected expression. Claire could have just as easily said, "Hitler's a nice man."

Anne recovered first. "What do you mean, there are Americans in our barn?" People in a confused state of mind often repeated the comment that made no sense, as though repeating it helped.

Claire spoke slowly, as though to a less intelligent person, "I mean, there . . . are . . . Americans . . . in the barn. They need our help to escape back to England."

Anne's hand flew to her mouth. "Dear God, what are they doing here?"

"Their airplane was shot down and they parachuted near here. They have one injured man."

"How do you know they're Americans?" Philippe looked like he was about to get his back up on this. "They could be Germans dressed up as Americans to trick us."

"Oh, Papa, the Germans are too busy to play dress up to catch a poor French girl."

"They caught Antoine didn't they?" As soon as he said the words, Philippe's face fell, ashamed.

Claire moved over and put a hand on her father's shoulder. "Papa. It's all right. I know you're just worried. But the Germans didn't just catch Antoine. Someone betrayed him. It happens. I just wish it hadn't happened to Antoine." She stepped back, grabbed her father's big farmer hands in her small ones and pulled. "Come. We have to help. I want you to meet them and then you can get in touch with Antoine's group."

Philippe got up and hugged his daughter. He was amazed by her internal strength. Where had it come from? How could she be so strong, when she had barely survived at all? Philippe raised his head and glanced at his wife, who was smiling. She nodded, to encourage him, and Philippe realized he was a fortunate man, to have not one, but two marvelous women in his life.

Claire let go of her father and turned around. "Mama, the men are hungry." With her eyes, she pointed at the eggs and bacon sizzling on the stove. "Can we make more?"

Anne was already moving to the ice box.

52

The Oval Office
Washington, D.C.
18 June, 2359 Hours, Eastern Daylight Time

"Mr. President?"

"Hmm?" Roosevelt raised his head, which he'd been supporting with a hand on his forehead. The long days and nights were taking their toll on the sixty-two year old man's body and mind. His spirit, however, remained as strong as ever. "What is it, Betty?"

Betty Nichols, Roosevelt's private secretary, was standing in the curved doorway leading to the outer office. "Sir, it's the Prime Minister."

The President glanced at the grandfather clock by the door and did a time calculation, an immediate reaction nowadays. Almost 5:00 A.M. in London. He rubbed his eyes with the palms of his hands, then blinked away his sleepiness. "All right, I'm ready."

"Yes, sir." Nichols disappeared and seconds later the transatlantic phone on Roosevelt's desk rang.

"Hello, Winston."

"Franklin!" Churchill's voice boomed across three thousand miles of wire. "Good news, my old friend."

Roosevelt's heart skipped a beat. "The missions were successful?"

"Indeed they were and in a spectacularly unexpected way."

"What? How's that?"

"It seems that one of your pilot chaps flying escort for the Horten mission decided on his own that it might be better to just steal the damn airplane rather than blowing it up. He flew it all the way back to England. Your Northrop boys are heading over here. I imagine they're licking their chops at getting into the guts of the airplane."

Roosevelt laughed. "That's excellent, Winston. I'll need to make sure that pilot gets a medal. What's his name?"

"Captain Norman Miller of the 357th squadron. As I understand it, his commander will be turning in the paperwork for a Distinguished Flying Cross."

"Good. Very good. What about the lab?"

"Completely destroyed. Our reconnaissance flight just reported the lab is a smoking crater, the entire hill is gone."

"The men used that much explosives?"

"No, the fighter escort leader reported a mushroom shaped cloud rising from the site that reached perhaps fifty or sixty thousand feet in altitude. We think that the team somehow triggered the atomic weapon."

"Oh my God. It does work."

"Yes."

"When will you have pictures of the site?"

"Another few hours. I assume you want to see them?"

"Yes." Roosevelt sent a sigh of relief down the line. "At least that threat is gone."

"Yes." Churchill's tone changed, as he said, "Franklin?"

Roosevelt knew Churchill well enough to recognize the change for what it was. "What's happened?"

"The lab mission team's plane was shot down and the men parachuted into occupied France. We think they all made it out of the plane."

Roosevelt's stomach dropped. *You'd think I'd be used to this kind of news.* "Has there been any word from them?"

"No."

"I don't suppose there's anything we can do to help them?"

"No, they're on their own."

"In occupied France."

"Yes."

"Thank you, Winston."

"Of course, Franklin." The line went dead and Roosevelt put the phone back. "Betty?"

From the outer office, Betty answered, "Yes, Mr. President?"

"Call Donovan and Stimson. I want them."

"Yes, sir."

Roosevelt spun his wheelchair around and rolled to the window. Pulling the blackout curtains aside, he looked out into the darkness of wartime Washington, D.C. In the moonlight, the fifty-five story, white marble obelisk for George Washington seemed to stab the sky. Dear God, the weapon works. What if we hadn't found out in time? How destructive was it? He couldn't wait to see the photos of the explosion site. He had no doubts that he could order its use, whether against Germany or Japan was yet to be decided. He thought Japan, since Germany seemed to be on its last legs and Eisenhower should reach Berlin by Christmas. The war in Europe could be over by the end of January. America could then turn all of her might against the Japanese. He released the curtains and turned back to his desk. "Betty?"

"Yes, sir?"

"Get Oppenheimer on the phone."

"Yes, Mr. President."

53

The Philippe Gereaux Farm
19 June, 0923 Hours

Dunn woke up wondering where the hell he was. He opened his bloodshot eyes and peered out from underneath his helmet, which was tipped down to block the light. He groaned and lifted his left arm to see the time. Three hours sleep.

Claire had come back to the loft, her parents trailing behind, carrying a huge platter of eggs and bacon and, bless their hearts, hot coffee. While his men ate, Dunn visited with Mr. Gereaux and they made plans for the farmer to make contact with the resistance group and ask for help. When the men had depleted the pile of food, the family departed, taking all evidence with them.

Dunn had fallen asleep almost immediately, leaving Morris on guard duty. Now he spotted Morris doing his own snoozing. He noted that Wickham was missing, so he must have taken over for Morris.

Standing up slowly, Dunn stretched, then promptly yawned.

"You should sleep longer, Sergeant." Dr. Herbert looked at Dunn steadily, fatherly concern on his face.

"Hello, Doc. No, I'm fine." Herbert was sitting in a corner, his legs sprawled out in front of him. Dunn moved over to sit beside him. "So, tell me, Doc, do you think the bomb went off?"

Herbert shrugged. "I don't know, maybe. It's too hard to say with any accuracy." He was too much of a scientist to give a precise answer without facts. "But I sure as hell hope so."

Dunn grinned tiredly. "Me too. I've had enough of this damn war." Dunn regarded Herbert quietly for a moment. "Why'd you decide to change sides, sir? I mean, you're in charge of one of the most important weapons development programs in history. With a success, you'd be famous and maybe even a little bit wealthy."

"Do you understand what 'success' means, Sergeant?"

Herbert had spoken these words in such a flat tone that Dunn was suddenly unsure. Wasn't the most powerful weapon on earth important?

Herbert didn't wait for Dunn's answer. "It means killing on a scale previously unheard of. Complete destruction of entire cities may be possible soon. In the hands of someone like the madman Hitler, who has no internal restraint, the world would become a flaming hell."

Dunn lifted his eyebrows. It seemed weird to hear a German bad-mouthing the dictator. "Not a fan any more?"

Herbert shook his head. "My wife is a Hitler fanatic. Has been since the election in 1932 when the Nazis won a third of the Reichstag's seats. She came home from their victory party singing Hitler's praises." He averted his eyes for a moment, then said, "I guess I got sick of the song."

"Who was the guy trying to kill you?"

Herbert sighed. "Gunther Winkel. An extremely intelligent man with no social graces whatsoever. I didn't even know he suspected me." Herbert ran a hand through his hair and some pieces of hay fell out. "Maybe I wasn't as clever as I thought." He held his hand out to Dunn. "Thank you for saving my life."

Dunn smiled and shook the man's hand. "Glad to do it, Doc. You were a terrific help to us."

Herbert nodded at the compliment, then glanced around at the sleeping forms and swept his hand in their general direction. "These must be special men. They seem smart and tough. Have you been through a lot together?"

"Yes, we have. They're all good men and they're good at their jobs. I'm proud to be with them."

"Tell me, Sergeant, do you think we're going to escape safely to England?"

"I've been in worse spots before and managed it. Of course, I had help."

"Tell me."

Dunn related the story of being in the Gestapo's hands in the Calais hospital and his escape.

Herbert grinned. "I am heartened to see you're not opposed to accepting help."

"Got to be smart, right?"

"Yes."

"I'm going to go relieve Wickham. You should get some rest yourself."

"I think I will. Nice talking with you."

"You, too." Dunn climbed out of the pit and joined Wickham, who was struggling to stay awake.

Beaux's bark drew Claire to the front door. He was alerting them to company coming up the long dirt driveway. A small black car threaded the narrow drive, leaving a plume of dust in its wake. Claire didn't recognize the car and she was suddenly filled with dread. "Mama?" She called, without taking her eyes of the car.

"Who is it?"

"I can't tell."

The car turned into the barnyard and headed straight to the house. After it stopped, the car door swung open. A policeman stepped out and Claire sucked a breath. "Oh, no. Mama, it's Dubois!"

Anne ran to the door and peered out. Not normally prone to swearing, she muttered, "Damn it." She grabbed Claire and pulled her back from the door. "Remember our story, now. Be careful." They'd made plans for this, but had hoped they wouldn't need it.

Claire nodded. "I will."

Together they opened the door and stepped out into the suddenly chilly air.

Officer Gaston Dubois was a Gestapo stooge and he made sure everyone knew it. Small-minded and mean, a poor combination, he worked hard at providing the Gestapo valuable information whenever possible. Still unmarried at the age of twenty-nine, Dubois was always on the lookout for a Mrs. Dubois. Claire had come into his sights when she was only fourteen and he'd fancied her ever since. Even though he'd never asked Claire out, he kept his eye on her over time. When she announced her engagement to Antoine, he'd started making his own plans to take care of her fiancé. Being a policeman had its advantages. It was no accident that Antoine had been captured.

Claire and Anne waited at the bottom of the steps. Beaux sat on his haunches beside Claire, a low rumble in his throat. Claire bent down and patted him on the head. Whispering she said, "Beaux, stop that. It's all right." Beaux looked up at her, doubt on his face, but he stopped growling. He settled to the ground and put his head on his front paws.

Dubois approached the women and tipped his black, Gendarme style hat. "Good morning, Mrs. Gereaux, Miss Gereaux. How are you ladies this fine morning?" His tone was friendly.

"Hello, Officer Dubois. We're fine, thank you. And yourself?" Anne forced herself to smile and match his tone.

"Oh, please, no formality. Call me Gaston. I'm fine, too, thanks."

"Of course, Gaston."

Dubois looked left then right, scanning the yard, house and the field south of the house. His demeanor turned officious and he said, "Is Mr. Gereaux working in a field farther from the house?"

"Papa had to go into town for something. He should be back soon." Claire shot Dubois a dazzling smile and he nodded acceptance of the lie.

"There was a report this morning of an American airplane crashing a few miles west of the city and another said paratroopers were spotted drifting to the ground not far from here." He raised a hand and pointed to the east. "Out that way. I think they started toward Saverne and decided to find a place to hide during the daylight. Have you seen any Americans?"

"Why, no, we haven't, Gaston." Anne's expression turned worried. "You don't think we're in any danger do you?"

"They're bound to be dangerous, so we mustn't take any chances." Looking over his shoulder, he eyed the barn for a moment said, "Have either of you been in your barn this morning?"

Claire immediately answered, "I was. I went out to milk the cows around five-thirty."

"You saw and heard nothing?"

"No, I didn't."

"Did you go up in the loft?"

Claire's heart jumped, but she kept her voice even. "Yes, I needed another bale of hay for the girls." Dubois regarded Claire steadily and she could tell he was debating with himself. She wanted to embellish the story, but fear of saying the wrong thing caused the words to stick in her throat.

"I'd better go check again. Perhaps they came after you returned to the house." He started to turn away and Claire stepped forward quickly. She put a hand on his shoulder and he stopped, surprised by her touch. He smiled and said, "What is it, Claire?"

Claire lowered her hand. She hadn't exactly batted her eyelashes at him, but she might as well have. "Do you think you should go in there alone? I mean, if they're that dangerous?"

Dubois puffed up. "Claire, it's my job to protect citizens."

You arrogant liar, Claire thought, but said, "Well, if you must." She was trying to think of a way to warn the Americans, but nothing came to mind. She glanced at her mother, who lifted one eyebrow just a tiny bit, as if to say, 'we can't stop him.' To Dubois, Claire said, "Do you want us to come with you?"

Dubois snorted. "No, Claire. That would be improper, to take you into possible danger. No, I'll be fine." He tipped his hat again, "Ladies." He spun around and marched off toward the barn.

Anne and Claire watched his retreating back. When he was out of earshot, Anne said, "I hope he doesn't find the Americans. They won't know not to trust the weasel."

"Maybe they'll kill him, Mama."

Anne stared a her daughter with a rush of sadness at what the war had done to her little girl.

Dubois reached the barn door and Claire thought he hesitated before opening it and disappearing from view. Was he fearful? She hoped so.

Dubois stepped into the gloom of the barn and, as his eyes adjusted, looked around. He'd forgotten to get his flashlight from the car and now he couldn't go back and get it without looking the fool. He turned around and pushed the door all the way open for more light. Ah, much better. He walked the length of the barn and back, peering into each stall in turn. Satisfied that the only occupants were the two cows, he put a foot on the first step going up to the loft.

54

The Philippe Gereaux Farm
19 June, 0932 Hours

Gereaux drove his dilapidated truck as fast as he could without causing the engine to take its last breath. Antoine's friend and contact, Remi Laurent sat in the seat beside him. It had been easy to find him; he owned a feed store on the eastern side of Saverne. He was a little younger than Gereaux, maybe five years. He was short and powerfully built, making the carrying of one hundred pound bags of feed a simple task. After Gereaux pulled Laurent aside and explained things, Laurent told his assistant he was going with Mr. Gereaux to check out the farmer's grain.

The drive from the store to the farm took ten minutes and Laurent had grilled the farmer for every detail the whole way. Gereaux had answered the questions the best he could and Laurent seemed satisfied for the time being.

Gereaux turned the truck onto the long dirt driveway. As they rounded a tree-lined corner and had a clear view of the barnyard, he saw a black car. "Uh, oh."

Laurent saw it, too. "Who's car is that?

"I don't know."

"Be prepared to talk with me about your grain. We have to keep our stories straight."

"I will." Gereaux guided the truck the last fifty yards into the barn yard. Anne and Claire sprinted toward the truck, their faces wearing the same expression, fear. Gereaux's pulse quickened and he swallowed hard. The truck skidded to a halt next to the car and Gereaux jumped out. Anne flew into his arms. "What's wrong?" He could see his wife and daughter were unhurt and was thankful for that.

"Dubois is here. He's in the barn looking for the Americans."

"How long ago?"

"He just now went into the barn."

Laurent, who had joined the Gereauxs, said, "Ladies, I think you should go back in the house as though nothing is wrong. Philippe, we best get in there and take care of this before it's too late."

"Yes, Anne, Claire, do as Mr. Laurent said, please." Philippe patted his wife on the shoulder. "It will be all right."

"Yes, Philippe." Anne turned and walked away, Claire by her side.

Gereaux looked at Laurent, who simply nodded. Moments later, they arrived at the open barn door. Gereaux stepped in and Laurent followed. A rustling sound came from above and Gereaux called out, "Dubois, are you up in the loft?"

Dubois didn't reply and the two men exchanged glances. This might not be good.

Gereaux started up the stairs. "Dubois? Are you up there?"

"Yes, I'm coming down." Dubois appeared at the top of the stairs and started down. When he reached the bottom, he said, "Looks like your barn is safe from the damn Americans."

Gereaux acted surprised. "What Americans?"

Dubois frowned. "Didn't your wife tell you? I just left her and your daughter a moment ago."

Gereaux shrugged. "They must have gone back in the house before we got here. What Americans?" he repeated.

Dubois explained.

"I see." Gereaux didn't want to, but lives were a stake, his family's and the Americans', so he put his hand on the policeman's shoulder in a grateful gesture, "Thank you, Dubois. I appreciate your checking for me while I was away. I want to keep my family safe."

Dubois grinned. "Of course you do. Any man would. Laurent, what are you doing out here?"

"Philippe has some grain he wants to show me. Might be a good switch from our usual stock."

Dubois showed no signs of interest in the grain or doubt that Laurent was telling the truth. "Oh. I must be off. More farms to check."

"Thanks again, Dubois. Do be careful."

"I always am." Dubois left the barn.

Gereaux and Laurent watched him march back to his car then drive away.

"Damn prick bastard," Laurent muttered. "We're going to have to kill him someday. Let's go meet the 'damn Americans' shall we?"

Gereaux chuckled and started up the stairs. At the top, he raised his voice, "Sergeant Dunn, Philippe Gereaux."

Dunn, Herbert, Cross and Marston were all awake and had listened to the exchange, with Marston whispering the translation. At the sound of his name, Dunn climbed up and raised a hand. Gereaux waved. Dunn looked down at Herbert and Marston. "I need you to come with me."

"Of course," Herbert replied.

"Sure thing," Marston said.

"Cross, keep an eye out, in case that cop comes back."

"Yes, Sarge."

The men scrambled out to join the Frenchmen while Cross took up his lookout station.

Laurent took an involuntary step back at the sight of Marston, even though Gereaux had forewarned him on the drive out to the farm.

Dunn shook hands with Gereaux, then offered his hand to Laurent, "Thomas Dunn, U.S. Army."

Herbert acted as the go between.

Laurent grasped Dunn's hand, "Remi Laurent, French Resistance. I'm glad to finally meet an American soldier. Let's have a seat." He swept a hand toward several bales lying at the base of the main stack.

The men pulled the bales around to form a circle, each sitting on his own scratchy chair.

Laurent, who was sitting directly across from Dunn, glanced at Marston and said, "I must say it's quite disconcerting to sit in such proximity to a Waffen-SS Colonel."

Marston replied in impeccable French, "I quite understand, sir. I must say it's quite odd to sit here *wearing* the uniform of a Waffen-SS Colonel."

"You do know if you're caught in that, you'll be shot."

Marston shrugged. "I've been in Berlin for four years with that very thought in mind daily."

Laurent gave Marston a rueful smile. "I see." He turned his attention to Dunn, "I'm here to offer whatever help I can to get you and your men home."

"Thanks." Dunn leaned forward, elbows on his knees and hands clasped. "I've already checked the map. We're a long way from the coast and I don't see how we can all travel to Calais together, either by train or truck."

"We could manage papers for all of you. There are ten of you?"

"Yes."

"You are correct. There would be many perils traveling by train. The Gestapo has check points at each town and often unexpectedly ride the trains, searching for anyone out of place. I take it that only these two men speak French?" he indicated Herbert and Marston.

"That's right. If anyone asked the rest of us a single question, we'd be in trouble. We have to find another way. Are there any airfields around here?"

"There's one about five miles from here. South."

"What kind of planes to they have there?"

"I have seen some fighters, but mostly it seems to be troop transports and cargo planes."

Dunn's heart jumped. "Troop transports? How heavily guarded is the airfield?"

"It has several anti-aircraft guns."

Dunn shook his head. "No, I mean on the ground."

Laurent's eyebrows knitted together as understanding settled in. "You are kidding, of course."

"Nope."

"Do you know how to fly a plane?"

"I can do better than that." Dunn stood up, then climbed to the top of the hay. Morris, who was awake, looked up.

"Wake up Clark and have him come out here."

"Okay."

A few minutes later, the sleepy-eyed copilot joined them. "Yes, Sergeant?"

Dunn made the introductions, then said, "Can you fly a German transport?"

Lieutenant Clark shrugged. "Sure. It'd just a take a few minutes to figure things out."

Laurent was shaking his head. "This is madness. Do you expect to walk in and 'borrow' an airplane from the Germans?"

Dunn smiled and lifted a hand in Marston's direction. "I prefer the term 'requisition.'"

Laurent shook his head. "That's still risky."

"What choice do we have?" Dunn spread his hands wide.

"I take your point. What do you have in mind?"

"We need a way to the airfield after dark. Around midnight would be best. Do you have a radio we can use to call London? We need to let them know what we're doing."

"I can bring one to you. It's not safe to move you around during the daytime."

"How soon?"

"An hour, maybe less. Is there anything you need?" Laurent gestured to Marston. "Medical supplies?"

"No, we have enough. I can't think of anything else."

Laurent rose and the others did, too. "We'll be back as soon as possible."

"Thanks. Be careful."

"Yes."

After Gereaux and Laurent left, Marston's expression was incredulous as he said, "You think we can pull this off? I mean, I blustered my way to get the truck, but I had a forged letter from Himmler. An airfield is something entirely different."

Dunn smiled. "I have confidence in you."

Marston looked doubtful. "I hope it's well placed."

55

Laurent Feed Store
Saverne
19 June, 1011 Hours

Madeline took a puff from the cigarette dangling from her lips and blew the smoke toward the light hanging above her. The fog swirled around the lone bulb, then dissipated. She was in a small room under the feed store where Laurent kept tools and spare parts for the grain elevator's upkeep. Behind her was a recently built doorway, a second one. It led out under a big barn-like structure farmers used to unload their grain. It was a well hidden door used only at night. Although not technically a safe house, the room acted as a good place for the group to meet on occasion.

Today, Madeline was biding her time until the rest of the local resistance leaders could get together later tonight. She was ready to plan Luc's execution. After the Calais disaster, she'd tried for two weeks to track him down, but no one had a lead to his whereabouts. Until Henri saw a Gestapo agent in Saverne order ten men murdered in front of their church.

When Henri had returned home and told her, Madeline's fury and hatred flared all over again, reaching a point higher than ever. She reaffirmed her vow to kill Luc, but she would ensure the traitor knew who his executioner was and why he was dying.

Madeline picked up a black Luger from the table. Holding it in her left hand, she used her right to open the chamber and begin the disassembly process. For fun, she closed her eyes and completed the job, carefully setting each piece on the old wooden table. Madeline opened her eyes and picked up an oiled cleaning cloth and gave the inner workings, the spring and rods, a good going over. Using a cleaning rod, she ran an oiled swab through the barrel. She repeated the process three times, until the swab came out as clean as it went in. She closed her eyes again and reassembled the weapon in less than a minute. Wearing a satisfied smile, she opened her eyes and slipped a clip into place. At a sudden sound from the main door, Madeline chambered a round, flipped off the safety, and aimed the Luger at the door.

The door creaked open and Laurent stepped through. He held up his hands. "Please don't shoot, mademoiselle." Then he grinned.

Madeline smiled. "You could knock, you know."

Laurent shrugged. "Eh." He moved past Madeline, patting her shoulder.

"Where have you been?"

"It seems we have another mission tonight, Little One."

Madeline Laurent smiled. Her uncle had called her that ever since she could remember. Her father, dead now fourteen years, had made Remi Laurent promise to keep an eye on his wife and daughter when he learned he was dying of cancer. Even though Madeline and her mother lived in Calais, Remi kept his promise and made the six hundred mile round-trip every other month.

When Remi found out Madeline had joined the resistance, he had been furious, but no amount of talking could change this stubborn young woman's mind. In the end, he'd just made sure she teamed up with someone who knew what the hell he was doing. He'd been outraged when he'd learned of Luc's treachery, but intrigue had become a part of their lives.

Remi was rummaging around another table, set against the back wall. Madeline leaned over to see around his bulk. He was unhooking the radio. "What's the mission?"

"It seems a group of Americans have fallen from the sky and landed on Philippe Gereaux's farm." He turned to give Madeline a smile. "You remember him and his wife and daughter, don't you?"

Madeline's face brightened. "I do. His daughter's what, four or five years younger than me?" She frowned. "What's her name, Clarisse?"

"Claire."

Madeline nodded. "Yes, that's right. How are they?"

Remi's face grew sad as he related the story of Antoine's death.

Madeline shook her head slowly and pursed her lips, but shed no tears; sometimes she felt like there would never be any more. "When will it end, Uncle Remi?"

Remi lifted his shoulders and held his hands out. "I don't know. But I do know we can help these Americans get back home so they can fight another day." He lifted the radio and put it in a wooden box. "Their Sergeant Dunn said they—"

"Sergeant Dunn is here?" Madeline jumped out of her chair and ran to Remi.

Remi snapped his head back in surprise. "You know Dunn?"

"Yes. He was one of the team leaders on the mission Luc sabotaged."

"Good Lord. That's unbelievable."

"Tell me, is he all right?"

"Yes, he seemed fine. Why?" Remi caught Madeline's suddenly radiant expression and he said, "Oh."

Madeline simply smiled.

"Well, at least help me get this all together. I'm going back out to Gereaux's right now." Remi gave Madeline a teasing look. "You wouldn't want to go with me, would you?"

Madeline punched her uncle in the shoulder and stepped around him to help load the box.

Saverne City Hall
19 June, 1015 Hours

Gaston Dubois walked into his office and tossed his hat onto the rack. The office was small, the size of a small bedroom, but for Dubois it was sufficient. He went around his desk, sat down, then flipped open his wooden address book to the letter G. There were two entries: Louis Gaston, his father, and Gestapo headquarters.

After leaving the Gereaux farm, instead of driving to the next farm down the road as he'd said, he'd swung around east and parked near a grove of trees. Making his way through the pasture, he walked slowly, eyeing the ground with care. When he reached the trees, he let his gaze sweep across a large wheat field. Sure enough, someone had made a path recently. The ground at his feet was hard packed, which meant finding footprints was out of the question. The Americans would want to bury or hide their parachutes; the question was, where? What would they do if they were in a hurry? He mulled this over and decided they wouldn't take the time to dig a hole, but would instead find a way to quickly cover them, maybe under leaves or fallen branches. He spun around to face the trees and, deciding it had to be in there, moved into the grove.

He searched for ten minutes, finding nothing, no suspicious piles of leaves or tree branches. His frustration mounted and he began to wonder if he was right. No! I am right. Laurent's presence at the Gereaux's proves that. The resistance were all the same. They always thought no one knew. But I know.

Gaston smirked. Even though it had been blind luck, he had spotted Laurent and Antoine going into the back door of the Feed Store at 3:00 A.M. one morning. Guilty by association, was Laurent. This was a fact Gaston had kept to himself, even after Antoine had been captured, tortured, then executed. It was information currency to be spent wisely. Now was the time. If he could just find the fucking chutes!

Gaston lifted his gaze from the ground, if for no other reason than to rid his neck of the building soreness from being hunched over. And came face to face with a massive blue spruce. A smile crossed his lips as he trotted over to the tree, lifted some prickly fronds and found what he was searching for. It had taken him another ten minutes to gather them all and stuff them in the back seat and trunk of his little car.

Gaston picked up the phone and dialed the number. You

didn't just walk into Gestapo headquarters without an appointment, but he was pretty sure he'd have no trouble getting that appointment.

56

The Philippe Gereaux Farm
19 June, 1023 Hours

Everyone was awake and trying to make the best of the cramped quarters. Asleep, they all had plenty of room, but now, as restlessness settled in, it was too close for comfort. Dunn watched his men fidget for a few minutes, then said, "Okay. Everyone out. Go walk around the loft, do some exercises, then you can lay around out there instead."

Like kids escaping to recess, the men scattered, including Herbert and Marston, leaving Dunn sitting by himself. He sighed, got up, and stretched by lacing his fingers together, then extending his arms over his head. Inexplicably, the motion drew his mind back to the first time with Pamela, when she'd raised her arms to undo her hair. The memory drew a smile that grew wider at the recollection of the moments following her sexy motion.

The sound of a vehicle pulling into the barnyard reached Dunn's ears about the time Wickham hollered, "Sarge. We got company. Looks like the farmer's truck."

Dunn grabbed his helmet, threw it on, and picked up his Thompson. After double-checking the safety, he slid the weapon's green canvas sling over his shoulder and clambered out. He searched the loft, quickly spotted Marston near the stairs, then wound his way around loose hay bales to stand by the British agent. "Neil, I'll need you to translate some more. How are you doing?" Dunn gestured at Marston's chest.

"It only hurts when I breathe."

Dunn's lips curled into a half smile. "Doctor, it hurts when I do this."

Marston laughed. "Then stop doing that."

"Come on." They went down the stairs.

The barn door swung open and Laurent stepped in carrying a big box. Gereaux was behind him.

Dunn raised a hand in greeting, "It's good to see you back so soon, gentlemen."

Laurent and Gereaux waited for Marston to translate, then smiled.

Laurent said, "I've got the radio here," he tipped his head toward the box in his arms.

"Good. Let's get it . . . " A flash of red hair outside the barn door caught Dunn's attention. A familiar flash of red. What the devil?

Madeline entered the barn like a debutante. She flashed a dazzling smile at Dunn and her jade eyes danced. "Hello, Sergeant."

Dunn worked his mouth silently. Finally, he managed, "Madeline, what are you doing here?"

Madeline grinned. "I'm here to help."

"No, I mean *here* and not Calais."

A fierce expression flew across Madeline's face and disappeared. "Some unfinished business. I'll tell you about it after you're done with the radio."

"It's good to see you." To Laurent, he said, "Let's set it up in the loft. It shouldn't take but a few minutes to get the information through."

"As you wish, Sergeant. Lead the way."

Dunn shot a smile at Madeline, then headed up the stairs.

Laurent got the radio up and running in a matter of minutes, then turned it over to Dunn, who knelt beside it. Everyone gathered around, trying to get close enough to hear. Twisting the dial, Dunn zeroed in on the memorized frequency and spoke into the microphone, "Golden Guard, this is Devil's Fire Alpha Three, do you read?"

The response was immediate. "This is Golden Guard, Devil's Fire Alpha Three, go ahead."

Dunn relayed their predicament and an abbreviated, coded version of the plan for that night, ending with, ". . . we want to make sure our own people don't shoot us down. Please pass the word along."

"Will do, Three. Anything else?"

"Negative. No, wait, can you advise us on the success of our work?"

"Affirmative, Three. I have a message for you and your team from the top. 'Well done, Chaps. A complete success was verified a few hours ago.'"

Muted cheers went up around Dunn and he grinned at his team as they slapped each other on the back. Returning to the microphone, Dunn said, "Pass our thanks along. Just be sure to get the word out. We'll attempt to communicate once we've caught our ride. Three, out."

"Safe travels, Three. Guard out."

Dunn switched off the set and got up, smiling. He looked at each team member in turn, then said, "As always, men, I'm proud of you. Another job done well." The men beamed at him and each other.

Dunn turned to Marston and Herbert and said, "Gentlemen, your help was invaluable. My thanks to you, too." Both men nodded. "All right, listen up. We've got hours to wait and we need to get as much rest as we can. I want two men to stand watch through the afternoon. Everyone else can sleep out here instead of in the hole." When the men showed no signs of moving, Dunn said, "Shoo. I mean now." He was rewarded with some gentle laughter as the men wandered off trying to find a suitable place for a snooze. Dunn stifled a laugh at their resemblance to a dog turning in circles before lying down. Marston hadn't moved, although he clearly needed sleep.

To Madeline, Dunn said, "Can you translate for me, so my

German colonel can get some shut eye?"

"Sure. Be glad to." On the drive out to the farm, Laurent had, in turn, warned Madeline about the ersatz Waffen-SS officer accompanying the team.

Marston gave Madeline a grateful tip of the head and moved off in search of his own bed.

"Mr. Laurent, thanks for the radio. It improved our chances," said Dunn.

Madeline interpreted and Laurent replied, "You're welcome. I'll be back soon with a covered feed truck. We can use that for transporting you and your men to the airport."

"That's great." Dunn had decided to push up the timetable. Rather than wait until midnight, he wanted to get to the airfield as soon as possible after dark. He believed it would improve their chances. Dunn asked Laurent for directions to the German airfield and the Frenchman gave them to him quickly, then stuck out his hand and Dunn shook it briskly. Laurent began packing up the radio. When he finished, he looked at Madeline and said, "We should be going."

Madeline looked at Dunn and said, "No, Uncle Remi, I believe I'll stay here."

Laurent leaned over to peck Madeline's cheek. "See you later, Little One." With that, he left, Gereaux on his heels.

Dunn gave Madeline a questioning look. She hadn't translated her little exchange with Laurent.

"My uncle."

Dunn tipped his head in understanding. The two of them were alone, if you didn't count the over half dozen men who were already snoring, just that fast. Only Hanson and Ward were still awake, keeping watch.

Madeline stepped close to Dunn and whispered, she said, "Is there some place we can go talk for a little while?"

"Sure. We can go downstairs, if you like."

"That's fine."

After they got to the first floor, Dunn rounded up an empty bucket and a crate to serve as chairs.

Seated, Madeline asked, "So did you make amends with your girl?"

Dunn grinned like a schoolboy. "Yes. Pamela forgave me and

I know here," a tap on his chest, "that she's the woman of my life."

"I understand. Love is a strange and wonderful thing because it often comes when you are busy looking the other way." She pointed a finger at Dunn. "Now you listen to me. You have to survive and get home to Pamela because . . ." She stopped at a sudden change in his expression. "What is it?"

Dunn blinked. "She said the exact same thing."

Madeline laughed lightly. "Then she and I have something else in common."

Dunn laughed in return and grasped Madeline's shoulders. Leaning over, he kissed her on the forehead. "Madeline, I will always remember you."

"You, too."

The air seemed to change, as if an electrical charge had dissipated, and Dunn said, "Tell me what you're doing here."

Madeline sighed and her expression turned grim. "I've come to kill Luc."

Dunn's eye widened. "Luc's here? In Saverne?"

"Yes, we just found out for certain; Henri found him, by accident to be truthful. He's a member of the Gestapo."

"The bastard's a real traitor, then, isn't he?"

"Yes. And he's taken to their world all too well." Madeline's eyes flashed. "He executed ten innocent men about a week ago. He stood them up against their church and used one bullet to kill them all. Henri said he looked like he was proud of his accomplishment."

"Damn, Madeline."

"I'm going to kidnap and kill him tonight. We have everything planned. I'm going to make him suffer for what he's done and make sure he knows why I'm killing him."

"Won't the Gestapo punish the townsfolk again when they find Luc's body?"

Madeline smiled, but her eyes burned with a savage fury. Dunn's blood chilled at the contrast. "There won't be a body to find."

"Oh Lord, Madeline. What are you going to do?" He quickly raised a hand to ward of the answer. "Never mind. I don't want to know. He deserves it, whatever it is." He touched her shoulder.

"Promise me you'll be careful."

"I will. Don't worry. I'm good at this."

Dunn gazed at her. God, what has this war done to you? How can a woman talk about love one minute, then torturing and killing another human being the next? He wondered whether she would ever be normal again. Would he? Would any of them? He mentally shook his head. "I wish you all the best in the world, Madeline."

"Psst! Sarge!" Hanson hissed from the loft.

Dunn stepped back and moved to the foot of the stairs. "What?"

"That cop fellow is coming up the driveway."

"Get everyone up." He spun around and grabbed Madeline's hand, "We better get upstairs."

57

The Philippe Gereaux Farm
19 June, 1058 Hours

The Gereaux women ran to the front door at the sound of Beaux's warning bark. Claire was first to arrive and she pressed her palms against the glass. A black car crunched across the barnyard toward the house. A hand flew to her mouth. "Oh, no, it's Dubois. He's come back!" She whirled to face Anne with panic in her eyes. "What are we going to do?"

Anne put a hand on Claire's shoulder. "We have to stay calm. Remember, when he was here earlier he didn't find anything. We just have to stay with our story and not let him goad us into giving something away. Now, take a few deep breaths."

Claire did as her mother instructed.

"Isn't that better?"

Claire shook her head. "No, but I'll be all right."

"Let's go." To stay inside would have made Dubois suspicious. Farm folks always went outside to greet a visitor. Anne opened the door and she and Claire went down the stairs. They headed toward the gate leading into the barnyard and Beaux bounded ahead of them. The fence around the yard was taut cattle wire. On the house's side of the fence was a waist high by twenty-foot-long wood pile. Beaux nosed around the base of the wood, snuffling for something and his rump knocked over a single-bladed axe with a thunk. Startled, Beaux tucked his tail and ran back to the women. Claire wanted to laugh, but fear stopped her. The trio arrived at the gate and waited for the policeman.

Dubois got out of the car wearing a grim expression. Claire sucked a breath, then whispered, "Something's wrong, Mother."

"Stay calm."

"I don't know if I can."

"Yes, you can."

Dubois marched toward the women, his jaw muscles clenching. When he was a few feet away, he shouted, "Tell me where the Americans are."

Anne and Claire involuntarily stepped backward at Dubois' rage. "What, what are you talking about, Gaston?" asked Anne.

"I found the Americans' parachutes not one mile from here. I know they're here somewhere." He opened the flap on his holster and yanked out his prized Luger. He raised the barrel and pointed it, not at Anne, but Claire.

Anne slid in front of her daughter, her hands warding off the policeman. "No! You are wrong, Gaston. They're not here. You already checked, remember? Please, put away your gun. We've done nothing wrong."

Dubois' face turned a blotchy red and his eyes narrowed. "I know you think I'm stupid. Well, I'm not. I know for a fact that Laurent is a leader of the resistance. I know he was working with Antoine. How do you think I was able to capture Antoine so easily?"

"You! You betrayed Antoine!" Claire screamed. She tried to step around her mother, but Anne turned and pushed her backwards so hard she nearly fell. Claire turned her hate-filled dark eyes on Dubois.

Dubois stared back and said, "I do my job, Claire, to protect the citizens of Saverne. The resistance brings nothing but death to us. You should be grateful, not angry with me."

Claire was shaking with rage and could not speak.

Dubois turned to Anne and, in a suddenly calm and dangerous voice, said, "Tell me, why would Laurent be out here if the Americans weren't here, also?" Anne started to protest, but he shouted over her, "Tell me where they are!" He shook his pistol in her face.

Anne held up a hand as if to wave away the black weapon. "Please. We don't know."

Dubois lowered his weapon and smiled.

Unsure, Anne returned the smile, her lower lip trembling.

The policeman took a small step closer, still smiling. In a black flash, the Luger swept up and crashed into Anne's temple. Blood spurted. Anne's eyes rolled back into her head and she toppled over sideways, landing on the ground with a thud.

Claire shrieked.

Beaux snarled and leapt at Dubois, sinking his fangs deep into the man's left arm.

Dubois screamed. He started to bring his gun hand around.

Claire watched. Time slowed. Bright red blood poured from her mother's wound. Beaux's white muzzle turned red as he shook Dubois' arm like a rat. Something heavy was suddenly in Claire's hand. She gripped it with both hands and swung. The Luger fired. Beaux yelped and fell. Dubois uttered a single, gargling grunt and collapsed.

Claire stared at the strange sight on the ground in front of her. A man lay on the ground with an axe buried between his shoulder blades, the handle looking like a grotesque second left arm. *How did that happen?*

Dunn pushed open the loft's door a crack to get a better view of what was happening. Hanson and Madeline crowded in to see, too. Suddenly, Dubois struck Anne. The dog attacked the policeman. Dunn's mouthed dropped open at the sight of the French farm girl whirling around, snatching up the axe and swinging away like Babe Ruth. "Holy shit!"

"We have to go help, Thomas," Madeline was tugging at Dunn's jacket.

Motion caught Dunn's eye and he turned his head. He reacted in a split second. After yanking the loft door closed, he spun around and shouted, "Everyone up! Now. Get up. We're leaving."

"What is it, Thomas?"

"German troop truck coming up the driveway."

The men jumped up at Dunn's warning and ran to the stairs, Cross in the lead.

Dunn said to his second in command, "Out the back door. Get back on the other side of that rock wall. I'll caboose."

Cross nodded and bounded down the stairs.

Dunn turned to Madeline, "You go with them."

She nodded and joined the train of men.

While everyone was heading out the back door, Dunn checked the loft as quickly as possible, looking for any obvious evidence. Satisfied there was none, he ran down the stairs, across the barn's first floor, and out the door, taking care to re-latch the door behind him.

Dunn sped across the distance between the barn and wall, pulled the gate closed, looped the wire over the stone again, and ducked down. The group was tucked in, kneeling. He scooted to the front of the line. Tapping Cross on the shoulder, he pointed at himself, at Cross, then father down the wall. Cross nodded. Dunn and Cross slid down the wall until they cleared the front of the barn.

The truck pulled to a stop near the barn. A squad of ten soldiers jumped out, taking up positions around the front of the farm building, weapons ready. Luc stepped down from the cab and snapped his suit jacket into place. He said something to the sergeant in command. The man nodded, then shot a Hitler salute, which Luc returned. Luc surveyed the barn, then the barnyard. He spotted the black car and a frown creased his brow. *I told that simpleton to leave this to me.* He pursed his lips and strode off to see what the idiot policeman was doing here.

Dunn eyed Luc's position relative to the mess on the ground near the house. It was clear Luc couldn't see what had happened or he'd have been running. The policeman's car must be blocking his view. But it wouldn't for much longer. Dunn signed to Cross to get the rest of the team up along the wall. Hurry. Cross nodded and passed the signs. The men immediately began moving and got into position quickly.

Dunn checked Luc's progress. Another twenty feet before the

traitor would see what had happened. Dunn turned his head toward the German soldiers. They stood in a long line facing the barn, all standing with their left foot in front, rifle ready in their hands. Experienced men. Except that their backs were to Dunn and his team. A perfect flanking position for the attacker. A classic ambush, it would be over in five seconds.

Dunn glanced at Luc. The Gestapo agent seemed to stop in mid-stride, then broke into a run, his hand reaching for the Luger under the suit jacket.

Dunn snapped his Thompson up over the wall and fired. His team reacted. In less than five seconds, it *was* over. The Germans hadn't even been able to turn to see who was killing them.

Dunn turned his Thompson toward Luc. The man had stopped and was spinning around to see what had happened behind him. His gun arm was swinging in a wide arc trying to come to bear on Dunn.

Dunn shouted, "Luc. Drop your weapon."

Luc's head swiveled toward Dunn, as did the Luger.

"Drop it, Luc. You have no place to go."

Luc glanced over his shoulder. He was ten feet from the car. There was nowhere else to hide. If he could just get to the girl moaning over her mother. A hostage was always a good thing. He took a step back. Then another.

"You sonofabitch." Dunn snapped off two rounds. The first one struck Luc in the right shoulder, twisting him around. The Luger flew from his hand, landing in a puff of dust ten feet away. The second bullet pierced his upper back, just above the left shoulder blade, and he collapsed.

To Cross, Dunn said, "Check the Germans." Then he climbed over the wall and ran toward Luc. Sounds of light footsteps followed him and he glanced over his shoulder. Madeline was running a few steps behind him, a pistol in her hand and a determined expression on her face. Dunn wondered where the hell the gun had been hidden.

Luc was alive and writhing on the ground. Dunn came to a halt, standing near Luc's head. Luc's eyes were mere slits as he grimaced in pain, but he recognized his attacker. "You! It can't be."

"Yep. Howdy, there, Luc.

"No. You're supposed to be in a prison camp."

"Uh, nope. Try again."

Madeline arrived, standing behind Dunn, who grinned at Luc. "Someone else is here who wants to see you, Luc."

Madeline stepped around Dunn and smiled grimly at Luc. The traitor's expression told Dunn he knew what was coming.

Madeline put her foot on Luc's left shoulder and pressed down hard. He screamed. "Hurts, does it?"

Luc groaned.

"Sarge!"

Dunn turned around. Cross was pointing. Another truck was coming up the driveway.

He peered at it. It wasn't a German truck. Maybe it was Laurent's feed truck. When the truck entered the barnyard he could read the sign on its side, Laurent Feed Co. The truck skidded to a stop and Laurent and Gereaux jumped out, then ran toward Dunn. Gereaux's eyes zeroed in on something over Dunn's shoulder. He gasped and tore past Dunn.

Laurent joined Dunn and Madeline. He looked down at Luc, disdain on his face, then raised his gaze to Madeline. "Looks like the idiot came to us, eh?"

"Very convenient," replied Madeline, as she shot him a smile.

Dunn noted it was the same chilling smile he'd seen earlier. "I'm going to leave this asshole to you two. I've got to get my men out of here. The gunfire will certainly bring someone out here. Is there any way you can dispose of the German soldiers?"

"Yes, we can do that if your men can help load them into my truck. I assume you'll be taking the German truck?" said Laurent.

Dunn nodded, then pointed at the Gereaux family and the mess beside them. "Can you take care of that, too?"

"We will."

Madeline touched Dunn's arm. "Thank, you, Thomas." She nodded. "We'll take care of this bastard."

Luc's eyes grew wide, terror plainly on his mind.

Laurent pulled a leather sap from his pocket. With a flicking motion, he struck the traitor and the whites of Luc's eyes flashed.

Dunn trotted back to his men, who were gathering the German soldiers' weapons, mostly Mauser rifles, with a couple of MP40 submachine guns thrown in. He found Cross and Marston conversing and made his way over to them. "We have to accelerate the time table. Someone's going to be coming out this way. We don't know whether Luc told anyone he was coming out here, so we can't afford to dawdle. Marston, are you up to getting us a plane in the daylight?"

"Yes, I suppose so. Could be more difficult."

Dunn's gaze settled on the dead German soldiers and an idea crept up. "Here's what we need to do." He outlined his plan quickly. When Cross winced, Dunn simply said, "We have to, if we want to make this thing work."

"Yes, Sarge."

Dunn patted Cross's shoulder and headed toward the truck.

Claire sat on the ground, legs tucked underneath, holding her mother's bloody head in her lap. "Mama, wake up. Mama. Please." Anne's chest was moving rhythmically with each breath, but her eyes were still closed. Tears ran down Claire's face. She'd ripped a piece of cloth from her own dress and held it against her mother's temple.

Beaux whimpered and crawled over to Claire. He pried her arm up with his muzzle and she patted him carefully. Blood seeped from a wound on his scalp; the bullet had just grazed him. "Oh, Beaux, you are such a good dog."

Gereaux skidded to a stop and dropped to his knees next to Claire. Reaching out with a shaking hand, he gently brushed some hair from Anne's face, then stroked her cheek. "What happened, Claire?"

"Papa, Dubois struck Mama with his pistol."

Gereaux looked at the still form of the small policeman. "My God, Claire, did you do that?"

Claire's breath caught, "Oh, I've killed a man."

She began to wail and Gereaux put an arm around her. "Shh, shh. It's all right, Claire. God understands. Come now, let's see what we can do for Mama. You run in the house and get us a bucket of cold water and some bandages. I'll stay here."

"Yes, Papa." Claire got up carefully, with Gereaux helping hold Anne's head steady, and ran to the house.

Gereaux's hand was supporting Anne's head as he leaned

over and kissed her softly on the lips. "Wake up, Anne. Please wake up." His own tears began to flow and he put his forehead against hers.

A slim arm lifted and wrapped itself around his broad back.

Gereaux drew back in surprise.

Anne's eyelids fluttered.

"Anne! Wake up!"

"Stop shouting, Philippe. I can hear just fine." Anne opened her eyes fully and smiled up at her husband.

"Hello, Anne."

"Philippe."

"Claire went to get some bandages."

Anne's hand went to her head, but Gereaux's own hand was in the way. "What happened?" Sudden realization hit and she tried to sit up, but Gereaux held her still. "What happened to Dubois?"

"He's dead."

"Dead?" Confusion flew across her face. "Who? What?"

"Not now, dear. I'll explain later. You just rest."

"Yes, all right."

Laurent and Madeline manhandled Luc over to the feed truck and hoisted his limp body into the back. Flipping Luc over roughly, Laurent tied the traitor's hands behind his back with baling wire, then did the same with his feet. One more strand of wire connected the hands to the feet, legs bent upwards, and Luc looked like a cannibal's dinner, all trussed up on a spit.

Dunn found the keys in the truck's ignition. He got in, started the vehicle and watched the gas gauge move to the quarter full mark. Relieved there would be enough to make it to the airfield, he turned off the engine and jumped out to check on his men's progress.

The German soldiers lay on the ground in only their gray skivvies. Dunn's men traipsed around trying to make ill-fitting uniforms work. Ward pulled a pair of German pants over his left boot and when the heel caught, he started hopping in a hopeless and graceless effort to stay on his feet, then flopped onto his side with a thump. A few of his teammates clapped in appreciation.

Getting back to his feet, he bowed and finished pulling the pants on.

Dunn just shook his head, but he was grateful to see the men a bit loose. They weren't out of it yet, but like baseball players, loose soldiers performed better. It was as though it made the brain sharper and the reflexes faster.

Only two things left to take care of. "Cross?"

Cross was settling a German helmet on his head and he turned to Dunn. "Yes, Sarge?"

"Let's get the Germans into Laurent's truck right away so they can get out of here."

"Got it."

"Did you save a uniform for me?"

Cross bent over and picked up a pile of clothes. "Right here." He trotted over to his sergeant and handed the clothes over. "It was their sergeant's."

Dunn wrinkled his nose. "God, these smell like a wet dog."

Cross shrugged. "Don't worry, your sense of smell will be overloaded in about two minutes, then you won't notice it."

A doubtful expression crossed Dunn's face, but he started changing as Cross moved off to get things started. Dunn finished, then put his helmet on. He took a tentative testing sniff. Damn, Cross was right. I can't smell it anymore. Thank God. Picking up the Mauser rifle lying at his feet, he took off for Laurent and Madeline.

"Madeline, can you go with me? I want to say a quick goodbye and thanks to the Gereauxs."

"Of course."

When they reached Philippe and Claire, who were helping Anne get her bearings, Madeline said, "Mr. Gereaux, the Americans are leaving soon."

Gereaux patted his wife's hand, got up and turned. He looked Dunn up and down and replied, "I must say you'd make a fierce looking Nazi, Sergeant Dunn."

Dunn grinned. "Thanks, I guess." He peered around Gereaux and, concerned, asked, "Is Mrs. Gereaux going to be all right?"

Gereaux nodded vigorously. "Yes, yes. She'll be fine."

"That was something your daughter did. That took tremendous courage. Will she be all right, too? Killing has a way of sucking a part of you away."

"She did what she had to. We'll get through it."

Dunn nodded. "I wanted to thank you and your family for all your help. I'm sorry we brought all this on you."

Gereaux put a rough, tanned hand on Dunn's shoulder and squeezed gently looking up into the tall American's eyes, searching. "This is war. Just promise me that whatever brought you here made a difference."

Dunn put his hand on top of Gereaux's. "I promise you we made a difference. We're going to win this war. And we're going to give you back your country."

Gereaux flipped his hand over and grasped Dunn's, pulling it into a handshake. "I believe you. Thank you."

"You're welcome." Dunn gestured toward Laurent and said, "Mr. Laurent will be taking care of the German soldiers, that guy," he pointed to Dubois' body, "and his car, but you should rake the barnyard to cover the blood."

"I've been meaning to till the barnyard anyway." Gereaux smiled and turned back to his family.

Dunn turned around and saw that Ward and Morris were loading the last of the dead Germans. "It looks like you're ready to go, Madeline."

"Yes, we are."

The two, the American soldier in a German uniform and the French Resistance leader with the flaming red hair, jogged back to join the final preparations.

"Madeline, I wish you the best. Please be careful."

"I will, Thomas. Good luck getting home." She stepped closer and they embraced, then smiled at each other.

Madeline turned away and got in the truck. She didn't look back.

"Sergeant." Laurent held out his hand and Dunn shook it.

"Keep your niece safe, Mr. Laurent."

"I will."

While Laurent was getting into his truck, Dunn joined his men by the German troop truck.

His eyes swept the area. The men had picked up all the gear and loaded it into the truck. Good. His turned his attention to Marston and asked again, "How are you holding up?"

"I'll make it."

Dunn nodded. "I'll be your driver, everyone else'll be in the back, of course. Dr. Herbert, I'm afraid you'll have to be in the back, too." Dunn stifled a grin at the sight of the little scientist in a German uniform three sizes too big.

"Yes, Sergeant. I'm ready."

"All right, boys, load 'em up."

After the men climbed in the truck, Dunn started the engine and glanced over at the Waffen-SS colonel sitting next to him. "Colonel, ready or not, here we go."

58

German airfield
5 miles south of Saverne
19 June, 1153 Hours

"Do you have a plan in case my bluff gets called?" Marston asked Dunn, as the truck bounced along the main road leading to the airfield.

Dunn gave Marston a sidelong glance. "No. We don't know what we might be up against. For all we know, there could be an entire German platoon, or worse, sitting right on top of the field."

"That's comforting," said Marston wryly.

"Don't worry. We prefer to have a plan drawn out before hand, but we're pretty good at making things up as we go."

"You're saying that you'll figure something out, if all hell breaks loose, like you did back at the farm?"

"Um, yes."

Marston turned away to look out the window at a passing wheat field. "God, I hope this works. I didn't realize how much I wanted to get back home."

Dunn nodded. "I'm with you on that." He stepped on the

brake pedal and the truck's speed dropped. "That's the airfield's road up there." He pointed. About two hundred yards farther down the highway was a tee intersection, with the airfield road going off to the left. In the distance, three hangers sat in a long row. The control tower and administration building sat next to the nearest hanger. Behind the tower was a small barracks, big enough for maybe fifteen or twenty men.

Dunn made the turn and they could see four airplanes parked on the tarmac adjacent to the runway. Three of them were single engine reconnaissance planes, built to carry only two people, but the fourth one seemed to fit the bill. It had an engine on each wing, like the C-47, but also had one in the nose; a tri-motor. Dunn didn't know what kind it was and didn't care, either. He rapped the window over his shoulder and Hanson slid it open.

"Yeah, Sarge?"

"Get Lieutenant Clark up here."

"Okay."

A moment later, Clark's face appeared in the small window. "What is it?"

"Can you fly that tri-motor over there?" Dunn pointed with his head.

Clark had a clear view. He let out a low whistle. "Wow. Yeah, sure. That's a Junkers 52. It's a real workhorse. Very reliable. Touchy in rough air, but solid."

"All right then. That's our girl." Dunn turned right, onto a narrow service road leading up to the administration building. At a distance of fifty yards, he said, "Okay, Marston. I'm going to park the truck outside the building, facing the plane. You go in and convince whoever to give you the plane."

"And if I can't?"

Dunn gave Marston an evaluating look, then said, "Have you killed before?"

Marston nodded, almost reluctantly. "Once."

"Are you up to doing it again?"

"If necessary."

"If it comes to that, you get your ass back out here posthaste."

"Then what?"

Dunn smiled. "Then we start making things up."

"Lord, have mercy."

"I hope he does." Dunn stopped the truck. "Be careful."

Marston nodded and got out. He straightened his tunic, checked to make sure his Luger was where it was supposed to be, and marched into the building.

Dunn kept himself busy by taking in all he could see. The runway ran north-south with all the buildings on the east side. The truck sat at the southern end. From this angle he noticed a square structure between the first and second hangers that had been hidden from view earlier. It had a garage door on the front and a man-sized door on the right side. In front of each hanger was an anti-aircraft gun, barrel pointing up. There was no activity anywhere.

The sun was at his back, so he was in the shade, but it was still getting warm, now that no air flow was coming in through the window. He wiped sweat from his brow with the stinking uniform's sleeve. The heat seemed to be cooking the smell out again. The garage door suddenly lifted and a gas truck trundled out toward the runway. To Dunn's surprise, the truck rolled past the four parked planes. Curious, Dunn leaned forward, putting a hand on the steering wheel to pull himself up. When the truck reached the edge of the runway, it stopped. Something made Dunn glance up and his heart jumped into his throat. Two small black specs appeared low in the sky, planes coming in for a landing. Were they recon planes or fighters? They grew larger and larger and Dunn sucked a breath. Shit. Messerschmitts.

"Cross?" he called over his shoulder.

"Yes?"

"We've got two Me-109s coming in. It looks like all they want is fuel, but we'd better be ready. Make sure everyone's got their Thompson loaded."

"Got it."

Dunn heard Cross give the order as he continued watching the planes. They were over the far end of the runway. In a few seconds, their tires would be on the ground. He looked at the admin building, hoping to see Marston coming back out the door, but no such luck. Dunn tightened his grip on the steering wheel. If things went awry in the office, they'd never get off the runway before the 109s shot them to pieces. They'd have to take out the enemy planes before getting into the Junkers. Dunn ran different plans through his head, playing 'if they do this, then we do that.' His chief worry was whether the barracks held German soldiers. There was no way to know, for sure, until it was too late. It'd just be another problem to prepare for. Dunn estimated the distance from the Junkers to the barracks and decided where to park the truck if there *were* soldiers in there. The office door opened and Marston stepped out into the sunlight with a pleased expression on his face. Dunn sighed in relief then saw Marston turn his head. Clearly, he'd seen the Messerschmitts rolling down the runway.

Marston got in the truck and said, "What are we going to do about those fighters?"

"I don't know yet, I'm working on it." Dunn put the truck in gear and headed toward the Junkers while keeping his eyes on the 109s. They had come to a stop, one behind the other, and the fuel truck sat next to the first one. The driver dragged the heavy hose toward the plane. The pilots climbed out of their cockpits and stood near the edge of the runway. A moment later, one of them pointed skyward and ran to his plane. The other pilot ran over to the man fueling his plane and began gesturing wildly. He obviously wanted to get off the ground.

Dunn leaned over and looked up. A flight of B-17s soared overhead. Dunn reacted immediately by turning the truck to the left.

Marston looked over at Dunn in surprise. "What are you doing?"

"We have to destroy those fighters. There's a bunch of B-17s flying right over us, heading home." Over his shoulder Dunn said, "Cross."

Cross was sitting right by the window and answered, "Yes."

"We're going to have to blow up these two planes. I'm going to pull up fifty yards from them. I want half to the right and half to the left. Right side target the right hand plane, left side target the fuel truck, then the left hand plane, if it doesn't go up with the truck. I'll go left, you go right. Got it?"

"Got it."

"Pass up a Thompson."

A wooden shoulder stock appeared through the window and Marston grabbed it for Dunn, putting the weapon in his lap.

Dunn stopped the truck, facing the planes, thus hiding the

back of the truck. "Stay here," he said to Marston as he got out. He stuck his hand back in and Marston passed over the machine gun. Dunn pulled the cocking knob back and turned off the safety. Hanson and Morris rounded the back of the truck and joined Dunn by the front bumper. They lined up abreast of each other, a step between them. Dunn glanced over the truck's hood. Cross, Ward and Wickham were lined up.

The fuel truck driver turned. Seeing soldiers here surprised him.

Dunn and his men went down one knee and raised their weapons.

The driver let go of the hose and ducked under the 109.

Dunn's team opened fire.

The fuel truck went first, with a thumping sound that Dunn felt in his chest. A fireball shot skyward. The second Messerschmitt burst into flames as its remaining fuel exploded from Cross's group's bullets. The 109 next to the flaming truck exploded in sympathy and hopped into the air, then settled down on its shattered undercarriage.

"Cease fire! Let's get the hell out of here."

The men jumped back into the truck and Dunn gunned the engine. They were only two hundred yards from the Junkers. Dunn kept his eye on the barracks.

Cross hollered through the window, "Sarge, the guy in the office is outside. We'll get him."

Dunn couldn't see the man, but heard a short burst. Marston leaned out the window and reported excitedly, "We got him!"

They were ten yards from the four planes when the barracks' door opened. Two men in mechanic's overalls ran out to stare at the dying fireballs.

Dunn stopped the truck. "Out!"

Dunn got out, ran around the front of the truck and lifted his Thompson. He fired a burst and the two mechanics crumpled.

The men ran to the Junkers and climbed aboard. Dunn got the men seated while Clark ran forward and climbed into the cockpit. Satisfied everyone was ready, Dunn started toward the cockpit, but stopped to tap Herbert on the shoulder. "Okay, Doc?" Herbert grinned and gave Dunn a thumbs up. Dunn grinned back and moved on. When he reached the cockpit, Clark was putting a hand on a red switch, one of three. Dunn sat down in the copilot's seat.

Clark flipped the switch and the port engine sputtered to life. In quick succession he started the other two engines. He tapped a dial on the console and turned to Dunn with a grin. "Good thing we didn't need that fuel truck."

Dunn looked at the gauge. Full. "Thank God." He hadn't thought about that.

"Too right." Clark put his hands on the steering yoke. "Look out the window and tell me if the little wings at the back of the aircraft move, up first, then down." Clark leaned to see his side.

Dunn complied and watched the elevator move as expected. "Yep."

"Good. Now watch the back of the big wings. Same as before." Clark turned the wheel right, then left.

"They moved."

"Okay. Here we go." Clark released the brake and pushed the throttles up. The Junkers rolled forward. Two minutes later, they were on the runway, far from the still-burning piles of twisted metal.

Clark shoved the throttles all the way forward and the plane shot into the wind.

59

In Flight
Over France
19 June, 1242 Hours

"Where do you think we are now?"

Clark glanced at his watch, then looked at the map he'd managed to grab before leaving the doomed Gooney Bird. The map was now hanging on the console from a toggle switch, which poked through the top of it. The pilot tapped a spot in France, near the Belgium border. "Around here. I'd guess we're about a hundred and twenty miles from the Channel and then another ninety or so to home."

"I think I'd better radio London and tell them we're in the air. Wouldn't do to get shot down by our own."

"No, that wouldn't do, at all."

Dunn slipped on the headset and tuned the dial to the frequency he'd used earlier. Pressing the mike key, he gave his call sign and waited.

Immediately, came a reply, "Go ahead, Devil's Fire Three, this is Golden Guard."

RONN MUNSTERMAN

Dunn explained where they were and what kind of plane they were in.

"We read you, Devil's Fire Alpha Three. We're scrambling a flight of Mustangs to greet you."

"Thank you, Golden Guard. Devil's Fire Alpha Three, out."

"Golden Guard, out."

Dunn took off the headset and said, "They're sending an escort to meet us. When do you think we'll meet up with them?"

"Give me a minute." Clark stared out the windshield as he calculated, muttering under his breath, "If two trains leave . . ."

Dunn smiled. He hated word problems, too.

A couple of minutes later, Clark said, "Assuming five minutes to get airborne, about forty minutes."

"Where will we be?"

"Almost to the coast."

"This is going to be a long forty minutes."

"Yep."

60

The Reich Chancellery
Berlin
19 June, 1306 Hours

Göring and Speer tried to stare each other down, but Hitler's secretary interrupted to tell them to go in. They both moved toward the door at the same time. Fortunately, it was a double door and wide enough for them to pass side by side.

Hitler watched them approach and sensed tension between his two chieftains. He liked and fostered the discord. Better to keep them on their toes. A little rivalry among his underlings was a good thing. He put his hands on the desk in front of him, waiting, curious. Both Göring and Speer had phoned earlier in the morning requesting an audience, but he had been asleep with strict orders not to be awakened for anyone.

Göring and Speer stopped in front of him. "Sit down."

The men sat down, looking uncharacteristically nervous, even unsure of themselves, Hitler thought. He lifted his eyebrows. "What's troubling you?"

Göring and Speer glanced at each other, then back at Hitler.

Neither spoke.

Hitler frowned. Usually they were fighting for his attention like two puppies. A few heartbeats passed. Hitler drummed his fingers on the desk. "I have no patience today. What is it?"

"*Mein Führer*, I'm saddened to report that the Hortens' plane was destroyed this morning," said Göring, evidently deciding that going first would be best.

Hitler jerked upright. "What happened? Did it crash?"

"No, there was an explosion at the hanger. We don't know what happened yet."

"When was this?"

"About three in the morning, *mein Führer*."

Hitler's expression turned incredulous. "A plane just exploded in the middle of the night? By itself?"

"We don't know what happened. The entire hanger and everything in it was completely incinerated. Nothing was left."

"How soon can they build another?" Hitler looked hopeful.

Göring swallowed. "Six months at the earliest."

"Six months! That's almost next year!"

"Yes, *mein Führer*."

"You tell them faster, or else."

"Yes, *mein Führer*."

Hitler turned his snake eyes toward Speer. "You don't have bad news for your *Führer*, too, do you, Speer?"

"I'm afraid so, *mein Führer*, there's been a terrible accident at the atomic bomb lab near Stuttgart."

"I know where the lab is, you idiot," growled Hitler. "What kind of accident? Someone get exposed to that radiation again?"

"No, it seems one of the weapons exploded. The lab is gone, as is the entire top of the hill it was under. The entire complex is nothing but rubble."

Hitler's face paled, lips trembling, and his eyes darted left and right, as though searching for an escape route from this horrible news. His jaw muscles clenched. "What about the scientists? Are they still alive? Can they build another one? I must have that bomb."

"All but two are safe and accounted for." Speer frowned. "But we think Herbert and Winkel may have died. We can't find them."

"They can be replaced. Move some of the others up in rank and start rebuilding. By the time the Hortens give me a New Year's present of a new airplane," he shot a threatening look at Göring, "the bomb will be ready."

Now it was Speer's turn to swallow. "*Mein Führer*," he started softly, "It took three years to build the lab and accumulate the required amounts of uranium and heavy water. We will never have enough heavy water again. The Americans have contaminated all that was left in Norway."

Hitler slammed his hands on the desk top and jumped up. His chair rolled backwards and crashed into the wall three meters behind. Pointing a bony finger at Speer, Hitler shouted, "Are you telling me I'm not ever going to have my bomb? My miracle? My salvation for Germany?"

It was clear from Speer's face that was exactly what he was saying, but he nodded. "Yes, *mein Führer*. Never."

"Get out! Both of you! Before I order you hanged as traitors!"

Göring and Speer jumped to their feet and practically ran to the door. As they were closing the door behind them, they heard the crash of something heavy hitting the wall.

61

In Flight
Over France
19 June, 1312 Hours

"There's the coast, Sergeant." Clark tipped his head forward.

Dunn nodded. They were flying at 8,000 feet and not only could they see the Channel, but farther out, the white cliffs of Dover appeared as a thin chalk line at the far end of the blue water. "A beautiful sight. The only thing that'll make me happier is the sight of our escort."

"Me, too. Shouldn't be much longer now."

Ten minutes later, Dunn said, "I think those might be our friends." He pointed at eight silver dots about five miles ahead and a little above them. In less than a minute, the Mustangs roared past them.

Dunn craned his neck to watch them out his window. Another minute passed, then the P-51s slid alongside. "God, it's good to see those guys."

Clark glanced over and saluted Captain Miller, who returned it. Clark grabbed the headset that Dunn had used earlier and slipped it on. "Good to see you again, Captain."

"You too. We'll get you home and on the ground safely."

"Many thanks."

"You're welcome."

"How much longer, now?" Dunn was getting out of his seat.

"Half hour."

"I'm going to let the men know."

62

Whitehall
10 Downing Street, London
19 June, 1403 Hours

Finch woke up to find an army corporal roughly shaking his shoulder. He groaned, then asked, "What is it?"

"Sir, you're wanted in the Prime Minister's office."

"I'm up."

"Yes, sir." The corporal left.

Finch and Lawson had gone down into the bowels of the massive underground bunker to grab some shut eye after they'd first heard from Dunn. They'd had to walk bent over to avoid knocking their heads against the pipes and low ceiling.

Finch slid his legs off the side of the bed and got up carefully, mindful of the concrete just inches above his head. Finch only had his skivvies on because he'd draped his clothes over the end of the cot, so as to keep his promise to himself to never appear disheveled in front of the Prime Minister again. He dressed quickly and took off down the claustrophobic, narrow hallway. Lawson was still sleeping, as far he as knew, but he didn't go check. One didn't keep the Prime Minister waiting.

As soon as Finch stepped into the outer office, Simon Coulter smiled. "Mr. Finch, the Prime Minister said to send you on in."

"Thank you, Mr. Coulter."

"Please, sir, call me Simon."

Finch nodded gratefully and replied with a tired smile, "All right, Simon." He checked his suit, saw a big clump of lint on the left lapel, picked it off with a sigh, then stepped into Churchill's office. His mind switched back to the first time he met the great man. *Was that only a few weeks ago?* He smiled at the memory, his nervousness, Churchill's unexpected kindness. He walked to the front of Churchill's desk and waited.

Churchill was, as always, reading a situation report. He flipped over the last page and closed the file, then looked up at Finch. A broad smile made his doughy cheeks rise. "Mr. Finch, sit down, son. Did you get some rest?"

Finch dropped into the old leather chair and said, "Yes, sir, thank you. I feel a little better."

Churchill grinned. Finch's eyes had that sleepy, watery look and underneath, dark circles hung like sacks. "Mr. Finch, Alan, I've been very impressed by your work on this mission." Churchill grabbed his cigar from the ashtray and took a puff, blowing the smoke out over his head.

"Thank you, Prime Minister."

"I talked to your boss a little while ago."

Finch's eyebrows lifted slightly, but he said nothing.

"He wanted to pass along his own congratulations, too."

"Thank you, sir." Finch wondered what this was all about.

Churchill's expression turned mischievous "You know, it'll probably be awhile before he sees you again."

Finch's expression gave way to confusion. "I, I don't understand, sir."

"I know." Churchill leaned forward, resting his hands and forearms on the desk. "I'm pulling you out of MI-5, effective," he glanced at the big clock on the wall, "now, 2:11 P.M. I'm reassigning you to my personal staff with a promotion, no, let's make that two promotions. What do you say?"

Finch swallowed hard. Work for the Prime Minister? My God, what an opportunity. "I say yes, Prime Minister. And thank you."

"You're welcome, my boy. You earned it on this one." Churchill sat back, took another puff and blew smoke out as he said, "Between you and Lawson, you helped put an end to the largest threat to freedom ever conceived. By the way, Lawson said to tell you goodbye. He's on the way back over the pond. Evidently, Mr. Roosevelt wants to have a similar conversation with him."

"He's a good man, sir."

Churchill nodded. "As are you, Alan Finch. I'm sure your wife would have been proud."

Tears appeared in Finch's eyes. He was surprised and grateful that the Prime Minister would even recall his comment to the insufferable Kenneth Moore at their first meeting. He made no attempt to hide the tears. "I believe she would, sir."

63

Camp Barton Stacy
19 June, 1423 Hours

The ready room sounded like a party house and Dunn let the men go, even though the strongest drink was coffee. In addition to his own team, Saunders and his bunch had joined them, as had all of the pilots, Mustangs and C-47s alike. Marston and Herbert were there, too. Marston had gotten a fresh bandage and a clean bill of health from the doctor on duty. Herbert was bemused by all the goings on. Clearly, the life of a soldier was far different from that of a scientist.

Dunn and Saunders stood near the door, chatting, and Dunn saw Kenton coming up the steps. He opened his mouth to call, "Ten-hut," but Kenton held up his hand, shaking his head. Dunn closed his mouth and smiled.

Kenton stuck out his hand. "Sergeant Dunn."

Dunn took the proffered hand and was surprised when Kenton pulled him into a hug, patting his back.

In Dunn's ear, Kenton said, "I was really worried this time. I'm relieved you're back safe."

"Me, too, sir."

Kenton pushed back and smiled. "I'm proud of you and your

336   RONN MUNSTERMAN

men."

"Thank you, sir."

"I'm going to speak to them, just for a few minutes, then let them go back to their party."

"Sir, first I'd like to introduce you to someone."

Kenton looked surprised, but nodded.

"I'll be right back," said Dunn and he walked away. Soon, he was back with Herbert in tow. Dunn put his arm around the small scientist's shoulders and said, "Colonel Kenton, may I present Dr. Franz Herbert of the German Atomic Lab."

Kenton stared at Herbert for a long moment, as if sizing him up. He couldn't believe it. This was an intelligence coup akin to finding the atomic lab. He gave Dunn an appreciative glance as a small smile lifted his lips, as though saying, 'very impressive.'

Dunn nodded.

Kenton held out his hand to Herbert. "Pleased to meet you, Dr. Herbert."

"You too, Colonel. I am glad to be here. I suppose I should officially request asylum or whatever the right term would be."

"That'll do fine, sir. I'm sure there are a few people who will want to talk with you. I believe a trip to the United States is in your near future."

Herbert's face lit up. "Really? I want to go to your country. I want to become an American." He turned to look up at Dunn with near adoration in his face. "This man saved my life in more ways than one, Colonel. I must say, that if he's an example of your best, then Hitler is doomed. As he should be."

"He *is* a perfect example of our best. It's been my honor to serve with him."

"Colonel?"

"Yes, Tom?"

"Dr. Herbert is the one who helped us create the atomic explosion." Dunn explained briefly how Herbert had packed explosives around the uranium.

Kenton whistled. "That's amazing. The reports we got said that the entire hillside was gone and much of the land as far away as two miles was stripped of all vegetation. It's like a giant crater now. I'll show you the pictures later, if you like."

"Yes, sir."

Kenton turned to Herbert, "Tell you what, Dr. Herbert, I'm going to speak to the men for a few minutes, then let them celebrate. I'd like to invite you to join me for a late lunch. That way, we can chat in relative peace."

Herbert grinned. "I'd love to."

Kenton patted Herbert's shoulder and moved over to the front of the room.

Dunn hollered, "Ten Hut!"

This immediately quieted the room.

Kenton surveyed the room, taking in the exhausted, but success-filled eyes that stared back at him. "Gentlemen, congratulations on jobs well done. I'm not going to waste your time by talking on and on—" Sudden clapping and whistles interrupted Kenton and he just smiled, then held up his hands for silence. "All right, you've had your laugh. Very nice."

His face grew somber as he continued, "Men, you've done a great service to the war effort. Ordinarily, I wouldn't give any more information than you need to know, and I'll probably get court-martialed for telling you this, but that bomb you destroyed was probably headed for either New York or Washington, D.C." The silence that greeted this announcement told Kenton the men hadn't completely considered what they had done. "It was to be delivered by the plane captured by Captain Miller and Sergeant Saunders and his team. That airplane was the first of its kind. A transatlantic bomber, capable of flying at such an extreme altitude that we'd had never seen or heard it coming. On top of that, the plane was made of a composite that would have been invisible to our radar." He let that sink in. "Our own engineers are on the way over here to examine the airplane to see how soon they can create a working American version. This could well shorten the war.

"Gentlemen, you saved thousands, maybe hundreds of thousands of innocent American citizens, men, women, . . . and children, from an unimaginable death." Kenton suddenly snapped to attention and the men looked toward the door, expecting a high ranking officer to appear. No one was there. Kenton raised his right hand slowly, rising to the bill of his officer's hat in a solemn and perfect salute. "I salute you."

As one, the men returned the salute, then Kenton lowered his hand. He unbuttoned his breast pocket and pulled out a slip of paper. "Gentlemen, a telegram from the President of the United States."

The men snapped to attention. Kenton managed to suppress a smile at their reaction. He carefully unfolded the paper and read, "To the men of Operation Devil's Fire: Your successes this day will live on as one of the most daring and crucial secret missions ever conducted by our Allied Forces. Your efforts will not be forgotten. I am proud of you. May God bless you. God bless America. Best regards, Franklin D. Roosevelt, President."

Kenton folded the paper, walked over to Dunn, who had moved closer, and handed it to the sergeant. "Tom, this is for your safekeeping."

"Thank you, sir."

"Tom, I did like you asked and called your girl, Pamela, when your plane went down. I'm sorry, but I haven't been able to reach her to tell her you were coming home."

Worry settled on Dunn's face. "Sir, I—"

"My jeep is outside, Tom."

"Thanks, sir."

"Don't mention it." Still looking at Dunn and in a drill field voice, Kenton said, "Sergeant, you may tell the men they may continue their celebration and I have arranged for a local church to provide . . . refreshments." The stunned men stared at him. "I meant a local . . . pub."

The room burst into cheers and whistles. Kenton squeezed Dunn's shoulder, walked over to Herbert, and with a wave, invited the doctor to precede him out the door.

Dunn faced the men, who were talking loudly about everything from baseball to girls, and shouted, "In case you didn't hear the good Colonel, you may begin your celebration."

The noise now threatened to pop eardrums and Dunn headed for the door. Saunders stepped in front of him and held out his hand. "I'm glad this one worked out, Sergeant."

Dunn shook Saunders' hand and replied, "A much better outcome than before."

"No fuck ups this time."

Dunn smiled. "No fuck ups." Then he turned and darted out the door toward the jeep.

64

Dunn had stopped at the Camp Barton Stacey hospital, but the nurses said Pamela had called in sick. He went to her apartment and pounded on the door so long an elderly man finally peeked out his door, opposite Pamela's. In a gruff voice, he'd said, "Stop that. She's not here." Then he'd slammed the door.

Dunn was barreling down the road leading to Pamela's farm. He was approaching the hairpin curve too fast and jammed his boot onto the brake to keep the jeep on the road. "Shit." To get home after all that and then die in car wreck. Dunn kept the jeep's speed down.

His mind had been in a whirlwind since leaving Hampstead Airbase. He was of single-minded purpose: find Pamela. He knew he loved her and he knew she loved him, although why that should be escaped him. A few miles from her, he began to doubt himself. What would she say? What he would he do if she said no? Would she want to move to America? To Iowa?

Finally, he spotted the Hardwicke's driveway and slowed the jeep, turning onto the dirt road. As he drew closer to the woman he loved, Dunn suddenly realized he didn't have a ring to offer Pamela. Then it occurred to him that he'd been on a mission, killed more than a few Germans, slept in a hayloft, worn a stinking German uniform, and hadn't even bathed himself. Smooth, Dunn, real smooth.

He pulled the jeep into the barnyard. The similarities between this one, the one he'd just left a few hours ago, and the one where Allen had died, struck him. He stopped the jeep and stared at the barn off in the distance. He suddenly saw his nightmare, Allen's fall, his outstretched fist with a torn piece of white shirt in it. Dunn recalled that for months afterwards, Paul had been the one doing the comforting, not the other way around, telling Dunn there was nothing he could have done. Paul believed that, so why can't you? You have to forgive yourself, no one else can do it for you. Dunn came back to the present and looked skyward. Relief and forgiveness washed over him and tears leaked. "Thank you, Paul." He turned off the jeep's engine and jumped out. He wiped his eyes and looked at the house, inside of which was his destiny. He knew what the answer would be to his question.

Pamela's dogs trotted around the side of the barn and spotted Dunn. Recognizing him, they began barking happily and bounded toward him. The screen door opened and Mrs. Hardwicke peeked out. Her face lit up and she waved.

Dunn lifted a hand.

Mrs. Hardwicke disappeared. A second later, Pamela burst through the door and sprinted toward Dunn.

Dunn took off himself. They met and fell into an embrace while the two dogs circled them, barking and hopping up and down. Dunn kissed Pamela, holding her tight. She ran her hands through his hair, knocking off his hat. The Border Collie snatched it up and ran off, shaking it like a rabbit.

"Tom. I've been a mess since Colonel Kenton called."

"Pamela, I'm sorry. I shouldn't have asked him to do that."

"No, no. Don't be sorry. This just proved to me how much I do love you, Tom."

Dunn kissed Pamela's forehead, then her cheeks. He put his lips next to her ear. "I love you, too, Pamela." He pulled back, enjoying the sight of her deep blue eyes. "I've known fear, before, all soldiers do. Fear of dying. That's the nature of combat." He stopped, fighting back a choking cry. "But when we were shot down, I realized I wasn't as much afraid of dying as I was of never seeing your beautiful face again. Of holding you like this."

"Oh, Tom."

Dunn pulled Pamela's head down onto his chest and caressed her back gently. He saw Mrs. Hardwicke in the door and smiled at her.

She waved and mouthed the words, "Ask her." Then she held up her left hand and pointed to her third finger, where a gold band rested.

Dunn's mouth dropped open. How could she know? Then he winked and she grinned, stepping back from view.

"Pamela?"

"Hmm?" Pamela's voice was soft, a wonderful purr against his chest.

Dunn decided he liked that very much. He put a hand on Pamela's shoulders and gently pushed her back a bit. She looked up, curiosity on her face.

Dunn went down on one knee, taking her left hand in both of his.

The black Labrador licked Dunn's cheek. Dunn somehow kept his composure.

Pamela's eyes widened, her mouth formed a silent 'O,' and her right hand flew to her throat.

"Pamela Hardwicke, will you marry me?"

Pamela lowered her right hand to stroke Dunn's cheek. He leaned his head in to the touch, keeping his eyes on hers. "Yes, Thomas Dunn, I will marry you."

Dunn got up and kissed Pamela.

The Border Collie rejoined them, minus the hat, but with a pleased expression.

Pamela grabbed Dunn's hand and started toward the house. "Let's go tell Mother and Father."

Dunn muttered, "She already knows."

Pamela glanced over at Dunn. "What did you say, Tom?"

Dunn grinned. "Oh, nothing, dear."

Author's Notes

Stop! Did you read the book? I warned you there is a spoiler here.

Readers love to ask writers, "Where do you get your story ideas?" Most writers have a generic answer for this question, but for me generally speaking the story idea just comes of its own accord, usually when I'm thinking about something else. In the case of this novel, my answer is more precise. In the fall of 2003, after I sold my first short story, "He Wasn't Always Old" which you can read on my website www.ronnmunsterman.com, I decided it was time to write a novel. I knew I wanted to write about WWII because I've always been very interested in it, and because I had many relatives who lived during that period, several of whom served our nation in the military, as listed in the Acknowledgments.

The question was, what would be a good story line? I'd been noodling some ideas and saw a show on the History Channel about the Horten brothers and their "flying wing." About half way through the program, I knew what my story line was going to be: the Germans did indeed have an atomic bomb program and they had an airplane that could deliver it to the U.S. There! Just that simple. Quite naturally, I took liberties with the timeline and juggled a few facts. The Hortens really were building the Horten 18, but when the U.S. Army found the manufacturing site in the spring of 1945, the plane was incomplete. There are conflicting reports regarding the Nazi's atomic bomb program, but most indicate the Germans were not as close to a completed weapon as I depict. But that's wonder of fiction!

Part of the fun of writing, for me, is the research. The internet and Google Earth became my friends as I looked up facts, locations, and historical people. Here are some of my favorites: the P-51 Mustang gun camera switch used by Captain Miller works exactly as described. Colonel C.E. "Bud" Anderson, (USAF, Retired) WWII Triple Ace, and author of *To Fly and Fight*, was kind enough to help me with that piece of technical information. Check out his website: www.cebudanderson.com. The Star and Garter Hotel in Andover is real and the exterior description is accurate. The hotel still exists as The Danebury.

Winston Churchill's War Room is based on WWII era photographs, as is the Transatlantic phone room, and how the phone system actually worked including the encryption process is accurate. The Castle of Rohan in Saverne, France really is red sandstone and stunningly beautiful. Do yourself a favor and do an online search to view it. Descriptions of the German Chancellery eagle, the long marble hallway, and Hitler's office are accurate. As a tidbit update: the location of the razed Chancellery building is now covered with apartment buildings.

Now as for the spoiler, please stop here if you haven't read the whole thing yet.

The information about setting the plastic explosives around the U-235 is all my idea. Whether it would really work is up for grabs. What I can tell you is that the American Manhattan Project's first weapon that was tested, *Trinity*, on 16 July 1945, was a plutonium bomb using the "implosion" design. The first bomb dropped on Hiroshima on 6 August 1945 was a "gun" design. Oppenheimer and his team were so certain it would explode no tests were made. A contributing factor to not conducting any tests was the limited supply of U-235. And yes, there were some scientists who believed the atmosphere would ignite if an atomic bomb was exploded as related by Göring to Hitler.

Any mistakes you find in fact or otherwise, are all mine.

I'd love to get feedback from you. Please send me an email at this address: SgtDunnNovel@yahoo.com.

RM
Iowa
June 2011

About The Author

Ronn Munsterman is an Information Technology profess-ional of nearly twenty years. He loves baseball, and as a native of Kansas City, Missouri, has followed the Royals since their beginning in 1969. He plays golf, usually with his son or oldest granddaughter, and even enjoys the occasional memorable shot. Other interests include reading, some selective television watching, movies, listening to music, playing and coaching chess, and photography. Visit his website for a list of his favorites. www.ronnmunsterman.com

He also writes short stories, two of which have been published, and they are available for free download on his website. Ronn says his first short story was written at the age of 14 for a high school literary contest . . . no, it didn't win. His lifelong interest in World War II history ultimately led to the writing of *Operation Devil's Fire.*

Ronn does volunteer chess coaching each school year for elementary- through high school-aged students, and also provides private lessons for chess students. He authored a book on teaching chess: *Chess Handbook for Parents and Coaches*, available on Amazon.com.

He lives in Iowa with his wife, and enjoys spending time with the family.

Ronn is currently busy at work on his next novel.

Made in the USA
San Bernardino, CA
23 September 2018